"Ms. Creed. Get i

Annja hesitated, but realiz
to run had passed.

"If you attempt to flee, I will shoot you in the legs and pull you into the car." The speaker was a man of medium height and Asian ancestry. He held the pistol with a steady hand.

"You'll shoot me with the police just up the street?" Annja asked calmly.

"I will. And I'll get away with it." He waved the pistol. "Now, get in before I have you put in. We won't be gentle."

She'd escaped many traps in the past. Sometimes it was better to step into them. Annja folded herself into the backseat of the car. Another man, also Asian, sat in the front passenger seat, a pistol in his lap. Once she was seated, the two other men got back in. She was sandwiched.

At a word from the driver, the car pulled into traffic as smoothly as wax running down a candle.

Annja sat quietly between the men on either side of her. "Do you want to tell me what this is about?"

"It's simple." The man in the front passenger seat turned to face her. "We want the magic lantern."

Titles in this series:

ROGUE Angel

Alex Archer

MAGIC LANTERN

A GOLD EAGLE BOOK FROM

WORLDWIDE®

TORONTO • NEW YORK • LONDON
AMSTERDAM • PARIS • SYDNEY • HAMBURG
STOCKHOLM • ATHENS • TOKYO • MILAN
MADRID • WARSAW • BUDAPEST • AUCKLAND

Recycling programs
for this product may
not exist in your area.

First edition May 2012

ISBN-13: 978-0-373-62156-9

MAGIC LANTERN

Special thanks and acknowledgment to
Mel Odom for his contribution to this work.

Printed in U.S.A.

The
LEGEND

...THE ENGLISH COMMANDER TOOK
JOAN'S SWORD AND RAISED IT HIGH.

The broadsword, plain and unadorned,
gleamed in the firelight. He put the tip against
the ground and his foot at the center of the blade.
The broadsword shattered, fragments falling
into the mud. The crowd surged forward,
peasant and soldier, and snatched the shards
from the trampled mud. The commander tossed
the hilt deep into the crowd.
Smoke almost obscured Joan, but she continued
praying till the end, until finally the flames climbed
her body and she sagged against the restraints.

Joan of Arc died that fateful day in France,
but her legend and sword are reborn....

PROLOGUE

Les Carrières de Paris
Paris, France
1793

In the darkness of the tunnel, the strong smell of old death struck Michel Toussaint like a sharp blow to the face. He barely managed to keep from turning and leaving as the hair on the back of his neck rose.

Even the Revolution sweeping through Paris these past four years hadn't affected him this much. Possible sudden death in the streets at the hands of madmen was not the same as death of an arcane nature.

Gulping back bile, he wrapped his arm over his mouth and nose and breathed through his rough coat sleeve. He peered at the darkness outside the reach of the lantern light. Most of the others in their group—three abreast in this dank passage—complained loudly.

"Where are we?"

"What is this place?"

The sound of their voices echoed and echoed again as it got lost in the long tunnel.

Their young guide raised the lantern above his head. The

orange light cascaded over the nearby cave walls, chasing the shadows. The white limestone seemed to warm from the glow, but the chill air rattled Michel. He couldn't forget that he was now dozens of feet below Paris.

God willing, he would go home again tonight.

A fat man in expensive business attire tried to seize the lantern from the guide. Michel recognized him as one of the wealthy merchants who had convinced Michel's editor to assign him the task of covering Anton Dutilleaux's show. As a distraction to the conflict raging throughout the city.

The boy refused to part with the lantern. Michel didn't know if that was out of ownership or fear of the dark, which steadfastly lay in wait.

"Give me that light, you rancid bit of flotsam," the fat man snarled. He swung his walking stick with considerable force at the boy's head.

Outmatched, the dirty-faced street urchin let go the lantern and retreated with one hand raised protectively, scarcely avoiding the stick. Metal gleamed in the boy's hand, and Michel knew the urchin had drawn a knife. For a moment the reporter thought blood was about to be spilled.

"I hope the ghosts get you, you oozing pox," the boy called belligerently, backing away. He pocketed his knife and no one except Michel seemed the wiser.

The fat man snarled an oath at the retreating boy, then shined the lantern's beam farther ahead into the waiting catacombs.

Michel hoped the man's cruel act didn't curse them all. Michel believed in ghosts and curses. He never walked across a grave and always went in the opposite direction if a black cat crossed his path.

I am, he thought miserably, without doubt the last person that should have been assigned to this story. Before he'd left the offices of the newspaper, he had made certain the editor had known that. Shaking just a little, he pulled his cloak more tightly around him.

"Dutilleaux!" the fat man roared. "I demand that you show

yourself! I didn't come all this way to be made to wait!" He paused as the thunder of his voice rolled down the throat of the tunnel. *"Dutilleaux!"*

"Quiet." From out of the shadows, a man calmly asked, "What are you trying to do, Gervaise? Wake the dead? We all know that is my job."

Anton Dutilleaux stepped from the shadows, but they didn't easily part company with him. Rather, they lingered in his dark hair, his dark gaze and his black evening suit. Black gloves covered his long-fingered hands.

The three women in the crowd drew back with small, frightened cries.

"Pardon me, ladies. I didn't mean to startle you." Dutilleaux smiled disarmingly and bowed deeply.

Liar, Michel thought unkindly. You meant to scare them. He was even angrier because Dutilleaux's appearance had scared him, as well.

"Is that your fancy, then, charlatan?" the fat man named Gervaise demanded. "Spending your nights with the dead so you can scare women and children?"

Dutilleaux smiled a second time, and it was a good smile. Michel had heard that the magician excelled with women. A number of scandalous stories had followed him through Europe.

"I didn't mean to scare anyone," Dutilleaux replied innocently. "I merely stayed overlong at my studies. I've not lost my keen fascination for the things I'm about to show you. In fact, I'd wager after I reveal them to you that you won't soon find them far from your mind, either."

The mocking certainty in Dutilleaux's voice served to further unnerve Michel. He cursed himself for not having the foresight to bring a handful of candles. They would have been better than nothing should he need to…leave these others behind.

"Well, I hope to see these *fascinations* of yours before I grow much older," Gervaise groused. "Otherwise, you won't see a single franc from me."

Michel gazed at the other men and women gathered around the fat man. Nearly all of them appeared to be his toadies and hangers-on. Gervaise didn't attract friends as much as he did dependents. Michel was certain the merchant was paying for everyone.

"Please come this way." Dutilleaux gestured.

"How much farther?"

"Only a little." Without another word, Dutilleaux walked into the darkness as if he could see in it.

They all hesitated. Then Gervaise took a fresh grip on his lantern and walking stick and started forward. The crowd seemed to shrink in on itself as everyone began to move.

Swallowing his fear once more, Michel cast a last glance back the way they'd come. The urchin had disappeared. Doubtless he knew his way to the surface, but Michel wasn't so sure he could find his way back even with the marks on the walls. He turned and followed the light down into the tunnel.

"AS YOU MAY HAVE HEARD," Dutilleaux said as they walked, "I've recently returned from an extensive stay in the Orient. Shanghai, actually."

Michel knew that because he'd written the piece on Anton Dutilleaux divulging that information. The reporter had interviewed one of Dutilleaux's servants the previous week.

"While there, I learned much about the spirit world," Dutilleaux said. The lantern light revealed him ducking beneath a low arch. "Do watch your heads here, please." He continued down the steep incline. "The Chinese spirits and ghosts are quite active, you know. Have you heard of the *huli jing?*"

"No," one of the women answered. Others echoed her answer.

Michel followed cautiously. His fingers trailed over the rough stone as he passed beneath the arch.

"The *huli jing* is a fox spirit," Dutilleaux continued. "It takes the form of a beautiful maiden and seduces men, turning them weak or cruel. There are a number of stories about them."

"Have you ever met a *huli jing?*" the woman asked with keen interest.

"No, sadly."

"Why do you say sadly?"

"Because the amorous nature of the fox spirit is legendary." Dutilleaux turned and smiled at his small audience. "I'm told it would have been quite the experience. I embrace challenges on the field of ardor."

A couple of the women laughed.

Gervaise glared them into silence. "Dutilleaux, if I don't see something soon, I'm going to—"

Dutilleaux clapped his hands. Immediately pale yellow flames jumped from his palms and raced along the walls to outline a small chamber filled with stacks of bones.

"God help us," one of the men said.

"Witchcraft," one of the women gasped.

Cotton-mouthed, Michel stared at the flames. For the first time in his life, he felt he was in the presence of something truly arcane.

As if entertaining in a well-appointed drawing room instead of beneath the city, Dutilleaux turned to face his audience and spread his arms wide. "Come. Don't be afraid. I won't let anything you see here harm you in any way."

"Where—?" Gervaise raised the lantern and walking stick before him. "Where did you get all these skeletons?"

"He's brought us down here to kill us," a woman whispered. "Those are the bones of his previous victims."

"I should think I would have been quite busy, if that were true." Dutilleaux smiled and shook his head. "These poor souls aren't here through any doing of mine." He gazed at the stacks of skulls and long bones. Rib cages lay in another pile. "The church is responsible for their presence with us. Everyone interred at Saint-Nicolas-des-Champs is being moved here." He shrugged. "The church takes care to work at night. It wouldn't be seemly for people to see them trundling around wheelbarrows filled with skeletons, would it?"

"Dutilleaux is telling the truth," an older man said. "I've

talked to some of the priests. They're emptying the graveyards so Paris can grow."

The flames in the room continued to burn. Upon closer inspection, Michel noted that gutters had been cut into the wall for oil. Dutilleaux had simply—through some sort of sleight of hand—lit the oil.

"Did you want to talk about real-estate possibilities, gentlemen?" Dutilleaux asked. "Or did you want to talk about what I discovered in my travels?"

"Show us," Gervaise ordered. "I've not got all night."

"Don't be so demanding," Dutilleaux cautioned. "The spirits of China can be quite vengeful. I thought I'd already apprised you of that."

The fat man scowled at him and his jowls quivered as he restrained what was no doubt a sharp retort.

For a time, Dutilleaux talked about his journey to the old empires of China. He mentioned the people he'd met and the places he'd seen. As he spoke, the flames depleted the oil in the gutters and the room grew gradually darker.

IT WASN'T UNTIL FULL DARK had almost returned that Michel wished Dutilleaux would hurry up his presentation. Dutilleaux was an excellent storyteller, though, and his trained orator's voice filled the cavernous space with excitement.

"Though I saw all these things," Dutilleaux concluded, "I saw nothing as stupendous as that which I'm about to show you." He paced the room like a wild animal, and the darkness settled about him like a favorite cloak. "I found a way to open a gate to the Celestial Heavens. I can visit the Oriental afterlife. Tonight, I can take you with me."

Michel leaned against the cold stone wall and waited. The room seemed colder, and he didn't think it was his imagination.

"I don't see a gate," Gervaise grumbled.

"That's because your eyes aren't finely attuned to the spirit world. But perhaps I can help you to bring the spirit world into better focus."

Michel's heart thudded in his chest and blood roared in his ears.

Theatrically, as if all of this was taking place on one of the stages where he'd first honed his showmanship, Dutilleaux gestured to either side. Gray smoke billowed up from the stone floor.

It's just a trick, Michel reminded himself. It's nothing you haven't seen in theaters.

But the unsettling sensation within him grew stronger. The smoke continued to swell till it nearly filled the room.

Then a glowing shape appeared in the haze. Indistinct at first, the image gradually grew sharper, till it revealed itself as a beautiful young Oriental woman. Dressed in a long flowing red gown and with her black hair pulled up, she hovered there in the smoke.

"My lady," Dutilleaux greeted warmly. "I bid you welcome to the earthly realm."

The apparition nodded slightly but did not speak.

"I crave a favor," Dutilleaux said. "I have friends with me tonight. They wish to look upon the Celestial Heavens."

Just a trick, Michel thought. It's all done with lights and painted glass. No one is there.

But the woman in the smoke moved and pointed to her right. A moment later, a doorway appeared and hung in midair.

The crowd sat silently. Michel didn't know if they were even breathing.

Slowly, ponderously, the doorway opened within the smoke. On the other side of the doorway, a beautiful land filled with flowers and trees lay waiting.

"Do you see it?" Dutilleaux asked softly. "Do you see the Celestial Heavens?"

"Yes," a woman said in a strained voice. "I do. I see it. I can't believe I see it, but it's there. Right there."

Dutilleaux basked in the glory of the moment. He turned to the crowd and bowed deeply.

"We must be careful at this point," he told the audience. "We have to keep a wary eye on the gateway before someone—or some*thing*—manages to get through."

"You brought us here to endanger our lives!" Gervaise shook his walking stick and the cover fell away to reveal a gleaming sword cane.

Dutilleaux raised his hands in a placating manner. "There is nothing to be afraid of."

"I'm not afraid," Gervaise insisted. "But I won't allow you to endanger these women."

"I'm not endangering them. I can control the ghosts."

"Listen to him," another man, this one's voice harder and more confident, interrupted. "There *is* nothing to be afraid of—because there's nothing there."

"Who's speaking?" Dutilleaux demanded. The confident smile never left his handsome face.

Another man stepped from the back of the crowd. He peeled back his cloak and revealed saturnine features. "I am."

For a moment, Dutilleaux seemed at a loss. Then he smiled and said, "Professor Étienne-Gaspard Robert. Welcome to our festivities."

Michel recognized Robert's name. The man was Belgian by birth but had recently moved to France to pursue a career in art. He was also reputed to be a professor of physics.

"Not festivities," Robert stated. "This is merely a parlor show." He turned to the audience. "What you're seeing is an illusion. A play of light and shadow. Less substantial than an early-morning fog."

"Are you so sure, my friend?" Dutilleaux asked in a calm voice. "Perhaps you'd like to be the first to go through the gateway."

Michel stared at the professor.

"There is no gateway there." The people nearest Robert stepped back as though afraid of being struck down by any forces that chose to punish him for sacrilege. Robert sneered at the audience. "Superstitious fools. You're letting this bag of wind with a handful of tricks sway your good judgment." He locked eyes with Dutilleaux. "Permit me passage, then, charlatan. Show these sheep your power. Or be cursed for your fakery."

Boldly, Robert strode forward.

An eerie hiss came from within the mystical doorway. Michel tried to remind himself that everything he was witnessing was a trick, but the mood Dutilleaux had established held him firmly in place.

Before the Belgian professor reached Dutilleaux, a garish figure with a horribly white face darted out of the doorway. The figure raised a long-bladed knife in one hand.

Robert stepped back with a curse.

But the figure wasn't hunting him. The phantom turned on Dutilleaux. The knife flashed down and the flames went out.

Men and women cried and screamed as they stood in the meager pool of light provided by the lantern. None of them were close to where Dutilleaux had stood.

Trembling, Michel scooped up the lantern and carried it toward Robert and Dutilleaux. The light crept across the stone floor with him.

Robert stood against the nearby wall, obviously fearing for his very life. "That *thing* was here. I felt it. By God, it was real."

Michel turned the lantern toward Dutilleaux and found the man stretched out on the stone cavern's floor. Several skulls and bones littered the ground around him.

And the large knife the phantom had carried stuck out of the phantasmagorist's chest. Dutilleaux's face was already pale white in death.

1

London, England
Current day

"Couldn't you have worn something a little more...revealing?"

Annja Creed frowned as she considered the question over the Bluetooth earpiece that linked her with her satellite phone. She stood in the middle of a dank alleyway stinking with rotting garbage and Chinese takeout. Dark rain clouds hung in the sky visible between the buildings. Sporadic smog patches drifted past.

"Doug, I'm way underdressed for a potential mugging as it is." Annja wore a silver calf-length duster over black pants and a pearl-gray silk tie-waist blouse. Slouchy microsuede boots pushed her five-ten up to something over six feet. The boots were comfortable, stylish, and she could run for her life in them if she had to. She wore her auburn hair clipped back.

"This guy's not a mugger." Doug Morrell sounded put out. The producer of *Chasing History's Monsters*—the syndicated television show Annja costarred in with Kristie Chatham—was twenty-two, young and driven by all things Twitter.

Despite the fact that he wasn't really interested in history or archaeology, Annja genuinely liked Doug. He was like the younger brother she'd never had.

"I know he's not a mugger." Annja walked through the alley with her hands in her pockets. "He's killed three women that the Metro police know about."

"I saw those reports, too, which is why I want you to be careful."

"Careful, but less dressed."

Doug hesitated only a moment. "Yeah."

"Not happening."

"You could at least get rid of the jacket."

"And give it to Igor to carry?"

"Don't make fun of your bodyguard."

Annja resisted the impulse to look back at Ray Venard, the guy Doug had hired for the shoot tonight. Venard was a large, hulking brute who had played professional rugby before he'd gotten caught shaving points, then was injured by outraged fans. He'd gotten through the court system unscathed, but the fans had left him with a knee that would never be the same.

"I thought he was a cameraman."

"He is. He's both. Kind of like a Reese's Peanut Butter Cup. Bodyguard and photographer."

"Did I mention to you that when I met him in his office he was taking pictures of women for a skin magazine?"

Doug sighed. "You did."

"So not only am I *not* going to take my coat off to be more revealing in this cold, rat-infested alley, I'm also not going to take it off in front of Igor."

"I only mention the coat because it could help ratings."

"The ratings are fine. We just got a two-year renewal."

"So we could work on the next two-year deal."

Annja kept walking. Working for the television show was sometimes a pain, but mostly it was fun. And there was Doug and a few of the other people she liked who were connected to the production. Not only did she get to travel, but the salary and bonuses were nice and allowed her to follow up on other explorations and digs.

She watched the shadows carefully. Detective Chief Inspector Westcox hadn't been happy when she'd come to his office to discuss the recent murders that the media was attributing to "Mr. Hyde." Of course, the reporters were only doing that because "Mr. Hyde" had written in, claiming responsibility for the murders.

Westcox had shown Annja the morgue photos of the victims. The DCI was closemouthed and professional, and he'd thought to frighten her off with the brutality of the killings. The victims had been stomped to death, their faces pulped by size eighteen Rufflander work boots.

What DCI Westcox hadn't known was how much violence Annja Creed had seen. The police inspector had assumed she was a young woman inquiring into things much too bloody for her.

"I'm keeping my clothes on for the next two years, too."

Doug whined. He was a good whiner when he wanted to be, but Annja was impervious.

"You have Kristie for the T and A ratings. With me, you've got history and archaeology ratings."

The fact that Kristie Chatham was the fan darling because of her habitual loss of clothing and "wardrobe malfunctions" bothered Annja more than she would ever tell anyone. But she accepted it. She had her fans, too.

"Would Kristie agree to walking in a rat-infested alley at midnight so a serial murderer could leap out of the shadows and murder her?"

"No, of course not. If she got hurt, she wouldn't be able to work."

"And I would?"

"You're not going to get hurt. You have Igor. Besides, you're only there tonight to shoot a little mood footage. Igor also tells me the fog is going to have to be enhanced. Says it's really weak."

Annja looked back over her shoulder at the lumbering shadow that trailed her. Igor carried a portable video camera in one giant paw. "You're talking to him?"

"Texting. I'm talking to you."

"Great. So you're distracting my bodyguard."

"He'd probably be more focused on you if you weren't over-dressed."

Turning her attention back to the alley ahead of her, Annja shook her head. Sometimes—*most* of the time—Doug had a one-track mind. "About the Mr. Hyde thing."

"You said you loved the Mr. Hyde thing," Doug said, instantly wary. "You said the Mr. Hyde thing was awesome. You couldn't wait to do the Mr. Hyde thing."

Annja had said that. But that had been when she'd thought her schedule wasn't going to be so tight. She'd hoped to get out to Hadrian's Wall. That had been the site of her first dig, and the place still held a special spot in her heart.

Then, when she'd seen those poor women in those police photographs, she realized that the "investigation" bordered on sensationalism. That the women were going to be fodder for the conspiracy mill *Chasing History's Monsters* routinely set into motion didn't sit well with her.

"You do realize Mr. Hyde isn't real."

"When you meet Mr. Hyde, tell him that. Either we've got one of London's oldest and eeriest monsters returned from over a hundred years of being missing, or we've got someone who rediscovered Dr. Jekyll's secret potion. I don't care which it is. It's a great story."

"That's what it is—a story. *Strange Case of Dr. Jekyll and Mr. Hyde* was a novella written by Robert Louis Stevenson. An allegory some say was based on Victorian views of sex."

"Yeah, yeah, yeah. You told me that already. And I agreed that you could put that stuff in there. As long as there's not too much of it. Which is why we're picking up the tab on your date with Professor Beeswax."

"Professor Beswick. And it's not a date. He's an expert on film, literature and myth."

"I suppose it doesn't hurt that Professor Beeswax is good-looking, though. I ran a Google search on him. I see what you saw."

"Really? You thought Professor Beswick was attractive?"

Doug nearly choked. "No! That's not what I said. Are you recording this?" He cursed. "Now I've got Diet Coke up my nose. Don't *do* that."

Annja chuckled. Doug was easy to set off.

"As for this Mr. Hyde thing, I got a very convincing email stating that the Dr. Jekyll formula had been discovered on the internet and someone had re-created it."

"Who was the email from?"

"An anonymous source."

"Doug, it's me and you. You can tell me."

"I can't. That's how the writer tagged the email."

"And you bought into this based on that." Annja couldn't believe it, then reminded herself she'd been in the same situation with Doug dozens of times before.

"Sure. There are the three murders. Mr. Hyde claims to have done them."

Annja bit her tongue. She was looking forward to her stay in London and dinner tomorrow with Professor Beswick appeared promising.

Ahead, one of the doors suddenly banged open and four figures spilled out into the alley. Three of them were young Asian males dressed in dark clothing backing out of a restaurant. One of them held a young woman trapped with an arm across her neck. Her eyes rolled fearfully and she hung on to the man's arm to keep her balance.

The woman was dressed in black pants and a white shirt, the typical server's uniform for a lot of restaurants. Light shined from the open doorway and revealed tattoos on the necks of two of the men. All of them carried pistols. A handful of pound notes drifted from the cloth bag one of the guys fisted.

"Doug, I'm going to have to talk to you later." She unclipped the Bluetooth earpiece and shoved it into her pocket. Annja was calm as she surveyed the scene. Her heart went out to the frightened young woman.

An older man in a suit raced through the back door and quickly stopped when he saw the gunmen. "Laurel."

"Get back, old man." One of the youths took a step forward and pointed the gun at the businessman.

"Please. You have the money. Don't take my daughter."

The youth opened fire. Annja didn't know if he was trying to hit the man or not, but one of the bullets chewed into the door and the other went through the doorway.

The man dropped to the ground, covered his head with his arms and screamed for his daughter.

"Papa!" The young woman cried out in fear and tried to free herself. One of the men not holding her backhanded her across the face.

"Hey!" Igor's loud voice thundered in the alley. "You blokes want to put the guns down before you get hurt?"

Glancing back, Annja saw that Igor had a gun in his own hand instead of the camera now. He stood holding the revolver like he knew what to do. Unfortunately, so did the three Asians. Two of them opened fire while the third hung on to their hostage.

Annja pressed herself flat against a building.

The bullets drove Igor back into cover. He rose up just long enough to fire two rounds. Both bullets went wild, and one of them came dangerously close to Annja.

In the next moment, a car roared into the alley behind Igor. The bright lights pinned him for a moment as he threw up a hand in front of his eyes. He stepped aside, but the driver opened the door and hit the bodyguard hard enough to bounce him off a brick wall. Igor rolled and dropped as the car roared by.

The driver brought the car to a rocking halt only a few feet from the three men. They opened the doors on the passenger's side and started to get in with their captive.

Annja sprang for the driver, shoved a hand into the car and caught the man by the jacket front. She yanked hard and the man's head cracked against the window's edge. The driver's eyes rolled up and showed white just before he slumped across the steering wheel. His foot pressed against the accelerator and the car sped forward before the others could climb in.

Reaching into the otherwhere that contained her sword, Annja drew the blade into the physical world. Moonlight glinted along the three-foot-plus polished steel blade. The hilt was plain, unadorned, wrapped in leather strips, and it felt completely at home in Annja's hand. The sword had been forged for Joan of Arc and only the one destined to take up Joan's crusade could wield it.

Annja shot forward as the car passed, and she knew she was moving too fast for the men to track. To them it would have looked like she'd appeared out of nowhere. She drove a double-fisted blow into the face of the man on the right. Propelled by the great strength she had when she wielded the sword, the man sailed backward and thudded against crates of trash. Rotted vegetables and refuse tumbled over him. Rats scattered and ran.

Whirling, Annja lashed out with the sword as the man holding the money took aim at her. Beyond him, the out-of-control car rammed into a streetlight, shuddered and died with an explosive release of steam. Her blade caught the man's pistol as he lifted it, and drove it from his grip. She took two quick side steps forward, then raised her right leg and drove her foot into his face.

He went down in a loose jumble of flesh and blood, unconscious before he hit the ground.

Still holding his hostage, the third robber fired again and again.

Annja ducked and went low. She shoved her left leg out and swept the legs of the man and his hostage from the ground. As they fell backward, the man kept firing, wildly spraying the stone walls on either side of the alley. Trapped between the buildings, the sharp reports rolled like thunder.

She swung the sword at the gun and knocked the weapon from the man's grip. He tried to get up, made it to his knees, but she met him with the sword hilt between his eyes. The impact snapped his head back and he sank.

Satisfied that the immediate danger was over, Annja released the sword and the weapon vanished. She walked over to the young woman and helped her to her feet.

"You're all right." Annja cradled the woman in her arms. "You're going to be fine." When her father reached them, she released the woman into his custody and went back to check on Igor.

The big man was just coming around, groaning and still trying to get his breath back.

"C'mon. Let's get you up and get out of here." Annja pulled him to his feet.

Igor held an arm across his ribs and stared at the men lying in the alley. Cooks and waitstaff were already taking them into custody.

"What happened?"

Annja shrugged. "The driver's brakes must have gone out. He hit them and knocked them down."

"The girl's not hurt?"

"We got lucky." That was an easier story than telling the truth to the police. "Let's go. I really don't want to spend the whole night in a police station being questioned."

"Shouldn't we stay?"

Annja looked at him.

Igor grinned sheepishly. "I mean, I did try to save the girl. Maybe a little publicity will help the business, you know."

"Right. And that way Doug Morrell will know you got taken out by a couple thugs. Think he's going to want to keep you around protecting me from Mr. Hyde?"

"On second thought, I've never been a glory hound."

"Right."

"But we can't leave just this minute." Igor looked at the side of the alley. "I have to find my pistol. I must have dropped it. Can you help give us a look?"

2

Professor Edmund Beswick stood on the curb in front of Carlini's Magic Bullet Club when Annja arrived by cab. He was a few years older than Annja, in his mid-thirties, and was about the same height. His black hair brushed the tips of his ears and he wore a neatly trimmed goatee. His olive complexion hinted at some Indian or Middle Eastern ancestry and lent him an Old World elegance. The dark blue tux and top hat made him look like he'd stepped from the pages of a Charles Dickens novel.

He opened the cab door for Annja and thrust pound notes at the driver.

"I can get that." Annja had her pocketbook at the ready.

"Nonsense. This evening is my treat. I insist." Edmund offered her his gloved hand.

Annja took it, then held on to his arm. She wore a simple black dress, but it was one of her favorites and she knew she wore it well. Still, she couldn't help feeling underdressed.

"I wasn't expecting anything so formal."

Edmund grinned. "You look marvelous, and you'll find that not everyone inside is dressed as pompously as I am." He waved a dismissive hand. "I tend toward the exotic when I'm given my head. I do hope you'll forgive me my eccentricities this evening, but this is a special occasion."

"You look dashing."

"Thank you. You are most kind."

Annja surveyed the front of Carlini's Magic Bullet Club. The first floor of the small building was covered in wooden gingerbread that made it look positively ancient. Red velvet curtains covered the large plate-glass windows. Torchlight created golden pools against the material and shadows moved inside. A red carpet under a small canopy led to the front door, which looked like it would open to a dungeon.

"Now, that looks foreboding."

Edmund's smile was so big and innocent, Annja was certain she could see the twelve-year-old he had been. "Doesn't it just?" he replied.

"And I notice there's no doorknob."

"So it's mysterious, too." His dark brown eyes twinkled. "Carlini's is a very special place. No one gets in here who isn't invited." He waved a hand and suddenly there was a single red rose in it. He offered it to Annja.

Smiling, she took the rose in her free hand and smelled it. The fragrance was subtle and sweet. "You're a magician?"

"Alas, you thought I was merely a literature professor?" Edmund feigned a look of pain.

"From what I've heard, you're an authority on English literature. I saw you in an interview on the History Channel and was impressed. When I got this assignment, I knew I wanted you as a guest speaker."

"I'd wondered about that. Your program doesn't draw immediate confidence from a cursory look."

"No." Annja knew that was true, and it was one of the things she had to accept about the opportunities *Chasing History's Monsters* afforded her. "I like to go below the surface of a story."

"That was true of most of your segments that I saw."

"Sometimes a good deal of what I've prepared ends up on the cutting-room floor. So I have to warn you that some of what I'm doing could end up in the same place."

"Well, we'll just have to roll the dice, won't we?"

"I do put interviews on the television website." That was a deal Annja had recently negotiated. "Added-value pieces I believe are interesting."

"Then I shall endeavor to be interesting. I consider it a challenge."

"That's hardly fair for you."

"Trust me when I say that I am a fierce competitor."

"All right." Annja grinned in self-satisfaction. She'd known Edmund was going to be intriguing. She was happy to be proven right.

"So how goes your hunt for our new Mr. Hyde?" Edmund looked troubled.

"We're still looking."

"Please don't hold it against me for hoping you're not the one who finds that man." Edmund shook his head. "I saw some of the pictures and videos they released of those poor women. I would hate to think of you facing such a brute."

"I don't think that's going to happen. Not with Metro increasing surveillance on the streets." Annja looked at the pub. "Tell me about this place."

"Carlini's has been a home to magic for over a hundred years. All the great masters have come here. Magicians. Escape artists. Illusionists. Mentalists. And prestidigitators of every stripe—fair and foul. They've had just as many villains as they've had heroes." Edmund smiled fondly at the pub. "Houdini was here. Sir Arthur Conan Doyle, though he came looking for *real* magic and a way to contact the spirit world. Walter B. Gibson. Robert Harbin. Chung Ling Soo. David Nixon. David Copperfield. Penn and Teller. You've heard of the Magic Circle?"

"The organization committed to sponsoring and reimagining magic. Of course."

"They formed here in London in 1905. Carlini's predated them. The Great Carlini preferred to keep a lower profile and only invited in the very best in the field. They gave private shows to the royals and other important people, perfected their craft and studied other masters. This was the place where they could be themselves and enjoy magic without the stress of an unfriendly or doubting audience. The people in this place appreciate the orchestration of a skilled magician."

"It sounds like the hardest audience in the world to play for."

Edmund grinned. "No. And do you know why?"

Annja shook her head, enjoying his enthusiasm.

"Because magicians *want* to believe in magic." Edmund's eyes sparkled. "Carlini's guests are the best audience. They live to be astonished, amazed and entertained. Now, observe." He gestured at the door.

In response, the door quivered, rattled and slowly pulled inward with a theatrical creak that gave Annja goose bumps. She'd been in scary situations before, circumstances that would have gotten her killed if she hadn't been quick enough or strong enough or lucky enough to get through. But there was something about the atmosphere of the pub, Edmund's story and her own awakened childish fascination with magic that affected her.

Edmund took her arm and guided her inside.

After the outside door closed, a small yellow light flared to life overhead. The tiny bulb was barely enough to reveal the three wooden doors at the end of the hallway. One door lay dead ahead and the two others were on either side. The doors were unmarked.

"Magic is all about choices." Edmund waved toward the doors. "Tonight you have three."

"And if I choose wrong?"

"We go hungry and I don't get to show you my biggest surprise." Edmund grinned. "But I have faith in you." He gestured her forward. "Please have a look. This challenge has been designed for you."

Annja cocked an eyebrow at Edmund. "You realize we could go hungry."

"I've always found that risk increases appetite and appreciation for a meal." Beswick looked at her. "I wouldn't have figured you for someone unwilling to risk."

Amused, Annja advanced. As she did, a slot opened up in each door and a three-by-five notecard slid out to hang from each of them.

"Kind of creepy."

Edmund just smiled and waited.

Examining the cards, Annja discovered the one on the left door had a drawing of a chicken in charcoal-gray ink. The middle door had a drawing of an egg in brown ink. The third one she wasn't quite sure of but it was black and the drawing was etched deep into the card. She pointed to it. "What's this?"

Edmund shook his head. "The best I could do at drawing a chicken nugget."

"A chicken nugget?"

"Yes."

"So the obvious correlation would be that I'm supposed to pick the door that comes first?"

"If that's what you think."

Annja examined the cards again, more closely this time. She paid particular attention to the drawings, the ink and the shape of the lines. She even smelled them to confirm her conclusions. "If you listen to a biologist, the biologist would say that the egg comes first. But a theologian would insist that the chicken came first."

Edmund's face remained unreadable.

"However, a mystery lover could be tempted to pick the chicken nugget simply because it doesn't fit, or because it's not a natural thing, as the chicken and the egg are." Annja smiled. "You went to a lot of trouble."

"Then you already know the answer?"

"Yes." Annja knew she'd surprised him. He hadn't thought she would fail, but he hadn't expected her to succeed so early. "But only because you went to such great detail to make your clues."

"Elucidate."

"The answer is in the inks, and somewhat in the drawings, but not in what was drawn."

Edmund smiled in startled appreciation. "You *are* good."

Annja pointed to the egg. "That ink is atramentum, or it's supposed to be. It's a replica of a Roman ink made about sixteen hundred years ago. You can tell because it's faded out and has turned brown. That's because it was made from iron salts and tannin. It goes on bluish-black, then fades to brown."

She moved on to the nugget. The image was drawn deeply into the card with fine, black lines. "This ink was called masi and was created in ancient India about 400 BCE. The drawing is deep and thin because they used needles to write with. So did you. Quite a good touch on that, actually."

Edmund inclined his head in thanks.

"This, however, was the first." Annja touched the drawing of the chicken. "The ink is graphite based and it was drawn with an ink brush. When you look closely, you can see the brushstrokes. This ink, or at least the original, was created by the Chinese about 1800 BCE. Definitely the first."

Edmund quietly applauded her. "Bravo, Ms. Creed. Quite the performance."

Annja curtsied, thoroughly enjoying herself. "Did you think of this little test yourself?"

"No. I must admit that I had help. After all, I'm just a professor of English and literature. This was beyond my ken." Edmund walked to the door with the chicken on it and the door opened before he reached it.

A large man in a good suit greeted Edmund with a warm handshake. He had a high forehead and glasses and looked to be in his sixties. "Welcome, Ms. Creed. It is indeed an honor."

"Annja Creed, may I present Gaetano Carlini, the current owner and host of the Magic Bullet Club. Gaetano, my beautiful guest, Ms. Annja Creed."

Totally charmed by the big man, Annja offered her hand and he took it, bowed deeply and kissed the back of it. "Please come in and make yourselves at home. I have your table this way." Gaetano swept them into a large dining room.

"OVER THE YEARS, MS. CREED—"

"Please call me Annja."

Gaetano nodded solemnly. "Annja. Over the years, Carlini's has been host to a number of important and famous people." He gave a careless shrug. "And, at times, some who were more infamous than famous."

"But no one that was ever shot or hanged for their crimes." Edmund swirled his wine around in the fluted glass.

"Thankfully, no. We've never had that notoriety." Gaetano pushed the glasses up on his nose. "But we do ask one favor of those guests, other than to enjoy themselves while they are here."

Annja sat at the small, intimate table in the center of the ornate dining room lined with stage magic memorabilia and framed caricatures of magicians. Her red rose occupied a small vase in the middle of the table. They were adjacent to the small, curtained stage. Noises came from the back, so Annja knew something was going on. Her curiosity was getting the better of her.

"What would that favor be?" Annja nibbled on a piece of Havarti cheese.

"To allow me to sketch a caricature to hang on our wall."

"Gaetano is very good. Very knowledgeable about a great many things. Including history." Edmund sipped his wine. "He's the one who helped me figure out your puzzle."

Gaetano waved the compliment away.

"In another life, had not magic called to him so strongly, I fear he would have been a forger."

"Oh, now I'm offended." But the big man's boisterous laugh plainly indicated he was more flattered than anything.

"I would love for you to draw a caricature of me. But I'm not a magician."

"I beg to differ." Gaetano sat up straight in his chair. "I have seen many episodes of your television show. You are a great performer at revealing some of history's best-kept secrets. I knew who you were before this youngster did."

Edmund held up his hands in surrender. "Sadly, that's true. I told him I'd gotten an email from an American archaeologist regarding the Mr. Hyde murders."

"He was set to turn you down." Gaetano shook his head in mock exasperation. "Silly boy."

"In my defense, it was only because the murders were so heinous. I didn't want to contribute to the gratuitous exposure of the misfortunes of others. That was before I spoke with you and you assured me that would not happen."

"It won't." Annja fully intended that the Mr. Hyde piece, if it aired, wouldn't dwell on the murders as much as it did the legend. Hopefully the London Metro police would have the killer in hand by then, as well.

"He might not have called you at all had I not shown him one of your programs." Gaetano chuckled. "He was, of course, instantly smitten."

Annja laughed. "Obviously he's easy to impress."

The meal came then, thick steaming platters of pastas and seasoned vegetables along with crisp salads. Annja ate with gusto, listening to the familiar camaraderie of the two men as they played off each other and took turns telling her stories.

While they dined, several magicians from other tables went to the stage and performed their acts. The audience oohed and aahed in approval and delight as things disappeared, reappeared and changed into other things.

Annja loved every moment of the shows, from the theatrics to the conversational patter that established the history and the obvious familiarity the men and women all had with one another.

"If you'll excuse me, I'll return shortly." Edmund left the table and headed for the kitchen area.

Gaetano kept Annja enthralled with stories about his adventures as a magician. He also kept the wine flowing and managed small sleight-of-hand tricks with dinnerware, napkins and coins between magic acts.

Then the stage curtain parted and Edmund passed through. He no longer wore the old-fashioned suit. He was dressed in a swimsuit and carried swim goggles in his hand.

Instantly, the dining area filled with catcalls and good-natured teasing.

"I see you've got nothing up your sleeve, Professor Beswick!"

"And chicken legs."

Edmund held up his hands in surrender. "Go ahead, mates. Take your shots. Make them the best you can, because I'm about to amaze and astonish you."

After a few more catcalls and hoots of laughter, the crowd settled into an expectant hush.

"Tonight I'm going to attempt my grandest escape ever. As many of you know, I've been studying to become something of an escapologist. I'm going to perform this escape in honor of my guest—Ms. Annja Creed of *Chasing History's Monsters* and something of an escape artist herself, according to the stories I've read about her."

An enthusiastic burst of applause followed the announcement.

"Stand up. Let them see you." Gaetano pushed back out of the spotlight that suddenly fell on Annja.

She stood, waved and bowed, and felt more than a little embarrassed. She sat back down and glanced at Gaetano. "Does Edmund bring all his dates here?"

Gaetano smiled. "You are the only person Edmund has brought here in all the years that he's been coming."

Flattered, Annja turned her attention back to the stage.

"You have all heard of the Great Houdini, and you have heard of the Chinese Water Torture Cell. Or, as the master himself called it, the Upside Down." Edmund stepped back and swept a hand toward the stage.

The curtains parted and a large glass-and-steel box filled with water was revealed. A beautiful young woman walked out of the shadows. Like Edmund, she wore a swimsuit, except hers was a spectacular yellow bikini designed to draw the attention of every male in the room.

Annja kept her focus riveted on Edmund. The assistant locked his feet into stocks, then operated a mechanical winch to lift Edmund off the stage floor, suspend him in the air and place him headfirst into the water tank.

Despite the fact that she knew the trick was part of a planned show, Annja tensed as she watched Edmund submerge. He put his hands on the glass, steadying himself as he went into the water. His hair floated around his face. She caught herself holding her breath with him and felt foolish.

A moment later, the assistant locked Edmund in. Once the woman stepped back, Edmund started working to free himself. At first, his movements were controlled, smooth and confident. Then, as time passed, he became more frantic. His hands slammed against the glass walls as he jerked and strained to pull free of the stocks.

3

"Something's wrong." Annja started to get up. She was already reaching for her sword, thinking that she could break the glass walls and release the water.

Calmly, Gaetano put a hand on her forearm to restrain her. "Relax. This is part of the show." But he didn't take his eyes from the stage.

Annja forced herself to sit, but she noticed that several of the other dinner guests were ill at ease, as well. She didn't know how much time had passed, but she thought at least two minutes had gone by. Perhaps as many as three.

Abruptly, the assistant hurried forward and draped a bloodred curtain over the water tank. Maybe it was supposed to protect the audience from the horrid sight unfolding before them. Then the woman lifted an ax and prepared to strike.

The audience held its collective breath.

The only thing holding Annja in her seat was Gaetano's firm, unshaking hand on her arm. And that wasn't going to hold her back for much longer.

The assistant started her swing with the ax just as the curtain rose above the water tank. She dropped the ax and yanked the thick material away to reveal Edmund standing triumphantly on top of the locked water tank.

Annja released a tense breath as enthusiastic applause filled the dining room.

Dripping wet and looking magnificent, Edmund bowed theatrically. Then the stage curtains closed.

Gaetano smiled at Annja. "Now are you glad that I asked you to wait?"

"Yes, but that was nerve-racking."

"It was meant to be. Magic is meant to confound or astonish. But really good magic, the kind like Houdini practiced, was more in line with a circus performance."

"How?"

"An aerialist working without a net. A lion tamer sticking his head into a lion's mouth. A motorcycle daredevil whirling madly inside one of those steel balls. And even someone who allows himself to be shot from a cannon. They all flirt with death. At least, they do to an untrained eye. But the reality is that even the best performers sometimes catch an unlucky break. The audience never truly wishes to see something like that, but the expectation is there that it could happen."

"I suppose that doesn't speak highly of us, does it?"

"We're all human. What is life without spectacle? And risk?"

"I LOVE DOING MAGIC." Edmund, dressed again in his tux, sat at the table and walked a euro across his knuckles. The coin flashed in the light. "Ever since I was a boy, I wanted to know how magicians did the things they did. So I worked at it." He shrugged and smiled sadly. "Unfortunately, magic doesn't pay much unless you get very good and very lucky."

"Being good doesn't always help." Gaetano poured more wine all around. "Edmund, you are good. What you need is a dedication to your craft and luck."

"So why didn't you become a magician? The money?" Annja basked in the glow of the dinner, wine and company.

"I thought I needed a legitimate job. Something to fall back on. In addition to magic, I also loved stories. So I became a professor of literature."

Gaetano threw his arm around the younger man. "Edmund is being modest, which is no way for any self-respecting magician to be. He attracted the attention of Oxford University and is now one of their shining lights."

Annja grinned. "So I've been told."

Gaetano shook his head. "Modesty ill becomes a magician. A performer of magic must be unique and daunting and commanding, while being extremely skilled at his craft. Edmund lacks the callous disregard for others that a magician must develop."

"Appearing on *Chasing History's Monsters* should help correct that."

Gaetano licked his finger and mopped up graham cracker crumbs from the small dessert plate that had once contained an excellent blackberry cheesecake. "And that is precisely why I pressed him to agree to see you. Of course, that might not have happened, anyway, except for that little predilection of his."

Annja was intrigued. "What predilection?"

"Oh? Usually he's very prompt about mentioning it and the curse."

Annja studied Edmund, who looked even more pained. "Now I'm curious."

"Annja, you must be tired."

She shook her head. "Not too tired to hear about cursed predilections. And I hate mysteries. If you don't tell me, I'm going to be wondering all night."

Edmund grinned. "Well, we can't have that, can we?"

"WHAT DO YOU KNOW of phantasmagoria?"

Annja walked beside Edmund as they strolled from Carlini's Magic Bullet Club. Still feeling a warm glow from the after-dinner wine, she linked her arm through the young professor's. "It was theater, kind of early film. Phantasmagorists projected images on walls—usually of supernatural creatures—and told stories about them. But that's the extent of what I know."

Cars whizzed by on the dark streets. Windows of closed

shops caught their reflections as they passed. The wind held a chill and the fog had increased, but the weather was still pleasant enough.

"The images weren't just shown on walls. They were also projected onto smoke and semitransparent surfaces, which created even more eerie effects. Phantasmagoria began in France in the late 1700s and spread all over Europe during the next hundred years. People do love being frightened."

"The human culture seems to thrive on ghost stories. They address common fears and offer a backhanded belief in God."

"If demons and monsters exist, then so must God?"

"Something like that."

"You learned that in archaeology?"

"Anthropology, actually. All part of the same field."

"Interesting."

Annja patted him on the arm. She relished the conversation, and her curiosity about the young professor's pastime remained unanswered. "This has something to do with your predilection?"

"Everything."

"Good."

"Phantasmagorists owed their success to the magic lantern."

"That was made by the Chinese."

Edmund grinned. "Not according to the phantasmagorists. They claim that Christian Huygens invented it in the mid-seventeenth century, and that Aimé Argand's self-named Argand lamp made the device even better. However, I do know that the Chinese were the first to use lamps to project images painted on glass as storytelling devices. Actually, that comes into this story, as well."

Annja continued walking and listening.

"Once the magic lantern was successfully designed, others were quick to use it. To backtrack a little, Giovanni Fontana, a physician and engineer and self-proclaimed magus, used a candle-powered lantern to project the image of a demon. The idea of the supernatural became a fixture when it came to the magic lantern."

They paused at the street corner.

"Athanasius Kircher, a German priest, reportedly summoned the devil with his device. Thomas Walgensten called his projector a *lantern of fear* and used it to 'summon ghosts.' A man named Johann Georg Schopfer performed in his Leipzig coffee shop and summoned dead people, images projected on smoke. Later, he went insane—believed he was being stalked by devils and shot himself. He also promised he would raise himself from the dead."

"I take it that didn't happen."

Edmund grinned and shook his head. "No."

The streetlight changed and they crossed.

"The latter part of the eighteenth century and into the nineteenth century gave rise to the phantasmagorists. They began their craft in Paris, as I mentioned, but the use of magic lanterns spread quickly. At the same time, Romanticism and Gothic literature were growing. The timing for the magic lantern and the phantasmagorists, you might say, was dead-on."

Annja rolled her eyes at the pun.

Edmund chuckled. "Suffice it to say, I am smitten by the whole splendor of the phantasmagorists and their lucrative entertainment. During the heyday of the shows, many hosted gatherings within the catacombs beneath Paris." Edmund looked at Annja. "Can you imagine what that was like? There they were, deep under the city, and these phantasmagorists could make them feel as though they were walking through the bowels of hell itself."

"That doesn't sound like my idea of a good time."

"Ever watch horror films when you were young?"

Annja smiled. "I did."

"We take pleasure in tempting the dark, wondering if it will one day come out of hiding and pounce on us with a predator's fangs."

"Not me." Annja had been there too many times.

"And yet, here you are, Ms. Creed, tracking a man who has savagely beaten and killed three women."

Some of Annja's good mood evaporated, though she knew

Edmund hadn't intended for it to. And he was right about her being there in spite of the danger. She was never drawn to the danger, but she was attracted to the mysteries and curiosities. "I'm not afraid of the man who killed those women."

"I would prefer it if you were."

"He's just a man. The police will find him soon enough."

Edmund nodded. "I hope you're right. In the meantime, I'll tell you about the particular magic lantern I have in my possession."

4

"Anton Dutilleaux was a Parisian phantasmagorist in the late eighteenth century." Seated at the small table in the tea shop not far from the hotel where Annja was staying, Edmund added milk to his tea and stirred. "Have you heard of him?"

"No." Annja stuck with coffee and cupped her hands around her cup to absorb the warmth. She took a deep breath, enjoying the sweet baking smells.

"I can't say I'm surprised. Rather, I would be flabbergasted—very much so—if you *had* heard of him." Edmund reached into the messenger bag he'd brought with him from Carlini's. He took out an iPad and placed it on the table. The screen flared to life.

Not many people were in the tea shop at that late hour, and none of them paid attention to Edmund and Annja. They were mostly watching the television in the corner of the room. The low rumble of the news and casual conversation was a comforting undercurrent of background noise.

Edmund touched the handheld device and opened a folder. He sorted through images, then selected one. Immediately, a taciturn man with slitted eyes filled the screen.

"Anton Dutilleaux. This image was used on several handbills that advertised his shows. He toured Paris for three years.

I couldn't find much history on him, no parents and no idea where he lived. I just know that he traveled." Edmund sipped his tea. "And no one ever knew much about his murder."

That heightened Annja's interest. "He was murdered?"

Edmund nodded and grinned. "Intriguing, no?"

"It is."

"According to a newspaper account of the murder, Dutilleaux was stabbed through the heart by a Chinese ghost in front of several eyewitnesses." Edmund tapped the iPad screen again and shifted to a new image. "He was pronounced dead at the scene by a doctor in the audience. Do you read French?"

Annja nodded. *"Mais, oui."* And she read on.

Phantasmagorist Slain by Celestial Spirit!

On the eve of the twenty-first of June, in the catacombs, M. Anton Dutilleaux, late of Paris and previously from parts unknown, met with an untimely end at the hands of a supernatural murderer. M. Dutilleaux was a phantasmagorist conducting a group comprising this reporter and several others through a dark and winding tunnel under the city at the time of his death.

The reporter described several of the events leading up to the murder. The account meandered, as stories did in those days because the news was meant to be savored and enjoyed and—in this case—puzzled over.

M. Dutilleaux had barely begun what was to be a fascinating presentation, this reporter is convinced of that, when the crafty killer sprang from the darkness. Merciless and without hesitation, the apparition brandished a knife and drove it through M. Dutilleaux's heart with cold savagery, like a predator pouncing on much weaker prey. The stricken man had no opportunity to defend himself or call upon his Maker before he lay stretched out dead before us.

A few paragraphs of the reactions of the crowd, the panic that had ensued and the desperate attempts to revive Dutilleaux followed.

As of this morning when I write this piece for you, Dear Reader, the Parisian police have yet to decide who killed M. Dutilleaux. There are some who believe that the phantasmagorist was the victim of a Celestial spell that followed him from the Far East during his travels. Many readers this reporter knows believe in those curses. All I can tell you is that whatever killed the poor man was not human. I stared into that White Face of Death and knew fear the like of which I have never before known.

My only prayer is that the thing that killed M. Dutilleaux has completed its mission. Otherwise, that thing may yet haunt the catacombs. At present, the tunnel has been boarded up and placed under guard by the police until such time as they deem it safe.

Annja looked up at Edmund. "I assume you followed up on this story?"

The young professor nodded. "Of course. I've checked for months and years following. And I've gotten absolutely nowhere. No one ever mentioned Anton Dutilleaux again. Only a few magicians remember him. I wouldn't have known him at all if I hadn't discovered some of his handbills in a collection I purchased a year ago."

"Two hundred years is a long time."

"It is. But history has a way of making itself known, don't you agree?" Edmund sipped his tea.

"Tell me about this lantern you found."

Slipping his hands around his teacup, Edmund leaned conspiratorially across the table toward her. "Only a few weeks ago, I was at an estate sale."

"Looking for the lantern?"

"No. Merely poking about. A lot of magicians have made their home—temporary and permanently—here in London.

During my days off, I research those people. Occasionally I stumble across stage props or costumes while dissembling through estate sales."

"Treasure hunting?"

Edmund smiled in pleasure. "When history is not valuable or fashionable, it is garbage and people toss it out. Or they sell it to speculators for pennies on the pound. I have assembled quite the collection of mementos and collectibles. Trust me when I say I have made several acquisitions that other fans of magic envy, and that no one else would want." He shot her a rueful look.

Annja didn't doubt him for a moment. Passion showed in Edmund's dark eyes and she knew he wouldn't easily turn away from something he wanted.

"Have you heard of Étienne-Gaspard Robert?"

Annja thought for a moment, then shook her head. "Another phantasmagorist?"

"Yes, but he was also an inventor and physicist from Liège, Belgium. His stage name was Étienne Robertson." Edmund waited expectantly.

Annja shook her head again.

"Robertson, by either name, was one of the most important phantasmagorists who ever lived. I have copies of some of the lenses with which he used to conduct his magic-lantern shows. I can't afford the real lenses, not on a university professor's salary. Fascinating stuff. Especially for the time."

"I'll take your word for it."

"Do. Anyway, Robertson was there the night Dutilleaux was murdered by the Chinese ghost."

"Coincidence?"

"No. Robertson was there to take umbrage with Dutilleaux. Robertson felt certain Dutilleaux was copying aspects of his own magic-lantern show. Which I'm sure he was. But at that time, many people were copying Robertson."

"Was Robertson a suspect in the murder?"

"Of course." Edmund grinned, warming to the subject. "Robertson and Dutilleaux were rivals for a long time. But the murder occurred in 1793, four years before Robertson revealed his pièce de résistance at the Pavillon de l'Echiquier. That was when Robertson left his competitors in the dust, to use a colloquialism. During that time, Robertson perfected the magic-lantern craft by putting the projectors on wheels to create moving images as well as make the images larger and smaller simply by moving the projectors."

Annja sipped her coffee.

"The police never found any evidence against Robertson?"

"No. But Dutilleaux's magic lantern went missing that night. I believe that Robertson, or one of his assistants, liberated that projector while the gendarmes were en route. Or perhaps it was merely a spectator looking for a trophy. Or simply theft."

"And the lantern was taken even though it was cursed."

"Dutilleaux claimed that he could open a doorway into another world. Maybe they didn't think the projector was cursed so much as it was truly a miracle." Edmund smiled. "You have to remember—magicians, the really good ones, want magic to be real. Perhaps whoever took it believed the magic lantern possessed supernatural powers. Fast-forward two hundred years."

Annja finished the last of her coffee.

"I was tracking down Robertson's apprentices. There were dozens of them, by the way. In 1799, Robertson's phantasmagoria show had created such a stir that the courts ordered him to reveal his secrets to the public. Once he did that, there were many imitators. Some of them carried phantasmagoria back to the United States. Did you know that?"

"No."

"In May 1803, the first of the magic-lantern shows was presented at Mount Vernon Garden, New York, and the entertainment caught on readily enough." Edmund looked into his cup.

For the briefest moment, Annja felt uncomfortable, like someone was watching her. She glanced around the teahouse, but no one seemed especially interested. It was too dark to see much out the window. She returned her attention to Edmund.

"The point is, I tracked down some belongings of one of Robertson's assistants at auction those few weeks ago." Excitement gleamed in Edmund's eyes. "I think someone else was searching, as well, because after I bought the lot—for a song, practically—the auctioneer informed me there was an interested party asking about the lantern I'd bought. They told me I could more than double my money if I wished to sell it. Of course I refused. What I gave for the lantern was a pittance, and it was purely for my own amusement. Even doubling my money wouldn't leave me a rich man."

"So you now own Anton Dutilleaux's cursed magic lantern?"

Edmund nodded happily. "I truly believe I do." He hesitated. "What I'd like to ask, and I wouldn't want to impose in any way, is if you could look this magic lantern over and see if there's a possibility of authenticating it."

"Confirming that it was owned by Anton Dutilleaux would be extremely difficult if the man is as hard to trace as you say he is."

"He is, and I wouldn't ask you to do that. If possible, I'd like to confirm the approximate age of the lantern."

"I would love to."

"Good." Edmund checked the time on the iPad. "We'll have to save that for another day, though. I have a literature class bloody early in the morning, and none of my students is especially keen on *Beowulf.* I don't want to go dragging in looking like one of the underclassmen. But I had an absolutely brilliant time, Annja."

"Me, too."

EDMUND INSISTED ON WALKING Annja back to her hotel, then he flagged down a taxi and left, promising to see her the following afternoon so they could start working on the Robert Louis Stevenson piece.

Up in her room, still slightly muddled from the rich food and the wine but not quite drowsy enough to sleep, Annja exchanged the black dress for a T-shirt and flannel pajama pants. The room was just cold enough to make the flannel welcome.

She booted up her notebook computer and logged on to the

internet. She checked Google for Anton Dutilleaux but didn't get any hits on the name that had anything to do with magic lanterns or phantasmagoria.

Frustrated, but not surprised, Annja backtracked and book-marked sites that dealt with phantasmagoria, magic lanterns and Étienne Robertson. At least that way she could meet Edmund Beswick on a more equal footing when they were together again.

Her sat-phone chirped for attention before her head hit the pillows. Caller ID showed it was Bart McGilley.

Bart was a longtime friend, a detective on the New York City Police Department and a guy who had ended up being a big part of her life—on and off. There was a definite attraction between them, and they'd been the "plus ones" for each other several times as well as going out on legitimate dates. However, the only permanent thing they had between them so far was friendship.

The caller ID picture showed Bart in his shirt and tie, which was how Annja usually saw him. He wore his dark hair cut short and was square jawed, the kind of guy women would want to have children with.

"Hey, Bart."

"Hey. Not calling too late, am I? Wherever you are." He sounded distant and a trifle off his game.

"London. Only a five-hour time difference."

"It's midnight there."

Annja looked at the time on the computer. "Yes. But I'm not asleep. Still working on New York time at the moment."

"Morning's going to come early."

"Morning is six hours away no matter how you look at it. I go to sleep and I'm awake six hours later. I don't have to be up till eight. I've still got a couple hours." Annja waited. Bart McGilley wasn't one to call frivolously.

Bart hesitated. "Maybe I should call at another time."

"You've got me now."

"Yeah."

Annja waited.

"We caught a bad one tonight. I don't really want to get into it. I just wanted to hear a friendly voice."

"Sure."

"So what are you doing in London?"

Obviously the Mr. Hyde story wasn't going to fly. That would have reminded Bart of his own problems as well as put him into worry mode. Instead, Annja talked about phantasmagorists, magic lanterns and what little she knew of Étienne Robertson.

Mostly, Bart listened. She'd seen him like this before and knew that he appreciated her talking about something, *anything,* while he sorted himself out. Chances were, she'd never know what he'd gotten into unless she went back and researched the news. Usually, she chose not to do that.

Finally, Bart thanked her and said he had to go. "You should be careful while you're over there. There's some creep in the city calling himself Mr. Hyde who's killing women. I was watching CNN while you were talking."

"Yeah, I heard about that."

"Well, be careful. According to the news release, he just killed his fourth victim tonight."

5

The streets were packed near the East End alley where the fourth Mr. Hyde murder had taken place. Annja instructed the cabdriver to get as close as he could, then paid him and walked the rest of the way.

She didn't like being at a crime scene. Several of the digs she'd been on had been crime scenes, as well. But there wasn't the immediacy of present-day death.

A logjam of onlookers, police and emergency teams filled the narrow street. Flashes went off from cell phones and pocket cameras. A cold breeze, shot through with patchy fog, blew in from the Thames. The blue lights of the police cars whipped across the apartment buildings and stirred the shadows.

Despite the number of people, Annja got close enough to see a middle-age woman sprawled half on the curb and half in the street between parked cars. Blood darkened the sides of the cars. Bloody handprints streaked the back windshield of one.

"She fought him." A woman in her late forties or early fifties stood in front of Annja in a faded house robe with a grape Popsicle in one hand, talking to an older man. "'Course, didn't do her no good. Poor thing couldn't get away from that madman."

Annja nudged closer. "Excuse me."

The woman looked back at her.

"Did you see what happened?"

Her eyes narrowed. "You're American?"

"Yes."

"Thought so. I recognize the accent. And yes, I did see what happened. I called in the bobbies. My name is Jane. Jane Morris."

"It's nice to meet you, Mrs. Morris."

"Are you a reporter?"

"Something like that."

Jane regarded her suspiciously. "I don't see no notepad."

"I've got a very good memory."

"No camera, neither."

Annja nodded toward the policemen as they started out into the bystanders. "Anyone who's taken a picture is likely to have their phone or camera removed as part of an effort to collect evidence."

The woman watched as the police officers gathered the cell phones and cameras. Of course, the law enforcement officers didn't get them all because the crowd started dispersing. The ones who had their grisly souvenirs were intent on keeping them. They'd pop up on Facebook, blogs and Twitter within minutes if they hadn't already.

"This is my first murder," Jane said in a low, confiding voice.

"Could you tell me what you saw?"

The woman pointed the Popsicle at the murder victim. "I saw that poor thing fighting with a proper big bloke. He was huge. Like some kind of gorilla. Shoulders out to here." She placed her hands about three feet apart and the Popsicle dripped on the neck of the man ahead of her.

The man cursed and shot her a nasty look. He took a step away.

"Sorry, love." Jane licked the Popsicle momentarily dry. "She hardly had time to cry help. I was standing up there." She pointed at a balcony on the third floor of the nearby building. "I called the police immediately." She shook her head sadly. "But I knew it was too late."

"The man got away?"

"Of course he did. A man who can stomp in a woman's head like he's stepping on a peanut? No one around him is going to stop him. We don't carry guns like you Yanks."

"Do you know who the woman was?"

Jane shook her head. "Looked like she was a waitress, from the way she was dressed."

Feeling ghoulish, Annja surreptitiously took out her sat-phone and brought up her Twitter account. Keeping the phone hidden from the police, she scrolled through the news and didn't have to go far before she found the first tweets about the dead woman.

Audrey McClintok. A twenty-seven-year-old waitress at a diner.

Annja put her phone back in the pocket of her Windbreaker. So far, none of the victims had anything in common except for being women. The ability of the man to kill and disappear was chilling.

"Well, now here's something." Jane sucked on her Popsicle.

Two uniformed policemen pushed through the crowd, backing people off and heading straight for them. Probably wanted to talk to Jane, since she'd reported the murder, Annja thought.

They stopped in front of Annja. The oldest of the two was grizzled, and his bleak eyes indicated he'd seen too much over the years. "Ms. Creed."

She nodded.

"DCI Westcox would like a word with you, miss."

"Now?" The last thing Annja wanted to do was get involved in the murder investigation.

"Yes, miss. Now."

The two policemen had flanked her and she got the distinct impression turning down the detective chief inspector's invitation wasn't an option.

"This way, miss." The older policeman waved her forward and the crowd parted once again.

Along the way, bright flashes from cell phones and cameras temporarily blinded Annja.

"DIDN'T TAKE YOU FOR A looky-loo, Ms. Creed." DCI Alfred Westcox was a tough, no-nonsense cop. Probably ten pounds underweight, he looked as if the excess had been hammered off him. He wore a trench coat and hat, and the tie clipped to his chest lifted as the wind gusted. His cottony white hair matched his eyebrows and mustache. He wore thick glasses over his watery blue eyes.

"I'm not." Annja respected how the chief inspector ran his business, but she wasn't happy with the way she'd inadvertently ended up on the wrong side of him.

Westcox didn't like her any more than he did any of the other media people gathered around for the story. In fact, she didn't know why he'd singled her out. There were plenty of others on hand.

"Yet here you are, Ms. Creed. In the middle of my murder investigation."

"I came out to see if I could help."

"Really?" Westcox cocked a dismissive eyebrow. "You? I don't know why that idea never crossed my mind."

"Your time would be better served solving Audrey McClintok's murder, than coming down hard on me."

Westcox took a deep breath and his nostrils flared. "Who gave you that name?" He glared at the two policemen who had fetched her.

"Not me, sir." The grizzled man stood his ground.

The younger man took a step back. "Nor me."

"Brought her here straightaway. Just as you said."

Annja didn't like the two men taking heat for something that wasn't their fault. "It wasn't either of them. I got the woman's name off Twitter."

Westcox turned his glare on her.

"Someone tweeted about the murder. Probably someone in the neighborhood who recognized her."

"Or it was the killer." He raised his voice to call, "Peters!"

A younger detective in a Windbreaker turned toward his superior.

"Get your mobile and give the lab a ring. Put one of the computer lads on to the Twitter accounts. Find out who put up posts regarding this unfortunate girl. I want their names, addresses and a chat with them."

"Yes, sir." Peters turned away and pulled out his cell phone.

Another uniformed policeman trotted up to Westcox. "The coroner is here, sir."

At the end of the street, Annja saw a new vehicle with flashing lights.

"Get him over here so we can shut this circus down."

"Yes, sir." The policeman turned and fled.

"Now you, Ms. Creed."

"I don't know why you're taking such issue with me." Annja met the man's gaze full measure.

"I was told this absolutely amazing story about a botched robbery last night. Apparently a few young Asian gang members held up a restaurant not far from here."

Annja kept her face devoid of emotion.

"The restaurateur and his lucky daughter—and even the gang members—all tell the same fabulous story of a red-haired American woman with a sword who interfered with the robbery."

"Okay."

"Would you happen to know anything about that?"

Annja didn't like lying, but in this case the truth wasn't something she was prepared to tell. "No."

"Why would the woman with the sword run off like that?"

"Perhaps she heard how appreciative you were of anyone trying to help with your investigation."

The grizzled officer laughed, then quickly covered it with a coughing fit. "Sorry, sir. It's this bloody fog."

Westcox glared at him, but the man stood with his eyes averted.

"You're not here to help me with my investigation, Ms. Creed." Westcox returned his attention to Annja. "If you interfere, or turn vigilante with a sword, I'm going to lock you up."

"All right."

That answer seemed to take Westcox by surprise. He stood there for a moment. "I don't much care for your nose in my case. Your particular television show seems dedicated to prattling on to the feebleminded about ghosts and ghoulies."

The accusation touched a nerve. Annja liked what she did for *Chasing History's Monsters* and was tired of defending her work.

Before she could speak, Peters turned back to him.

"Chief Inspector."

"What?"

"I've accessed the Twitter feed regarding the murder." Peters pointed at Annja. "They also appear to be aware that Ms. Creed is with you." He held out his cell phone for Westcox to see.

Annja saw it, as well. Someone had snapped a picture of her talking to the detective chief inspector.

"Whoever took this is assuming you called Ms. Creed in for a consultation regarding the Mr. Hyde murders."

Westcox looked apoplectic. "No one has even said this is a Hyde killing."

"Actually, someone has. Mr. Hyde himself has tweeted in and claimed credit."

Annja responded immediately. "Trace the tweet."

"Computer forensics is already on it."

"This is a break," Annja said to Westcox. "Hyde has never tweeted before."

"And he may not have…have *tweeted* now. Someone else may have done that. We can't jump to conclusions." Westcox shoved his hands into his trench coat.

"I wouldn't dream of it, Inspector." Despite her respect for the man's job, Annja had had enough. She wasn't the only person interested in the Mr. Hyde story. The number of people taking note of the murders was growing every day. He had no right to lean on her while she was simply trying to do her job. "Are we done here?"

Westcox hesitated. Finally he gave a brief nod. "We are. But watch your step, Ms. Creed."

"I always do, Inspector." Annja walked away as the haggard-looking coroner hunkered down beside the woman's corpse. She headed into the crowd without looking back. She'd seen more than she'd wanted to.

"Annja! Annja!" A young female reporter with blond highlights held out a microphone while a camcorder operator trained his sights on Annja. She raised a hand to block the sudden bright light.

"Ms. Creed, what kind of help do you expect to give Detective Chief Inspector Westcox regarding the Mr. Hyde killings?" That came from another journalist, one with an Irish accent.

Annja ignored them and headed for the other end of the street. A few of them followed her, but gave up when she hit the cross street.

Her phone rang. Caller ID showed it was Doug Morrell. She didn't want to take the call, but she knew if she didn't Doug would just keep calling back.

Just as she started to answer, a dark Jaguar S-Type glided to a stop at the curb. Both passenger doors opened and two men holding pistols got out.

"Ms. Creed. Get in the car, please."

6

For a moment, Annja hesitated.

"If you attempt to flee, I will shoot you in the legs and pull you into the car." The speaker was a man of medium height and Asian ancestry. He held the pistol with a steady hand.

"You'll shoot me with the police just up the street?" Annja asked calmly.

"And I'll get away with it. They are compromised in this area. Before they can mobilize and get here, we'll be gone." He waved the pistol. "Now get in before I have you put in. We won't be gentle."

She'd escaped many traps in the past. Sometimes it was better to step into them and work on the fly. A moving trap couldn't stop and think, or reset itself. At least, not most of the time.

She folded herself into the backseat of the car. Another man, also Asian, sat in the front passenger seat. He held a pistol in his lap. Once she was seated, the two men who had gotten out got back in. She was sandwiched between them.

At a word from the driver, the car pulled into traffic as smoothly as wax running down a candle.

Annja sat quietly between the two men on either side of her. "Do you want to tell me what this is about?"

The man in the front passenger seat turned to face her. "It's simple. We want the magic lantern Edmund Beswick purchased from the antiquities auction."

The answer surprised Annja. "I don't know where it is."

The man's expression remained flat and unreadable. "That's too bad. My employer will not believe you. It would be better if you knew where the lantern was."

"Why would anyone think I knew where it was?"

"Because Edmund Beswick has shown you the lantern."

"No, he hasn't."

"Then he planned to. My employer knows this."

"Planned to. *Didn't.*" Despite her anger, Annja was worried about Edmund. Why hadn't the men gone to his flat first?

"My employer will believe you're lying."

"Why would I lie?"

"I only asked you so that we could stop and pick up the lantern before I take you to him." He shrugged. "It's too bad you don't know. He is a very determined man. Many people fear him, and with good reason." He turned back around and watched traffic, then gave directions to the driver in Chinese.

Annja couldn't understand what was said, but she guessed it wasn't good. She shifted in the backseat. "How did you find me?"

One of the men sitting beside Annja showed her his cell phone. The picture of her talking with Detective Chief Inspector Westcox. He grinned. "We have been watching you. We only just missed you in the hotel."

The commander flicked his gaze to the rearview mirror and spoke harshly.

A scowl darkened the face of the man beside Annja. He put his cell phone away.

Even in the shadows of the car, Annja saw the tattoos ringing the guy's neck. As with the Japanese Yakuza and the Russian Mafiya, in the Chinese Triad, tattoo designs were badges of office and warnings to everyone else.

How had Edmund's magic lantern drawn the attention of the Triad?

Since she didn't know where the magic lantern was, she had to escape.

Her captors wouldn't hesitate to harm her. The only edge she had was that they hadn't been given permission to kill her.

She hoped.

At a traffic light, the car came to a stop. The man in the passenger seat turned up the radio. Techno-pop filled the Jaguar.

Focusing on what she was going to do, she breathed deeply enough to charge her lungs without drawing the attention of the men beside her. Then she threw a backfist toward the man on her right. As she expected, he was prepared for the attack and caught her arm. However, he wasn't prepared for her to shift and slam her forehead into his face as an immediate follow-up. She repeated the move and heard the man's nose crunch under her assault.

He cried out once, then lapsed into unconsciousness.

As the other man tried to bring his pistol into play, Annja fell into the lap of the unconscious man, lifted her left leg and thrust her foot into her second attacker's face.

The kick slammed the man against the window and shattered the glass. His pistol fell to the floor. Annja kept her foot pressed against his jaw to hold him in place. He struggled weakly, obviously dazed from the impact.

The man in the front passenger seat swung quickly and threw his gun arm across the seat. Annja didn't wait to see if he was going to threaten her before he opened fire. She reached up and seized his wrist, then yanked down hard and snapped his elbow.

The man screamed hoarsely and dropped the pistol.

Committed now, aware that her life was possibly measured in heartbeats, Annja opened the passenger door, pushed off the guy she had trapped against the broken window and rolled onto the street. She got to her feet at once, cognizant that the conscious men inside the car were clawing for their weapons. Even the man with the broken arm was determined to get his pistol, or maybe he had another.

Annja vaulted to the back of the car and headed for the

roof. Bullets ripped through the back windshield, blowing out chunks of glass, and punched calderas in the car's roof. She never broke stride as she ran across the hood of the car and leaped onto the next stopped vehicle.

Jumping, vaulting and changing directions like a fleet-footed deer, Annja crossed the stalled traffic and reached the sidewalk just as the light turned green. She kept running as car horns, shouts and pistol shots made a huge cacophony behind her.

At the corner of the nearest building, she risked a quick glance back. Bullets tore into the bricks and threw dust in her face. She ducked out of sight, then dared another look. Two of the men had started after her, but their hearts weren't in it and they'd retreated to their vehicle. Annja resumed running.

SEVERAL BLOCKS LATER, ANNJA slowed to a walk. Thankfully London stayed busy nearly twenty-four hours. She called Edmund Beswick's cell several times but didn't get an answer.

She also debated calling the Metro police, but decided against that until she knew more of what was going on. Detective Chief Inspector Westcox was going to have a lot of questions, and she didn't have any answers.

Doug Morrell called again and this time she picked up.

"Hey," he whispered irritably.

"I need you to do me a favor."

"Me? I was calling you."

Annja would've smiled at that, but she was too worried about Edmund Beswick. "Still need the favor, Doug."

"Fine. What did you find out from the police?"

"What?" For a moment Annja was thrown for a loop.

"I saw the pictures on Twitter. You and Detective Scarecrow."

Annja couldn't believe it. Then she checked herself. Doug Morrell lived for Facebook and Twitter. It only made sense that he'd be trailing any mentions of her or *Chasing History's Monsters*. "His name's Westcox."

"Whatever. Man looks like an advance warning for a famine."

"He's not that thin."

"Your perspective is skewed because you're always looking at mummies and skeletons. Skinny living guys must look obese to you."

Annja shook her head. "Let's talk about the favor."

"Let's talk about Detective Scarecrow."

"Westcox. Get his name right. The lawyer will need to know it."

"Lawyer?" Doug's tone changed immediately from irritated to anxious. "Did you do something?"

"No, but the chief inspector is threatening to deport me if I don't stay out of his investigation."

"He can't do that, can he?"

Annja loved putting Doug on the spot. "Not if I have a lawyer. A good one."

"We do have a good one."

Curiosity got the best of Annja. "Why are you whispering, Doug?"

"We're having a council meeting."

"Who?" Then it clicked. Doug Morrell belonged to a group of would-be vampires. That was one of his hobbies and one of the interests that endeared him to the production company that underwrote *Chasing History's Monsters*. "Right. You're with the Bat Boy Legion."

Doug refused to take the bait and stayed focused. "Did you find out anything more about Mr. Hyde?"

"No."

"Why not?"

"Because there's nothing to tell."

"Mr. Hyde just took his fourth victim."

"I know. I was there." Annja looked up and down the street for a cab. If the men who had kidnapped her hadn't doubled back around and found her by now, she felt fairly sure they wouldn't.

"Oh, yeah, the Twitter feed. And there are a couple You-Tube videos up now."

Annja groaned.

"In fact, I think maybe *Chasing History's Monsters*—" Doug's voice grew louder "—is the only program not getting video of your meeting with Scotland Yard."

"Shhh, you'll wake the baby vampires."

"I'm just saying…"

"Westcox isn't with Scotland Yard. He's with Metro. And he called me over when he saw me at the crime scene to warn me away. Actually, warning is too soft. It was definitely a threat."

"Well, we're not going to put up with that crap. He's not going to threaten us and get away with it. We're going to follow the Mr. Hyde story no matter where it goes."

"You do realize that I'm the only person in danger of going to jail, don't you?"

"There's Igor."

"He's missing in action tonight."

"What? He should be there with you."

Annja silently disagreed. The last thing she needed was Igor going all macho. "I need the favor."

"What favor?"

"I filled out paperwork on Edmund Beswick."

"Professor Beeswax."

"I need his home address."

Doug chuckled. "Don't tell me you couldn't get that from Professor Beeswax. I mean, c'mon, Annja. A professor of reading? That should have been a slam dunk."

"He's a professor of literature. Are you sure you went to college?"

"Business degree with a minor in video productions. Got the diploma on my office wall."

"I haven't seen it for all the action figures and comic books."

"Hey! Graphic novels."

"I need Beswick's address from the file."

"Do I look like a walking computer?"

"You don't go far without your computer. Just look up the

information for me so you can go back and play with the other vampires."

"We don't play." Sullenly, Doug put her on hold.

After a couple minutes, during which the light changed and Annja crossed the street, Doug was back on the line with the requested information.

"And keep me up to date. We're paying for your little trip over there and we don't want to have to put this program together from YouTube videos. Make sure Detective Scarecrow keeps you in the loop."

"I'll get right on that." Annja broke the connection, tried Edmund's number one more time, got no answer and flagged a passing taxi.

7

A few tense minutes later, Annja got out of the cab in front of Edmund's apartment building in Chelsea. She paid the driver and walked up to the security door. Frustrated, she rang Edmund again, but he still didn't answer.

She knew it was possible the professor was asleep and had turned his phone off. However, she couldn't get the Triad members—if that's who they were—out of her mind. She didn't doubt they'd go after Edmund.

She retreated to the back of the building. Studying the old metal fire escape, she leaped up, caught hold of the bottom rung on the ladder leading up to it and was pleasantly surprised when the ladder rolled down more quietly than she would have figured.

For a moment, she lingered in the shadows, watching the windows of the back apartments to see if any lights came on or if anyone looked out to check on the sound. Then, when nothing happened, she went up the ladder. There was still the chance that someone could have called the police, but she was willing to take the risk.

On the third-floor landing, she stayed low, duckwalking under two windows to reach Edmund's flat. The window was locked. The room was dark. When she peered inside, she couldn't see anything.

She liked Edmund. She wanted to know he was all right. But if she got caught breaking into his flat—either by Edmund or by the police—the situation was going to be really embarrassing.

She could finesse Edmund. He'd wanted to show her the magic lantern, and her news that someone was searching for it, even to the point of shooting at her, would gloss over the forced entry.

The police would be a different matter.

Taking out the Leatherman multitool she'd purchased after arriving in London, because she hated to travel without some sort of tools, she opened the longest blade. Working carefully, she ran the blade around the glass and removed the plastic liner that held the window together.

When she finished, she set the liner aside, then used the knife blade to leverage the glass free. The pane popped out easily and she set it aside, as well. She folded the knife and put it away. Then she stepped into the flat.

Inside the room, after negotiating a small sofa, Annja moved to one side and waited for her vision to acclimate to the darkness. She also listened intently. Someone in another flat was watching television, a program with an obnoxious laugh track. In another flat, farther down, people were in the midst of an argument. And there was a crying baby somewhere in there.

Annja wished she had her backpack, where she kept her Mini Maglite. Abruptly, she realized her possessions might not be safe in the hotel. Her mysterious abductors had mentioned that they'd missed her there, but she didn't know if that meant they'd broken in or merely seen her leave.

Eyes adjusted, Annja looked around the small studio flat. It was basically a tiny office under a miniloft that held a modest bed. Two separate areas for Edmund to work and sleep.

Clutter covered the floor. Most of the mess was books and papers, but Annja knew Edmund wouldn't have left them like that. He was responsible for the corkboards on the walls and the books piled on the small dining table, but not for the haphazard way everything had been thrown.

The door was ajar and light from the outside hallway leaked in. Someone had broken in.

Remaining calm, Annja closed the drapes over the windows and crossed the room by memory to find the lamp mounted on the wall. She switched it on with a curled knuckle and soft yellow light filled the studio.

She closed the door, then picked up three of the biggest books she could find. She used her sleeves to cover her hands so she wouldn't leave fingerprints behind in case any crime scene techs got overly industrious.

Moving quickly, she stacked the books against the bottom of the broken door. They wouldn't keep anyone out, but they would serve as an early warning system if anyone tried to enter.

The small desk had once held a notebook computer. A network cable lay abandoned on the desk. She checked through the drawers, but it was obvious they had been searched. Judging from the clutter in front of the desk, the searchers had simply emptied the drawers onto the floor.

There were no thumb drives, no CDs or DVDs, nothing that could have been used to store files. A business card file folder lay abandoned upside down. Evidently the searchers had been instructed to find anything high-tech.

Again using her sleeves, Annja picked up the folder and flipped through it. Most of it was contact information for various agencies, libraries, library staff, other Oxford professors, plumbers and electricians. She guessed that Edmund didn't entirely trust his computer to remember everything for him. She didn't blame him. She didn't, either. That was one of the reasons she maintained her journals as well as her private blog.

One of the cards caught her attention.

Gaetano Carlini stood out in a heavily embossed but simple font against the grayed image of a rabbit peering over the edge of a top hat. The number on the front of the card was to the club. With difficulty, Annja extracted the card from the plastic holder using her sleeved fingers.

When she flipped the card over, she found another telephone number. Feeling a little better, she tucked the card into the back pocket of her jeans, then continued her search.

Twenty minutes later, Annja was satisfied she'd combed the entire flat. Edmund Beswick lived the cramped life of a confirmed scholar with too much to do and too little space to do it in.

Although Edmund had spoken proudly of the collection of magical props he'd assembled, only a handful of small things occupied the built-in bookshelves in the office area. Decks of playing cards, coins, scarves, cups and balls, and even a gibecière, the large pouch street magicians used to hold props while putting on shows, shared space with the books on magic.

That meant Edmund kept his collection somewhere else.

Annja returned to the card file and flipped through the thick plastic pages till she found three business cards for storage units. Two of the storage businesses were in Chelsea and one was in Mayfair.

She'd been relieved to discover there was no blood in the apartment. If the men had gotten to Edmund, they'd taken him easily enough. She didn't know if he would tell them about his storage unit. Then she realized almost in the same thought that he would. He would be fearful for his life, for good reason, and wouldn't hold back when asked.

But what would the Triad do with Edmund when it recovered the magic lantern?

Antsy, ready to move, Annja retreated to the window and climbed out. She took a moment to replace the glass pane in the window so others—less altruistic—wouldn't be tempted by an easy mark. Then she clambered back down the fire escape.

ANNJA BOUGHT A CUP OF COFFEE at a pub around the corner, fended off a couple halfhearted attempts at picking her up and retreated to the back area and the phone. She was happy to find one there because public phones were a dying business now that everyone had cell phones. Still, cell phones were known to go dead at inopportune moments.

She switched off her sat-phone because it had a GPS chip in it that would allow police to track her if they wanted to. After she finished speaking with DCI Westcox, she was pretty sure the man would want to find her.

She dialed Westcox's office and was greeted by a polite male voice. She identified herself and asked to speak with Westcox.

"I'm afraid DCI Westcox is unavailable at the moment, Ms. Creed."

"I know. He's working the fourth Mr. Hyde murder."

The assistant didn't respond to that.

"I just left him less than an hour ago."

"I understand that, Ms. Creed, but DCI Westcox asked not to be disturbed—"

"A man has been kidnapped and it might have something to do with Mr. Hyde. Do you think that will interest DCI Westcox?"

"Wait a tick, Ms. Creed."

Annja sipped her coffee and waited anxiously. She didn't know if Edmund's disappearance was connected with the Mr. Hyde murders or not, but it was a way of getting Westcox's attention. She didn't have to wait long.

"Ms. Creed, where are you?"

Annja ignored that, but she felt certain that the chief inspector already knew. The landline would show up immediately. If he really wanted to see her, a patrol unit would already be en route.

"Professor Edmund Beswick has been kidnapped."

"Who is he?"

"I don't have a lot of time to get into this."

"Why?"

"Because I'm trying to find him. I think it would be better if you were looking, too."

"Come into my office. We'll talk."

"Haven't you already sent someone to pick me up?"

Westcox didn't bother to deny the charge.

"I don't know what Professor Beswick is involved in—"

"The Mr. Hyde murders?"

"I doubt it. Saying that was the only way I had of getting your attention."

"That also constitutes interfering in a police investigation. I'll have you up on charges."

"Fine. If that's what it takes to get you looking for Professor Beswick, do it. In the meantime, he needs to be found. His life is in danger."

"What makes you so certain of that?"

Annja peeked down the hallway to assure herself the police had not yet arrived. "Because the men looking for him also kidnapped me."

"Really?" Westcox's tone indicated he wasn't happy, and he wasn't entirely convinced.

"Yes. Right from under your nose. Now that I think about it, maybe calling you is a waste of time."

"Ms. Creed, you're not doing much to endear yourself to this office."

"You're not very endearing, either, Inspector. I need you to help me find my friend."

"I was given a report only a short time ago. Something about a shooting involving an automobile loaded with possible Asian gangsters and a young red-haired woman spotted fleeing the scene. Would you happen to know anything about that?"

"Have those men been taken into custody?"

"Not as yet. We're searching for them. Nor do I intend to discuss this over the phone with you, Ms. Creed. We'll talk in my office."

"Thanks for the invitation, Inspector, but I'm going to decline for the moment."

Westcox's voice was hard as he replied, "That course of action wouldn't be prudent."

"With all due respect, you weren't in the back of that car when the guns came out. I like my chances on my own at the moment. Find my friend. Then I'll be happy to speak with you." Annja hung up.

She regretted not having gotten her backpack from her hotel room, but it was possible that Westcox already had men there. Or that the Triad had set up camp there.

Or both, which would have been interesting.

She started for the front of the pub, noticed the police car pulling to a stop out on the street in front of the building and headed for the back door. She was in the wind before the police arrived.

8

A few blocks from the pub, Annja stopped at a bodega and used the pay phone. She called the number she'd found for Gaetano Carlini's home and listened to it ring twice before it was picked up.

"Hello?" Gaetano sounded half-asleep.

"It's Annja Creed. I'm sorry to be calling so late." Annja glanced at the clock on the wall behind the counter. The young Indian male working the counter watched her, though whether he just liked looking or was suspicious she couldn't say.

"Ah, Annja." She heard fumbling noises over the line. "It's very late, isn't it?"

"Or very early, depending on your point of view."

Gaetano chuckled. "Yes, it is. Are you all right?"

"I am, but I'm afraid something's happened to Edmund. He's not with you, is he?"

"No. Why would he be with me?"

"I was just hoping he was there because he's not at home." Annja quickly brought Gaetano up to date on her attempted kidnapping and Edmund's probable abduction.

"Oh, dear. You've gone to the police?"

That required a further explanation.

"I see." Gaetano sounded thoughtful and more awake. "I

could, as Edmund's friend, insist that something be done to find him. You said this inspector's name is Westcox?"

"Yes. But I was hoping you might be able to help out a little more."

"How so?"

"What do you know about the magic lantern Edmund bought from the auction house?"

"Only what he's told me, but I can find out more. I have a number of contacts throughout the city. I'll try to uncover what I can."

"That would be awesome."

"What about you? Are you safe?"

"I think so."

"But you can't go back to your hotel, can you?"

"Not without a forced audience with DCI Westcox. And he might be successful in putting me on the first plane out of London."

"Well, we won't let things go that far. However, it's plain that you can't do anything else until we know more, and you require safe habitation while we look. Would you feel comfortable coming here? There's an extra room in my quarters, and I don't mind putting you up."

Annja almost sighed in relief. Being on the run in London, which she was partially familiar with as a tourist but definitely not as a fugitive, sounded horrible. Her chances of getting caught by the police grew exponentially the longer she stayed on the streets. The trip to London wasn't turning out the way she'd expected it to.

"You don't mind?"

Gaetano laughed. "One of my neighbors is an old spinster who is convinced that—because of the magic—I am in league with the devil. I can't wait for her to catch a glimpse of you arriving at all hours."

Annja didn't much feel like laughing.

"Meet me here at the shop. I'll put on some of that terrible coffee that you Americans treasure so much. And try not to fret about Edmund. He's a resourceful lad and a skilled escapologist. I'm sure he's handling himself just fine."

Even though she wanted to believe that, Annja didn't hold out much hope. Escapology was all about knowing the traps inside and out. It wasn't about escaping from people determined to kill you.

FIFTEEN MINUTES LATER, ANNJA stood in front of the entrance to Carlini's Magic Bullet Club. The morning had grown colder and the fog had gotten more thick.

Less than a minute later, it opened with the same theatrical creak as before. The weak light in the corridor flared to life as the door closed behind her. For just a moment as she stood there, alone, Annja felt nervous.

Her chances of getting out of the corridor if this turned out to be a trap weren't good. Just as she felt ready to explode, the door on the right opened and Gaetano stuck his head through. He wore a colorful bathrobe over flannel pajamas.

He waved her forward. "Come on, then."

Annja walked through the door. As she'd noticed earlier, all the doors actually led to the foyer outside the dining area. The puzzle was that in name only. Of course, a guest could still be wrong, but he or she wouldn't be turned away.

"You haven't heard from Edmund?"

Gaetano shook his head as he led the way back into the dining room. "No. I've tried some of the friends we have in common. Woke them up and worried them, as well."

"Then he *is* missing." The news hit Annja hard. She'd hoped that the break-in at his flat only signified that his home had been violated and that he might yet be free.

"Yes. I'm afraid so. Please. Sit." Gaetano gestured to the table he'd set up with a coffee and tea service.

Annja slipped out of her coat and draped it over a chair. She sat in the chair Gaetano pulled out for her, then watched as the man took a seat across from her. He poured coffee and pushed the cup and saucer across.

"Would Edmund call you if he was in trouble?"

Gaetano poured a cup of tea for himself. "About something like this? Something involving magic?" He nodded. "Of course he would. In addition to knowing a lot about legerdemain and the art of illusion, I also know a great number of people. Like, for instance, the auctioneer that worked the estate sale where Edmund picked up Anton Dutilleaux's magic lantern."

Gaetano poured milk into his tea before continuing. "There was nothing special about the sale. Merely a descendant of a collector getting rid of items no one else cared about." He set the creamer down and looked at Annja.

She blew on her coffee and waited. She wrapped her hands around the cup to absorb the welcome heat.

"In the case of Dutilleaux's magic lantern, there was another interested party, but he learned of the sale too late to bid. This is where it gets interesting. And, perhaps, more troubling." Gaetano laced his fingers. "Have you heard of a man named Jean-Baptiste Laframboise?"

From the way Gaetano said the name, Annja knew the person wasn't a good man. She missed having her computer and a ready internet connection. In seconds she could be infinitely more knowledgeable than she presently was. "No."

"Neither had I, but the auctioneer told me about him. As it turns out, Laframboise is a black marketer. One of those chaps who can—no matter how difficult or how illegal it is—get it for you. For a price."

"Laframboise deals in antiquities?"

"Not as a regular field of operations, no. In fact, the auctioneer inquired after Laframboise to a policeman friend of his. A man in Scotland Yard who deals with forgeries and the like. According to the detective at the Yard, he's made quite the name for himself in the drug trade and human trafficking."

"Then why is he after Dutilleaux's magic lantern?"

Gaetano shook his head. "I have no earthly idea. The auctioneer went on to tell me that Laframboise was quite distraught when he discovered the magic lantern had been sold."

"When did Laframboise find out?"

"He talked to the auctioneer two days ago."

"When was the sale?"

"A few weeks ago."

"Laframboise just found out about it?"

Gaetano shrugged. "Evidently. The auction was a small thing. I remember that Edmund was worried someone might snatch up his prize. Professors don't make a lot, you know."

Annja nodded. She knew. That was one of the reasons she didn't teach full-time. But the main reason was because she'd rather be at a dig getting her hands dirty. The chance to see something no one had seen in a very long time was exciting. A lot of archaeologists lived for it.

And a lot of them had died for it.

"How did Laframboise find out about the auction?"

"My friend didn't know."

"How did Laframboise track Dutilleaux's lantern to Edmund?"

A deep frown creased Gaetano's face. "Two of Laframboise's bullyboys showed up on my friend's doorstep and assaulted him."

"He didn't think to tell you or Edmund?"

"This only happened a few hours ago. And they threatened him if he told anyone. He has a family to think of. He was very scared the whole time he was talking to me. Had I not gone to him and had we not been longtime friends, I don't think he would have told me."

Taking a deep breath, Annja pushed her anger away. "There are a lot of innocents involved in this."

"Exactly my thoughts." Gaetano sighed. "I fear I, too, have been remiss in the assistance I could have given Edmund."

"What do you mean?"

"Edmund was thrilled with his acquisition. I'd promised to help him research the matter and Anton Dutilleaux and I hadn't. I'm currently endeavoring to correct that oversight by calling in some favors."

For a moment, Annja was silent, chasing thoughts of her own. "There is one other possibility."

Gaetano cocked an eyebrow.

"I was at Edmund's flat. His collection of magic props doesn't appear to be there."

"No. He keeps them in a storage unit."

"Do you know which storage unit?"

Gaetano smiled when he realized what she was actually asking. "Of course I do. That's where Edmund shows off his collection. There's no room at his flat." He pushed himself up from the table. "Let me go change clothes. I have a car around back."

While waiting for Gaetano to get dressed, Annja wandered the dining area and stared at the caricatures. Most of the names were unfamiliar to her, but she recognized the famous ones.

Then, on the third wall she examined, she found a caricature that she recognized immediately, though the name was new to her. It had been drawn thirty-three years ago.

The man in the picture hadn't changed in the intervening years. He was gaunt to the point of emaciation, had white hair that hung to his shoulders and a beard that extended to his chest. He held a long staff in one hand and was dressed in a robe and tall, pointed hat. His eyes were deep-set and she knew the color of them even though the caricature had been done in charcoal and sprayed with a fixative.

Roux.

9

The name came unbidden to Annja. She was aware that she smiled and grimaced at the same time. Roux and Garin Braden were the two people who, like her, were somehow connected to the mystical sword she carried.

Five hundred years ago, Roux had been charged with watching over Joan of Arc, and he had failed. As penance, he and his apprentice, Garin, had been assigned—or cursed—with finding Joan's broken sword, reforging it and placing it once more in the hands of a champion.

Most days, Annja was pretty certain a mistake had been made regarding her role as a champion. But she had to admit that the sword had changed her life in a number of ways.

"What do you see?"

Startled, Annja looked at the doorway where Gaetano stood. She didn't know what to say.

Gaetano walked over to her and pulled on a pair of glasses. He studied the picture. "Ah, yes. The fabulous Raymond the Red." He smiled happily. "He was quite an amazing performer."

"Was he?" Annja looked closely. "He looks kind of crotchety and unpleasant."

"If you can see that, then my father truly captured the essence of this man in his sketch." Gaetano shook his head. "Raymond the Red had a sweet-and-sour disposition. You never knew what you were going to get with him. Children and women loved him, though."

"Seriously?" Annja's own experiences with Roux had left her between camps. She loved him as a mentor, and perhaps even as a father figure—though she couldn't be sure since she hadn't known her own father—but he often got on her last nerve. Roux could be vexing and irritating, and incredibly demanding.

Over the time they'd known each other, she'd come to look forward to and dread every moment they spent together.

"Oh, yes. I was just a boy when I first met Raymond the Red. Perhaps eight or nine. The adults didn't care for him so much. He was far too opinionated for their tastes, and he didn't seem to delight over magic the way they did. But he had the gift."

"The gift?"

"For magic." Gaetano shook his head. "He was fantastic. Things appeared, disappeared and changed into other things. Even as practiced and experienced as the audience here was, there were a number of his tricks no one could explain. It was as though he were truly able to work magic."

Annja didn't comment on that. "Raymond the Red asked to be drawn as Merlin?"

"No. That was my father's idea. I asked him about it once, but he told me Raymond could be no one else." Gaetano gestured toward the door with his hat. "Shall we?"

"Yes." Annja led the way, but she couldn't resist taking one more look at the drawing.

SINCE THEY WERE IN GAETANO'S car and moving through the early-morning London traffic and wouldn't be easily traced if DCI Westcox had assigned someone to look for her, Annja turned on her phone and called Roux. The phone rang three times.

"What?" Roux sounded as gruff as always.

"Dutilleaux's magic lantern. Have you ever heard of it?"

"You called me for a game of Twenty Questions?"

"No. Actually, I don't have a lot of time."

"Neither do I. I'm in Atlantic City and the tables are running hot. I've got a private poker game set up in…twenty minutes."

"I'm in London and the police are looking for me. Do I win?"

Roux harrumphed theatrically. "Okay. Tell me about it."

Annja grinned at that. Roux treated her like she was a pain, like she was the child that kept returning to the nest, but he cared about her.

"I don't have time to go into all the particulars. I'm trying to help a friend. He got mixed up with something called Dutilleaux's magic lantern. From the old phantasmagoria shows."

"I know what a magic lantern is and I'm familiar with phantasmagoria. Childish theater for adults. Shameless." In the background, a croupier called for bets.

"I thought it might be one of those things you sometimes look for. This one's supposed to be cursed."

"No. Not to my knowledge. I'll have a look around. Later."

"Sure. Just any time. I'm sure I can keep the police waiting till you decide to act. And as long as I don't actually have the magic lantern, it's not like the curse can harm me or my friend."

"Sarcasm isn't an endearing trait."

"It wasn't intended to be."

"Did you kill someone?"

From anyone else, the question would have been ludicrous. But not from Roux. He was serious. He had been with Annja when they'd left dead men lying in their wake. "No."

"And you're not with Garin?"

"No."

"Because getting in trouble with the police is something I'd expect from Garin."

Garin Braden lived outside the law but he was so rich that a phalanx of attorneys protected him from most repercussions.

"It's not like I planned this."

While he drove, Gaetano glanced at her with polite but definite interest. He had an easy touch on the wheel and the sedan glided through the traffic.

"Are you going to be in London long?" Roux sounded only mildly interested.

"Maybe longer than I'd planned to if this doesn't work out right."

"I'll text you the number of a private inquiry agent there in London."

"A private inquiry agent? Like Sherlock Holmes? I've got goose bumps already."

"Don't be insufferable. Do you want the number?"

"Yes."

"I'll text it to you now."

"Just tell me. When I get off the phone with you, I'm turning the phone off. I've got the police looking for me, remember?"

"How am I supposed to know if anything happens to you?"

His concern warmed Annja, but she wasn't going to relay that to Roux. They'd only both be embarrassed. Roux was as uncomfortable with airing personal feelings as she was.

"Even the London police give me one phone call. I'll call you."

Roux sighed. "You know, I just got away to do a little gambling. It's truly depressing when an old man can't relax in his twilight years."

"As long as you've lived, you've already passed your twilight years."

"Don't be impertinent." Roux gave her the phone number and made her repeat it. "Should you contact her, give her my name. Tell her she will be compensated for her time."

"I can pay my own way."

"This woman is one of the best I have ever seen, Annja. She'll surprise you."

Roux didn't speak highly of many people other than himself.

"Whatever she tells you to do, or even suggests, don't take it under advisement. Just do it."

"All right."

"And take care of yourself, Annja. I still find you more interesting than vexing." Roux hung up before she could respond.

For a moment, Annja sat there dazed and a little mystified. Roux and Garin were part of her life because of the sword, which Garin wanted to destroy or control, but she sometimes forgot that their relationships went deeper than that. Roux and Garin had started out as master and apprentice and often carried on more as father and wayward—very wayward—son. Now, when they weren't operating under a truce, they occasionally tried to kill each other.

It was all very complicated.

She remembered to shut off the phone, then dropped it into her pocket.

"An old friend?" Gaetano glanced at her.

"Yes."

Gaetano was waiting for her to reveal more, but magicians weren't the only ones who could keep secrets. She glanced at the dash clock. It was 2:48 a.m. She decided to wait till later in the morning to call the number Roux had given her.

If she didn't have Edmund Beswick back by that time.

FIFTEEN MINUTES LATER, Gaetano pulled to a stop at the curb in front of the storage facility. He got out of the car and fished a walking stick from the backseat. He looked a little embarrassed as he carried it.

"I don't like walking into a potentially dangerous situation without some kind of weapon." He used a swipe card to open the storage building's security door, then led the way inside.

"I don't suppose you have a key to Edmund's unit." Alert to everything around her, Annja trailed after the big man. She felt into the otherwhere and briefly touched the sword. The weapon was ready to spring into her hand.

"No. Then again, locks have never been a problem for an escapologist. I'm certain we'll manage." Gaetano winked at her and followed the twisting labyrinth without hesitation. Weak yellow bulbs lit the way.

Annja noted the numbers and tried not to think about what might be happening to Edmund at that moment. Jean-Baptiste Laframboise didn't sound like a forgiving man—or one who would want to leave a witness behind.

She heard furtive jostling and a muttered curse ahead.

Annja caught Gaetano's elbow and guided him back against the wall. She put a finger to her lips. His face tightened in consternation as his hands worked along the walking stick, but he nodded his understanding.

Edging forward, Annja peered around the corner. Halfway down the hall, three men snapped a lock with a large pair of bolt cutters. Their casual clothes gave nothing away, but they kept glancing around.

One of them took out a cell phone and said in French, "Yes, we're here now. Number three twenty-seven. There are two locks, Mr. Laframboise. We'll be through them in just a moment." He nodded to the one with the bolt cutters.

Annja pulled back around the corner and glanced at Gaetano. "Three twenty-seven?" she whispered.

Gaetano nodded.

"Laframboise's men are breaking into the unit now."

He scowled. "Well, that isn't good."

"Can I borrow your walking stick?"

Gaetano hesitated, then handed it over. "What are you going to do?"

"Try to keep them from taking Dutilleaux's lantern. Once they have that, they might not need Edmund anymore." Annja focused on what she was about to do, not what might happen. She took a deep breath, kept a loose grip on the walking stick and spun around the corner. Calmly, almost nonchalantly, she walked toward the three thieves breaking into Edmund Beswick's storage unit.

10

Annja walked as if she'd been inside the storage facility several times. She acted a little wary, as any woman would bearing down on three strangers in a close hallway. She didn't meet their gazes, but she could feel them on her, and she nodded politely. She kept the walking stick tucked behind her right leg. Despite her efforts at hiding her weapon, she knew the subterfuge wouldn't last.

The ringleader caught sight of the walking stick, doing a double take. "Look out!" He slid a hand inside his jacket.

Reacting swiftly as the two other men started to stand, Annja brought the walking stick up. The ringleader expected her to swing at his head, so she feinted the swing. When he raised his left arm to block, she took a quick step forward, whipped the stick around in her hands and jabbed him in the stomach with it.

The air gusted out of the man and his face turned pale. He had a small pistol in his hand now, but he lacked the strength to raise the weapon.

Annja snap-kicked the pistol from the man's hand and sent the gun spinning down the hallway with a rasp of metal. Then she whipped the stick around again and delivered a line drive to his temple. The man sank bonelessly.

Instantly, the man with the bolt cutters lunged forward and snapped the razor-sharp edges at Annja's face like a maniacal bird beak. She managed to elude the attempt, but only just. When the bolt cutters closed, a lock of her hair fell away. He immediately thrust again and she gave way before him, measuring his stride and getting his rhythm.

"Get the lantern, François! The lock is open!" The bolt cutter operator snapped at Annja again and again.

She kept giving ground, not wanting to do battle over the body of the unconscious man. When the man lashed out once more, she jammed the walking stick into the jaws of the bolt cutters, then twisted hard.

Yelping in pain, the man lost his grip. Annja flung the tool away. The man immediately drew a locking knife from his pants and took up an experienced stance with the blade reversed and laid along his arm.

"That's right, girl. Come on. I'll take your head off." He spoke in heavily accented French to himself, obviously not knowing or even thinking she could speak French fluently.

Annja dropped into a crouch and swung the walking stick only inches off the ground. The hardwood shaft contacted explosively against the man's ankle. In the next instant, the numbed foot gave way under him. She blocked a feeble thrust of the knife with the stick as she stood, then kicked the man in the crotch.

He screamed high and thin, like a dying horse, and fell over. The knife tumbled from his hands as he reached for his ankle and his crotch.

Annja stepped past him and saw that François had opened the storage unit door and gone inside. She stepped through the door and was amazed to see all the boxes and crates piled inside.

A small stainless-steel table, like something salvaged from a hospital, stood against the wall on the right. Several objects sat on it, and chief among them was a lantern.

The device looked like a dragon rearing on its hind legs. Crafted out of brass, the dragon held a round glass lens in its mouth. Heavy coats of lacquer covered the dark wood at the lantern's base, but it was scraped and scarred from rough handling and hard years.

For a moment, Annja just stared at the piece and wondered about all the stories it held. How many people had stared enraptured at the ghostly images Anton Dutilleaux had projected for them in the Parisian tunnels? Where had the stories come from? Were they ones Dutilleaux made up? Or were they ones he'd borrowed from the places he'd traveled?

Then the present rushed at her again as François grabbed the lantern and wheeled around. He wasn't any bigger than Annja and he had his hands full. The only problem was making sure the lantern wasn't harmed.

Slowly, Annja spread her arms out to her sides, the walking stick still in her right hand. She spoke in French in a calm voice. "François, I don't want to hurt you."

He sneered and produced a knife. "You will not hurt me."

Annja smiled. She let go of the walking stick.

François got the wrong idea. He started forward with the knife held out before him. "Now go away before I carve the face off you."

Reaching into the otherwhere, Annja drew the sword into the room. The dulled lighting ran along the razor-sharp edges. "Mine's bigger. And I promise, I will hurt you if I have to."

"Where did you get that?" François backed up.

"Where is Edmund Beswick?"

The Frenchman looked uncomfortable. Nervously, he glanced past Annja toward the door.

"Your friends aren't coming. I made certain of that. Tell me about Edmund Beswick. I'm not going to ask again."

"Laframboise has him."

"Jean-Baptiste Laframboise?"

François nodded angrily.

"Where?"

"In a warehouse on the Isle of Dogs. I don't know the address. This city is new to me."

"Is he all right?"

"Yes. Laframboise gave us instructions that the professor was not to be harmed until we had the secret of the lantern."

Her relief was short-lived when Gaetano called hoarsely from outside, "Annja!"

Moving back cautiously, keeping the sword between her and François, Annja peered out into the hallway. Down at the corner, Gaetano pointed at the other end of the corridor.

Three Asians in jeans and a whole lot of leather approached the locker.

Annja ducked back inside. There was *no* way those men happened to be here by accident. She looked at the Frenchman. "Who are the Asian guys?"

"Chinamen." François spat, but he looked afraid. He clutched the lantern close to his chest. "They work for a man named Puyi-Jin."

"Who's he?"

"A Triad boss. He hired Laframboise to find the lantern."

"If your boss is supposed to get the lantern for him, why is Puyi-Jin sending people after me?"

"Once my boss figured out where the lantern was, he tried to cut a new deal with Puyi-Jin." François grimaced. "They haven't reached an accord."

"So whoever has the lantern gets to negotiate the new deal."

"You see how it is."

"Great. Your boss gets greedy and I've got Chinese gangsters after me."

François shrugged. "Puyi-Jin must have figured Edmund Beswick told you about the lantern."

"No." Not yet. Annja drew in a deep breath and took a fresh hold on the sword. "Do you know why everyone is after the lantern?"

"No."

"You realize it's supposed to be cursed?"

François didn't look happy all of a sudden. "Laframboise didn't mention that."

"Yeah. Well, it is. And guess what? Now we've got the Triad out in the hallway. You'd think the curse is working."

"We can give them the lantern," François said hopefully.

"Do you really think they'll just let us go?"

"Probably not."

Annja didn't think so, either, and she wasn't going to lose the opportunity to get Edmund away from Laframboise. She glanced around the shelves, looking for anything she could use. The possibility of getting out of the storage facility unscathed was dim.

Edmund had a storage chest against one wall that had paraphernalia from his magic act. She looked through the contents, searching desperately for an advantage.

"Annja!" Gaetano sounded positively panicked.

She heard footsteps and quiet voices speaking Chinese.

Spotting a box marked Flash Paper, Annja grabbed a handful of sheets and a lighter. The next shelf yielded a gallon jug of cleaning solvent that smelled properly combustible. She took the jug, added it to her collection and hurried back to the door.

"Annja Creed." That wasn't Gaetano.

She opened the gallon of solvent and poured it at the edge of the door. She'd already seen the fire extinguisher out in the hallway. She hoped it would be enough to take care of the fire. Or that the fire department would get there in time to save everything.

"Come out." The speaker sounded young and irritated. "Otherwise, we're coming in to get you."

Once the gallon jug was empty, Annja placed it behind her. The sword had vanished the moment she'd let go of the hilt, but the weapon was still there waiting for her.

"What are you doing?" François shifted nervously farther back in the storage unit.

"Trying to save us. Get ready to run." Annja watched as shadows fell across the doorway. She held the lighter and flash paper ready.

A moment later, a young Asian man rounded the corner and came into view of the doorway. Metal studs glinted on his face, and tattoos snaked up from his neck to his chin. He held a pistol before him. Satisfied Annja wasn't holding a weapon, he grinned. "I have her."

Shielding her movements in her hands, Annja lit the flash papers. There was an instant flare of bright light and heat. She threw them at her attacker.

The flaming sheets sailed into the young Triad member's face and dropped to the floor. The solvent started to burn at once and the harsh chemical smell grew even stronger.

The gunman's feet caught on fire from the burning solvent that had coated them in the doorway. He screamed and backed away, but his finger was on the trigger and he fired three times in quick succession as Annja pursued, jumping over the solvent trap. Safely inside his gun arm so the bullets couldn't hit her, she punched him in the throat and ripped the pistol away from him.

As the man staggered backward, flames wrapping his feet, Annja moved out into the hallway and used the man for cover. The two other men with guns weren't standing in the growing pool of fire.

Annja shoved the staggering man into the others and tossed the captured pistol away. She wasn't going to kill anyone if she could help it. She was already in enough hot water with Westcox and the Metro police. But she wasn't going to let her or Gaetano be killed, either. With her right hand now free, she reached for the sword and pulled it into the hallway with her.

The element of surprise was only going to last a moment. She stayed low as she stepped over the gangster on fire. The man was too distracted by kicking his shoes off to be a threat at the moment.

The pool of solvent that had collected in a depression worn into the hallway ignited in a rush that sent flames spiraling three feet high, much higher than Annja had anticipated. She threw her left arm across her face as she charged through them, keeping the flames from her face and eyes and hair.

On the other side, the two remaining Triad members took hasty steps back from the fire and their fallen comrade. They lifted their pistols and fired, and the crescendo of sudden thunder pealed through the hallway. At the same time, the fire alarm stuttered to life.

One bullet plucked at Annja's jacket sleeve. The other five or seven—she lost count—screamed off the walls.

She swung the sword and caught the weapon of the man on the left in midrecoil. The slide snapped off the pistol, flying through the air and leaving the weapon useless. She set her left leg, pivoted and drove her right into the man's face.

The second man whirled on her and fired again. Annja dropped into a crouch and the bullets cut the air over her head before thudding into the wall behind her. She stepped forward and drove the sword into the man's shoulder just deeply enough to cause him to drop the pistol. Blood streamed from the wound but she knew it wasn't life-threatening.

The man stumbled back and clasped his good hand over his injured arm. Annja kept moving forward and kicked him in the crotch. When he bent over, she brought a knee up into his face and left him sprawled on the floor.

The man whose shoes she'd set on fire had scrambled out of them and was batting at sparks on his pant legs. He caught her looking at him and quickly backed away.

The fire in the hallway licked at the walls, seeking fresh footholds in the building. Annja let go of the sword and sprinted a few steps down the hall to grab the fire extinguisher from the wall.

As she returned, the man she'd kicked in the face was scrambling for his weapon. She swung the fire extinguisher against his head and he dropped like a rock.

Aiming the fire extinguisher at the base of the flames, Annja yanked the safety pin and squeezed the release handle. A cloud of white chemicals boiled from the nozzle and spewed over the fire. When it finally cycled dry, the flames were out and only scorch marks remained.

Annja ran back to Gaetano and found him nursing a large bump on his forehead. His eyes looked glassy. "I'm afraid we've lost Edmund's magic lantern. I tried to stop the Frenchman, but he got away. I wasn't strong enough to overpower him."

"That's all right. We've got a lead on where Laframboise is keeping Edmund. That's more than what we had when we came here." Annja pulled Gaetano into motion and herded him toward the door as the fire alarm continued to shrill.

Thankfully, none of the combatants she'd left behind were in any shape to pursue.

11

The sign on the door was professional and understated. Bronze letters barely stood out against the simulated wood. Fiona Pioche, Private Inquiries.

When Annja knocked, the solid sound told her the wood was merely a veneer over a security door. Fiona Pioche's offices were in the upscale Mayfair district of London. She had a downstairs corner office, which would be even more expensive. Annja decided that whoever Fiona Pioche was, she must be doing quite nicely for herself.

And she wondered how Roux knew the woman. Of course, Roux and Garin knew all sorts of people, from refined gentry to cold-blooded killers. Unfortunately, both Roux and Garin seemed more at home with the latter. And that made Ms. Pioche even more interesting.

Gaetano stood unsteadily at Annja's side. He blinked repeatedly, trying to bring his vision into focus. Seeing her concern, he patted her on the shoulder, missing the first time before correcting his aim.

"I'm perfectly fine. Don't worry about me."

"I wish you'd let me take you to see a doctor. You could have a concussion."

"It won't be the first concussion I've had. We need to find Edmund."

"If you're not feeling any better when we finish up here, you're going to see a doctor."

"I fear the chief inspector will have you locked up and possibly deported if he gets his hands on you."

Annja worried about that, too.

The door opened and a young man about Annja's age stood there in an expensive suit. His black hair was neatly cropped and he wore a tailored Savile Row suit that emphasized his lean athleticism. "Ah, Ms. Creed, we'd been wondering when you would show up."

He opened the door wider to reveal a large and expensive office filled with modern furniture.

"My name is Oliver Wemyss. You may call me Ollie, if you like." He waved Annja and Gaetano to plush seats in front of the desk. "Would you care for a refreshment?" He crossed the room to a service bar. "We have tea and coffee, and a large selection of juices, liquors, beers, wines and soft drinks."

Annja shook her head. "No, thank you."

Gaetano declined, as well.

"Come, Mr. Carlini, you simply must have a spot of tea. I have some analgesics for that headache you're obviously sporting, and you need something to wash them down."

"You're right. And thank you. Tea with milk, please."

Ollie poured and brought a steaming cup and saucer over to Gaetano, who managed to take it in shaking hands.

Efficient and crisp, Ollie folded himself into the chair behind the big desk and studied the three monitors in front of him. He tapped the keyboard in rapid syncopation, then looked up at Annja. "Were you at the Cleburne storage unit this morning?"

Surprised, Annja nodded. "How did you know that?"

"It appears Detective Chief Inspector Westcox has interviewed men taken from there who named you as their attacker."

"Preposterous." Gaetano was so upset he almost lost his tea, but he recovered quickly. "Those men attacked us."

Ollie typed more. "Oh, I'm certain their claims will fall apart once the inspector pulls their records. They each have long criminal histories. I'm quite convinced you'd be exonerated even without Ms. Pioche's help."

Watching Ollie work both impressed and irritated Annja. She shifted in the chair, wishing she could just take a quick nap, but knowing she wouldn't be able to until Edmund was safe.

"We've got a friend out there who's in trouble. If it's going to be a while before Ms. Pioche can see us—"

"Ms. Pioche is already working on that. That is to say, *I* am already working on that. Your friend's troubles—Professor Beswick's kidnapping—is precisely the reason I have broken into the Metro Police Division's files." Ollie shot her a small smile. "If I am discovered, they will be properly vexed."

"I'm sure they would." And I'm going to be one step closer to deportation. Annja sat tensely. "But shouldn't we have some kind of arrangement before she starts working?"

Ollie glanced at her and raised his eyebrows. "You should. Ms. Pioche assures me that we don't need the usual contract agreement in your case. She considers you...*special*."

"Why?"

"She did not see her way clear to elucidate. Mystifying, actually." Ollie shrugged. "I have been through your files and see nothing that connects you to Ms. Pioche."

"Until this morning, I'd never heard of her."

Ollie grimaced at that. "Oh, dear. She's quite well-known. And getting her known—to the right people—is part of my job description."

"Maybe I'm not the right people."

Ollie nodded and smiled. "Judging from the background checks I've done on you, you seem to travel in areas outside Ms. Pioche's normal purview. Though you both certainly have been in the news regarding aggressive involvement with criminal types."

"One of the drawbacks of the job."

"As a television personality?"

"As an archaeologist."

"Ah." Ollie nodded again. "To be sure. There are any number of unsavory types in that job field. Ms. Pioche has dealt with some of them, as well."

"She's an archaeologist?"

"No. But she has worked for those who are." Ollie cocked his head to one side. "Yes, Ms. Pioche?" He listened for a moment, then nodded. "Of course, Ms. Pioche. Straightaway." He stood and looked at Annja and Gaetano. "Ms. Pioche will see you now."

Gaetano frowned. "If that was supposed to be ESP, I'm not impressed. All you had to do was set up a prearranged time to make that announcement."

Ollie grinned. "Nothing so esoteric, I'm afraid. I have an earbud that keeps me in touch with her. Would you like another cup of tea, Mr. Carlini?"

THE INNER OFFICE WAS AT ONCE imposing and impressive. Blond wood covered the walls and Italian marble covered the floor. Persian rugs added a layer of wealth that the paintings and sculptures might not have fully expressed.

Annja stood in awe of the artifacts that were on such casual display. Arranged as they were, though, she didn't get the sense that they were shown to intimidate prospective clientele. Rather, the pieces were there as keepsakes of an extraordinary life.

Drawn to a brass gladiator mask, Annja noted that it hadn't been restored. Instead, it showed the scars of having been taken in battle centuries earlier.

And beside it was a ceramic Russian icon, an image taken from Christian stories of Christ, which showed an angel Annja assumed was Archangel Michael. The figure brandished a flaming sword.

"That one is a particular favorite of mine."

At the sound of the woman's voice, Annja turned. "Ms. Pioche?"

"Yes." The woman sitting behind the desk was in her late fifties. Her silver hair was cropped at her jaw and parted on the left side. She wore red lipstick that enhanced her dark blue eyes. Diamond earrings glistened from under her bob. Her white cashmere sweater, black skinny pants and black boots suggested wealth, class and good taste.

"I apologize. I just didn't expect to see anything like this here."

Ms. Pioche's right eyebrow arched. "What were you expecting?"

"For starters, a much smaller office."

"Roux told you nothing of me?"

Annja couldn't decide whether the older woman sounded angry or hurt. Of course, with a man in the picture—especially with a man like Roux—the one wasn't very far from the other.

"Only that you were very good at what you do."

"I am." She glared at Annja.

Annja folded her arms and returned the woman's challenging gaze full measure. She didn't know the source of the animosity between them, but she wasn't simply going to roll over. "Perhaps coming here wasn't a good idea. I'm sorry to have imposed." She turned to Gaetano, who appeared to be too dazed to know what was going on. "Let's get you to a doctor."

"Nonsense." The woman's voice was a razor claw in a velvet glove. "That poor man is almost out on his feet. If you ask him to move from that chair, he might well collapse."

Gaetano started to force himself out of the comfortable chair in front of the massive Louis XIV desk. "Madam, I am quite capable of—"

"Oh, do sit down, Mr. Carlini, before you topple over." She never took her eyes off Annja.

"Quite right, madam." Annja didn't know if it was Gaetano's realization of his own infirmity or Ms. Pioche's imposing will that motivated him, but he sat.

"Ollie, be a dear and ask Dr. Whitehead to come around."

Ollie took out a small, slim cell phone and punched a single digit.

"I'm awaiting orders, Ms. Pioche, but I have yet to figure out whether you're helping this young woman." Ollie beamed at Annja.

"Oh, God." Ms. Pioche leaned back in her chair. "Annja Creed, I apologize for my behavior and would like to do my best to help you rescue your kidnapped friend."

The woman stood and offered her hand. "Although you obviously do not know the history involved in this situation, I hope we can put that aside and bring your friend—Mr. Edmund Beswick—home safely."

Annja took the offered hand and felt the calm, cool strength of it. "Roux said you were the best at this. Please, call me Annja."

Her blue eyes glittered. "I am. On that we can agree. My name is Fiona." She waved Annja toward a chair beside Gaetano.

Ollie spoke rapidly on the phone and put it away. "The physician is on his way."

Gaetano shifted in his chair. "Being able to call a physician in so quickly is most impressive."

"Not so impressive. He has an office in this building."

"Still, proximity alone—"

"I also own the building."

Gaetano was silent for a moment. "That, too, is most impressive."

Well, that explains the office space. Annja settled into her chair as Fiona did the same across the wide expanse of the ornate desk.

"Ollie has been sending me files all morning, since I got Roux's call predicament. Apparently, Jean-Baptiste Laframboise is a criminal of the worst cut. And you don't know where your friend is."

"I have a lead."

Fiona looked at Annja.

"He's being held somewhere on the Isle of Dogs. And by now Laframboise also has the object he's been searching for."

"How do you know this?" Her blue eyes searched Annja's face.

"Because it was in the storage unit and I lost it to one of Laframboise's men."

Gaetano sat up straighter. "*We* lost it."

"Ollie, be a dear and have Jenkins bring the car around." Fiona Pioche stood, opened a locked desk drawer and took out a small black automatic. She slipped the pistol into place at the small of her back, then turned and opened a hidden compartment in the wall. She took out a thigh-length shapeless beige jacket and pulled it on.

"Would you like me to accompany you, Ms. Pioche?" Ollie asked.

"That won't be necessary." She nodded at Annja. "Annja and I should be able to handle things for the moment." She took out extra magazines for the pistol and an elegant cell phone, then dropped them into her jacket pockets. "I'll need you to take care of Mr. Carlini and keep me apprised of any developments we may need to know about."

"Of course." Ollie was all business now.

The woman took a tiny earpiece from a small box and slipped it into her ear. She looked at Annja. "Are you ready?"

"Yes." Annja had chafed at waiting. If she'd known where to go, she'd have gone already.

Fiona walked to a back corner of the room, pressed a hidden button, and a section of the wall swung out to reveal a passageway. Without another word, she stepped through the secret door.

12

Evidently once Fiona Pioche made up her mind about a course of action, things happened quickly. Annja was hard-pressed to keep up with the woman as they strode down the long, narrow tunnel.

"Private route to the parking garage." Fiona had her hands in her jacket and her eyes fixed straight ahead. "That's one of the reasons to own the building."

"It wasn't just the office space?"

Fiona laughed in delight. "Don't make me laugh. I'd rather not like you."

"Why?"

"Because you're with Roux."

Annja thought about that for only a moment before the ramifications of that declaration set in. "Eww!" She looked at the older woman. "When you say *with,* are you talking about—" She couldn't go on.

"Sleeping with him?" Fiona's eyebrows arched. "Of course. What else would I be talking about?"

Annja cringed.

Her response obviously puzzled the other woman. "Do you mean to say you're not?"

"*No!* Pigs will fly before that happens. On second thought, there will be flying pigs and it still *won't* happen."

Fiona chuckled. "I have to beg your pardon. It appears I have jumped to an incorrect assumption. When Roux called me and spoke so glowingly of you—"

"Glowingly?"

"Yes."

"Roux treats me like I'm a pain in the butt most of the time. Like I'm some kind of kid that prattles on incessantly about things he has no interest in."

"That part, unfortunately, is probably true."

"That I prattle?"

"No, that Roux would find you boring."

"Thanks."

She smiled again, then reached over and took Annja by the hand and squeezed. "Given his background, I think Roux finds most people boring. Don't take it personally."

Annja looked at Fiona as she took back her hand. "What background?"

"The fact that he's lived five hundred years. He told me that you knew."

"You know about that?"

"Yes, and I rather think he's lying about his age. I think he's lived considerably longer than that."

"He *told* you he's lived that long?" Annja couldn't wrap her head around that. Roux had told her only after the sword had reforged itself and she'd needed some kind of confirmation. His age wasn't something he talked about.

"Yes. Of course, at the time he thought he was dying. Someone named Garin had tried to kill him. I arrived in time to get Roux to a physician." Fiona shrugged. "Even given his inexplicable existence, there are things that can still kill Roux."

"I know." Annja remembered how frail the old man had looked in the hospital bed after that business in Loulan City. She'd thought Roux was going to die then, and she'd been distraught when faced with the possibility. Until that point, she hadn't known for certain how much he'd meant in her life.

"Well, since I was wrong and you're not sleeping with that old goat, I insist you call me Fiona."

"And I'd really prefer Annja."

"It's a pleasure to meet you, Annja, and this time I mean that. I look forward to knowing you better. There aren't many people I can share stories with about Roux."

Fiona reached the end of the corridor, pressed her hand against a section of the wall and stepped back as a door flipped inside on well-oiled hinges. On the other side of the threshold, a small office space overlooked the parking garage. She led the way to the office door, then through it.

No sooner did they reach the curb than a sleek, silver sports coupe pulled to a stop. The gullwing doors opened like a raptor about to launch itself after prey and a small man climbed from the driver's seat.

"'Ello, Ms. Pioche." The man smiled and helped Fiona into the car as Annja climbed into the passenger seat.

"Good morning, Mr. Jenkins."

"She's filled with petrol and clean as clean can be. Do try to bring her back in one piece."

"I shall so endeavor, Mr. Jenkins." Fiona pulled the seat belt around her and buckled in. As soon as the connection snapped together, the door lowered. She pulled on a pair of supple driving gloves.

Annja buckled in, as well, and the door folded in.

Fiona hit the accelerator and the powerful engine roared to life. The sudden acceleration shoved Annja back into the seat and she closed her eyes twice during near-misses with a support pillar and a wall as the coupe shot out of the garage and screamed into early-morning traffic.

"Where did you meet Roux?" Fiona drove effortlessly and with audacity, as if nothing on the street would ever cause her any harm.

"In France. On a dig. I was looking into a local legend. Roux was there." Annja braced her feet against the floorboard and tried to control the fight-or-flight instinct that screamed through her. She told herself that Fiona knew what she was doing. "Do I need a crash helmet?"

"No. Of course not. I don't intend to crash. That would interfere with the whole rescue mission we're undertaking." Fiona jetted into the oncoming lane, downshifted and accelerated, breaking the rear wheels free and throwing them into a tire-eating skid across an intersection. Horns blared all around them as she cut the wheel, upshifted, found traction again and veered off in a ninety-degree turn just ahead of the panel truck she'd outrun.

"And you don't have a death wish?"

A faint smile crossed Fiona's red lips. "If that question should be asked of anyone, it would be you."

"Me?"

"I haven't had a single shoot-out on the streets in…oh… weeks, I suppose. Things have been dreadfully dull." Fiona slewed around another two cars, then jumped back into her lane just in time to avoid a head-on collision. Then she turned the next corner into a skid across cobblestones.

Annja braced her hands against the roof of the car.

"Don't be silly. Get your hands down. You're going to give the other drivers the impression that I'm holding you at gunpoint."

Annja dropped her arms at her sides and held on to the bucket seat instead. The scenery blurred by as Fiona roared through the streets. They narrowly missed locking bumpers with a bright red double-decker bus, buzzed through a red light that had just changed and juked back and forth into momentary voids in the traffic.

"For someone Roux obviously puts stock in, I'd expected you to be made of sterner stuff."

Annja closed her eyes as a maintenance vehicle filled the windshield. Then she was slammed against the side of the car as Fiona applied acceleration, brake and acceleration. Annja would have sworn she'd heard metal scraping as they passed, but it might have been the maintenance vehicle's worn brakes protesting.

"I'm pretty stern."

"Yes, well, perhaps under other circumstances. Obviously you have no qualms when it comes to personal combat. Driving, however, seems to be another matter."

"I'd prefer to be the one driving. And that term seems to be used loosely at the moment."

Fiona grinned and slipped on a pair of wraparound sunglasses from the glove box, then smoothly shifted gears again, once more accelerating. "I'm an excellent driver, and this coupe is an excellent machine. Bristol Fighter Turbo. First in its class."

"Did it rate well with the crash test dummies?"

"Your friend's life is in danger. We are in something of a hurry."

Grudgingly, Annja admitted that was true. "We don't even know where he's being held."

"Isle of Dogs, you said. We're off to see if we can narrow that down a little."

"How?"

"We're going to talk to a…an *associate* of mine. Over in the East End. If there's anything to know about Laframboise, Paddy will know."

Annja dug her feet harder into the floorboard. "How did you meet Roux?"

"I was a girl. Twenty, I think. Still in university at Oxford."

"You went to Oxford?"

"That surprises you?"

"The people I've known from Oxford are generally a little more reserved— *Look out!*" Annja pointed at the delivery truck that nosed out of an alley.

Fiona blasted her horn, cursed, then downshifted again and managed to pull into the alley the delivery truck had just vacated. Annja stared at the rapidly passing brick wall only inches on the other side of the window. The roar of the car engine trebled inside the enclosed space.

Unbelievably, Fiona was once more accelerating. "I was reserved at that time. Running with Roux changed me. I'll be the first to admit that." She pulled on the wheel hard and slid out into the next street, then jockeyed for position in the traffic.

A taxi driver, forced over to keep from colliding with the sports coupe, made a gesture.

"Some days I like the changes, but other times I wonder what kind of person I'd have been if Roux hadn't become infatuated with me."

"Infatuated with you?"

"Does that seem so difficult to believe?"

"No, but it's Roux. He has a thing for younger women. I've seen that."

"When Roux met me, I was a younger woman."

"Okay, but he wasn't a younger guy. He was old then. Really, really old." Despite her fear of impending doom, Annja couldn't help but be curious. "You became infatuated with Roux?"

"He's a deeply complex man."

"I know he likes young girls. Girls. Plural. You had a relationship?"

"We did." Fiona grimaced. "And he does like girls. As I said, he's something of a randy old goat. But while he was with me, I believe he was monogamous."

"You're blowing my mind. Seriously. I don't want to think about Roux's sex life."

"Well, we won't talk about that." Fiona smiled. "But I have to admit, he opened my eyes to a lot of possibilities. There's nothing like the touch of an older lover who knows what he's about."

"Don't. I'm going to be sick."

"Is it the car?"

"It's this conversation."

Fiona grinned. "You're the one that asked."

"Maybe we could just stick to the highlights." Annja closed her eyes again as the woman briefly left the street and zipped along the sidewalk.

"Remind me to have Jenkins take a look at the suspension when we get back." Fiona checked the traffic, spotted a gap and got back over just as an early-morning breakfast crowd fearfully vacated the tables of an open-air restaurant. "At any rate, I was working my way through university. I answered an ad for a personal secretary."

"In London? I thought Roux lived outside Paris."

"Does he? I didn't know that." Some of the lightheartedness deserted Fiona then. "So close, and he's never once…" She frowned.

"The ad was for a personal secretary?" Annja couldn't help prompting.

"Yes. You do know that Roux looks for legendary objects from time to time?"

"I do."

"Such as those stupid sword pieces he was forever going on about. Did he talk to you about those, too?"

"Uh…" Annja wasn't sure she wanted to get into her relationship with the sword.

"Of course he did. I don't know why I bothered to ask. The man was—and probably still is—obsessed with finding the lost pieces of Joan of Arc's sword." Fiona shrilled around the next corner. "I spent years helping him look for it. But they weren't all bad years. We had a lot of fun traveling around the world."

"But when you found out how old Roux was, didn't that kind of creep you out?" Annja held her thumb and forefinger marginally apart. "Just a little."

Fiona laughed. "You look at Roux and see an old man."

"Um, yeah. Gray hair. Wrinkles. Skinny. Yeah, definitely an old man."

"That's because you're superficial."

Annja couldn't believe what she was hearing.

Fiona reached across and patted her on the knee. "Don't take it to heart, love. Everybody's superficial to a degree. Roux certainly is. Some sweet young thing would walk by, his head would nearly twist off turning to look."

"Gross."

"Is it, now?" Fiona laughed. "Just means he's alive, is all."

She accelerated around another car. "Do you want to know what I saw when I looked at Roux?"

Annja gave the question considerable thought. She didn't want to be scarred for life. And she was comfortable—mostly—with how she dealt with Roux. She didn't want that to change.

Evidently Fiona decided not to wait on her answer. "I saw a man who was on fire to live."

"Roux?" When Annja thought of Roux, she thought of sloth and selfishness. The old man never truly did anything unless it suited him.

"Yes." Fiona smiled in memory. "Just thinking about him makes my heart beat faster. I used to watch him play baccarat. That was his game."

"He plays Texas Hold'em now."

"Does he? Probably with the same zeal." Then Fiona grimaced and tightened her grip on the steering wheel. "Of course, I also think about how the weasel ran out on me in the middle of the night." She jerked the car violently and avoided another vehicular encounter, leaving horns blaring in her wake.

"He just left?" That was the Roux Annja knew. Of course Roux didn't give an answer about something unless someone was holding a blowtorch to his face.

"He did. We were together eighteen years. Then, one day, he went out and never came back. For a while I was convinced someone had killed him. He has quite a number of enemies, as you might know."

"Yes."

"Then there's that man, Garin."

Annja decided not to say anything about that.

"And out of the blue, Roux calls me and asks me to look after you." Fiona glanced at Annja. "You can see how I might not have been as friendly as I could have."

"Did you ask Roux why he left?"

"My pride may be tattered, but I do still have it. I most certainly did *not* ask him that."

"Don't you want to know?"

"Yes, but do you think Roux would tell me? The truth, I mean?"

Annja shook her head. "Probably not."

"But I know he still cares."

"How?"

"Because he knew how to get hold of me, and that I would be able to help you. If he didn't care about me, he wouldn't have known that. Since he left, I've made something of myself. Adventured for a while, mostly hoping to run into him again in our old haunts, and continued working."

"Private inquiry work?"

"Among other things. I made a fortune from some of the things I'd done with Roux, and some of the things I did afterward. After a while, I came back to London to live, but I still couldn't settle down. I opened up the business to keep from being bored, and because I found out I enjoy helping people." Fiona smiled grandly. "And I love nettling Scotland Yard and those stuffed shirts when I get the opportunity."

Abruptly, Fiona braked and pulled the car to the curb. She parked in front of an old two-story building a block off Cheshire Street, if Annja had managed the geography correctly.

A sign out front declared Snooker.

Fiona pressed a button and the gullwing doors opened. "Come along, then. Paddy practically lives here. We'll see what he knows about Jean-Baptiste Laframboise."

13

Annja had definite misgivings as she stepped into the snooker hall. Although much of the East End had undergone reconstruction and refurbishment, seedy patches remained. This was one of them. Even at this early hour, men were at the tables, drinking and smoking, and talking to one another in language better used on the docks and in the factories where they normally worked.

The interior was dark and stank of smoke and stale beer. Curtains covered the windows, but thin lines of sunlight fell through gaps and drew lines on the stained wooden floor. Billiards cracked sharply somewhere in the back.

Voices quieted as the crowd spotted Fiona. She also drew a number of salacious comments, but she ignored them.

Annja flanked the older woman as they walked to the bar on the other side of the room.

A scroungy man in a red shirt unbuttoned to the navel tended bar. He leaned over the scarred surface, pencil in hand as he worked a Sudoku puzzle. His limp black hair fell into his face. Eyeliner outlined his dark eyes and made them look sad and sensitive.

"You're in a bad place, love." He spoke softly so his voice didn't carry. He didn't look up. "You should pack up and go back to wherever it is you come from."

"I've been in worse places. I don't suppose you have a pot of tea back there, do you?"

"I do." The bartender left the Sudoku puzzle lying on the counter. "Milk?"

"Please."

The bartender glanced at Annja. "Would you like tea, as well?"

"I would. Thank you."

A grin thinned the bartender's lips. "You're an American."

Annja nodded.

"Interesting." The bartender threw a towel over one shoulder and retreated to the back. He returned a moment later with two steaming cups of tea. With polite deliberation, he put the teacups in front of them. "Brace yourselves. Here comes the bloody cock of the walk."

Annja glanced at the small mirror on the wall at the back of the bar and watched a stout man approaching the bar. Three younger men trailed after him. With the builds they had, lean and muscular, they probably worked the docks. Or they had in their past. The hardness of their expressions marked them as something other than warehouse employees.

Fiona turned casually, leaned back against the bar and hooked her elbows over it. She looked like a cat stretched in the sun, but Annja read her wariness. A small grin pulled at the corners of her mouth.

Annja hoisted herself onto a bar stool a few feet from Fiona and waited. She hoped the woman knew what she was doing.

The big man leaned on the counter. Then he swiveled his attention to Fiona. "My name is Leon Copely. I've got a nose for cops. My nose is telling me you're a cop."

"You need to check in with your otolaryngologist at your first opportunity, Mr. Copely."

The big man frowned, held his gaze on Fiona for a moment, then looked at his nearest lackey.

Fiona leaned over to the man and added in a low voice, "An otolaryngologist is an ears, nose and throat physician, Mr. Copely." She tapped her nose. "He should be able to help you with your sense of smell. I'm certain he can put things to rights. He might even be able to recommend someone to straighten it."

The man grimaced with cold deliberation. "I don't need help with my nose. I don't need it straightened. And you're a cop."

"I'm not a police officer."

"You don't belong here, neither. So I'm only gonna ask you one time—what are you doing here?"

"I came for some information."

The man scowled. "You ain't getting nothing from me."

"I didn't ask you, now, did I? You didn't even know what an otolaryngologist was. I suspect you may be pathetically deficient in information." Fiona sipped her tea. "As far as I'm concerned, you can go back about your business."

Annja couldn't believe the way Fiona was deliberately antagonizing the man. Something bad was going to happen.

Copely bristled and his jaw worked as if he was chewing cud. "You got a smart mouth."

"Trust me, the smart mouth suits the rest of the package." Fiona eyed Copely coolly as the man stood straighter. "Have a care that you don't bite off something bigger than you can chew."

"Haddock." Copely's voice had turned to gravel.

The biggest of his three companions started forward. He knotted his hands into fists, his intention clear.

Unable to sit back, Annja slid from the bar stool. She took one step forward, hooked her hand in the man's shirt collar from behind and yanked at the same time she kicked his supporting knee.

The big man fell with a squawk. Annja stepped back at once, already aware of a second man setting himself and throwing a punch at her. She slipped under it, then twisted and caught the extended arm by the wrist. Shifting her stance, she set herself, redirected the man's forward momentum and took the captured arm down and around. Pivoted by his own strength and the fulcrum of his shoulder, the man screamed in pain as he landed flat on his back.

An amateur enthusiast rather than a trained fighter, the third man rushed at Annja. She hooked a bar stool with her foot and propelled it into the man's path. He tripped over it, caught himself and tried to fight his way clear. Annja whirled into a spinning back kick that caught the point of the man's jaw and stretched him out on the floor.

By that time, the big man she'd choked and tripped was getting his feet back under him. He reached into his pocket and flicked open a knife as Annja seized another bar stool and broke it across his teeth. Bloody and unconscious, the big man toppled to the floor.

Still holding the stool, Annja threw it down and turned back to Copely. He had already reached under his jacket and was coming out with a pistol.

A few of the other men in the room had started approaching with pool cues.

Fiona flicked out a hand quick as a striking snake, seized Copely's thumb and snapped it like a breadstick. The pistol fell from his grasp and he yelled in pain. Still holding on to the man's injured hand, Fiona locked her prey in place, then shoved her pistol into his ear. She pulled the trigger and a spray of blood misted over Copely's shoulder.

Copely screamed.

The bartender cursed and jumped back.

Half the room away, the men with the pool cues pulled up and watched in fascination.

For a moment Annja thought the woman had shot her opponent in the head and that she'd watched a cold-blooded murder. Instead, she noted the small hole in the center of his stippled and charred earlobe and knew that Fiona had deliberately not killed the man.

Fiona shoved the pistol into Copely's mouth. Copely stopped screaming as he choked on the heated metal.

Almost politely, Fiona leaned forward to the man's uninjured ear. "Do I have your attention, Mr. Copely?" She had him turned so she could watch the other men in the snooker parlor.

Weakly, eyes glassy and not properly focused, probably concussed by the detonation in his ear, Copely nodded.

"That's good. I'd hate to repeat myself, and it would be only a waste of time because then you wouldn't be able to hear me at all. You only have two ears." Fiona smiled and Annja's estimation of the woman shifted. She decided she wouldn't want Fiona Pioche as an opponent for any reason. "I want you to go away now, Mr. Copely. Pick up your friends and go wherever it is when you're not here. And as free advice, don't ever be anywhere around me again. Do you understand?"

Shivering, Copely nodded.

"I hate a bully, Mr. Copely, and I do business on this side of the city. If I have a client who has a problem with you in the future—no matter how far away—I will help them for free. And when I am finished with you, you will be dead or in prison. I hope I make myself clear."

"Yeah."

"On your way, then." Fiona gently pushed Copely into motion.

He stumbled, touched his ear and stared at the bright blood. Then he motioned to the other man who was still conscious and they started working on their two unconscious friends.

Fiona placed the pistol on the bar and sipped her tea.

"Never a dull moment with you, is there, Ms. Pioche?"

Annja tracked the man's voice upward to the second story overlooking the first. He stood at the railing dressed in a double-breasted suit. He looked almost as wide as he was tall and wore a salt-and-pepper goatee. His dark hair was slicked back. He wore rimless glasses that made him look professorial.

Fiona smiled. "Hello, Paddy."

"You're a pip, my dear." Paddy smiled for a moment, then his face hardened. "Mr. Copely."

Copely stood with one of Haddock's arms across his shoulders.

"You're no longer welcome on these premises."

"That would be a mistake." Copely had some of his nerve back. "I throw you a percentage of everything I do."

"I know that." Paddy fixed the man with a harsh stare. "And I run an establishment that's safe for everyone that comes through those doors, whether it's for snooker or… You know that."

Copely's face darkened. "You can't talk to me—"

"Eddie." Paddy's voice was sharp with rebuke. "If that imbecile insists on continuing to waste his breath and my time, blow him out of his shoes."

The bartender reached under the bar and took out a sawed-off double-barreled shotgun. "Yes, sir." He ratcheted back the hammers and the clicks sounded ominous in the silence that filled the big gaming room.

Without another word, Copely staggered out under the weight of the big man. His other two companions leaned on each other and followed.

"Now, Ms. Pioche, I am to assume you are here on business and not merely to harass my patrons?" Paddy peered down at Fiona.

"The only reason I have for ever coming here, my dear man, is to be enchanted by your charm and wit."

"And my information, of course." Paddy grinned.

"Merely part of your charm."

"Well played, Ms. Pioche. Please come up."

THE SPACIOUS UPSTAIRS OFFICE contained a great many books on built-in shelves. Most of the volumes looked as if they'd been read.

"Annja Creed, it is my pleasure to present Mr. Paddy McGurk."

Paddy smiled and inclined his head. "Ms. Creed, this is indeed an honor. Judging from your articles and your books, we share similar interests."

"We do?"

"Antiquities. Legends. Stories of long-lost things."

"You're a collector?"

"An appreciator of fine arts." Paddy bowed and took Annja's hand briefly before gesturing her to one of the plush sofas on either side of a glass-topped coffee table.

Fiona busied herself at a tea service on one side of the room while Paddy took a seat on the sofa across from Annja. "What he isn't telling you is that he collects antiquities for other people who aren't too picky about how he got his hands on them."

Apparently embarrassed, Paddy waved Fiona's words away. "Avarice is a mean thing. First cousin to jealousy. And I don't hide away every antiquity that I set my sights on. Some of them end up in museums. I'm very careful to…give back."

"You are." Fiona brought the tea service over and put it on the coffee table. She poured the steaming liquid into cups.

"Thank you. You spoil me." Paddy lifted the cup and blew on the tea.

"Another thing Paddy won't mention, unless he knows you *very* well, is that he is a gifted forger." Fiona settled onto the couch beside Paddy with her own cup of tea.

"I wouldn't say gifted."

"He has seven pieces hanging in various museums."

"*Nine.* Nine pieces, actually." Paddy grimaced.

"See? He does have an ego."

"Only when you're around, love." Paddy shifted his attention back to Annja. "Since you're in Ms. Pioche's company, I assume she is helping you find something."

"*Someone,* actually."

"Mr. Hyde?" Paddy shook his head. "I've been following the media and I'm afraid I can't help you with that. I apologize, but crime like that isn't especially my field."

"What the old dear means is that he hasn't yet found a way to make money from it."

Paddy slapped a hand over his heart. "You wound me, woman."

"I seriously doubt that."

Paddy nodded thoughtfully. "Who are you looking for, Ms. Creed?"

"Edmund Beswick."

Cocking his head to one side, Paddy thought for a moment. "I'm afraid I can't help you there, either. I'm not acquainted with Edmund Beswick. Never heard of him."

"He's a friend. He was kidnapped last night by a man named Jean-Baptiste Laframboise."

Sipping his tea, Paddy appeared troubled. "Now, that's a name I am familiar with. Laframboise is a horrid man. No appreciation for the finer things in life. He's a ruffian and a scoundrel. Why would your friend be kidnapped by the likes of Laframboise?"

"For a magic lantern that supposedly had its origins in China."

"Why would anyone want a magic lantern from China? Perhaps Laframboise doesn't know that he needs a Middle Eastern lamp if he's looking for a genie and three wishes." Paddy smiled at his own wit.

"Laframboise was supposed to turn over the lantern, if he found it, to a man named Puyi-Jin. Instead, Laframboise has double-crossed his employer."

Paddy trailed his fingers through his goatee absently. "The name Puyi-Jin is known to me, as well, and he is as much an animal as Laframboise. The thing I keep stumbling over, though, is that neither of these two men are collectors. Why would they be interested in this magic lantern?"

"I don't know. All I've managed to discover is that Edmund is being held on the Isle of Dogs."

Paddy brightened at once. "So he would have to have a base of operations."

Fiona nodded. "That is what we were thinking."

"Then that is something I can help you with." Paddy took out a cell phone. "Ever since the construction and rebuilding began in that area, there have been many hiding places criminals have used for all sorts of purposes. Let me see what I can find out."

"That would be lovely, Paddy." Fiona stood.

"Leaving?" Paddy looked disappointed.

"Yes. Ms. Creed and I have things to do. Policemen to upset.

While you're ferreting out Professor Beswick, we need to pursue what we can of the magic lantern. As much as I love to watch you work, you'll be calling people I'd rather not know about. Until I have to."

"Right you are." Paddy got to his feet and accepted the peck on his cheek that Fiona offered. "I have your mobile number. I'll give you a ring as soon as I have anything to report."

Annja shook Paddy's big hand. "Thank you."

"Before you leave London, I'd love to take you and Ms. Pioche to dinner. If you will allow me the privilege."

"When things are settled and Edmund is safe again, I'd like that."

"Then I shall endeavor to work harder and swifter."

Although she didn't say it, Annja felt certain that news of Edmund wouldn't come swiftly enough.

14

"Professor Beswick."

Edmund struggled against the heaviness that kept his eyelids closed. He wanted to see, but he just couldn't open his eyes. In the distance, he heard boat motors and machinery that weren't the normal morning noises around his flat.

"Professor Beswick."

He tried to open his eyes again. This time he also moved his head slightly, but it felt as if someone had filled his skull to bursting with wet cement.

The man cursed in French and it was so fast that Edmund couldn't follow all of it.

"Why isn't he waking?"

"The chloroform takes a while to wear off." This second voice was cold and impersonal.

Hearing that sent a charge of adrenaline through Edmund's body. Frantic, he tried to gather his scattered thoughts. The last thing he remembered was working in his flat.

No, that wasn't right. The last thing he remembered was *walking* into his flat. He'd been looking forward to working, and he'd especially been looking forward to seeing Annja Creed again.

Except he hadn't been alone in the flat. He vaguely remembered a shadow stepping away from his office area. Before he'd been able to react, someone had hit him. The left side of his jaw felt tender.

"Then chloroform wasn't the best idea, no?"

"No, sir. At the time, we wanted to control him without having to hurt him." The impersonal voice held a note of resentment.

Edmund succeeded in lifting his head a little. A rough hand touched his face. A thumb pried open one of his eyelids. Someone shined a bright light into his eye. He tried to protest, but he couldn't get his voice to work.

The eyelid was released and the hand drew back. Edmund's head dropped heavily to his chest. Then something slammed into the side of his face, he felt a searing blast of pain and everything went dark.

WAKING THIS TIME WAS EASIER. Edmund even managed to crack his eyes as he raised his head. His mouth was dry as a sock and he tasted salt, which he assumed was blood. His mouth was swollen and felt crooked. Harsh chemicals stung his nose.

A quick glance revealed that he was sitting in a dilapidated warehouse. Piles of debris sat in corners of the big, wide-open space. The place had been gutted. Black and gray and white utility cables hung from the ceiling like dead snakes.

"Professor Beswick."

The hard-voiced Frenchman lounged in an office chair in front of a battered desk that had only three legs and listed heavily to one side. The Frenchman had his boots on the desk.

"I am Jean-Baptiste Laframboise." The man obviously had a lot of ego. Self-satisfaction resonated in his voice and he smiled. He was lean and muscular, probably nearing forty, and had short black hair and a short matching beard that crowded his cheeks and eyes. The overall effect of all the hair made him look like an eight ball on a human body.

He dropped his boots to the floor and faced Edmund. The man wore what looked like designer jeans and shirt—gray. With a dark pin-striped vest. A coat hung on the back of a nearby straight-backed chair. He held a very large stainless-steel revolver in his right hand.

"Do you know me?"

Not trusting his voice, Edmund shook his head. He instantly regretted the motion. Pain speared his skull and his stomach twisted.

Laframboise's mouth screwed up in irritation. He lifted the revolver and laid the long barrel over his shoulder. "You will come to know me. Have no fear of that."

Edmund didn't know what to say to that, so he didn't speak. He glimpsed two armed thugs standing slightly behind where he was sitting.

"I have Anton Dutilleaux's lantern." Laframboise gestured with the revolver and pointed at the magic lantern sitting in a box beside the desk.

"How did you find my storage locker?" Talking made Edmund's left jaw ache and he knew it was swollen.

Laframboise paced. "You told us where it was."

Edmund couldn't remember doing that, but there was a lot he didn't remember. Despite the plywood sheets that covered the warehouse windows, enough light leaked in that he could tell it was daylight outside. He wondered how long he'd slept.

"Unfortunately, you haven't told us much else." Laframboise sat on the corner of the listing desk and laid the revolver across his thigh. "You're going to—" he hesitated over his word choice "—amend that now, *non?*"

"What do you want me to tell you?" Edmund shifted slightly and discovered he was bound to a steel folding chair. For the first time, he realized how much his body hurt from being restrained. Wide bands of green tape wrapped his ankles. His hands must've been trapped behind him with the same tape.

"I want to know about the lantern."

Edmund sucked in a deep breath and felt blood clots inside his mouth shift. Sickened, he spat them out onto the cement floor. Bright red blood mixed with older stains. "It...reportedly belonged to a man named Anton Dutilleaux."

A few of his teeth felt loosened, but they all seemed to be

there. The inside of his cheek was swollen and torn. In all his life, he'd never been hurt so badly. He just wanted to go home. Better yet, he wanted to go to the emergency room, then home.

"Have you heard of a man named Puyi-Jin?"

"No."

Laframboise tapped the revolver muzzle against his thigh irritably. "You're certain of this?"

"Yes."

"He is a Chinaman."

Seeing the man's obvious frustration with him, Edmund grew more afraid. "I don't know anyone named Puyi-Jin."

"A few days ago, Puyi-Jin came to me and asked me to acquire this object for him." Laframboise tapped the box containing the lantern with his boot. "Why is he so interested in this thing?"

Edmund hesitated only a moment, then realized that Laframboise at least knew part of the story concerning Anton Dutilleaux's magic lantern. Sensing that his life was on the line, Edmund resolved to tell the truth.

"You're sure this man, Puyi-Jin, is Chinese?"

"With a name like that, I should hope so." Laframboise smiled at his own wit and his two thugs laughed.

"Just because he has a Chinese name doesn't mean he's Chinese. There are many people of Chinese heritage born in London."

The Frenchman's face hardened. He stood and walked over to Edmund. The big revolver rose to touch the end of Edmund's nose. The cold steel felt alien. "Are you trying to be the wise mouth with me?"

"No." Edmund could scarcely speak for the fear that coursed through him. "It helps to know this man's culture. To know where he would have picked up knowledge of the lantern." He sipped his breath, his eyes crossed as he stared at the revolver muzzle. "The lantern has a lengthy history."

Laframboise considered that. "Keep talking."

Edmund licked his lips and tasted more blood. "I just don't know what you're looking for. Anton Dutilleaux's lantern has inspired many rumors. The foremost is that it's cursed and brings bad luck to anyone who owns it. That story rose predominantly after Dutilleaux's murder in Paris, but I believe the lantern already held a malign aura about it from China before then."

One of the thugs shifted uneasily.

Laframboise leaned in and the barrel of the revolver mashed Edmund's nose hard enough to bring tears. "Men *run* from curses. They don't *chase* them."

"There's also the belief that the lantern actually opens a gateway to the dead. Or at least to another place."

"Now you're trying my patience."

Edmund blinked the tears from his eyes and concentrated. He didn't know what his captor wanted. He was going to die and there was nothing he could do to stop it. "It's also rumored that the Nazis chased after the lantern." Actually, he'd never confirmed that was a rumor, and he'd never particularly cared because his interest in the lantern was as a keepsake, nothing more.

"Why would they do that?"

"During World War II, Adolph Hitler organized special units to search for things related to Aryan history, and for things repudiated to have mystical properties." Edmund's jaw ached as he spoke, but he forced himself to go on. As long as he was talking, he was staying alive. "One of the sources I turned up about the lantern suggested it was on those lists, but I couldn't confirm that."

Laframboise breathed out in exasperation. "I get the notion you are trifling with me. This is a very dangerous thing."

"I'm telling you everything I know." Edmund felt desperate, caged and as though he were looking death in the eyes. And, in that moment, he knew that he was.

"Then Puyi-Jin knows more than you do. Pity." Laframboise didn't seem happy about that.

"I had only just acquired the lantern." Edmund swallowed and tasted blood again. "I have not even been able to verify that the lantern I bought at the estate sale truly belonged to Anton Dutilleaux."

Laframboise tapped the pistol barrel against his thigh. "This is very upsetting. I have betrayed an employer in order to get you and the lantern." He shrugged. "Not such a big thing, usually, but I always turn a profit. On this, I am not so sure I will profit." He frowned. "Sadly, I have made a very power-ful enemy."

Edmund forced himself to think. He was an escapologist. He'd trained himself to pay attention to an audience. One of the basic tenets in dealing with an audience was to always give them what they wanted. Obviously Laframboise wanted to be-lieve the lantern had some secret. So Edmund had to manu-facture one. But it had to be based on truth.

"Has Puyi-Jin told you anything of the lantern?"

Laframboise scratched his beard with his free hand. "No. The only reason he came to me was because I had people in London who could snatch you. He didn't want to trust the young thugs he has access to. They tend to be messy and not so trustworthy."

And trusting you turned out so much better, Edmund thought, but didn't say. Desperately, he focused on Lafram-boise, seeking some kind of leverage. All he needed was a hint of doubt. "But you have your reasons for betraying Puyi-Jin."

The Frenchman's eyes slitted.

"What I'm saying is that you have your suspicions about why Puyi-Jin wants the lantern. Tell me what you think and I'll see if that information triggers something I may know."

"You said you know nothing more."

"But I might know and not be aware." Edmund licked his split lips. "I read a lot of information about phantasmagoria and phantasmagorists. I'm not at my best at the moment. Not like this." He strained against his bonds but didn't get anywhere. "What you tell me may trigger something. So please, if you want answers, tell me."

"All right." Laframboise rested the long muzzle of his pistol over his shoulder again. "The Chinaman is certain the lantern marks the location of a treasure."

"Whose treasure?"

Laframboise looked displeased.

Nervously, Edmund hesitated for just a moment. "There is a rumor, but it's only a rumor, mind you, that Dutilleaux had hidden away a fortune in gold."

For a moment, Laframboise looked unmoved. Then interest flickered in his dark eyes. "Gold?"

Edmund nodded. "I couldn't confirm it, and I thought it was just a legend."

"You're saying it isn't?"

"I'm telling you I don't know." Edmund gathered himself the way he would before he got ready to free himself from a trap and cleared his mind of fear. It was harder than during a performance. "But I do know that Anton Dutilleaux worked in Shanghai before he came to Paris."

Laframboise shrugged. "So? This means nothing to me."

"He worked as a stockbroker in the International Settlement. A lot of money flowed through that city after the Treaty of Nanking opened China to Western colonialism. A man in the right place at the right time, with a plan, could have made a fortune. Several men did."

For a moment, silence filled the large warehouse. Edmund sat strapped in the chair, and he thought he could hear his heartbeat echo throughout the emptiness, but that was just the blood rushing in his ears. He kept his expression calm. He was a showman.

And he was certain he was about to die.

"Interesting." Laframboise smiled. "I'd like to hear more, *mon ami.*"

Edmund didn't know what he was going to do next. He was all out of rabbits. That little tidbit about Dutilleaux's life prior to his arrival in France was all he had. He didn't even know much about Shanghai.

And then the double doors of the warehouse exploded inward and a van screeched to a halt a short distance inside the building. The doors flew open and armed Asian youths bolted from the vehicle and took up positions behind piles of debris and crates.

Bullets filled the air and the world turned into a rolling crash of thunder.

15

"Shouldn't we call the police?" Annja unbuckled her seat belt and stepped from the low-slung sports car. The gullwing door protected her from the misty fog rolling in from the river for just a moment, then the cold damp reached her. Fiona had parked the car in a narrow alley between two-story run-down warehouses being eaten away by rust.

The Isle of Dogs wasn't truly an island. It was a peninsula surrounded on three sides by the Thames. It wasn't a home to dogs, either, though there were several stories to that effect.

Canary Wharf Tower stood eight hundred feet tall and cast a long shadow over the area. Anyone looking at it would think the whole region was affluent, but Annja knew that wasn't true. The Canary Wharf office complex tilted the odds on the per capita breakdown. Slums and poor neighborhoods stood shoulder to shoulder with the wharf area.

They were in one of them now, parked in Blackwall not far from the condemned warehouse where Laframboise was supposed to be holding Edmund Beswick.

Fiona slipped off her jacket and left it lying on the car seat. "Do you really want the police?"

Annja hesitated. The police would complicate things, and there was no guarantee they could ensure Edmund's safety.

On the other hand, they weren't even sure Laframboise and Edmund were there.

"How certain of Paddy's information are you?"

"Very. Otherwise, we wouldn't be here."

Annja gazed at the warehouses ahead of them, vaguely aware of the clang and chug noises of the nearby port. The one Paddy's informants had fingered was three down and to the left. The news had come from a man also doing illicit contraband business in the warehouses.

Out on the river, tugboats and other ships hauled cargo or sat in port awaiting loads or unloading.

"All right. No police."

Fiona smiled at her. "Brilliant. I do hate working alongside the police when time is of the essence. Oh, don't get me wrong, those lads are useful, but they tend to move in large groups and get noticed rather more than we will." She clicked her key fob and the car's trunk swung open to reveal an arsenal. "Care for a shotgun? Or do you prefer a minisubmachine gun?"

Stunned, Annja gazed at the weapons. They lay in neat order in special boxes. Along with Kevlar vests. "Do you drive around with a weapons locker all the time?"

"Don't be ridiculous. I had Jenkins load the car before he brought it around." Fiona glanced at Annja, then pulled out one of the Kevlar vests and handed it to her.

Annja started putting it on. "Why?"

"Because I thought we might need them. Things to do with Roux often have a way of going sideways. I've been caught unprepared before. I was lucky to get out with my life." Fiona reached in and took out a military shotgun with an abbreviated barrel. "You do know how to use weapons, don't you?"

"Yes."

"I rather thought you might. Did Roux teach you?"

"No. I've picked it up here and there. The first guys to really teach me how to handle a pistol and a rifle were SAS soldiers working security on a dig at Hadrian's Wall."

"Do you see anything you like? Don't be shy."

As a general rule, Annja didn't like guns. They were noisy and violent and the people using them often tended not to be discriminating in a pitched battle. She preferred her sword, and she preferred not to have to kill.

However, both Laframboise and Puyi-Jin didn't seem to have those qualms.

Annja chose a Glock 21 .45 ACP for the knockdown power. She belted that around her hips, tied the holster down and slid the pistol in and out a few times. The belt came with four extra magazines in pouches. She also picked up a military shotgun that had been cut down. She added ammo for the shotgun and a Mini Maglite.

Fiona reached back in for an H&K MP5 submachine gun and slung it over her shoulder. The woman was turning out to be quite the surprise.

Annja indicated the naked weapons. "Not exactly on stealth mode here."

"You fret entirely too much. Men never understand women's fashions." Fiona reached into the trunk and pulled out two brightly colored plastic rain ponchos with collar snaps. She handed one to Annja and pulled her own over her head. The folds covered the weapons easily. "This isn't my first time at this particular dance."

Annja pulled hers over her head, too. Then gathered her hair in one hand and pulled it back. She secured it with a hair band from Fiona. The woman thought of everything.

"Right now we're just trying to help your friend." Fiona closed the trunk and set the car alarm. She took the lead.

Annja followed behind, overly aware of the weapons she carried. Unconsciously, she felt for the sword hilt and touched the blade. Knowing it was there made her a little more comfortable.

FIONA WAS A FAST MOVER ON foot as well as in a car. Annja had to step up her pace to match the woman. She didn't know where Fiona got the energy, but she was definitely a power walker.

"These men are dangerous." Fiona's voice was flat and neutral. "If we engage them—*when* we engage them—I want you to remember that. They chose their own fates before they stepped foot inside that warehouse."

Annja wiped a wet layer of fog from her face.

Fiona glanced at her. "You're not as hard as I am."

"I've done what I had to to survive."

"And you still have to make your peace with that, don't you?"

Annja didn't say anything. Every time she'd taken a life, it had been to save one.

But she had taken lives. And they did weigh on her.

"You're different from the young women Roux has taken up with before."

Startled, Annja looked at the older woman.

"He's told you about his past?"

"Never intentionally."

"But he's told you about the things he's seen? The people he's met?"

"Not while he was sober. He would never do that sober."

Annja turned that over in her mind. "Do you realize everything he's seen? All the history?"

"You mean all the violence and bloodshed?" Fiona's voice had turned harsh. "That's what much of history boils down to. Greed, murder, torture, rape. It isn't all pomp and pageantry."

"I know."

"Good, because for a moment there you looked like a dewy-eyed romantic."

Annja didn't say anything.

"Not that I have anything against dewy-eyed romantics. As long as they realize there's another side to history."

"What we're living in now is going to be history one day. I don't think things are any easier now than they were."

Fiona blew out a breath and her voice softened. "You're

right, of course. I'd like to think that we've come further than those bleak times."

"Fiona, we're walking into a warehouse to rescue a man that might already be dead. And we're probably going to have to kill men to get that done. I don't think much has changed."

"Right you are." Fiona nodded. "As I was saying, though, you're a different kind of young woman than Roux usually keeps time with."

"More of a dewy-eyed romantic?"

Fiona chuckled. "To be quite candid, yes."

"Maybe I am." Annja thought back to all the violence that had been in her life since she'd claimed the sword. Or since the sword had claimed her. She was never quite certain how that worked.

When she thought about it, she was surprised at how easily she'd adapted to the violence. And sometimes she was ashamed of herself and the way she craved action. But it was who she was now. Maybe it was who she'd been all along.

"When we get inside the warehouse, you won't have to worry about me or what I'll do."

Fiona patted her on the shoulder. "You will do what is necessary. I can see that in you. I just wish you wouldn't have the regrets."

"That's part of what keeps me who I am…. And, just so we're clear, I'm not keeping *time* with Roux."

WHEN THEY REACHED THE TARGET warehouse, Annja realized almost at once that her uneasiness came from the men she saw in front of her. They weren't office workers or dockworkers. They weren't even the homeless, beggars or blue-collar workers barely getting by.

The young Asians stood out against the warehouse background because they were clearly gang members. Tattooed Triad thugs with their low-slung street bikes. They wore black wraparound sunglasses that hid their eyes and long dusters that concealed whatever weapons they carried.

Annja put a hand out to Fiona, but the woman had already stopped.

"It appears we're not the only ones to discover M. Laframboise's hiding spot." She smiled mirthlessly. She looked at Annja. "There's no question about this turning bloody now, I'm afraid. What do you wish to do?"

Taking a deep breath, Annja shook her head. "We don't leave Edmund in their hands."

"Agreed. Follow me."

Fiona led the way through a small alley that went by the warehouse where Edmund was probably being held. At the corner of the building, a yellow-and-black-striped fence circled a manhole cover. She knelt down and a wicked pry bar appeared in her hand. She inserted the pry bar into the keyhole in the manhole cover and pulled the lid up a few inches.

"Give us a shove."

Annja knelt, as well, and grabbed the manhole cover. It had to weigh seventy or eighty pounds. She shifted it to the side to reveal the opening. Foul odors drifted up from below.

"At least it will get us into the warehouse." Fiona pulled out a Mini Maglite and flicked it on. "When the East India Docks filled with cargo ships and extra warehouses were needed, tunnels were built under the buildings to allow small cargoes to be shifted in and out. Also, coal was brought in underground, as well. These tunnels are filthy things at best."

Annja grabbed the edge of the manhole and swung down into the darkness. She breathed shallowly, hoping the sewer gas wasn't powerful enough to cause respiratory problems.

At the bottom of the ladder, Annja stood in a couple inches of drain water that ran through the irregular bottom of the tunnel. She pulled the poncho off. A rat sloshed through the water only a few feet away and scurried into the darkness. She took out her borrowed flashlight and scoured the tunnel bottom for a rock.

"What are you looking for?" Fiona stepped down beside her and removed her poncho, as well.

"A rock. I want to mark this ladder. If we're in a hurry coming out of that warehouse, I want to be able to find the way out immediately."

"Good thinking." Fiona pulled a small cylinder out of one of the pockets on her Kevlar vest. She sprayed a quick yellow X on the wall beside the ladder. "Phosphorescent. We'll be able to find it in the dark. Now let's move along, shall we?"

16

The tunnel ran straight for forty yards, then arrived at a four-way intersection. Annja went to the right, following the new passage toward the warehouse. Although she listened intently, all she heard was the trickle of water, the rapid smacking of rats frantically avoiding them and the echo of their own movements.

The flashlight beam picked up the occasional pair of red eyes over whiskered snouts as well as other flotsam and jetsam. She ignored all that and concentrated on Edmund, hoping fervently that he was still alive. And that they could bring him out that way.

Twenty yards later, she found another ladder mounted on the wall. She switched off the flashlight and put it away, secured the shotgun behind her and glanced at Fiona.

The older woman held her MP5-SD3 in both hands while managing her own flashlight and gave her a quick nod. "Keep your head down."

Annja climbed the ladder rungs. Her wet boots slid on the metal, but she forced her way up. She bumped her head on the manhole that covered the opening.

Locking a leg and an arm in the ladder, she reached up with her other hand and pressed her palm against the manhole cover.

One-handed, she lifted the heavy disc out of place and shifted it to the side. The manhole cover made only a slight grating sound as she let go.

Above her, the crescent-moon-shaped opening let in weak yellow electrical light. Men's voices sounded far away, not on top of her.

Cautiously, she reached up with both hands and gripped the manhole cover. Lifting it by the edge to move it quietly was difficult. She'd always been strong, but since the sword had come into her possession, she was stronger and faster, as if some new part of her had blossomed.

She set the cover aside, then gripped the sides of the tunnel mouth and pulled herself up. When she peered over the edge, she discovered she was in a small office bereft of furniture. The walls went only halfway up. The rest was window and venetian blinds in disarray.

She hauled herself up but remained in a crouch, then brought the shotgun around. Just as she turned around to help Fiona, the woman pulled herself up.

Fiona crossed the room in a crouch and took up a position on the other side of the open doorway. Together, they peered out into the warehouse.

In the center of the open space riddled with remnants of walls, Edmund Beswick sat tied in a chair. Jean-Baptiste Laframboise stood before him with a big pistol in one hand. Annja recognized the man from the crime photos.

Two other men stood in the room slightly behind Edward, both armed with assault rifles.

"Just three of them, then," Fiona whispered. "Shouldn't be too hard. When you're ready."

"All right." Annja flipped the safety off the shotgun, held it in both hands before her and stayed low as she went through the door.

The gloom that filled the warehouse helped keep her in shadows. Laframboise had lights in the area where he held Edmund and plywood sheets covered the windows. She took advantage of the partial walls to hide her approach.

Twenty feet away, at the edge of the pool of light where Edmund was, Annja stopped behind the low remnant of a wall. Fiona crept to a support pillar and readied her submachine gun. She looked at Annja, waiting.

Annja stared at the men around Edmund. From all accounts, Laframboise was a murderer and a thief. He'd left the bodies of victims and betrayed partners scattered in his wake. She had no doubt that the Frenchman fully intended to kill Edmund once he had everything from the professor that he thought he could get.

But she couldn't just kill someone in cold blood. The heat of battle was another thing. That felt right. But this…

Annja steadied herself and prepared to step out to confront the men, hoping she could dissuade them from taking action. Fiona stared at her as if she'd gone mad, then whirled around the pillar quickly and lifted the MP5 to her shoulder.

At the other end of the warehouse, the door suddenly exploded open, propelled by a van. Sheet metal screeched as it tore and the vehicle's motor howled inside the building. Men carrying weapons flung themselves from the van. Annja recognized the gang tattoos at once.

Gunfire erupted, but instead of coming from Laframboise's group or the Asian gang, it came from Fiona. With two quick bursts, she put down the armed guards around Edmund. Laframboise was on the other side of the professor, in the line of fire.

The Frenchman fired at the men ahead of him and squalled for reinforcements. He dove into hiding as bullets sliced through the air where he'd been standing.

Annja ran toward Edmund, slung the shotgun over her shoulder and dug out her Tinker knife. Kneeling beside him, she sliced the tape binding his hands and feet.

"Annja." Edmund looked nonplussed.

"Run." She shoved him forward, then had to catch him as his legs gave way beneath him. He'd been tied too long and didn't have control over his body. She hauled his arm across her shoulders and supported him as they ran toward the back of the warehouse.

Fiona hosed the van with the submachine gun. Bullets tore through the body and smashed holes in the windshield. Annja glimpsed at least two of the Asian gang members sprawled on the floor.

By that time Laframboise knew he was under attack on two separate fronts. He aimed his big pistol at Fiona and fired twice, but both rounds went wide of the target.

When her weapon cycled dry, Fiona ducked back behind the pillar, dropped the magazine and inserted another one. She wheeled back around and started firing again, meeting a wave of Asian gang members who had chosen that moment to try to gain ground. Her bullets slapped one of them back.

Other gang members closed on Laframboise's position. The Frenchman fought desperately, trading shots. Then he gained a brief respite when a group of his men poured into the building. The new arrivals took up positions and attacked the gang members, but they also fired back out the door they'd come in, obviously under attack from outside.

With Edmund's arm pulled across her shoulders, Annja kept running. He pounded along beside her and his rhythm came to him before they reached the back office area. She got him settled behind the wall.

"Does Laframboise have the lantern?"

He stared at her. "Yes."

Annja peered around the doorway as Fiona skidded into the office in a crouch. "Where?"

"You're not seriously thinking of going back there."

Annja was, though she didn't see how she could do it. But the first priority was to get everyone to safety.

"No." Even as she said it, Laframboise broke from cover and ran back toward the desk. He yelled orders into a phone as he sprinted and fired blindly at the gang members. He hunkered down beside the desk.

"We've got to go." Fiona radiated calm on the other side of the doorway from Annja.

"I know."

Beside the door Laframboise's men had come through, the wall suddenly exploded as a heavy sedan smashed through it. The vehicle immediately drew fire from the gang members, but it was apparent that the sedan was armored and had bulletproof glass. Bullets ricocheted off the body and left only tiny spiderwebbed cracks behind instead of punching holes through the windshield.

The driver pulled the car between Laframboise and the gang members. Instantly, the Frenchman scooped up the box near the desk and clambered into the rear of the sedan.

"Laframboise has the lantern." Edmund peered through the glass above the half wall.

Annja felt a pang of frustration. She still hadn't even held the lantern.

The sedan reversed and sped, mostly, back through the hole it had made. Some of the gang members went after the fleeing car, but others raced toward the back office where they were taking cover.

Annja grabbed Edmund's arm and shoved him toward the manhole. "Time for our disappearing act."

Edmund reacted immediately and dropped down the opening.

Fiona recharged her weapon and glanced at Annja. "You're next. I'll hold them."

Arguing with the woman hadn't proven successful, and there was no time under the circumstances. Annja rushed over to the opening as Fiona leaned around the doorway and opened fire. The staccato string of explosions blotted out her hearing as she went down the ladder.

At the bottom, Annja took out the Mini Maglite and started off. Edmund followed close behind. Conversation was impossible in the tunnel with all the gunfire echoes. She kept the flashlight moving, knowing their entrance could have been discovered and that someone could be in the tunnel with them. Rats ran for cover and she had to keep from blasting them with the shotgun.

The phosphorescent X glowed on the wall ahead of them. The opening stood out in the darkness.

Annja slung the shotgun and went up the ladder. Her attention was torn between what lay ahead of her and whether Fiona had made it into the tunnel with them. She didn't see the men waiting for her till one of them had her by her hair.

He yanked her head back and another man thrust a pistol into her throat. The second man grinned. "Found your back door. Now you come up out of there or I'm going to shoot you."

For a moment, Annja held her position. She thought she could break away from the man holding her hair, and she believed she could knock the pistol aside. But Edmund was below her, already on the ladder, and that was going to be a problem.

Worse, the two men weren't alone. Three others with submachine guns stood around the manhole.

"I won't tell you again." The man with the pistol was hard and his eyes were empty of compassion, almost feral.

Slowly, Annja climbed up. As she emerged, the gang members stripped her of the shotgun and the pistol. Two of them grabbed her by the wrists and held her arms behind her back. They pulled her back from the hole and pushed her facedown on the ground.

The man with the pistol leaned out over the hole. "Come up now or I'll shoot you where you stand."

A moment later, Edmund crawled out of the hole. He was patted down, then pulled back and forced to the ground, as well.

"There's another one in the tunnel." The leader readied his pistol. "These two were too close to the opening to be shooting back in the warehouse."

Fiona was going to be ambushed. If she fought, which Annja felt the woman might do, she was going to be killed. And if she surrendered, they were all going to be in the hands of the gang. Annja had no doubt about their eventual fate.

The men focused on the hole as someone sloshed through the water below.

Annja rolled to her left, jerking her right arm violently in an attempt to break free of the man holding her. He managed to hang on, but he was off balance. She swung her right leg up and swept his feet out from under him, knocking him backward.

The man on her left tried to aim his submachine gun, but he'd retained his hold on her left wrist, as well. Anna reached back with her right arm, caught the back of the man's shirt and yanked him over her body to trip him. He fell heavily and his grip on her wrist broke as he tried to keep his face from striking the pavement.

Still in motion, Annja rolled to her feet, reached for the sword, and the blade nestled easily in her hands. Mercilessly, knowing their lives were measured in heartbeats now, she struck. The blade glittered as she swung and took off the head of the man on her right as he brought up his weapon.

Stepping toward the man on the left, Annja turned the blade and brought it down in an overhand strike that caught her opponent between his neck and shoulder. Almost cut in half, he dropped without a sound.

The man at the opening lifted his pistol and snarled with rage and fear. Annja ducked and followed her blade home as she took another step. The point crashed through the man's breastbone and skewered his head. He fell backward just as Fiona appeared in the opening.

Annja spun back toward the men she'd knocked down behind her. They were getting up, grabbing for their weapons. Before she could move, Fiona blasted them with the MP5.

On solid ground now, Fiona dumped her empty magazine and put a fresh one in. She glanced at Annja. "Is that the sword Roux was looking for?"

Not knowing what else to say, Annja nodded. She let the

sword disappear, then picked up the shotgun and pistol that had been taken from her.

"We have a lot to talk about, don't we?" Fiona smiled grimly. "So let's try to stay alive over the next few moments." She shifted her attention to Edmund, who was slowly getting up from the ground. "Come along. We've a car waiting."

They ran through the alley as gunfire echoed all around them.

17

The dock area in front of the warehouse had turned into a bloodbath as Laframboise's men battled the Asian gang members. Bodies lay strewn across the pavement. Klaxons rang out across the river and boat traffic had powered to the other bank.

Annja sprinted at Edmund's side. He was in good shape and had made a quick recovery. Fiona led them toward the Bristol Fighter, skirting along the warehouses so they wouldn't be immediately noticed.

Their luck didn't hold, though. Two of the gang members on motorcycles spotted them and gave chase. The high-pitched whine of the engines cut through the noise of the firefight like buzz saws.

"Fiona!" Annja brought up her shotgun.

Ahead, Fiona swept around and threw a protective arm across Edmund, grasping his shirt and yanking him off balance. He fell and covered his head with his hands.

Annja aimed at the lead motorcyclist as he fired a machine pistol left-handed. Bullets stitched the warehouse wall near Annja and the ringing sounds of the rounds tearing through the sheet metal sounded like steel rain. She squeezed the trigger and rode out the recoil as the shotgun fed another shell into the chamber. The empty cartridge dropped as she sighted in again.

The initial double-ought burst caught the man in the chest and tore him from the motorcycle. The machine fell on its side and skidded across the ground while the man tumbled forward like a rag doll.

Annja squeezed the trigger again and caught the second man in the head. He jerked sideways, parting company with his ride.

A third motorcyclist who'd joined the chase broke his approach and wheeled to his left. Unfortunately, that was directly in the path of Laframboise's escaping sedan. The big car hammered the motorcycle. The rider tore loose and bounced across the hood and the windshield before dropping in its wake.

For a moment, the sedan got caught up on the fallen motorcycle. Sparks flared from the machine as it ground to pieces beneath the bigger vehicle. The driver stopped, reversed and left the motorcycle debris on the pavement. He whipped around the wreck.

Fiona already had Edmund moving again. They were less than fifty feet from the sports car.

Annja fed more shells into the shotgun as she raced over to the nearest fallen motorcycle. She slung the shotgun and righted the motorcycle. Everything looked fine and the handlebars remained straight, in alignment with the front wheel. She threw a leg across, pulled in the clutch and pressed the start button. The engine caught immediately and she stepped the gearshift into First.

Other gang members on motorcycles roared by in pursuit of the sedan. None paid any attention to Annja. She twisted the accelerator and raced over to Fiona.

"I'm going to follow Laframboise. See where he goes. The car only has two seats."

Fiona hesitated for just a moment, decided arguing was obviously not going to work and nodded. "Be careful."

Annja rolled the throttle and shot off in pursuit. Four motorcyclists and a car trailed after the sedan. A gunner leaned out of the sedan, took aim at the car following and unleashed a spray of bullets that smashed into the vehicle's windshield. Annja was close enough to see the driver jerk with the impacts of the bullets.

The driver tried to maintain control but lost the battle, swerving to the left and cutting off two of the motorcycles without warning. One of the motorcycles went down under the car's wheels. The other got clipped by the front bumper and spun out of control. Still accelerating, the dead man's car hit the end of a dock and sailed out into the river.

Annja downshifted, swerved and powered out of a slide, narrowly missing the crushed motorcycle. She checked her mirrors and saw that Fiona was in hot pursuit.

The two gang members remaining on motorcycles hadn't given up. They dodged and weaved behind the sedan, making hard targets of themselves. They didn't try to return fire because they'd realized the car was armored and because it took all their skill to manage the rough road and dodge the gunner.

The sedan smashed through cargo loads and sent dockworkers scattering. One man barely had time to leap off his forklift before the sedan smashed into it. The collision ripped the sedan's fender away and mangled the steering. Annja didn't imagine that the passengers inside the car fared much better. Despite the damage, the sedan was slowed only for a moment and continued more or less on course.

Less than a hundred yards ahead, the sedan slewed around in a ninety-degree turn that left it broadside in the middle of the road. The move caught one of the motorcyclists unaware and he smashed into it. Annja and the other gang member braked to a halt, then sped away as the gunner in the sedan opened fire again.

The sedan drove forward toward one of the docks. For a moment Annja thought it was out of control and was going to go over the side. Instead, the driver brought the vehicle to a skidding halt that left the right front tire hanging over the dock's edge. The passenger doors opened and Laframboise and his lackeys scrambled out toward the water.

The last gang member on motorcycle fired at them, then got picked off by one of the Frenchman's gunners. Annja remained behind a parked car and ducked as a swath of gunfire took out the windows. Safety glass rained down over her.

When she stuck her head back up, Annja saw a speedboat racing away from the dock. She caught just a glimpse of Laframboise as he ducked belowdecks. In seconds, the speedboat zipped through the lazy river traffic and was gone.

Fiona braked the sports car in front of the car where Annja had taken cover. Peering through the window, Fiona nodded in the direction of the speedboat. "That was Laframboise?"

"Yes."

"Ah, well, there's nothing to be done for it now."

"You don't have a boat handy?" It was a joke, but Annja did halfway expect the woman to have one waiting somewhere.

"Disappointing as it may be, no, I don't. Nor helicopter, either. I do have a helicopter, just not at the ready." Fiona shot her a rueful look. "I hadn't planned on this."

"Me, neither."

They could hear sirens coming closer with each passing second.

"Be a love and put your weapons in the back." The sports car's trunk flipped up. "Wouldn't do any good to get caught with those. There would be far too many explanations for us to make at this juncture. The game is afoot, so to speak, and it wouldn't do to break stride."

Annja rode the motorcycle over to the car and dumped her weapons into the trunk. Edmund watched her in fascination.

"You know, Ms. Creed, I don't believe any of this was covered in the information you sent me." He looked slightly pale.

"No. I try not to get involved in things like this." Annja closed the trunk lid. "But they seem to keep…involving me."

In the rearview mirror, Fiona was smiling knowingly.

There were going to be a lot of questions. Annja got back on the motorcycle and followed the sports car away from the docks as the arriving police tried in vain to contain the area.

They made their escape at a leisurely pace.

"I'M REALLY NOT SURE THIS is a good idea." Self-conscious, Annja walked beside Fiona Pioche into the hotel. Annja tried to remember how many nights she'd actually stayed there and couldn't. She remembered the first night, but thought maybe she'd only caught a nap there before heading out into the streets looking for the new Mr. Hyde.

"I *know* this isn't a good idea." Looking guilty and somewhat like a vagabond after all his rough handling, Edmund trailed the two women. "After all that shooting on the docks, I should quite imagine most of the Metro police are looking for us."

"No one got a good look at us." Fiona nodded to the concierge and headed for the elevators.

"There are security cameras over there, you know."

"Well, we'll just have to see how good their systems are, won't we?"

"You drive a rather distinguishable car."

Fiona pressed the elevator button. "I believe at the time we would have been spotted, Annja and I were freeing you from kidnappers."

"True, but—"

Smiling sweetly, Fiona turned to Edmund. "But nothing, dear man. Relax and enjoy the adventure."

"Adventure?"

"Yes. Events like this remind us why we're alive."

"After this morning, we're lucky to *be* alive."

"That's part of the package. So few people get to enjoy adrenaline like that anymore." Fiona faced the elevator doors as they opened. "I know I've missed it."

Edmund shot Annja a look of disbelief.

Annja smiled at him and stepped into the elevator after Fiona. "I don't have to collect my gear. I can get internet access practically anywhere."

"True. But these are your tools we're after. I think a professional should have access to her tools. This thing—whatever it is—is going to require some serious effort. I think you'd be at your best working with tools you're comfortable with."

"Detective Chief Inspector Westcox is going to have a man stationed on my door."

"There was a policeman in the lobby. I'm sure he's already phoned the inspector."

"Was there?" Annja hadn't seen the man.

"Yes. Callow fellow. Gray suit and a bad haircut. He was reading a fishing magazine. That's what gave him away. Well, I'd already sussed him out, of course, but the magazine confirmed it."

"How?"

"It had an address label on it. The magazine wasn't one provided by the hotel, and it wasn't one bought in the shop, or in any nearby shop."

"He brought it from home."

"Exactly."

Standing there beside the older woman, Annja felt foolish. "I wouldn't even have thought of looking for something like that."

"But now you'll never forget it." Fiona reached over and took Annja's hand. "Don't waste time chastising yourself. We all have our specialties. This one happens to fall within my bailiwick. I don't know as much about archaeology and antiquities as you do. And I definitely cannot pull a sword out of thin air even if my life depended on it."

Edmund stood there and looked fondly back toward the front door.

Fiona held the door and waited for him. She lifted her eyebrows quizzically. "Are you coming? If you don't, there's a good chance you'll never see Anton Dutilleaux's magic lantern again. Or learn why so many people seem to prize it."

With a piteous snarl of self-loathing, Edmund stepped into the elevator. He wrapped his arms around himself. "I'm going to regret this."

Fiona smiled. "Only if you live long enough."

The elevator doors closed with finality and they started to rise.

"Normally, I'm braver than this." Edmund pursed his lips.

"Then again, normally I don't have to face gun-toting criminals who tie me to chairs and hit me. Seriously, that's something that doesn't happen every day." He paused. "If it did, I'm convinced I'd find another line of work."

"We'll see." Fiona took out her small pistol and checked it. Satisfied, she put it away. "You might be surprised how quickly you become accustomed to such a lifestyle."

That was true. Occasionally, when she thought about her own life, Annja marveled, as well. But the action was addictive.

Edmund shook his head. "Absolutely brill."

When the elevator stopped without fanfare at the correct floor, Annja stepped out first. After she turned the corner to the hallway leading down to her room, she saw the big man standing beside a chair in front of her door. He surely hadn't been standing long.

"Ms. Creed?" The man faced her with his hands at his sides, his jacket unbuttoned, and the blue-and-yellow bulk of the X26 Taser nestled in a hip holster. He smiled, but it didn't reach his eyes.

"Yes?"

"I'm Constable Stanbrook."

"Is there something I can do for you, Constable?"

The smile stayed in place. "Detective Chief Inspector Westcox would like a word with you."

"I'm not interested in talking to the inspector."

The constable's smile disappeared. "I'm afraid the inspector has insisted."

Fiona stepped in beside Annja. "On whose authority?"

Stanbrook looked momentarily flummoxed. "On his own authority, of course."

"Balderdash. What you're doing here is illegal."

"Back off before you get hurt, gran. I'll be deciding what's legal here and what's not."

Fiona kicked the constable in the shins.

Yelping, the man stepped away and bumped into the wall

behind him. When he bounced off the wall, Fiona grabbed his jacket lapels in one hand, stuck out a foot and tripped him with an economy of motion. Stanbrook fell heavily to the carpeted floor. He reached for the Taser. Fiona was on him in a flash, controlling the man's arm as he came up with the weapon. She helped him fire the Taser and both dartlike electrodes lanced into his crotch. He cried out in pain, then shivered as the current hit him and he finally relaxed into unconsciousness.

Fiona stood and ran a hand through her platinum hair. "Gran, my arse." She nodded at the door. "Let's go in, shall we?"

Still stunned at how quickly events had escalated, Annja fished her room key card from her pocket and slotted it. She was surprised when the lights turned green and the locking mechanism worked. She opened the door and went inside.

18

Laframboise sat in a small bar just off the Thames. On the television above the bartender's head, police boats rocked on the river current as they tried to contain the Isle of Dogs crime scene. Several uniformed officers stretched yellow warning tape around the area. Other constables put up sawhorses to block vehicle access.

The news reporter covering the story talked excitedly, but the conversation buzzing around the bar was too loud for Laframboise to make out what she was saying.

"Another drink, sir?" A thin server with black skin and close-cropped blond hair and electric-blue highlights stopped beside his table.

"Please." Laframboise tapped his wineglass.

The waitress took it and scurried back to the bar.

Laframboise swiveled his attention to Gilbert Campra, his majordomo. "Those were Puyi-Jin's people?"

Campra was a large man, over six feet tall and steroid-enhanced. He shaved his head but grew a thick goatee that was artificially colored black. Silver hoop earrings glittered in his ears. He wore loose-fitting gym pants, a T-shirt and a light-weight jacket that covered the pistols he carried. Red-lensed wraparound sunglasses masked his eyes.

"Yes." Campra wore an earpiece that kept him in contact with the rest of the security team.

"How many are still on our tail?"

"Three."

"That we've found."

Campra nodded. His team was good at surveillance, but Puyi-Jin's people were good at not being surveilled.

The two women at the ambush had been a surprise.

The server brought back another glass of red wine. Laframboise paid her, tipped generously and swirled the glass by its stem. The wine had a good nose. He sipped. It was far from the best he'd ever had, still, it was good.

"Do we know who the woman was with Annja Creed?"

Campra shook his head. "Not yet."

If the woman had shown up in Paris, Laframboise would have known who she was within minutes. "Where are the rest of Puyi-Jin's men?"

"Nearby." Campra frowned. "They appear to be closing ranks." The big man had spent time in the military before turning mercenary. The other men who worked with Laframboise didn't hang out with Campra. To them, he was dangerous and unpredictable. Campra would rather kill someone than worry about them.

Laframboise found that Campra's most endearing quality. Laframboise didn't believe in leaving witnesses alive behind him, either. He hated that Annja Creed had gotten away with Professor Edmund Beswick.

"They're closing ranks?"

Campra nodded again and sipped his water. He never touched alcohol. "Evidently they're satisfied that they know where you're going."

Laframboise fully intended to return to Paris. That was where he felt the safest, and that was where Anton Dutilleaux had lost the lantern—along with his life.

"Then what do you think they're going to do?"

Campra shrugged. "Kill you."

He grinned at that. People had tried to kill him before. He carried scars and two bullets from those encounters.

"Are you certain the professor didn't know anything more about your little party favor?" Campra glanced at the shopping bag in the seat next to Laframboise. Inside, a specially constructed protective box held the magic lantern.

"He's not the kind to hide the truth when he's being physically punished. Everything he knew, he told us."

Campra ran a hand through his goatee. "Something you have to ask yourself."

"What?"

"Is the lantern worth going up against Puyi-Jin?"

Laframboise smiled at the other man. "Are you afraid of the Chinaman?"

A grin twitched Campra's lips but failed to light his eyes. "Afraid, no. Wary, yeah. The guy is dangerous."

"So are we."

Campra nodded. "I still can't help thinking you're making a very powerful enemy for no reason. Puyi-Jin hasn't been able to figure out the lantern, and that professor doesn't have a clue, maybe you should cut it loose."

Campra's opinion was valued in his organization and he was offered the opportunity to propose courses of action. "Do you think I could buy Puyi-Jin's forgiveness for betraying him with that act?"

The red lenses remained focused on Laframboise. "No." Campra sipped his water again. "Not forgiveness, but he's losing money and men on this, too. Several of his people have been arrested, chasing Annja Creed. He's lost some good men."

"I don't want to give the lantern to him."

Campra didn't say anything.

"I didn't get where I am by letting people push me around, my friend."

"I know that."

"And I'm curious." Laframboise upended his wineglass and drained the dregs. "I hate being curious. Especially if there's money involved. The professor mentioned that Dutilleaux was around Shanghai when money was flowing. You and I both know that a smart man, one willing to take risks, can divert some of that free-flowing money into his own pockets." He tapped the shopping bag with his hand. "I have a feeling about this—a very *strong* feeling—that there's something to the story of Anton Dutilleaux's lantern." He smiled. "Annja Creed being involved is most interesting. Have you seen her show? *Chasing History's Monsters?*"

"Not much of a TV watcher."

"Pity."

"You're a fan?"

"Of Annja Creed?" He shook his head. "No. I am, however, a fan of Kristie Chatham, the cohost of the show. Loses her clothing in all manner of delightful ways during most episodes."

Campra shook his head. "You through with that wine?"

"I am." He set the empty glass on the small table.

"Then we should be going. The car is here."

"Of course." Laframboise picked up the shopping bag and followed Campra through the crowd.

Research he'd done into the lantern had included scouring old photographs of Dutilleaux standing in front of wild phantasms in the catacombs. Laframboise had gone down into the catacombs to the exact spot where the phantasmagorist had been stabbed to death.

Laframboise liked to believe he was psychic. His mother had told fortunes when he'd been a boy. He remembered watching her spread the large tarot cards on a black felt cloth.

From the moment he'd put his hands on the magic lantern Puyi-Jin had offered to pay him so handsomely for, he'd felt certain the device would change his life forever. His mother's gift was real enough and he'd inherited it. He was convinced of that.

OUTSIDE ON THE DOCKS, THEY headed for the rendezvous point. Despite the mad rush from the warehouse, everything else had gone according to plan.

Out of the corner of his eye, he spotted the three Chinese men trailing him. The men were dressed in street clothes, but the loose shirts and light jackets easily concealed whatever weapons they carried.

Laframboise felt alive. He didn't know where Puyi-Jin had come from or what the man had been forced to do to create his empire, but Laframboise had been killing for survival since he'd turned fourteen. He fisted the big pistol in his jacket pocket.

"Campra?"

"I see them." The big man's voice was flat and hard. "We don't have to take them on ourselves. We have men nearby."

"Worried?"

Campra snorted. "Not about me."

"I want one of them left alive."

"I can't guarantee that."

Laframboise turned right and took the next alley. "Work on it."

He guessed that the three Chinese men would meet him on the other side. They gave themselves a moment and then wheeled and ran back out of the alley, hoping to double back around behind their stalkers.

Shoppers and tourists, already edgy from the police boats out on the river and the reports cycling through the media, hurried out of the way.

The three gangsters had no clue they'd been outfoxed. They'd spread out at the end of the alley Laframboise had initially taken, waiting.

A few yards away, holding the shopping bag in one hand, Laframboise lifted the Colt .44 Magnum and squeezed the trigger. The heavy round cored through the head of the closest man. The detonation sounded like an artillery shell going off, so near the narrow confines of the alley.

The .44 Magnum bullet nearly decapitated the target. Already dead on his feet, the man stumbled onto the man in front of him. The other two men tried to turn and draw their weapons from under their jackets. One of them was blocked by the dead man, but the other took a step to the side.

Campra's bullet snapped into his face and drove the man backward. He jerked and fought for his balance, then sank to one knee. Campra shot the man twice more in the chest, making certain of the kill.

The third man finally managed to get the corpse off him. Covered in the other man's blood, his young face tight with fear, he lifted his weapon.

"Alive, Gilbert." Laframboise held his weapon in a relaxed grip. He wore body armor and didn't think the man would get a shot off, anyway, but he was prepared to put a round into the man's chest if he had to.

Campra didn't speak. His weapon barked twice.

The Chinese gangster shuddered at both impacts, and the pistol fell from his nerveless fingers. At different times, Campra had explained the shot to Laframboise, how the round could tear through the brachial nerve cluster in the shoulder and leave a wounded man unable to use his hands.

The shot was difficult, but Campra was a master.

He strode forward, keeping the wounded man covered. "Get down." He waggled the pistol for emphasis. "Down on your knees. Do it now."

Off balance, the man did as he was told. He barely managed to stay upright. He couldn't raise his hands because his arms wouldn't obey him, but he held them out from his sides.

"Don't shoot." The young man blinked fearfully.

"You work for Puyi-Jin. Tell me a lie and I'll kill you."

He hesitated only a moment, then nodded. His eyes were glazed and otherworldly. Between the fear and the pain, he was barely hanging on to consciousness.

"What did Puyi-Jin send you to do?"

The man clenched his teeth and swallowed hard. He was afraid. He wanted to run. All of that showed in his eyes. "To kill you. To get the lantern."

Laframboise smiled. "All right. I want you to do something for me."

He didn't respond.

"If you're not going to do it, I'll kill you and leave you with your friends."

"It will be done."

"Give Puyi-Jin this message—I'm not easy to kill. Tell him that and tell him to stay away from me. Otherwise, I'll come after him."

He nodded.

Lowering his weapon, Laframboise strode past the wounded man with Campra at his side, heading to the black luxury sedan idling down the street.

The driver got out and opened the back door. Laframboise holstered his weapon and slid in. Campra joined him a moment later.

In the space of a drawn breath, the chauffeur put the transmission into gear and eased into the morning traffic.

Calmly, Laframboise shook the empties from his pistol and replaced them with fresh cartridges. "Do you think Puyi-Jin will get the message?"

"Yes. But he's not going to listen."

"You don't think so?"

Campra snorted. "Would you?"

Laframboise grinned. "No." He put the pistol away. "Puyi-Jin's continued involvement will only make things interesting."

"Isn't that an old Chinese curse? May you live in interesting times?"

"I suppose it is." Laframboise looked down to the magic lantern in the bag at his feet. There was something there, something just beneath the surface. He sensed the darkness inside the device and it called to him. "A curse can be a powerful weapon against people who believe it. We'll make it our weapon."

19

"You travel light."

Zipping her duffel bag, Annja glanced up at Fiona Pioche. "It's a gift. And a necessity in my line of work."

Fiona stood at the window with her arms crossed, looking out over the city. "And which line of work would that be? The television personality? The archaeologist? Or whatever it is you are when you draw that sword?"

"Sword?" Sitting in the small straight-backed chair beside the equally small writing desk, Edmund perked up at once. "There was a sword, wasn't there? And you had it. What happened to that sword?" He didn't look happy at all.

Annja dropped the duffel on the floor. "I don't have it anymore."

"I didn't see what you did with it."

Annja ignored him and went back to the bathroom to make sure she'd got everything. Satisfied everything was packed, she returned to the bedroom.

Someone knocked on the door. Fiona casually drew her pistol and nodded at Annja.

At the door, Annja stood to the side, almost inside the small closet. "Who is it?" She'd seen nasty things happen to people who made the mistake of looking through the peephole.

"Ms. Creed, it's Detective Chief Inspector Westcox. I'd like a word if I might." The man sounded irate.

Fiona put her pistol away.

Annja opened the door.

Westcox stood in the doorway with his hat in one hand.

"I was just leaving."

"That might not be as easy as you like. There are several matters I need to discuss with you."

Fiona stepped forward. "If I may be permitted, Annja."

Westcox gritted his teeth. "Ah, Ms. Pioche. I would say it's nice seeing you again. If that were true."

Fiona smiled thinly. "Likewise, I'm sure." She waved a hand toward Annja's duffel and backpack. "As you can see, Ms. Creed *was* on her way out. If you'd like, you could help carry."

"No, I don't think I would. Furthermore, I was just thinking of escorting Ms. Creed—and you—down to the station for questioning."

"We have rather pressing business to attend."

Westcox worked his jaws and his color deepened.

"Unless your offer wasn't an invitation? In that case, I'd have to get my barrister involved. And as you know, Chief Inspector, Maurice doesn't care for the bullying tactics you sometimes employ." Fiona's smile was saccharine.

Distaste compressed Westcox's lips. "There's no need to get that man involved."

"So this is an invitation?"

Westcox hesitated, then nodded reluctantly. "Of course."

"Then we decline." Fiona turned to Annja. "Grab your things. The car should be out front by now."

Annja retreated long enough to pick up her duffel, backpack and leather coat.

"Chief Inspector." The constable who'd been guarding the door stood in back of Westcox with a hand held protectively over his groin. His voice had risen a full octave. His eyes looked watery and his face was red. "You can't just let that woman go. Not after…not after what she did."

Westcox glared at Fiona. "My constable says you assaulted him."

"With his own Taser. And he's a head taller than I am." Fiona shook her head sorrowfully. "Do you really want something like this to end up in the papers and on television, Chief Inspector?"

The constable tried to edge forward.

Westcox held the man back with an arm. "Walk away, Constable."

"But—"

"I said, *walk away.* Do it now."

Cursing, the constable turned and walked down the hallway.

Westcox shifted his focus back to Fiona. "You're going to involve yourself in this, Ms. Pioche?"

"I'm afraid I am already involved."

"Why?"

"At the behest of an old friend, Chief Inspector. And you know how I treasure my friendships."

"I also know that the moral nature of your *friends* is often questionable."

"Merely part of what makes them interesting."

Westcox glanced at Annja. "What has made this woman so interesting?"

Annja objected to being casually dismissed, but she allowed Fiona to handle the situation.

"After you get to know her, Ms. Creed is quite endearing."

"Endearing or not, the two of you are in a mess." The chief inspector reached back over his shoulder. A serious young woman in uniform stepped into view in the open doorway and handed him a file. Westcox opened it and took photographs out. "I just got these from a security camera on the Isle of Dogs where an apparent skirmish was fought between known criminals—and yourselves." He handed them the pictures.

Annja studied the images with a sinking feeling. They were of Fiona, Edmund and her fleeing the scene.

Fiona took one of them and pulled a pair of reading glasses from her jacket. She put them on and studied the photograph.

"Tell me what you were doing there," the chief inspector said.

"I don't think these images are high quality enough to prove that the people in these pictures are us."

"That car of yours is sufficiently distinct to mark you. Your ego is going to drive the nail in your coffin."

Fiona handed the photograph back dismissively. "If you'd like to take your chances before a judge, Chief Inspector, then, please, by all means. I keep Maurice on year-round retainer. It would be good to see him work for some of that."

Westcox returned the photographs to the folder and handed the file back to his young subordinate. "Tell me what you were doing there, Ms. Pioche."

"You haven't proven I was there."

Edmund cleared his throat nervously and spoke up. "Actually, they were there to rescue me. I'd been kidnapped, you see."

Westcox rounded on Edmund like a cat that had just swallowed the canary. "And who are you?"

"Professor Edmund Beswick." He brushed ineffectually at his ruined and bloody clothing. His face was swollen and bruised and his hair was in disarray.

"Pleasure to meet you, Professor." Westcox stood a little taller. "Ah, it appears I have a witness that can put you at that scene, Ms. Pioche."

"Wait," Edmund said frantically. "Did you not hear me? I said I was kidnapped."

"I'll be glad to take you down to the station where you can fill out a report." Westcox reached out for Edmund.

"No. I'm no longer kidnapped."

Fiona looked amused. "If you choose to go with the inspector, Professor Beswick, I think you might as well consider yourself kidnapped again. And the process will be about as regrettable."

Westcox snorted.

Edmund looked confused. "What I'm trying to tell you is that Ms. Pioche and Ms. Creed had a reason to be there."

"They could have contacted the police, Professor Beswick. That's what we're here for."

Fiona yawned. "Police take forever and a day getting paperwork together."

"But those men had guns. Really big guns." Edmund still seemed to be impressed by that.

Westcox scowled. "We can get guns when we need them. Now come along."

Edmund stepped back. "On second thought, I wasn't kidnapped at all. And I was never there."

Anger boiled behind Westcox's features. "If I have to, I'll take you into custody."

"For what?" Fiona moved into position to confront Westcox. "There's no law that says a man has to report his kidnapping, is there? And wouldn't that make a fine headline?"

Westcox looked apoplectic. With an effort, he peered past Fiona to Edmund. "You're making a mistake. Ms. Pioche is a loose cannon." Westcox flung a forefinger in Annja's direction. "And I'm working on getting this one deported."

Fiona glanced at Annja. "Sounds as though you might need a barrister. I know a good one."

Annja checked her own anger with difficulty. Nothing that had happened to her had been her fault. She was just experiencing an incredibly bad run of luck. "If it goes that far, sure. I'm also convinced that the media company I work for wouldn't like the idea of getting pushed around, either." She wasn't certain of that, but Doug Morrell and the production staff had interceded on Kristie Chatham's behalf a number of times.

Westcox fixed Fiona with his stare. "You cannot just circumvent the law."

Fiona stared up at him. "Until Ms. Creed releases this room, it's still hers and she has a right to expect privacy."

For a moment, Annja didn't know which way the situation would go. Then Westcox stepped back from the doorway.

Fiona took the lead out of the room. Annja followed and Edmund fell into step behind her.

"Be careful, Professor." Westcox's voice was chipped ice. "I get the distinct feeling that you're a lamb among lionesses."

"Flatterer," Fiona muttered without turning around.

ANNJA AND EDMUND FOLLOWED Fiona to a long limousine waiting outside the hotel. The chauffeur opened the rear door for them. Two other men, both dressed in dark suits, stood around the luxury car.

"I thought it would be better if we improved security." Fiona slid across the seat and patted the one next to her.

One of the security men relieved Annja of her backpack and duffel bag. Before he spirited them off to the trunk compartment, Annja slipped her notebook computer out of the backpack.

Edmund sat on the seat across from them. Annja indicated the notebook computer. "Do you mind? I've been out of touch."

"Of course not. We need information."

Annja booted it up.

Fiona took out a small notepad and pen. "Now, Professor Beswick, it seems we have time for a little chat."

Edmund nodded. "Definitely." He grimaced. "Sorry about that back in the hotel. I was trying to help."

"Of course you were." Fiona held her pen poised over her pad. "You said a man named Laframboise kidnapped you."

Annja lost touch with their conversation as she immersed herself in the thread she'd created on alt.history. Anton Dutilleaux's magic lantern had sparked more interest than she'd anticipated. She started reading and taking notes as the limousine wound through the London streets. She was hunting now, and she knew on some level that Fiona Pioche was doing the same thing.

20

In addition to the offices she kept on the bottom floor of the building, Fiona Pioche also reserved the top floor for herself, which she'd remodeled into spacious living quarters. She told Annja that she also maintained an estate in the country, if they had to leave the city, and that it was a proper fort.

"Good afternoon, Ms. Pioche." Oliver Wemyss held open the door to the foyer of the top suite of rooms. He took jackets and weapons without hesitation, storing them in a secure closet off to one side of the foyer. "Everything went well, I trust."

"Well enough, Ollie. We're still alive and several of our opponents are not."

"Cutting down the odds already. Sounds as though you've had a productive day." Ollie grinned at Annja and lifted an eyebrow. "Does Ms. Pioche surprise?"

"Every minute."

"One of her more endearing and consistent qualities, rest assured." Ollie glanced at Edmund. "And you're the erstwhile Professor Beswick." He offered his hand. "Oliver Wemyss at your service. I work with Ms. Pioche. Please be at ease."

"Is that possible around her?"

"On most days, no. But occasionally it does happen. This

way, please." Ollie swept an arm toward the open room on the other side of the foyer.

Annja kept her backpack and duffel with her.

The immense living room was filled with plush cream and tan furniture—easy chairs, two love seats and a huge modern couch. An enormous Persian rug anchored them all. The walls were a rich gold, with deep brown curtains over arched lattice windows. Pink and white lilies filled a gold vase on the large coffee table.

Annja just stood there a moment, taking it in. "Wow."

Ollie beamed at her, then shifted his attention to Fiona. "Ms. Pioche, I've taken the liberty of assigning rooms."

"Thank you, Ollie." Fiona went to the wet bar in the corner of the large room and began preparing a drink.

Ollie stood before them like a tour guide and Annja slightly resented his energy. "I thought the three of you would like to freshen up first. I'll have sandwiches and fresh fruit laid out, or you can have something more substantial if you wish."

"Sandwiches will be fine. I think we'll want to talk and finger food will be excellent." Fiona lifted her glass to Annja and Edmund, but both politely declined.

Edmund glanced down at his clothing self-consciously. "I'm not exactly dressed for lunch."

"I took the liberty of ordering a suit and other clothing for you," Ollie said. "You'll find them in your room."

"I have other clothes at my flat."

"I thought it best you stayed away from your flat until we got the lay of the land. Safer all around that way, I think."

"I suppose. But how did you know what size to get?"

Ollie grinned. "I'm a very good judge of a man's clothing, Professor. If I'm wrong, I'll have it attended to."

Fiona smiled and sipped her drink. "He won't be wrong."

"Ms. Creed, I took the same liberties for you."

Annja lifted a speculative eyebrow. "Good at guessing women's sizes, as well?"

"Very dangerous territory, that. I followed Ms. Pioche's direction." Ollie shook his head. "Americans are also rather too casual for my expertise, I'm afraid. When it comes to style, I don't speak American."

Fiona waved a dismissive hand. "Cut Ollie and he'd bleed Brit aristocrat."

Ollie grinned. "And be smug about it the whole time."

THE BEDROOM PROVED TO BE as incredible as the living room, with a view of the Thames from the king-size bed.

Evidently when Fiona Pioche decided to put a guest up, she did so in style.

Boxes of clothing in the correct size sat on the bench at the foot of the bed. Annja went through them in short order, picking out a pair of olive khakis and a fitted black T-shirt, before heading to the bathroom.

She started the bathwater, added one of several floral bath gels and stripped.

No one appreciated a bath the way an archaeologist did. They often spent days and sometimes weeks working on location without the benefit of anything other than makeshift showers at best.

She retrieved her notebook computer and power cord, crawled into the spacious tub and logged on to the internet using the pass code Fiona Pioche had provided.

Dozens of emails had come in since she'd last logged on. Several of those were from Doug, and a glance at her phone confirmed that he'd even started calling her. She put the phone away and filed the emails in the folder she'd set up for Doug. Chances were good he'd call again before she got back to him.

She dug into the responses to her posts about Dutilleaux's lantern. Several of them were without basis and she dismissed those. The ones that looked promising she copied and filed into a folder.

As she soaked, she reviewed the more promising posts from alt.archaeology.esoterica.

Hey, Lantern Girl,
Your mysterious lantern looks cool. I'm an American college

student in France and have been doing a doctoral thesis on popular illusionists, primarily Étienne Robertson (I'm sure you know who he was, but if not, hit me up for the 411). I came across some flyers from Anton Dutilleaux's shows as part of my research.

Dutilleaux was amazing for the time. A lot of people were convinced he was doing actual black magic. Getting killed like that kind of sealed the deal.

Anyway, I also found out that Dutilleaux's lantern was on Adolph Hitler's short list of things to acquire during World War II.

Is that news to you?

The message was from eyesontheprize@doctororbust.com. And the information was news, although Annja wasn't convinced how important it was.

She knew about Hitler's efforts to track down supernatural artifacts, including the Spear of Destiny that had been used by a Roman soldier to kill Jesus Christ. Originally, Hitler had intended to gather items that belonged to Aryan history, but the stories had grown during the war, and after the war the stories had exploded into cryptohistory, providing so many tales that finding out the truth was almost impossible.

Eyes on the Prize had also appended photocopied pages of resource material. Annja flicked through both pages. Basically the mention was more or less a footnote, a tale that had spread from a Paris museum worker who'd cooperated with the Nazis.

The information wasn't what Annja was looking for, but it let her know that more people than Edmund Beswick, the mysterious French gangster and the Chinese crime lord had been interested in Dutilleaux's lantern.

She flipped through the next two entries. One of them insisted that Dutilleaux's magic lantern actually held a trapped demon who had eventually gotten out and killed him. The other presented an unsupported case that the lantern was mystical in origin and would give three wishes to its owner.

The three wishes smacked too much of genies, or *djinn*, which were from the Arabic culture. Neither Dutilleaux nor the lantern had been there as far as she knew.

However, melodybaby@toocooltobetrue.net had another tidbit.

Hola, Lantern Girl,
Interesting subject you have there. I've been writing an article on illusionists—prompted by my love of the very sexy Hugh Jackman in *The Prestige*. But I digress. *Sigh*
    I did a lot of research on Anton Dutilleaux but eventually dropped him—they cut my word limit! Don't you hate when that happens? Anyway, I found a diary entry in a journal written by one of Étienne Robertson's understudies that had been put online. It said Dutilleaux got the lantern in Shanghai, China.
    From what I've been able to piece together, Dutilleaux was an assistant banker for the French businesses there in Shanghai. But he also worked for the Shanghai bankers as a go-between for emerging international business interests. There was some kind of kafuffle there and Dutilleaux left the city—and China!—in a hurry.
    Hope this helps. I'm sending my research as an attachment.

Annja sent a quick thank-you to all those who'd written in to the thread. She opened her mail client and sorted through her email. Doug Morrell had sent another dozen emails since she'd filed his other ones.

She sighed, shut down the notebook computer and put it on the floor beside the tub. Then she held her breath and slid beneath the warm water for a thorough soak.

21

The phone rang just after Annja had finished drying her hair and putting on makeup. Caller ID told her it was Doug Morrell. He'd called four times while she'd been in the bath. Knowing she couldn't really put the call off any longer, she answered.

"You're alive!" Doug sounded more irritated than relieved.

"I am." Annja checked her hair in the antique full-length mirror in one corner of the room. She was having a surprisingly good hair day in spite of everything she'd been through.

"The bit about you being alive? That was sarcasm."

"Noted."

"See, I knew you were alive."

"Why the sarcasm?"

"Because I've been calling for hours."

"I've been busy."

"Working on the Mr. Hyde story?"

"Not exactly."

Doug groaned. His chair springs squeaked and Annja pictured him leaning back in his chair in his stuffed office. He kept a lot of vampire paraphernalia there, including an old original Revell Dracula model kit Annja had found on eBay.

Annja sat on the bed and pulled her computer over to her. "How did you find out I was alive?"

"Legal contacted me. They told me you're going to be listed as an undesirable in London. If you are, we don't get the Mr. Hyde story."

"That may not be a story, anyway."

"Somebody's killing those women."

Annja scanned her notes on Anton Dutilleaux and focused on the material concerning his job in the financial sector while in Shanghai. "I think that whoever the actual murderer is will probably turn out to be a regular serial killer—and I'm using *regular* loosely—not some college student who's discovered Dr. Jekyll's secret formula."

"You *think* that. You don't know it. We want the truth for our show. Our viewers deserve to know what happened to Dr. Jekyll's freaky little formula."

"Doug, listen to me a minute."

He sighed noisily and as unpleasantly as he could.

"Dr. Jekyll wasn't real. Neither was Mr. Hyde. They are fictional creations Robert Louis Stevenson made up during a bout of fever and sickness." She'd already *had* this conversation.

"Were you there? Stevenson got his inspiration from somewhere."

"He had a fever. He was sick. Chronically."

"So that means he knew a lot of doctors. *Doctors.* He lived in a lot of places. See? I was listening."

He had been. Annja was shocked.

"Since he met *lots* of doctors, Stevenson also could very well have met one like Dr. Jekyll. One who invented a formula that changed people into monsters. That's all I'm saying. Our viewers don't need much. Just a nudge in the direction of conspiracy."

For a moment, Annja was taken aback. Then she remembered how stubborn Doug could be once he had an idea in his head. "Look, I'm working on something else."

"*Annnnnnnnjjjjjjaaaaa,* please. You're killing me here. I've been covering for you. Tell me we're close to the Mr. Hyde story."

"Not even."

She heard a thumping noise over the phone.

"Doug."

The thumping stopped. "What?"

"How do you expect me to tell you when the London Metro police are going to catch this guy?"

"They don't have to catch him. It's better if they don't. More mysterious. Continuing danger. That sort of thing. All I need is a story that hints that Mr. Hyde is still out there roaming around. An interview would be cool, too."

"More people will be killed."

"Then the police should stop him. And we need to be there when they do. Or at least to film them trying to catch Mr. Hyde."

Annja took a breath, then repeated, "I'm working on another thing."

Doug's response was immediate. "No."

"I was nearly killed today."

"I understand. You're not easy to work with."

Annja almost argued. She knew for certain she was a lot easier to work with than Kristie Chatham was. "And if I keep poking around in the Mr. Hyde investigation, Inspector Westcox is going to put me on a plane."

"I'll get the lawyer working to fight that."

"Getting back to the me nearly getting killed part."

"Does it have anything to do with Mr. Hyde?"

"No."

"Annnnnjjj—"

"It has to do with a magic lantern that's said to be haunted and can give its owner three wishes." It was all she had to work with.

Doug stopped moaning. A beat passed and she could almost hear him thinking. "Wait. Did you just say a *magic* lantern?"

"Yes."

"And three wishes?"

"Yes." He'd registered that but he'd glossed over the fact

that she'd nearly gotten killed. Annja marveled at Doug's attention span.

"Cool. Three wishes is awesome. I don't think we've done a three-wishes story in a couple years." Doug's connection became fuzzy for a moment, then she heard the rapid-fire tapping of his keyboard. "Nope. We haven't since that well in Italy that Kristie did the story on."

"The one that was supposed to have the mummy in it?"

"Yeah."

"There was no mummy in that well."

"No three wishes, either, but the viewers loved the episode…. Three wishes. I'm sure I can get marketing to give this a special look."

"And the lantern is said to have already caused several deaths." That was also true. Annja knew for certain that several men had died earlier.

"Sweet." Doug lowered his voice. "Look. Right now we've got a little fat in the schedule. We've got some time—maybe a few days—before we have to wrap the next episode. I can let you do this if you bring in the lantern story *and* the Mr. Hyde story."

Annja let out a calming breath. She didn't know if she'd have either story. "All right."

"Have you made a wish yet?"

"No. I don't have the lantern."

"Not feeling the love right now."

"But I know where the lantern is. I don't know where Mr. Hyde is."

Doug was silent for a moment. "Three wishes, you said?"

"Yes."

"If you get the lantern, if there are three wishes, you get one, I get one, then we flip for the third. Deal?"

A FEW MINUTES LATER AFTER hanging up on Doug, Annja discovered the large library where Fiona and Edmund sat at a table with a buffet spread out before them. They hadn't hesitated about digging in. Edmund's new suit fit him well and he looked refreshed except for the bruises and small bandages on his cheek and chin.

"Sorry." Annja took a seat across from Edmund. Fiona sat at the head. "Didn't realize I took so long."

"You didn't take long." Fiona placed ham and cheese and vegetables on a flatbread wrap. "Edmund and I just got here a few minutes ago ourselves."

Annja picked up a plate and selected sliced meat, cheese, vegetables and a boiled egg, with a selection of fresh berries and cut melon on the side.

She glanced at Edmund. "Did you know that Dutilleaux's lantern was on Hitler's list of arcane items?"

Edmund nodded. "I did."

"You didn't think that was significant?"

"I saw no reason to give that particular myth credence. There was nothing to support it. Unless you've discovered something I couldn't… Did you find something?"

"Nothing to substantiate it, no. But I did hear from researchers in the field about some of the lantern's myths."

"Did they mention the legend about how Dutilleaux was using the lantern to enter the spirit world and steal gold and gems to finance himself in the real world?"

"No." Annja dug into her meal, surprised at how hungry she was.

"You'll get to that one eventually. Laframboise seemed to be particularly enchanted with the idea of the lantern's mystical properties."

"I suppose." Annja bit into a boiled egg, chewed and swallowed. "Did you know that Dutilleaux worked for the Shanghai banking companies?"

Edmund frowned and winced almost immediately as the expression caused him obvious pain. The bruises on his face and mouth had started to show up a little more. Some of the swelling had gone down, though. "Yes."

"Dutilleaux was an aide to the French businessmen trading with China through Shanghai."

Fiona sipped her drink and set it aside. "I thought the First

Opium War and the Treaty of Nanking were what opened the port cities to outsider trading. That was well after Dutilleaux died in the catacombs in Paris."

Annja raised an eyebrow. "History buff?"

Fiona smiled and reached for a peach. "Traveling for years with Roux."

Annja wiped a crumb from the corner of her mouth with her napkin. "The Opium Wars gave the Chinese no choice about opening the ports. Once that happened, the British, French and Americans were there to stay. Those were the big three. From the information I received, Dutilleaux was a banker first for the French, then worked for the Chinese."

"Why is that important?" Edmund pushed his plate aside. "And who is Roux?"

She ignored his second question. "Why did he take employment? Or why did the Chinese offer it?"

"Either."

Fiona held up a forefinger. "The Chinese would have wanted an insider. Someone they could trust who could explain to them the Western mind-set." She took another bite out of her peach. "They would have sought out someone they believed they could control."

Annja nodded. "They made a mistake with Dutilleaux. He worked there for three years, then was discovered to be pilfering gold and gems from the bank where he worked. According to the papers I was sent, Dutilleaux got out of Shanghai just ahead of the Qianlong Emperor's royal executioners."

22

"Anton Dutilleaux was just a common thief?" Edmund looked shocked and dismayed, and Annja couldn't tell which feeling was stronger. "That can't be."

"I'd hardly call a man who could steal a small fortune from under a Chinese emperor's nose a *common* thief." Fiona shook her head. "A walking dead man, perhaps. But never common. He had to have been very skilled at what he was doing, with nerves of steel."

Annja silently agreed. She watched Edmund and felt sorry for him because he'd obviously built Dutilleaux up into so much more. During her early years working in archaeology, heroes and legends had sometimes fallen like wheat before a thresher.

"The missing money could explain why Dutilleaux's murderer was Asian." Annja maneuvered a chunk of honeydew melon into her mouth.

"No one ever proved the nationality of Dutilleaux's killer. That person was never caught. Dutilleaux had rivals as well as jealous husbands of his lovers." Edmund returned his attention to the buffet, but his heart wasn't in it and he merely picked at the food.

"No matter what the truth is, the cold, hard fact of the matter is that we may never know." As always, Fiona looked unflappable. "Sometimes the truth does hide in history." She paused for a moment. "Ollie was able to put together quite the package on the man who kidnapped Professor Beswick. If we choose to pursue the lantern, we're up against an accomplished foe."

The doors to the library opened and Ollie strode in. "Did I just hear my name mentioned?" He carried a small computer tablet tucked under one arm.

"I thought I was going to have to call for you."

"Never." Ollie flashed a winning smile. He paused near the table and tapped on the computer screen.

A wide-screen television monitor dropped from the ceiling to cover a section of the bookshelves. Almost immediately, the image of the man Annja had noticed with Edmund in the warehouse filled the screen.

"As you know, this is Jean-Baptiste Laframboise, not one of the biggest criminals in Paris, but certainly one of the most lethal," Ollie said in a calm, clear voice. "He's never risen to the top of anyone's list, but that's more by design than ability. Laframboise has deliberately stayed away from high-profile crimes that caught the national eye, much less international attention."

Annja worked to build another sandwich. "He's been taking small jobs?"

"On the contrary, he's taken very lucrative jobs. But he's been careful to pick very *quiet* ones, as well. Things that ran under the radar when you consider the varied nature of criminal enterprise. He's done quite well for himself." Ollie tapped the tablet again.

On the screen, pictures rotated quickly, showing a penthouse, a country home, a yacht and Laframboise in either a Jaguar or a Lotus. There were also several pictures of him at big social gatherings.

"He's become something of a gentleman crook." Ollie smiled. "He's even ingratiated himself with the Parisian government by undertaking to buy back some paintings taken from the Louvre a few years ago."

Fiona stared at the screen. "Did Laframboise steal the paintings first?"

"No, surprisingly."

"Then who selected him as the go-between?"

"The thieves."

"Interesting. That means the thieves knew Laframboise had a connection he could go to. Are we aware who that is?"

"I'm afraid not, Ms. Pioche. At least, not yet."

Edmund frowned. "Laframboise's contact within the Parisian government, especially an entity like the Louvre, could explain how he knows so much about Anton Dutilleaux."

Annja regarded him. "Laframboise doesn't exactly strike me as the scholarly type. Is there anything in his background to suggest interests like that?"

Ollie sniffed delicately. "The man never even finished a secondary education. By all accounts, though, he's a reasonably intelligent man. I did discover one oddity that might be interesting to you. It appears that Laframboise's mother was a fortune-teller."

"What kind of fortune-teller?" Fiona looked surprised.

"Cards, Ms. Pioche. Tarot, to be exact, though the reports I've obtained from police records indicate that she was taken into custody a number of times with a regular deck of cards."

"Which is nothing more than an abbreviated tarot deck."

"She claimed she was a Gypsy and possessed otherworldly skills."

"Why was she arrested?"

"The bunco squad pulled her in. She was convicted of numerous cons. She even served jail time. No more than a few months at a stretch."

"Where's the mother now?"

"Dead, I'm afraid. Nine years ago from cancer."

"Was Jean-Baptiste Laframboise ever indicted in his mother's crimes?"

"No, but by then he was well on his way down the criminal career path. Robbery. Burglary."

"He had no ties to the metaphysical?"

"None that I've found."

Fiona leaned back in her chair and folded her arms. "Laframboise didn't find Dutilleaux's lantern on his own. He wouldn't have had an interest in something like that."

Annja picked up on the other woman's line of thinking. "I think we're safe in assuming Puyi-Jin brought the lantern to Laframboise's attention."

Edmund nodded and his eyes looked distant. "That's what Laframboise said. That Puyi-Jin had told him about the lantern. Had, in fact, hired Laframboise to get the lantern from me."

"Maybe Laframboise picked up on the lantern because of the supernatural story connected to it."

Fiona nodded. "Laframboise would have had to have a personal reason for betraying an employer—especially a *dangerous* employer—if there wasn't an immediate payoff of some kind. And I think we're all in agreement that we don't see one. The lantern, unless it is worth more somehow than its presence would suggest, is worthless for the simple materials involved in its construction. There has to be something more."

Stunned, Edmund looked at both women. "Are you saying you believe there's something magical about that lantern?"

Fiona smiled. "Do you mean, do I believe in magic, Professor Beswick?"

Edmund looked uncomfortable as he nodded.

"Of course I believe in magic." Fiona glanced at Annja. "I've seen it."

Annja felt the sword blaze hot for just a moment.

"But why should we go to such extreme lengths to get this lantern back?" Edmund shook his head. "People have died in pursuit of this lantern. You've already—" He stopped himself short.

Fiona tapped her glass with an elegant forefinger. "I've already killed people. Is that what you were going to say?"

Edmund squirmed in embarrassment. "I had no right to say anything about that."

"There is a distinction in how Laframboise and his Chinese counterpart are going about their business," Fiona said, her voice cool and soft.

If Fiona hadn't liked Edmund, Annja was sure she wouldn't be controlling herself so well. Roux and Garin tended toward a more simplistic view of life, of predator and prey, of kill or be killed. Annja had seen a lot of that life herself, but she hadn't quite bought into it. Killing, though sometimes necessary, was still something to be avoided.

When possible.

"Those men are killing to obtain the lantern, and to obtain *you*. I killed to save you."

"I know. And I'm grateful. Truly I am." Edmund knotted a fist uncertainly. "But at this point, I'm safe. We could step away from this thing."

Annja felt a sick twist in her stomach that told her she wasn't ready to let go of the hunt.

Fiona smiled. "Hasn't all of this made you curious, Professor?" She held up her forefinger and thumb a fraction of an inch apart. "Just a little?"

Edmund hesitated, then nodded. "Of course. I don't believe any of the stories that I've heard circulating about that lantern—"

"But you know there must be something there. Otherwise, Laframboise and his ex-employer wouldn't be working so hard to get it."

"They could be wrong."

Fiona shrugged, then glanced at Annja. "Maybe they are. But I feel certain Annja will attempt to find the lantern. Or am I wrong?"

"No." Annja shook her head. "You're not wrong."

Fiona shifted her gaze back to Edmund. "Furthermore, even should you decide to stay out of this, there is every possibility Laframboise or someone else looking for the lantern will think you know more than you're telling."

Edmund paled a little, and Annja didn't blame him. She'd thought the very same thing, but she hadn't wanted to mention it. Of course, not mentioning it would have been irresponsible.

Fiona continued in a deadpan voice. "Personally, I believe it would be better if we had the matter settled. Wouldn't you agree?"

"There's no guarantee you'll do anything except get yourself killed. And Annja."

Fiona pursed her lips. "We're going, Professor. All I need to know is whether I should make reservations for you, as well."

Edmund vacillated for only a moment. Then he took a deep breath and nodded. "But I want to stop short of getting killed for my curiosity."

"We're going to work on that."

DESPITE THE SPACIOUS TRUNK of the limousine parked in front of Fiona's building, Annja kept her backpack with her. Ollie stood by with his computer tablet and chatted on his Bluetooth headset while overseeing the loading of Fiona's bags by the chauffeur. A bodyguard in a black suit and wraparound sunglasses stood watch nearby.

With her backpack slung over one shoulder, Annja joined Fiona. The woman looked elegant in casual wear and sunglasses.

"I suppose you noticed the car across the street?" Annja shifted the backpack to a more comfortable spot.

Fiona pulled on a leather glove. "I did indeed."

"Are they police?"

"Yes. Some of Inspector Westcox's men. Ollie has already verified their identities."

A small knot unraveled in Annja's stomach. She hadn't noticed the car until only a few moments ago.

Ollie smiled. "I was of a mind to have them move by filing a harassment action with our solicitors, but Ms. Pioche told me not to."

"There's no reason." Fiona tugged her second glove on. "We've already tweaked the inspector's nose enough. Besides, those men will only follow us as far as the airport. There's really not much for them to see."

That was true and Annja tried to take solace in it. Being followed made her feel vulnerable.

"Did you find out anything about the Chinese gang that's involved with the lantern?"

"You mean Puyi-Jin?" Ollie reached into his pocket and pulled out a small thumb drive. "You can review the files at your leisure."

Fiona took it from him. "Good work."

Ollie's ebullient nature gave way to worry for just a moment as he gazed at his employer. "The gang members we've identified have led us to one man—Puyi-Jin. This man, Ms. Pioche, is much worse than anything we've seen from Laframboise. He has a rather long reach. I'm surprised he needed Laframboise." Ollie grimaced and nodded at the thumb drive. "You might want to skip over some of the police files. They're in color and they're very gruesome. Puyi-Jin is *not* a nice man."

Fiona patted Ollie's cheek. "I am not a nice woman when properly motivated."

"I do know that, Ms. Pioche."

"Do we have someone in Paris who can outfit us?"

"Yes. Georges will meet you at the airport with a car. He promised me that you would have everything you needed."

"Thank you, Ollie."

"My pleasure, Ms. Pioche." Ollie grabbed the limousine door before the chauffeur could. "As always."

23

Even though Fiona had her own personal jet, there was still a fair amount of red tape to go through to get airborne. Despite that, less than an hour later, they were wheels up in the small Embraer Phenom 100 microjet.

Annja had never flown in a jet so small. The four main seats sat in two-by-two formation and faced one another. Toward the rear of the jet, there were two more seats and a small toilet.

After stowing her gear, Annja strapped herself in. Edmund sat across from her. He looked tired and rumpled. The bruises on his face were even darker. He kept fidgeting after he'd strapped himself in, unable to relax.

Fiona handed him a glass of soda water and a pill. "Take this. It's an analgesic. It should help with the pain."

Obediently, Edmund tossed the pill back and drained the glass.

Annja pulled her computer out, then attached it to the outlet in the wall. In addition to the power, the jet also maintained a satellite connection.

She checked the alt.history sites again, looking for updates. Not finding any, she moved on to emails. There were three invitations from universities to speak, galleys for two articles she'd written for magazines and queries from her editor concerning her latest book. Business as usual.

Beside her, Fiona spoke quickly on her cell. Judging from the snippets of conversation Annja was privy to, Fiona kept her hand in several investigations at one time. After a few moments, she finished the calls and tucked the phone back into her jacket pocket.

Annja glanced at her. "You stay busy."

"I try." Fiona was contemplative for a moment. "After the time I spent with Roux, a mundane existence seems impossible. I kept telling myself I'd probably slow down at some point."

"But you haven't?"

"No. Roux used to always say there would be time enough to rest when you were in the grave."

"This from a man who seems determined to avoid that particular destination." Annja glanced over at Edmund, but amazingly, the pill seemed to have knocked him out in record time.

Fiona laughed. "True." Her expression sobered. "Despite all his years, Roux is vulnerable. He can be killed."

A chill crept over Annja as she recalled how Roux had looked in the hospital bed in China.

"Yet even facing death, he can be fearless. Not truly heroic, though, because he faces death for his own reasons, not necessarily for the greater good."

"I've also seen him be cautious."

Fiona regarded her. "What kind of relationship do you have with Roux?"

Annja thought for a moment, then answered, "Complicated?"

"I can believe that." Fiona took a breath as the jet taxied down the runway.

She stared out the window, but Annja knew that the woman didn't see a thing. "For a few days I was afraid the mysterious Garin person had finally succeeded in killing him. I kept watch over the newspapers and news channels. There was nothing."

"Until he called about me."

Fiona looked back at Annja. "Yes." Tears brimmed in her

eyes, but she blinked them back. "Surely between us we can find another topic. After all, we're potentially flying into the jaws of death."

The jet had reached cruising altitude after a steep climb and settled into a level course. Edmund was snoring softly in his seat. She looked at Fiona. "That wasn't an analgesic, was it?"

Fiona settled back in her seat. "Tell me about that sword."

AN HOUR LATER, ANNJA STOOD in line waiting for the French customs agent to clear her through Orly Airport. Air traffic was lighter at Orly than Charles de Gaulle. But the customs agents were no less demanding. She'd been separated from the other two by a few people and the conversations going on around her were in a half-dozen languages. Behind her, two women with Texas accents were talking loudly.

Annja took out her cell and punched in Roux's number.

The phone rang three times and she was sure it was about to go to voice mail. She didn't know if she hoped it would or if she wanted Roux to pick up. She liked Fiona a lot and hearing what her sometime-mentor had done to the woman was exasperating. Roux's behavior wasn't without precedent, though. Annja knew that neither Roux nor Garin invested too heavily in the feelings of others. They put their own welfare first.

"Must you keep interrupting me? I was playing cards."

"If you were at the table right now, you wouldn't have answered." Roux cared about her, though, or he wouldn't have taken her call.

Roux harrumphed. "For all you know, I just threw in a winning hand to answer this infernal device."

"Did you?"

"No, but that could have happened. Don't tell me you called just to ask what I was doing."

"I called to tell you you were an asshat," she snapped.

Roux didn't reply right away. "I don't think I'm familiar with the term."

"It means you wear your ass for a hat."

Roux was silent for another moment. "I suppose that isn't a sartorial comment."

"No." Annja moved forward, now only a dozen people from the customs agent. "It means you have your head up your ass."

"Since we haven't been in contact for hours, I assume you're basing this conclusion on something other than what I might have done."

"Oh, I'm definitely basing this on something you've done."

"Did Fiona Pioche not work out? I must tell you, Annja, that would surprise me. She's quite capable. Of course, she is older now, no longer the young woman I knew."

Okay, that ageist comment brought the anger back full force. "No, Fiona is great. Terrific, perhaps. She's tougher than any of the nuns that raised me in the orphanage, and she's entertaining and witty. Not only that, she helped me rescue Edmund."

"That's the professor you'd lost."

"Not exactly mine to lose, and I wasn't responsible for him when he went missing."

"But Fiona helped you get him back nonetheless."

"Yes."

"Then you should be happy."

"Why did you leave Fiona?"

The silence over the phone stretched out.

"Roux."

No response.

"Roux?" For a moment Annja thought he'd hung up on her.

"That is not a topic open for discussion."

"Why?" Annja shifted the phone to her other hand as the line moved forward.

"Quite frankly because it's no business of yours."

"It's Fiona's business."

"Then she should ask."

Annja took a breath. "She's not going to ask."

"Good."

"She's not going to ask because you hurt her."

"That was…regrettable."

"*Regrettable? Regrettable* is when you send a birthday card and it doesn't get there on time. *Regrettable* is when you burn the eggs for breakfast and you don't have any more. Leaving a woman without a word is more than *regrettable*. It's cowardly and selfish."

The phone clicked in Annja's ear. She stared at it. Roux had hung up on her. She couldn't believe it. Then again, she couldn't believe she'd had that conversation with him in the first place. She didn't like people prying into her business, either.

"He hung up on you, didn't he?" The Texan woman behind Annja spoke up. She patted Annja on the shoulder. "I could have told you he was going to. Men don't like confrontation. They know when they've been bad, and they don't like anybody rubbing their noses in it."

Annja put the phone away. She didn't really know what else she could say to Roux. Worse, she knew it wasn't her place to say anything.

"A pretty little thing like you?" The woman continued patting Annja. "Why, you don't have anything to worry about. If I was you, I'd move right on to the next one."

"Thanks." Annja gave the woman a smile and hoped the line would move faster.

"Men, most men, anyway, are just dogs, honey. Just *dogs*." The woman's companion nodded sagely. "They don't know the first thing about love. And you can't teach them no matter how hard you try. Why, let me tell you what happened to my friend Ethyl here."

Annja hoped the line moved a *lot* faster.

"Ms. PIOCHE!" A SMALL dapper man in a maroon sweater and khaki pants stood waving near the doorway leading out to the pickup area. He looked like a grandfather picking up a favorite grandchild.

"Georges!" Fiona changed directions and cut through the crowd to reach him.

Annja tried to keep up, but it was difficult. The crowd was thick and relentless, and she found herself momentarily carried along in its tide. Before she could turn back, a young Asian woman stepped in beside her. In the next instant, Annja felt the prick of a very sharp blade pressed into her side.

The Asian woman was in her thirties, compact, five and a half feet tall. She gripped Annja's arm above the elbow. A martial-arts hold.

"Remain calm, Ms. Creed," the other woman said in flawless English. "Do that and you will live."

Annja breathed in and out, thinking fast. There was no room to work in the crowd, and nowhere to run if things got out of hand. She kept walking forward, with the woman's hand on her arm, going with the flow of traffic.

"Are you with Puyi-Jin?" Annja glanced back at Fiona, who was looking at her in concern.

"Do not talk. Walk where I take you."

"Annja." Edmund was beside Fiona, staring at Annja in confusion. "Annja?"

Reluctantly, without a choice, Annja walked out through the door. As soon as she stepped outside the air-conditioned building, the foul odor of car exhaust and diesel smoke hit her, burning her nasal passages and tightening her lungs. Brakes squealed and horns honked as taxis jockeyed for position at the curb. Voices in a dozen different languages surrounded them. Twilight was already falling and the lights around the airfield shone brightly.

The woman redirected Annja to a black luxury sedan to her left. A uniformed airport worker stood engaged in a heated debate with the driver.

"Get this vehicle out of here, sir. I will not tell you again. You cannot pick up private travelers in this lane. You must go out and around." The airport worker glanced up and saw the woman approaching with Annja in tow. "Do you know this man?"

The woman answered without breaking stride. "I do."

"He can't park here. It's against the rules."

"I will explain that to him."

The airport worker shook his head wearily and held up his walkie-talkie. "You're lucky I haven't called a tow truck."

"Thank you." The woman guided Annja to the vehicle's rear door and opened it. "Get in."

Annja hesitated, but the woman pressed the keen blade into her side. Without a word, she climbed in, then she shot across the seat and tried to open the other door.

The handle lifted, but the lock remained engaged.

Wheeling around in the seat, Annja looked back as the woman closed the other door. Then Annja noticed the thick security acrylic that separated her from the front seat. She tried the release on the other door.

The woman smiled at her from the other side of the window. Then she opened the front passenger door. Moving easily, the woman took her seat as the driver pulled out into traffic amid screaming horns and a torrent of offensive language.

24

The driver maneuvered smoothly out of the airport. From her other visits to the city, Annja knew they were traveling the A6. The Autoroute de Soleil—the Sun's Motorway—was a nod to King Louis XIV, the Sun King. She'd never known if the highway's name was actually derived from an old trade route from Paris to the south of France and the French Riviera or if someone had just given the thoroughfare that as an honor.

Evidently their destination was Paris because the driver turned north.

Neither the woman nor the driver paid particular attention to Annja. They kept their eyes on the slowly darkening highway. The woman spoke on the phone, but the acrylic partition was soundproofed, as well.

Annja took her sat-phone from her backpack, powered it on and went to her contact list. She glanced at the names only for a moment, then decided to call the Parisian police. They would be able to track her GPS signal.

She opened up the maps app and waited to enter *Paris Police,* knowing it would give her the phone number. Instead, the phone remained blank. A quick glance at the bars showed that she was receiving no signal. Something inside the car was preventing the sat-link.

Frustrated and a little panicked, Annja returned the phone to her backpack, then leaned back in the seat so that her feet shoved forward. Thrusting violently, she lay on her back and drove her feet into the acrylic partition. The *thud* of impact echoed in the spacious backseat.

In the front seat, the driver glanced at the rearview mirror and the woman turned around to gaze into the backseat. Annja rammed her boots against the acrylic again.

The woman flicked a switch on a panel on the back of the front seat. Her voice came over a concealed speaker. "Stop that."

"Come back here and make me." Annja drove her feet against the acrylic panel again. Truthfully, she didn't feel the barrier giving way or loosening. It felt like she might as well have been trying to kick a hole through a steel plate.

Temporarily abandoning her efforts against the partition, Annja swung around and set herself to drive a boot against the passenger's-side window. Bailing out of a car doing sixty or seventy miles an hour wasn't something she wanted to do, but she had to have options. If the glass would break, the car eventually had to slow or stop. She'd seize whatever opportunity came along then.

But hammering the side window didn't help much, either. The acrylic there bore up just as well.

"You can't escape." The woman's voice was devoid of emotion.

Annja ignored her and turned her attention to the rear windshield. A quick examination assured her that it, too, was thick acrylic. Then she eyed the seat, wondering if there was a release that would let her into the trunk space.

A moment later, she gave up looking for it. She reached for the sword and it was there in her hand. Thankfully there was enough room for it to materialize in the back of the car.

On the other side of the glass, the woman's eyes grew huge. She spoke hurriedly to the driver, who glanced over his shoulder.

Annja drove the sword through the backseat cushions easily. Many cars now had safety releases in the trunk to keep people from getting locked up there. Of course, she'd again be forced to wait for the car to slow or stop before continuing her escape.

Fabric and stuffing came away in pieces as she bared the seat's steel frame. Disappointingly, the framework was too tight to allow her into the trunk. She released the sword and it vanished.

In the darkness filling the back of the car, Annja couldn't see clearly but she thought she'd revealed a thin backing that sealed the backseat off from the trunk. When she pushed against it, the backing moved easily. The steel supports across the backseat prevented her from crawling through. She seized one of them in both hands, set herself, one foot against the back of the seat, and pulled.

Nothing moved.

She tried again to no avail.

Just as she was thinking she might be better served using the sword as leverage against the support, Annja spotted a large gray sedan racing along on the highway shoulder. Her Asian captor and the driver hadn't noticed the vehicle rapidly gaining on them because their attention was on Annja.

In just a few seconds, the gray sedan pulled onto the highway and cut off a car trailing the vehicle that held Annja. At the same time, two other vehicles converged on the trailing vehicle. Windows rolled down on both those cars and muzzle flashes punctured the gathering darkness.

Wary of ricochets, Annja ducked down. The back window went untested, though. The driver hit the accelerator and the big car shot forward, only to slow again a moment later as traffic continued to block its progress.

Traffic quickly backed off. Drivers recognized gunfire and wanted no part of the battle. Cars, buses and shuttles gave ground to the large sedan holding Annja captive and the other cars in pursuit.

A large muzzle poked through one of the large gray sedan's windows and belched fire a moment later. In that instant, the wheel and axle assembly sheared away from the pursuit vehicle on the left and caused the car to swerve hard to the right.

The gray sedan met the other vehicle in full side-to-side contact. The smaller car, already out of control, rebounded from the larger vehicle and shot into the median. A deep scar snaked behind the car as it left the highway. Upon reaching the uneven ground, the vehicle flipped and rolled till it came to a rest on its side. The flaming wheel well blazed in the night.

In the front seat of her captors' car, the Asian woman pounded the dashboard and spoke frantically. Annja still couldn't hear her. In fact, she just realized she wasn't able to hear any of the gunfire or collisions. The soundproofing was excellent.

A moment later, the muzzle of the rocket launcher—and Annja knew that was what the weapon had to be—shoved through a window on the opposite side of the gray sedan. The smaller car tried to accelerate and get around in front of it.

The brake lights of the gray sedan gleamed red as the wily driver slowed to let the other car pass. As soon as it did, Fiona Pioche inched out the passenger window just enough to take aim with her rocket launcher.

Despite her trust in the woman, Annja sank down just a little in case the rocket missed its intended target or skated off a curved surface. The missile sped true, though, and caught the back of the second pursuit vehicle. Instantly, the car's rear section shredded and flames wreathed it. Lifted by the concussion, the car went airborne and spun in a hundred-and-eighty-degree turn that left it facing the oncoming sedan.

The gray sedan's driver accelerated and pulled hard to the right, going wide of the stricken car as it crashed down on the highway. Debris scattered across the pavement, but the traffic had already pulled to a stop several yards back. All of the drivers had recognized that they were in danger.

In the passenger seat, the Asian woman rolled down the

window and shoved her arm through. A large-capacity pistol in her hand jumped and spat bullets. Annja couldn't tell if her captor was missing her intended target or if the gray sedan was armored. The sedan had a lot more power than the car Annja was in. The driver closed the intervening distance quickly, then switched lanes and came up on the driver's side.

Frustrated and probably out of ammunition, the Asian woman dropped back into the seat and pulled her safety belt back in place. Concern tightened her features as she watched the gray sedan pull up alongside their vehicle. She yelled at the driver, who yelled back at her.

Swerving, the driver pulled the car into the sedan, but the other vehicle was larger and heavier, and all he managed to do was confirm his opponent's prowess. His own car shuddered and swerved, barely remaining under control.

Through the window, Annja stared at Fiona Pioche. The woman's hair blew back from her face and her black-lensed sunglasses looked implacable and unyielding. She no longer held the rocket launcher, which Annja was happy to see, but had pistols in both fists. Looking at her, Annja couldn't help but think how well Fiona must have fit with Roux.

At her age now, Fiona would fit even better with Roux. And that made Annja wonder even more why Roux had left her.

The dapper Georges, Annja could see, was piloting the gray sedan. He dropped back a couple feet, then pulled hard on the wheel. Guessing what was coming, Annja grabbed the nearest safety harness and held tight.

The sedan's front bumper slammed into the car's rear hard enough to break the traction the rear wheels had on the pavement. Hammered by the heavier vehicle, the car drifted sideways. The driver tried to recover control, but before he had the chance, Georges swerved and hit the car again.

This time the car tore completely free of the highway and went into a drift. The sedan muscled forward and hit the skidding car broadside this time, driving it in front of it. In the backseat, Annja bounced and ricocheted as the car left the highway and went onto the shoulder.

Dirt and grass flew in a maelstrom around the car as it went off-road. Something under the vehicle, a tire or a strut or the frame, buckled and dug into the ground. Caught for just a moment, the car almost stopped, then it was struck again. Driven forward once more, the car slid sideways, then went up on one side and rolled over onto its side, then onto its top and over onto the other side.

Annja bounced around the car's interior. The floorboard and the roof weren't covered in anything soft. The impacts hurt, but she kept her head and focused on escape.

The car warped as it rolled. The back passenger's-side door warped out of its frame. Standing on the left door, Annja reached up and shoved on the right one. For a moment, the door held, refusing to budge, then it gave way with a loud screech. She reached back and caught the straps of her backpack.

Movement on the other side of the acrylic partition, which was no longer in its housing and now had gaps around it, caught Annja's attention just as she shoved the broken door open farther. The Asian woman was struggling to shove her pistol into position to fire. The driver was immobile behind the steering wheel, held there by the deployed air bag.

Grabbing the sides of the door frame, Annja heaved herself up and out as the Asian woman started firing. Bullets bounced off the glass and the seat's reinforced undercarriage. Off balance and desperate, Annja threw herself from the car in an inelegant sprawl. She tried to hit the ground prepared to run, but the soft earth gave way beneath her boots and she went down to one knee.

The driver's-side door opened and the Asian woman popped up with her pistol in her fist.

Knowing she wouldn't be able to run without being gunned down, Annja released her hold on the backpack, took a step toward the car, another step on the driveshaft to propel herself upward again and launched a flying snap-kick. Her foot caught the woman in the face and knocked her backward. The pistol fell from her hands and tumbled to the ground. Unconscious, the woman dropped back inside the car.

Annja landed on her feet, listed badly to one side and quickly righted herself. She sprinted for her backpack, then raced up the small incline toward the highway.

The sedan had stopped on the shoulder. The cars Fiona had taken out were a football field away, and the traffic ahead of the accident had mostly kept going. Only a few drivers had pulled over to see if they could help or to gawk. Motorists on the opposite side of the highway were all gawking.

Fiona, Georges and Edmund stood outside the sedan. Evidently they'd been about to come to Annja's rescue.

Edmund looked enormously relieved. "You're alive."

"Of course she's alive." Fiona calmly lowered her pistols and smiled at Annja. "She's made of stern stuff."

Georges sighed theatrically. "Maybe you could give a smidgen of credit to my driving, eh? I am very good at what I do, Ms. Pioche."

"Yes, you are, dear man." Fiona looked down the highway.

In the distance, three men raced toward them and flashes lit up their hands. A moment later dirt clods lifted from the nearby ground and sparks leaped from the sedan's top. They heard the harsh pistol cracks shortly after.

"Maybe you could postpone the mutual admiration fest till after we've made our escape." Edmund held the rear door open for Annja.

Annja slid inside, quickly followed by Edmund, who slammed the door shut. Part of the backseat lay forward, revealing the armament hidden there.

Fiona passed the rocket launcher back to Edmund. "Be a dear and put that away. I don't think we'll be needing it any further."

Gingerly, Edmund took the weapon and shoved it into the recess.

More bullets thudded against the back of the sedan, but they didn't penetrate. Edmund ducked at the sounds, though. He glanced at Annja. "I know the glass is bulletproof, but I can't help it."

"It's not something you get used to easily." Annja had taken cover, as well.

"I have no wish to ever get used to it."

Georges pulled the sedan back onto the highway and roared into the night that now shrouded Paris.

25

Forty minutes later, Georges pulled to a stop in front of a small electronics store on rue Marx Dormoy in the 18th arrondissement in Paris just down from a streetlamp. The neighborhood was also known as Montmartre and was equally famous and infamous in history.

Georges parked the car and opened the door. "Come, come. We must step lively now."

Fiona got out at once and stood on the sidewalk, her sunglasses pushed up onto her head. She watched the lighted street as a parade of vehicles flowed through.

A lanky African-American youth in a soccer shirt and maroon hoodie stepped out of the shadows. "Georges."

Georges's face lit with a smile. "Ah, Hasan, it is good to see you. You are on time tonight."

"I try, *mon ami*." The young man spoke in a lilting accent that Annja placed as West African.

"It is good." Georges tossed the car keys into the air.

Hasan caught the keys with a quick flicker of movement and never broke stride as he walked toward the car. "What do you wish done with the vehicle?"

"Take it to Gardiah."

"And what should I tell him?" Hasan opened the sedan's door and glanced at the scars left by the bullets. He got in.

"That it needs a new face and a new name, okay?"

"Okay."

"There are things in the back I will need. You know the address?"

"I do. I will have them there in a few hours. When I am certain I am not followed." Hasan glanced over his shoulder and pulled out into traffic.

Georges turned to Fiona. "The car has to disappear as we do, true?"

"Of course."

"As you have heard, your things will arrive shortly. If not, I will replace them."

"You are as capable as ever, my friend."

Georges waved down a cab. "I have suitable quarters for you a short distance away. Hasan will meet us there with your things. Taking a few cabs along the way will ensure we are hard to follow."

The cab pulled to the curb and Georges opened the back door for Fiona.

FOUR CAB RIDES LATER, ALL of them sandwiched between walks of a few blocks—and sometimes split up into two groups of two and a mix of one and three to keep the numbers off in case the police were looking for four—they arrived at the studio apartments Georges had leased for their stay. Although they'd taken different cabs, none of them within sight of the other, they'd remained within the 18th arrondissement.

"The apartment will not be up to hotel standards, I'm afraid." The lower floor housed a shoe repair shop and a dress shop. Both businesses were currently closed and had steel curtains pulled down over the doors and windows.

"I'm more interested in privacy than in the accommodations." Fiona studied the street.

Edmund walked beside Annja. The air was cool enough that she felt a chill. Traffic noises and shouts of passersby and residents rang around them. Neon lights shone dimly from a bar on the corner and a small Chinese restaurant across the street. American rock and roll competed with Japanese pop and some Delta blues. Paris had always been an eclectic city. That was one of the things Annja loved about it.

The neighborhood was one of the rougher districts in the city. The street was paved, not cobbled, and some of the surrounding buildings had been made over, but everything remained old. It wasn't too hard for Annja to close her eyes and imagine the city as it had been two hundred years ago.

The 18th arrondissement had been the eye of the storm of political unrest in the city since the mid-1800s. The Paris Commune, with its focus on the rising power of the working class, had taken root here.

Edmund matched his steps with Annja's. "You've been to Paris before?"

"A few times." Annja had found the sword not far from where they now were, and she'd bearded Roux in his home outside Paris. Since then she'd visited Roux here on a few occasions, and come on her own, as well.

"Then you know this isn't a very good neighborhood."

"I think we'll be safe enough with Georges."

A frown knitted Edmund's brows.

Crime had favored the 18th arrondissement since the influx of workers had settled here to work at the coal mines and the factories that sprang up with the Industrial Revolution.

"What I'm trying to say," Edmund continued, "is that Laframboise may have spies everywhere, and he most assuredly has them in this place."

"We knew we were taking a chance in coming to Paris." Annja glanced at the traffic but saw no one giving them any special attention. "Fiona trusts Georges, and he risked his life to get me back. I think we're in good hands."

Edmund nodded but he wasn't happy.

THE APARTMENT DIDN'T HAVE much in the way of flash, but it held all the creature comforts they would need. Like a proud real estate agent, Georges conducted a brief tour of the rented rooms.

The apartment had two small bedrooms and a common bath, but Georges assured Edmund that the couch pulled out into a comfortable bed. There was also cable television and internet. A sprig of flowers sat on the dining table just off the small kitchen.

"Are you hungry?" Georges stood beside a pantry and waved, like a game show host presenting a prize. When he opened the door, shelves laden with canned and boxed items stood in neat rows. "The refrigerator is well stocked, also. Meat. Fresh vegetables. And there is a Russian bakery only two blocks away that makes wonderful breads." He closed the pantry door. "It will suffice, yes?"

Fiona crossed to Georges and kissed him on the cheek. "This is perfectly lovely. More than I had expected."

"Good, good." Georges rubbed his hands together. "But we should see to your armory needs."

"Please."

On the way out of the kitchen, Annja picked up a green apple from the fruit bowl on the counter. As she followed she bit into the apple, relishing the tart, sweet taste. Edmund still didn't look happy.

Georges apologized as he led the way to the back bedroom. "If this had been one of the usual safe houses I've used, I would have had a much better hiding place for these things. And more built-in security measures."

Fiona nodded in understanding. "But if this had been one of your usual haunts, someone might know about it and might take an interest in what we're doing here. I'd rather we remain off-grid as much as possible."

Concern filled Georges's face as he came to a stop at the back wall. "Laframboise is a most dangerous man, Fiona." He drew the heavy drapes over the room's only window, plunging the room into near-darkness till he turned on a bedside lamp.

"So I've heard. But you know yourself that I'm lethal when prompted to be."

"And then there is this Asian contingent that tried to kidnap

Miss Creed." Georges tapped his chin with his forefinger. "I suppose you know who they are?"

"I believe they were with Puyi-Jin, a Chinese—" She stopped when she saw Georges wince. "Have you heard of him?"

"Have you had dealings with Puyi-Jin before?"

"No. He's new to me."

"A very bad man. Is his interest in Miss Creed separate from your business with Laframboise?"

"They're tied together."

"Either one of those men would be daunting by himself, yes?"

Fiona smiled. "It is our good fortune, though, that Laframboise was working for Puyi-Jin and betrayed him."

Immediately, Georges brightened. "Ah, then we can use this to our advantage."

"I was hoping so."

"You've always been such a fascinating woman, Ms. Pioche." Georges turned toward the wall and took a small knife from his pocket. "I'm afraid getting to your armory won't be quick if you should need it in a hurry." The blade glinted as he pried molding from the corner of the wall, then from a decorative beam three feet away. "This wall adjoins the apartment in the next room, but the occupants living there have no idea what this space conceals."

When Georges finished removing the molding, he inserted the knife behind the wallboard and quickly pried the section out of place. He set the piece of wall aside and the lamplight played over the lubricated sheen of the weapons hanging on the wall. A dozen handguns and an equal number of assault rifles and shotguns hung from pegs. Boxes of ammunition sat neatly organized at the bottom of the space.

"The ammunition is color-coded for the weapons." Georges pointed to the small colored dots on the boxes and the matching colored stripes on the butts of the handguns and rifles and shotguns. "For speed."

"Wonderful." Fiona took out a pair of thin gloves, then selected a pistol and cut-down belt holster. She loaded the weapon's magazine and slammed it home. Methodically, she worked the action, stripped a bullet into the receiver, then popped the magazine and replaced the bullet. Satisfied, she tucked the weapon and holster at the small of her back.

Fiona looked back at Annja and Edmund. "Would you care to make a selection?"

Edmund shook his head. "No. I don't know the first thing about pistols."

"Well, we'll have to attend to that, won't we, Professor. And for you, Annja?" Fiona held out another pair of gloves. "Mustn't leave any prints, so don't touch the weapons without gloves on. Unless the situation calls for it."

Knowing Fiona wouldn't be satisfied until she picked something, Annja pulled on the gloves, then stepped forward and surveyed the pistols. After a moment, she found one she easily recognized. She plucked the Baby Desert Eagle 9 mm from the wall, then took time to load the weapon. Unlike Fiona, she didn't put a round under the hammer. She chose another of the cut-down belt holsters.

"Anything else?"

"No, thanks. I'm good." Annja stepped back.

Fiona chose a chopped semiautomatic shotgun with a shoulder sling. Meticulously, she loaded the shotgun, worked the slide and fed a last shell into it. Then she slid the weapon under the bed.

"I'll be taking this room, if that's all right."

Annja nodded.

Smiling, Georges clapped his hands. "Then, perhaps, we could return to the kitchen. I've laid in an excellent selection of wines, if I must say so myself. And I can show you the information I have on Laframboise."

HEAD SWIMMING A LITTLE FROM the wine, Annja settled into bed. Georges had departed, slightly tipsy but as professional as ever, in the company of Hasan and a couple other young men who looked capable of violence. Fiona had retired to her room, and Edmund was curled up asleep on the couch. His body wasn't used to being pushed so hard for so long.

Aches and pains plagued Annja, too, most of them from the car wreck, but she knew from past experience that she'd probably feel just fine in the morning. Since she'd found the sword, her recuperative powers had surpassed Olympic standards.

Hasan had brought them their luggage a couple hours after their arrival, and had stayed around for the wine. He had been watchful and intelligent, and Annja had recognized almost immediately that he was a street kid who paid attention. She had known kids like that while she'd been at the orphanage in New Orleans. Hasan, no matter where he was—West Africa or Paris—was a survivor.

So was she.

Dressed in gym shorts and a Yankees jersey, Annja opened up her computer and dug into the alt.history sites, hoping for more information. Several of the entries were just basic information on the magic lanterns, a few focused on different illusionists scattered across two hundred years of legerdemain, and there was even a flame war regarding Criss Angel's ability to do real magic.

Ni hao, Lantern Girl,

Don't mind the two rockheads arguing above. Apparently they didn't see Criss Angel's interview with Larry King when he said he didn't believe in magic. *Sigh*

Anyway, I was writing because the lantern you've got in this picture looks a lot like one I heard about while visiting one of my friends in Shanghai. Their family has some kind of legend about that lantern, about how they were disgraced by an ancestor or something. You know how big that is in Asian culture.

I'm adding a picture of the lantern my friend's grandmother told me about. The pic is in black and white and it's not very clear, but maybe this helps?

New Shanghai Girl

A surge of excitement stirred Annja as she clicked on the attachment. The photograph was large and it took a while to download, but when it had, the image was big enough to blow up and examine.

At first blush, the lantern resembled the one Edmund had bought. Then again, all lanterns looked a lot alike.

What most interested Annja was the two men in the photograph. Neither of them was Anton Dutilleaux, but they stood in front of a small building that had signs in the windows advertising banking in English, French and Chinese.

Her excitement grew.

26

"You think this is where Anton Dutilleaux worked?" Edmund looked doubtful.

Sitting at the dining room table the next morning, Annja stared at her computer studying the old Chinese picture. She spooned up another bite of key lime pie yogurt, not the most breakfasty yogurt ever made, but she liked it. "I don't know."

"Doesn't really look like a bank, does it?"

"Banks didn't always look like banks back then. China was expanding, growing rapidly. It took time for construction to catch up." Fiona poured milk over her cereal. She was already dressed for the day in pants and a loose pullover to cover her pistol. A thick folder sat at her elbow. "You have to remember, Professor, Shanghai was a budding community back then. Trade was opening up along the Yangtze River. The customs office was moved to Shanghai from Songjiang in the 1730s."

"Seventeen thirty-two." Annja's response was immediate and she didn't know she'd said anything until the others stopped to look at her. "Sorry. I suppose saying the 1730s was close enough."

Fiona smiled. "You must worry Roux to death with everything you know. He remembers events and people, but he's not one to keep dates in mind."

"I didn't exactly know the date until I refreshed what I knew last night." Annja said that, but she'd also been blessed with a near-photographic memory.

Annja glanced at the lower right side of her computer screen. It was 8:13 a.m., a lot earlier than she'd expected to get up, and much earlier than she suspected Jean-Baptiste Laframboise would be up. Still, it was better to get a lead on her quarry.

Edmund leaned back in his chair and sighed. "I truly don't know how your head can hold all that information without exploding."

She glanced at him. "Name the Romantic poets."

"William Blake, Lord Byron, William Wordsworth, Samuel Coleridge, Percy B. Shelley, John Keats, Matthew Arnold and John Clare."

"And why were they called Romantic poets?"

"Because their work contrasted sharply with previous literary styles, philosophy, the church and the problems and promise of industrialization." Edmund shook his head. "I get your point. I know the facts of my field as well as you know yours—history."

Annja swallowed another spoonful of yogurt. "But my field—history—touches your field—literature. The same period we're talking about? The one with these Romantic poets? That took place at the same time Shanghai was becoming a major trade franchise in China. Lord Byron died in the 1820s in the Greek War of Independence, didn't he?"

Edmund frowned. "He did. From illness. In 1824 at the age of thirty-six while preparing to battle with the Greeks against the Turks." He paused. "You know, I hadn't before thought of the relationship that period in Europe had with China."

Fiona stirred her cereal and spooned up a bite. "Yet Europe and the United States were bent on invading China through Shanghai at the same time to open up the opium trade, which they primarily owned and operated down in India."

Annja set the empty yogurt container aside and picked up a piece of toast. "Enough of the history lesson. Where are we going to find Laframboise?"

Fiona poured a cup of strong tea from the carafe on the table, then stirred in milk. "What do we know about him?"

"That he's a violent killer." Unconsciously, Edmund touched his bruised face.

Fiona waved that away. "He made a momentous decision to betray a very dangerous enemy. He's also come into possession of an artifact that might possess magical properties. We know from his upbringing, from his mother's interest in the arcane, that Laframboise is a man given to a belief in the supernatural. His world has been turned upside down. So where would he go?"

Annja glanced at the thick folder at Fiona's elbow. Georges had provided the information last night, and all of it concerned Laframboise and Puyi-Jin. She had a digital copy of the same information on her computer hard drive. Fiona liked hard copy. Last night she had spread it out around her and looked at photographs and documents. Judging from her responses and observations about the materials, Fiona was a much better hunter of men than Annja was. She was a remarkable woman.

"Getting out at all will be dangerous for him." Edmund steepled his forefingers under his chin. "He knows Puyi-Jin is looking for him. The attack on Annja last evening would have told him that. The story was all over the news last night and this morning." He nodded at the television against one of the living room walls.

Annja had picked the story up on her computer in her room last night. So far, the Parisian police and the Département de la Sûreté, the equivalent of the FBI, known locally as the Sûreté, hadn't identified Annja.

They had identified the Asians involved in the kidnapping attempt. They were all known Puyi-Jin gangsters. No one had a clue why the attack had taken place.

They had been lucky the story was so vague.

Fiona nodded. "The danger is something Laframboise will accept, though. That's the price he pays for doing business. What is the least known thing he's got on his hands at the moment?"

Annja understood where Fiona was headed now. "The lantern."

"Yes. Now that he has his hands on it, he'll want to know more about it. Where will he go?"

"A museum." Edmund sounded certain of himself. "Like me, he'll want to verify the authenticity of the lantern."

"I mean no disrespect, Professor, but Laframboise would take the lantern to a museum or auction house only if he were interested in the financial value of the piece. He's not interested in that, is he?"

"No."

Annja tapped at her computer and called up the file on Laframboise. She found what she was looking for quickly. "He's going to be more interested in the mystical aspects of the lantern."

Fiona set her teacup on the saucer on the table. "And where is he going to go to find out about that?"

"Georges has listed three fortune-tellers here in Paris that Laframboise sees on a regular basis."

"None of them will be able to satisfy Laframboise, because whatever knowledge they have is going to be incomplete at best."

Edmund tapped his fingers on the table nervously. "We have no way of knowing which one he'll see."

"On the contrary, I think he's going to see them all. He has no choice."

"Then we stake out these three people?"

"Georges has already put eyes on them. I asked him to do that last night."

Annja was impressed.

"So we're going to try to intercept Laframboise when he goes to see these people?" Edmund didn't sound happy.

"No. If we try to engage Laframboise in the streets, he'll be riding in an armored car. We won't be able to get at him." Fiona rummaged through the file and pulled out an eight-by-ten of a luxury car, which she spun into the center of the table. "This is his vehicle. Top of the line and very well equipped."

Annja glanced at the photograph. "Laframboise could always just have the fortune-tellers come to him."

"One of them does on a regular basis." Fiona drew out another photograph, this one of a young man with intelligent eyes and thin lips. "He'll have to go to the other two." She laid their photographs out, as well.

The first was a stylishly dressed young African woman. The second was an older Asian woman whose face was gnarled in wrinkles and flecked with age spots. Her hazel eyes glittered in an otherworldly way.

"The first is Magdelaine de Brosses, a popular Parisian psychic." Fiona touched the photograph. "She has a network set up. Phone lines and websites. She has a local television show and does private consulting in her office."

Fiona laid another photograph on top of de Brosses's. A tall building in downtown Paris.

"That building has considerable security and manpower." Fiona tapped the photograph of the old woman. "This is Bui Thi Trinh."

"Vietnamese?" Annja studied the picture.

"Yes."

Edmund leaned in. "I wasn't aware that the Vietnamese went much in for fortune-telling."

"Belief in the supernatural is cultural." Annja buttered a piece of toast. "Every primitive people developed some sense of the supernatural to explain things. You're thinking of the Vietnamese as they are now and were back in the twentieth century. Influenced by communism and torn apart by one outside nation after another. Back in the feudal era, the Vietnamese people believed in *thầy phù thủy.* Sorcerers or witch-men. They set up small temples all over the country. They also believed in *âm binh,* ghost warriors that could cure disease or insanity, or cast love spells."

"Interesting." Edmund leaned back. "Where does this woman operate?"

"In her flat," Fiona replied. "It's also interesting to note that this woman was one of those who taught Laframboise's mother fortune-telling."

Annja nodded. "So Laframboise's link to this one isn't just professional."

Fiona shook her head.

Edmund frowned. "Don't tell me we're going to go after this old woman?"

"No. She lives in a building that could be hard to control, hard to get into and out of." Fiona put Bui Thi Trinh's picture back into the folder. "We're going after the lantern when Laframboise goes to see Magdelaine de Brosses."

"I thought you said she worked out of a heavily secured office building."

"She does." Fiona smiled. "It'll make it *more* interesting, won't it?"

27

Annja sat at a small table in an internet café across from the building where Magdelaine de Brosses regularly delivered the future for her clientele. Jean-Baptiste Laframboise arrived a few minutes before noon. That saved Annja the hassle of finding a new observation post. She'd been rotating locations with Fiona, cycling through the internet café across the street, a bistro a half block down the street and a tourist shop in the bottom floor of the building.

Across the street, Laframboise got out of his car while one of his bodyguards held the door. The man looked good, sleek and rested, and that made Annja even more annoyed with him. Despite the solid hours of sleep she'd gotten the previous night, she still felt ragged and off.

Edmund Beswick's continued involvement plagued her. The literature professor was probably safer with them than he was in London on his own, but she was too aware that he was on the firing line with them when things went wrong.

And things were going to go wrong even if they went right, of that Annja was certain. Thankfully, for the moment, Edmund had agreed to remain with the car.

On the curb, Laframboise glanced around, spotted the window washers working on the eighth-floor windows, then he buttoned his coat and nodded to his bodyguard. The big man took the lead toward the building and Laframboise followed. Two more bodyguards came after him. One of them carried a case slightly larger than Dutilleaux's lantern.

Annja lifted the disposable phone Georges had given her to use. She punched in Fiona's number. The woman answered on the first ring. "He's here." Annja watched Laframboise pass through the building's double glass doors and into the foyer.

"I have him." Fiona's voice was cool and competent. She was currently inside the tourist shop. "We know where he's going."

Magdelaine de Brosses operated out of a small office on the sixth floor. According to the information Georges had provided, the fortune-teller's day began promptly at eight o'clock and was over by 5:00 p.m. Clients came and went every thirty minutes and stayed no longer than twenty minutes—unless they made arrangements to stay longer, and that was expensive.

Georges's information on the fortune-teller was extensive. Some of the background came from a man Georges knew inside the Parisian police. De Brosses and her operation had been under investigation for some time, but none of the law enforcement people had found anything incriminating. The woman claimed to deliver glimpses of the future, and she never took more money than she charged for her time.

"I'm on my way." Annja felt her pulse speed slightly as she got up from the chair at the table. She clipped the phone's earpiece to her ear and pocketed the cell, leaving the connection in place.

Out on the street, Laframboise's car pulled into traffic and glided away. There was a parking garage two blocks away. Georges had assumed the driver would take the car there, or he would simply circle the block until Laframboise reemerged. Either way would keep the man out of play.

In the foyer across the street, Laframboise and his retinue stood waiting for the elevator to arrive. Fiona was nowhere in sight.

Outside the internet café, Annja pulled her jacket a little tighter against the wind and walked to the corner to cross. She wore a black wig and wraparound sunglasses that dramatically altered her features. She felt confident that neither Laframboise nor his people would recognize her. They hadn't met, but *Chasing History's Monsters* had an extensive database of pictures of her online.

"He is going up to six." The detached male voice had a West African accent, but there was a lot of Parisian influence there, as well. He might have been born somewhere else, but Annja knew he'd spent most of his formative years in France.

She hadn't met the young technical wizard Georges had provided for their recovery effort. They'd talked briefly by phone before leaving the flat that morning, but there had been no face-to-face encounter. As Georges had explained, it was as much for their benefit as it was for his young technical wizard.

When the light changed, Annja strode across the street with the other pedestrians. She wore cargo pants and a T-shirt with a loose shirt and a jacket to cover the pistol at the small of her back. She didn't want to have to rely on the gun. She also wore the thin gloves so she wouldn't leave prints on the weapon. Thankfully, the weather was cool enough that gloves wouldn't draw attention.

"He's arrived at six." The tech spy had hacked into the building's CCT system. The closed-circuit television system showed all the public areas, the hallways and the elevators.

"Very good." Fiona's voice was calm, like she did this kind of thing all the time.

Maybe she did. Annja smiled at the thought, but she felt out of depth. She'd been involved in similar operations in the past, but she'd never grown comfortable with all the clandestine cloak and dagger.

"What about his associates?"

"They're with him."

"Let me know if there's any deviation."

"Of course."

Annja pushed through the double glass doors and entered

the building's lobby. A uniformed security guard stood at one post. He had a magazine in one hand and a cup of coffee in the other, but he was talking over a phone headset. Despite the man's inattention, Annja's stomach knotted.

Fiona fell into step with her and they reached the elevator together. She'd changed her appearance also, adding a long brown wig and different makeup.

"Are you ready for this?" Fiona stood beside Annja like she was in no hurry.

"As ready as I can be." Her heart was beating rapidly. She watched the elevator numbers drop lower as they neared the lobby.

"I always get nervous right before we get down to it."

"I thought you were born for stuff like this."

Fiona chuckled. She leaned over to Annja conspiratorially. "I just put on a good show."

"Yes, you do."

The elevator pinged and the doors separated in front of them a moment later. They were the only two people to get on.

Fiona snaked a hand to her back, checking on the pistol. "Are you still with us, Heimdall?" She glanced at Annja. "I feel ridiculous using that sobriquet."

"I see everything." The young man sounded amused over the headset links. "No evil shall escape my sight."

Annja grinned as she felt the elevator start up. "You're mixing your comic book cultures. Heimdall is from the Norse mythology in *Thor* as published by Marvel Comics. The bit about 'no evil' is from Green Lantern's oath, a DC Comics thing."

"Depends on your point of view. It's all Hollywood to me. Idris Elba and Ryan Reynolds. And how do you know so much about comics?"

"I'm a big reader. I was always a big reader."

Fiona smiled and looked at her. "You do surprise, Annja Creed."

"You should hear me talk about *Lost* and *Supernatural*."

"Given your schedule, I wouldn't think you'd have time to keep up with television."

"If it weren't for the internet, I wouldn't be able to keep up."

"Personally, I've always enjoyed *Gilmore Girls.*" Fiona briefly took out her pistol and racked the slide. "Shame they took it off the air." She put the pistol away again.

The elevator went past the sixth floor and stopped at the seventh. The doors opened and Annja went through at Fiona's side. The plan was to take the stairs back down to six. Magdelaine de Brosses's office was near the corner.

"Good morning, M. Laframboise." The young man seated behind the glass-and-chrome desk looked relaxed and cheery. He always did.

Laframboise couldn't recall the man's name and had never liked him. The man was too pretty, too perfect. But he suited Magdelaine well as an intermediary. He was handsome enough to keep the attention of young women and too laid-back to threaten the husbands of those women. He was also young enough to stir the fantasies of older women and make them wish they had a few years back, and at the same time make them look on him like a son or grandson.

Innocuous. That was the word that often came to Laframboise's mind when he dealt with the man.

Laframboise nodded.

"Would you care to have a seat?" The young man gestured toward one of the seats in the elegant room. Plants and art prints of scenic areas around Paris brought an Old World feeling to the modern room.

"No." Laframboise wandered over to look at a print of the Eiffel Tower. His mobile showed three minutes of twelve. Magdelaine wouldn't keep him waiting. She wouldn't dare.

Gilbert Campra took one of the seats and gave the appearance of relaxing. The news reports of Puyi-Jin's men attacking a woman who was doubtlessly Annja Creed had confirmed the Shanghai crime lord's continued interest in the lantern.

One of Laframboise's security guards sat in another chair, the case containing the lantern in his lap.

"Mademoiselle de Brosses should only be a moment."

Laframboise didn't respond. He knew for a fact that Magdelaine had finished with her prior client at eleven-fifty. The woman was prompt, conscious of time and never broke her rules. She always took ten minutes between clients to recover the psychic energies she expended.

The time he was kept waiting irritated Laframboise, but he knew better than to push it. In past visits, when he had made an issue of being kept waiting, the readings hadn't gone as well, and he believed Magdelaine needed time to gather herself.

He took a deep breath and tried to relax. He hadn't slept well last night, and only alcohol and drugs had put him out of his head at all. He had spent hours working on the lantern, trying to guess its secrets. One thing was for sure: the lantern possessed power. He could feel it. He was enough of his mother's son to sense that.

At precisely twelve, Magdelaine opened the door to her office and greeted him with a smile. "Jean-Baptiste, how pleasant to see you."

Laframboise put on his best smile. His wealth didn't impress her. Magdelaine had a number of wealthy clients, and she had considerable wealth of her own. Clients not only paid her steep prices, but they also befriended her, often giving her investment tips that had proven to be lucrative. Laframboise had done background checks on the woman.

"Magdelaine, you look positively radiant." Laframboise took her proffered hand and kissed the back of it.

"Flatterer." Her full, plump lips tweaked in a smile.

"But no, love, I'm only speaking the truth. As you do." Just as Laframboise was about to release her hand, he felt an electric tingle in his hand that coursed up his arm to his heart.

That had never before happened.

Magdelaine's smile faltered for just a moment and something flashed in her eyes. "You've brought me something to look at, haven't you?"

"I have."

"And it's very important to you."

"Yes." Laframboise released her hand and turned back to

the man holding the case. He gestured and the man came over at once with the case.

Campra never moved.

Laframboise held the case up for inspection. Magdelaine hesitated, then ran her hands over it.

"This is very powerful. Very dangerous." She looked at him. "But you already know this, don't you?"

"No." Laframboise gave her a smile he didn't truly feel. "That's why I brought it to you. To learn."

Magdelaine stepped back inside her office. "Bring it inside. Let's have a look at it."

28

Laframboise followed Magdelaine into her private office. The room was understated, darkened by the heavy drapes pulled against the noonday sun, and furnished in heavy wooden pieces that were more than a hundred years old. The broad desk was clear of everything except a black velvet spread.

"Put it here." Magdelaine gestured to the desk as she walked around behind it. She sat as Laframboise placed the case on one of the two chairs in front of the desk and opened it.

Gently, he lifted the dragon lantern from the foam padding and placed it on the black velvet. The dragon sat there, frozen in bronze and roosting on its wooden platform. Laframboise sat in the other chair and gazed at the fortune-teller.

"What is this?" Magdelaine studied the lantern but she made no move to touch it.

"It's called a magic lantern."

"Why?" Magdelaine's voice had taken on a dreamy quality, like she was half in the physical world and half somewhere else.

Laframboise was impressed. He'd seen her like this before, but she had never gone into a trance state so quickly. "It's an old magician's trick. A device used to project images to scare people. Illusionists used these before the digital age of holograms."

"This one—" Magdelaine's voice was almost a whisper "—is very old."

"Yes."

"Very dangerous."

"How so?"

"People have killed for this." Her dark eyes focused on him for a moment. "*You* have killed for this."

Laframboise didn't deny the charges, but neither did he admit to them. He trusted Magdelaine implicitly, but he knew that the police sometimes bugged her office while she underwent an investigation. As far as he knew, she wasn't currently under suspicion. But he didn't take chances.

Magdelaine shifted her attention back to the lantern. "You betrayed a man for this lantern."

Laframboise squirmed in the seat. He had known that Magdelaine would undoubtedly ferret that out, but it was the price of finding out more about the lantern. He remained silent. She didn't judge. Probably a lot of her business involved those who weren't good people.

"This man was very powerful. Very dangerous. You have made a mistake there."

He curbed a sharp retort. He didn't like being told about his mistakes or what he should do. "Tell me about the lantern. I want to know the secrets it holds. I know all I need to about its current history."

"Of course." Magdelaine placed both her hands on the desk, palms turned upright, but she still made no effort to touch the lantern. She certainly seemed wary of it. She was more tense than he could remember ever seeing her. Her eyes grew darker and looked through him. "This object belonged to a family. It was an heirloom, something they regarded very highly. It was taken from them, but not without their knowledge."

Laframboise considered that. He'd believed the lantern stolen by Anton Dutilleaux when he'd left Shanghai.

Magdelaine frowned. "There is something missing." She

cocked her head to one side. "Something that was *in* the lantern."

"Something was concealed in the lantern?" He wasn't supposed to ask questions that might shape Magdelaine's efforts or lead her astray. As she had explained her work, the connection she made to people, things and events was tenuous at best.

She shook her head and frowned. She closed her eyes for a moment. "Something valuable was hidden in the lantern. A fortune. A treasure."

Laframboise's heart beat faster and he had to restrain himself from moving. "Where is the treasure? What is it?"

Eyes still closed, Magdelaine shook her head. "You cannot demand. You know that."

Restraining his anger and impatience, Laframboise nodded. Magdelaine had been a favorite of his, and her glimpses into his future had nearly always been helpful.

Magdelaine took in a deep breath and let it out again. "One of the contents of the lanterns was hope. I feel that emotion very strongly. It was hope for the future, hope for an escape. It promised an end to very bad circumstances."

"For the man who owned this lantern?"

"Yes. But there were several who have owned this lantern. The bad circumstances belonged to the original owner. He made his life harder by choosing to take the treasure. But the hope he had then echoes still within this lantern."

He said nothing, but he was seething inside. He couldn't sell hope. There was no method of weighing or measuring it. He stifled a growl of frustration.

"The lantern was a doorway to another world."

Those words checked Laframboise's anger and he was certain he felt a cool breeze pass over his face. That told him he was in the presence of real magic, the kind Magdelaine had always brought. Once she had told him about an investigation by the Sûreté that could have gotten him in a lot of trouble, or possibly in prison for several years, in time for him to prevent it.

Magdelaine raised her hand before her, eyes still shut, as

though she was reaching for a door. "I can feel the door, and I can feel those who are just on the other side." She lowered her hand and placed it once more beside the lantern.

Another chill passed through Laframboise. Part of the legend that surrounded the lantern was that Anton Dutilleaux had been killed by a vengeful ghost. Laframboise had accepted the fact that the lantern might be haunted.

Magdelaine opened her eyes and focused on him. "Taking this lantern was a very bad thing, Jean-Baptiste."

"Not if it leads me to treasure."

Darkness clouded Magdelaine's face. "You will never see the treasure."

The chill returned, and this time it was almost cold enough to turn Laframboise's blood to ice. "Why?"

"Because this lantern is going to get you killed."

Frozen by her words, Laframboise was slow to react when a section of the wall slid open behind Magdelaine. From the hollow, two Asian men dressed in black stepped into the room. They held machine pistols equipped with laser sights.

The ruby dots centered on his chest.

A third man stepped from the recess, as well, and this one Laframboise could put a name to. "Zhang."

Zhang was Puyi-Jin's right-hand man. Although only in his early thirties, Zhang had killed dozens of men and steadily climbed to a position of prominence. There was even a story that when his predecessor turned and agreed to immunity in England in exchange for his testimony, Zhang had gotten himself sent to the same holding facility to kill him. And got away.

"Good afternoon, M. Laframboise." Zhang spoke French without an inflection. He was of medium height and compact; wearing black clothing and a long leather duster. To most observers, he didn't look like a dangerous man. His face was filled with hard planes, and his short-cropped hair was black. A scar ran across his chin and a wispy mustache drew a line over his mouth. He held no weapon in his hands.

Magdelaine stood up from the desk and retreated against

the room's back wall. "You promised me that there would be no bloodshed in this place."

Zhang's hard eyes never left Laframboise. "That promise is contingent on the behavior of your guest."

Laframboise turned to Magdelaine, hurt and confused. He thought of how the treasure the lantern hid was almost within his grasp. "You betrayed me?"

Magdelaine didn't answer.

"You *betrayed* me? *Me?* After all these years?" Laframboise couldn't believe it.

Zhang stood there complacently, his hands clasped.

Tears leaked down Magdelaine's cheeks. "I was given no choice. They knew you would come here to ask about the lantern."

"You could have warned me."

"I have warned you. What you do in this room, how you act now, will determine whether you live or die. Choose to live, Jean-Baptiste. What is on the other side will be very dark and cold for you. You must atone for what you have done in this life."

"My boss is being very generous today, M. Laframboise." Zhang spoke flatly, as if he didn't care about anything Laframboise said or did. "In spite of your treachery and deceit, he is willing to let you live. All you have to do is walk away."

Laframboise cursed the man, but he made no move to reach for a weapon. The laser sights remained unwavering.

Zhang didn't appear to take the abuse personally. Until his boss told him to kill, he wouldn't. And even when he did, the bloodshed would be impersonal.

Angry and trapped, Laframboise rested his hands on his thighs, touching the key chain in his pants pocket. Gently, he pressed the panic button, sending a silent command to Gilbert Campra in the outer room.

Laframboise fixed his gaze on Magdelaine. "You shouldn't have betrayed me, Magdelaine. That wasn't wise of you."

She shook her head. "I didn't have a choice. And the warning I gave you is true—the lantern will get you killed."

Zhang gave a command in Chinese. One of the men stepped forward and seized the lantern. Taking the padded case, the man placed the object inside and shut it. Laframboise had to restrain himself from lunging for the lantern.

"In the future, M. Laframboise, my boss will not be so generous." Zhang stared at Laframboise.

"Tell him that I was being generous, too. I only took the lantern. I didn't take his life. Now things have changed."

A smile touched Zhang's mouth, but there was no warmth in his expression. "I will tell him that. I hope that once I do, we will see each other again. Soon." He nodded at the man with the lantern.

Holding the lantern under one arm, the man stepped up into the recessed area behind the desk. Laframboise tried to peer into the darkness, but couldn't. There had to be a passage. He assumed it led into the room behind Magdelaine's office.

Zhang turned to follow.

At that moment, the office door burst open and Campra took cover to one side. He brought up his H&K MP5 outfitted with a sound suppressor. The machine pistol chugged to life.

29

"Guys, we have a problem."

In the stairwell just outside the door leading to the sixth floor, Annja came to a halt and looked at Fiona. The other woman drew her pistol from the folds of her jacket. Annja reached for the sword and felt it in her fingers but didn't pull it into the stairwell.

"What problem, Heimdall?" Fiona peered through the wire mesh window that looked into the hallway.

Annja leaned in beside her. Only a short distance away, a lone guard stood at the entrance to Magdelaine de Brosses's suite. Heimdall had told them about the man. The two other guards and Laframboise had to be inside.

"The psychic woman has just called the police." Heimdall's voice sounded more urgent. "I took the liberty of tapping her phone lines as a precaution."

Annja was impressed. This was way past television host skill sets.

"Why did she call the police?"

"There's some trouble in the office."

"What trouble?"

"I'm looking.... The psychic rents the room *behind* her office, as well."

Fiona glanced at Annja. "A bolt hole."

"Yes." Heimdall sounded more strained. "I'm checking through the security footage…. Late last night, a group of Chinese men entered that office. They haven't come out."

Fiona nodded. "Then we have to assume we aren't the only ones who know about Magdelaine de Brosses's second room. Can you identify the men?"

"I've downloaded images of them, but I don't have access to those kinds of databases. I'm limited to situations like these. I never cared to get into anything heavier."

"Understood. I have a chap who can take care of the identification. Just keep those images."

At that moment, the sharp cracks of gunfire sounded from inside the office. The guard drew his weapon and charged.

"Well, that's a sure indication that things have gone awry. The second room is just around the way?"

"Yes."

Fiona opened the door and raced into the hallway. "Since our quarry hasn't come back through this door, let's assume he—or someone—is going to come through the other one." She started running toward the intersection of hallways only a short distance ahead of her. Her feet made no sound on the plush carpet. Annja kept pace.

LAFRAMBOISE PUSHED HIMSELF up from his chair and snapped his right wrist, then twisted. Immediately a small, heavy-caliber Semmerling XLM derringer popped into his hand.

The weapon was almost a museum piece and hard to acquire. Once Laframboise had heard of the weapon, he'd had to have it. Chambered in .45 ACP and semiautomatic, the pistol was deadly in close quarters.

It was also painful to shoot. He squeezed the trigger and immediately felt like someone had struck his hand with a baseball bat. No matter how much time he'd spent at the target range, his grip and his reaction to the recoil couldn't prevent it. Shooting the pistol hurt.

But it also gave him a chance to get back the lantern. The

bullet struck Zhang high on the left shoulder and staggered the man, knocking him to the ground. Laframboise fired again but he'd hurried his shot. The bullet gouged the wood surrounding the hidden door and tore a white scar across the varnished surface.

With only three rounds left, Laframboise turned his attention to the man carrying the lantern. He aimed low, starting at the man's knees and letting the pistol rise naturally on the successive recoils. He fired the three remaining rounds in a thunderous roll.

The heavy-caliber bullets tore the man's legs out from beneath him and left him flattened on the ground, the lantern on top of him.

Partially deaf from the detonations in the enclosed room, Laframboise shoved the pistol back up his sleeve and locked it into place. Then he reached for the pistol at his hip.

Campra had already killed the other Chinese gangster. Blood splashed the wall behind the man and soaked the bullet holes. Magdelaine had shrunk down in the corner and was trying to wrap her arms over her head and hide herself. She was screaming, and Laframboise couldn't help but wonder what she might have seen in her immediate future.

"Gilbert, be careful of the lantern."

Campra nodded.

Holding his pistol before him in both hands, Laframboise took one step to the side to get around the desk. He intended to finish killing Zhang if the man wasn't dead.

Instead, Zhang seemed to return to life. The Chinese killer jerked and rolled over. In that brief second, Laframboise saw there was no blood on the man's back and knew that Zhang must have been wearing body armor. A pistol appeared in Zhang's hand as if by magic.

"Look out!" Campra brought up the machine pistol. Before he could fire, Zhang fired three rounds into him, knocking him back. The H&K flew from his hands.

Laframboise brought his pistol to bear and fired two shots.

He didn't think either of them hit his target, and then he was looking down the barrel of Zhang's weapon.

Cursing, Laframboise threw himself backward and down, seeking shelter as a bullet cut the wind near his ear. He took cover behind the desk. The wood vibrated as Zhang continued firing. The rounds cored through in a couple places, but most of them were stopped.

Magdelaine wailed and shrieked in the sudden silence. She was shaking uncontrollably now.

Laframboise cursed her silently. Even without psychic powers, she should have been able to see what was going to happen. Thinking that Zhang had cycled his weapon dry, Laframboise rose from behind the desk with his pistol gripped in both hands.

Zhang wasn't there. Neither was the lantern case. Only the wounded man remained, and he was trying desperately to escape by crawling away. Mercilessly, Laframboise shot the man through the head from behind. By the time the corpse collapsed, Laframboise was already moving toward Campra.

Blood matted Campra's left shoulder. Bullets had made holes in his jacket, and there was a tear on the right side where a round had ricocheted and tore through the coat. Campra wore body armor, as well. As Laframboise watched, the man finally managed to draw a deep breath. Then he rolled over, cursed and reached for the machine pistol.

"Did you get him?" Campra rose to his feet, dropped the empty magazine and fed another one into the weapon.

"Zhang? No. He's gone, and he's got my lantern."

A man filled the doorway behind them and they turned with their weapons. His other guard stood there with his weapon pointed at them. He lowered it.

Laframboise pierced the man with his gaze. "You saw nothing in the hallway?"

"No."

"Call the car and have it waiting in the alley. Call in the other team and let them know we're looking for Puyi-Jin's men."

"Yes, sir." The man fumbled inside his jacket and produced a mobile. He pressed a button and started speaking rapidly.

Campra glanced at the hidden door. "Cute." He pressed a hand to his side and winced. "The woman knew they were there?"

"Yes."

"What are you going to do about her?"

Laframboise glanced at Magdelaine. "Leave her." He pinned her with his hot gaze. "But if I lose my lantern, I'm coming back here to kill you."

The woman reached toward him with a shaking hand. Her face was racked with fear as tears streamed down her cheeks. "I'm sorry. I'm so sorry. Forgive me."

"Where does this door lead?"

"To the adjoining room."

"Then out into the next hallway?"

"Yes."

"There are elevators at the other end of the building?"

Magdelaine nodded and her head jerked with the movement. "Forgive me, Jean-Baptiste. Please. I beg you. I had no choice. You must understand that."

Ignoring her, Laframboise nodded to Campra. "Let's go get my lantern back."

Together, they plunged through the hidden door.

"I've got your target." Heimdall tried to speak calmly, but his excitement betrayed him.

Annja was a step behind Fiona as they rounded the next corner that took them to the hallway where the door to Magdelaine de Brosses's second room was.

"Where?" Fiona stared down the hallway at the scattered individuals cowering in the hallway at the sound of gunfire.

"Ahead of you. On the left. No. On *your* right."

Staring ahead, Annja spotted the Asian man just stepping out of a doorway less than ten feet away. Just before she asked Heimdall for further clarification, she spotted the familiar case tucked under the man's arm. When the man pulled up a pistol, he removed all doubt as to his identity.

He swung the case up as Fiona fired. The bullet screamed off the reinforced case and dug into a nearby wall only a few feet over the head of a reluctant observer. The man went flat to the ground immediately.

Fiona held her fire, obviously deciding unless she had a clear shot she didn't want to risk accidentally hitting a bystander. Never breaking stride, Annja plucked the sword into the hallway with her and swung. The blade flashed as it cut through the air and smacked into the pistol.

The weapon flew from the man's hand as he stared at the sword in surprise. He raised the case to block another sword strike and backed away, talking rapidly.

Annja didn't realize who the man was talking to until four men rounded the corner at the far end of the hallway. They opened fire at once. Deciding to cope with the more deadly threat, Fiona flung herself into a doorway and fired from cover.

One of the men sagged with a bullet between his eyes. Another lost interest in the gun battle when a bullet ripped through his throat. He stood, frantically using both hands to stem the tide of blood. His efforts were in vain and he staggered to one side, falling over a woman who went into immediate panic.

Brandishing her sword, Annja focused on the Asian man with the lantern case. She swung at his head, trying to scare him into stepping back against the wall. Once he was off balance, she intended to take him down.

Instead, the man spun, blocking her sword with the case, then coming around with a back kick that caught her in the middle of her chest. The air whooshed out of her and she went backward. Dumb, dumb, you should have seen that coming. He knew the wall was there, too.

As she fell back, the man spun again, lashing out with a foot and sweeping her legs out from under her. Reflexively, she reached out to break her fall and released her hold on the sword. It disappeared at once, returning to wherever it was when she didn't have it. She slammed against the floor. The only reason she didn't have the breath knocked out of her was because it was already gone.

Her vision turned spotty and she hovered on the edge of unconsciousness. The man loomed above her. He raised his foot and she knew he intended to drive it through her face.

30

Reaching up, Annja caught the man's foot. She stopped his boot sole only an inch or two from her nose. Her arms burned with the effort of keeping him at bay. He was quick, though, almost too quick. He let her hold on to his foot and used it to push himself up so he could drive the other foot down into her throat.

Lungs burning for air, a sudden headache splitting her temples and her vision grayed out at the edges, Annja wrenched her opponent's foot. Physiology and leverage created an insurmountable pressure. The man cried out in pain as his body torqued off balance. He came crashing down, arms windmilling, and he lost his hold on the case.

Annja rolled out of the way and air finally rushed back into her lungs just as she thought she was never going to breathe again. She pushed herself to her feet and grabbed the handle of the case.

"No!" The man scrambled to get up, but his wrenched ankle betrayed him and he crumpled to his knee. He lunged for the pistol but Annja got there first and kicked the weapon away.

Gunshots still rang out in the hallway. Only one of the gunmen had survived Fiona's marksmanship, but he had holed up around the corner at the end of the hall in another corridor.

Fiona took refuge in the recessed doorway and calmly reloaded her weapon. She took note of Annja. "You got the case. Good job."

"Let's get out of here before some of these people get hurt." Annja headed toward the opposite end of the hallway. Another corridor ran perpendicular to the one they were in. If she had the floor configuration worked out, there was another emergency stairwell and a set of elevators there.

Fiona released the slide on her weapon to chamber a fresh round, took another shot at the man around the corner, then turned the pistol toward the man Annja had fought. Annja didn't have any doubt that the woman would kill in cold blood if she had to. The man was already a recognized threat.

Before Fiona could pull the trigger, though, Laframboise yanked open the door the Asian man had come through. Another man with a machine pistol stood at his side.

"Fiona!"

Effortlessly, Fiona wheeled around and fired at the open door, triggering shot after shot. Annja was uncertain whether any of the shots hit Laframboise or his lackey, but both men dove back inside the room as splinters ripped from the door.

Fiona cursed and dropped the empty magazine, pulling still another from her jacket and slamming it home as she ran to join Annja. "Bloody cross fire is *not* where we need to be."

In full agreement, Annja ran after her. Bullets cut the air around them and punched holes in the wall at the end of the hallway. The percussions sounded impossibly loud.

At the end of the hallway, Annja started to go to the right, toward the second set of stairs and elevators. She'd barely managed two steps before she spotted another group of armed Asians sprinting toward them.

"Well, this isn't where we want to be, either." Fiona brought up her pistol and fired rapidly, scattering the new arrivals.

Retreating the other way, Annja ran hard but didn't leave

Fiona behind. The older woman kept up surprisingly well. "Heimdall, is the other stairwell and elevator bank clear?"

"Negative. You guys are boxed. I'm sorry. I'll call our friend. Perhaps there's something he can do. The police are on their way."

Fiona drew up alongside Annja and they ducked around another turn in the hallway. This one left them facing a wall of glass that looked out over Paris. The view was spectacular. In the distance, Annja could see the Eiffel Tower and perhaps even white crenellations of the Arc de Triomphe sitting in the Place de l'Étoile.

Annja took a breath. You're trapped. How are you going to get out of this?

Fiona stood at attention beside her. Gunshots rolled and echoed around them. She held the pistol, pointing at the ceiling. "You don't think they'd be willing to surrender, do you?"

"No."

"I didn't think so, either. But it's only because they don't know what they're up against."

Annja couldn't help but laugh. Fiona Pioche was irrepressible.

More staccato gunshots peppered the hallway.

"For the moment, they're distracted by each other, but they'll get round to us soon enough." Fiona brandished her weapon ruefully. "I'm down to my last magazine. And to be frightfully honest, I don't think either Laframboise or Puyi-Jin's group intends to let us survive this."

A flicker of movement on the other side of the window distracted her from the dark thoughts that crowded her mind. When she saw the second snakelike flicker slide across the glass, she recognized what it had to be.

She rushed over to the window, listening to the steady roar of weapons closing in relentlessly on their position. There, outside the window, the suspended scaffold she'd spotted earlier hung a floor below them and to one side, perhaps eight feet away. Two men dragged squeegees across the windows with iPod earbuds in their ears.

Annja turned to Fiona. "How do you feel about heights?"

"We're on the sixth floor. Jumping is *not* an option."

"It's the only option we have."

Fiona joined her at the window and peered down at the window-washer rig. "Oh, bloody hell. Surely you're joking."

"We're all out of places to run to." Annja stepped back from the window and drew her pistol. She aimed for the center of the glass and fired.

At first she thought the window was going to hold. Though the surface integrity of the glass had been compromised, with thin cracks that looked like spiderwebs spreading out from the bullet hole, it clung stubbornly to its moorings. The windows had been designed to handle the wind shear and accidental impacts.

Annja set down the lantern case and reached for one of the spare magazines she carried. Just as she slammed it home, the glass sucked out of the window and broke apart, leaving the space relatively empty. The pieces glittered as they sailed across the street, smashed into the building opposite, then rained down over the sidewalk as pedestrians ran for cover.

No one was hurt.

Breathing a sigh of relief, Annja holstered her weapon and picked up the case.

Below, the window washers were definitely aware that something was going on. Both young men looked up at the broken window and spotted Annja. They plucked the earbuds out of their ears and stood waiting. The gunfire was unmistakable, and they hunkered down immediately.

Annja didn't give them much more time to think. She climbed into the window, barely managed her balance against the sucking pull of the wind and the vertigo as she stared down at the street far below.

She blew out her breath, hefted the lantern case and brought it in close to her body to better manage the balance, then flung herself toward the nearest cable supporting the washing rig.

She clamped her hand around the wire rope and the rigid surface bit into her palm. Maintaining her grip, she wrapped her leg around the rope, as well, and then released her hand and wrapped the rope inside her elbow to protect her fingers. Holding on, able to somewhat control her descent, she slid down until her foot reached the scaffold's safety rail.

The wind caught her again, but she fought it and dropped onto the scaffold. The men stared at her in shock. Driven by Annja's landing, the scaffold swung sickeningly.

"Mademoiselle."

Ignoring them, Annja set the case down and turned to look up at Fiona. The woman stood at the window and gazed down. Gunshots cracked behind her and reverberated over the street. Sirens screamed, growing closer with every passing second.

"Fiona." Annja wished the scaffold weren't swinging. She hadn't considered the effect her jump would have on the platform. "Just get the timing and jump. Wrap your arms and legs around the cable. Don't try to hold on with your hands."

Cautiously, swaying with the wind, Fiona climbed into the window frame and gathered herself. Without a word, she leaped toward the scaffold.

Panic froze Annja for just a moment when she realized that something had gone wrong, that Fiona had misjudged the jump. Then the woman wrapped her arms and legs around the wire rope and she slid. She came too fast, though, and her foot hit a glancing blow on the scaffold's edge and bounced off. Her legs shot past the scaffolding and her grip with her arms was slipping.

Annja grabbed the back of Fiona's jacket, prayed that it would hold and yanked. Fiona came up a couple inches, giving Annja just enough purchase to catch her under the arms and start hauling.

"It's okay. I've got you. Just hang on."

The scaffold swayed and banged against the windows, jarring Annja as she pulled and fought against the changing leverage provided by the uncertain fulcrum of the safety railing. Before she could get Fiona onto the scaffold, an Asian gunman thrust his head and shoulders through the window above. He pointed his pistol and fired.

Bullets ricocheted off the scaffold and cracked into the nearby windows. The scaffold's wild swings and the wind shear hammering the gunman made them a harder target, but it was only a matter of time.

Fiona released her grip on Annja's arm with her right hand and drew her pistol. She had the weapon up and firing even as Annja set herself and yanked again. Fiona's bullets slapped into the man's chest. He struggled to step back or shoot, Annja wasn't sure which, but the wind caught him and sucked him out the window.

His screams echoed around them as Annja pulled Fiona onto the scaffold and fell onto her haunches.

Fiona rolled and contorted, then got into a crouched position with her pistol braced on the scaffold's safety railing for support.

Searching the scaffold, Annja spotted the control panel. The directions were simple and in French. But there was another problem. She looked at the men.

"Will the scaffold reach the ground?" Scaffolds were usually mounted on rooftops with parapet clamps and didn't necessarily reach the ground. They were designed to clean the upper-story windows of buildings.

"Second floor." One of the men answered in a stunned monotone. "It will go to the second floor. Perhaps a little farther."

"Thank you." Down, then. Up would have been more problematic, requiring them to escape from the building all over again. Annja pressed the button and the scaffold started dropping. "Heimdall, are you still with us?"

"Yes, but I thought you were dead when you jumped out of that window."

"Have the car brought around. There's an alley—" Annja

made sure she hadn't gotten her sense of direction mixed up during the excitement "—on the west side of the building."

"Siasia will be there. Don't worry."

Annja looked at the two window washers. "Can this go any faster?"

The man who had spoken pointed to the control panel. "The lever."

Spotting the lever, Annja threw it in the other direction. Immediately, the scaffold dropped almost as fast as an elevator. The dizzy feeling in her stomach was there, but it was constantly interrupted by the scaffold banging against the side of the building as the wind caught them again and again.

Fifty yards away, white Peugeot cars with Police on the sides in red and blue slewed to a stop in front of the building. Pedestrians ringed the dead man on the sidewalk only a few yards away. So far no one was paying particular attention to the window-washing scaffold.

Reaching the end of its tether, the scaffold swung six or seven feet from the ground. The motor hummed for a moment, then shut off automatically.

"I'm sorry." The window washer wrung his hands apologetically but didn't get up from his position on his knees. "This is as far as it goes."

"That's fine. Thank you."

He looked at her hopefully. "Will you be going now?"

"Yes." Annja grabbed the lantern case and clambered over the side of the scaffold, which was still swinging, though less so now that it had come to a stop. Several pedestrians stared at the scaffold as Annja heaved herself over the side and dropped to the sidewalk. Fiona dropped into place beside her.

"Well, that was certainly an adventure." Fiona tugged the bottom of her jacket into place. "Is it like this for you all the time?"

"More often than not."

"Does Roux accompany you much?"

"No."

"I didn't think so. I believe the life you lead is perhaps a little too exciting even for his tastes."

"It's a little too exciting for mine."

"Ah, Annja Creed, I don't think that's exactly true." Fiona grinned. "There's a certain glow about you that I see when we're under fire. Or jumping from tall buildings."

Several of the pedestrians called to the nearby policemen. One of the uniformed men came toward them, then saw the dead man lying on the pavement. He clicked his shoulder radio and more policemen came running with their guns drawn.

Annja shoved through the pedestrians and broke into a full run on the outside of the crowd. Fiona followed her. Together, they sprinted for the alley and she hoped the car would be there.

When she arrived, the alley was empty. She came to a stop and looked around. "Heimdall."

"Patience. He's almost there."

Three uniformed policemen had pursued Annja and Fiona, probably only because they had run. Pursuit was an instinct and man was, by nature, a predator.

"You two," one of the officers, a woman, said, in French. "Hold it there. We want to talk to you." She repeated her order in English.

Just as she finished, the car that had brought Annja and Fiona roared out on the street and swooped into a tire-eating turn. The police officers drew back as the vehicle bore down on them.

"Stop! Stop the car!"

The driver did stop, but he came to a rocking halt beside Annja and Fiona. In the backseat, Edmund flung the door open, his face tight with anxiety.

"Get in."

Annja wasted no time sliding in, and was immediately followed by Fiona. The police officer who'd first spoken yelled in protest and gave chase on foot, but none of them fired their weapons.

The driver, Siasia, was a young West African man who

wore his multicolored hair in dreadlocks and chewed gum incessantly. Despite the situation, he blew a pink bubble as he wheeled out onto the next street and churned through traffic.

Edmund stared at the case. "You got the lantern."

Annja nodded. "Now we get to see what secrets it holds."

31

Two hours later, back in the safe house Georges had provided, Annja had to admit she was stumped. If the lantern had any secrets, and she was certain it had to, then it was stubbornly holding on to them. Her back aching from the prolonged strain—and maybe from leaping out of buildings and wrestling thugs—she sat up straight at the dining table and massaged her back.

The bronze dragon held on to the lens in its mouth, as well as any secrets it had, and seemed to mock her. She knew that was just her imagination and frustration, but she couldn't keep from personalizing the little monster.

Fiona and Edmund sat across from her. Fiona occupied herself cleaning their weapons. Edmund had watched every move Annja had made but had thankfully kept his questions to a minimum.

"Is there anything at all you can tell us about the lantern?" Edmund looked a little desperate and worse for wear.

"No more than I've already told you." Annja glumly surveyed the object on the dining table. "The lantern is authentic. Handmade. At least three hundred years old." She shook her head. "Other than that, I can't find anything."

"No secret markings? No hidden code?" Edmund's disappointment colored his words and showed in the slump of his shoulders.

"None that I can find." Annja gestured at the array of chemicals and powders she'd used on the lantern. "There are no inscriptions, no contact points that could be braille or glyphs." The Chinese written language was a collection of strokes that fit neatly into a square shape, and those were sometimes referred to as glyphs.

Exasperated, Edmund leaned back in his chair and folded his arms over his chest. "But that doesn't make sense."

"I know."

"There has to be something."

"If there is, I haven't found it. The only discrepancy I've found is in the lens placement."

"The fact that there are three grooves for the lens in the dragon's mouth?" Edmund nodded. "I'd already noticed that."

"Do you know why they're there?"

"To focus the lens better during projection. Probably marked off for different distances. Depending on the image."

Annja looked at the lantern. The reasoning was as sound as anything she'd come up with. "The lens in the dragon's mouth isn't the original, is it?"

Edmund shook his head. "No. That was too much to ask for."

Annja leaned forward again and popped the lens from the dragon's mouth. It didn't come out easily.

"I got the best fit I could. I intended to have the lens ground to a better size at a later date. Once I'd figured out what I was going to have painted on the lens."

"What were you thinking of?"

Edmund frowned. "A black-and-white image of Anton Dutilleaux. Nothing terribly imaginative, I'm afraid."

Annja tried the lens on the other grooves and couldn't get it to fit. She finally surrendered and placed it back in the original groove.

Edmund drummed his fingers on the table nervously. "Men have been killed over that lantern. Not just now, but two hundred years ago Anton Dutilleaux was killed for it. There *has* to be something."

"I know." Annja wished she had more to say. She ran her fingers along the lens grooves.

"It could well be that the treasure, whatever it was, is already gone." Sitting nearby, Fiona poured herself a cup of tea. The aroma lifted Annja's flagging spirits. Noticing Annja's look, Fiona pushed the tea across the table to her. "I'll pour myself another." She glanced at Edmund. "Would you like one?"

"No. I couldn't." Edmund sighed. "Yes. Please." He ran a hand through his hair. "I simply can't believe that we would have to undergo all of this for nothing."

Annja sipped her tea. "Not every mystery gets solved. Not every treasure gets found. Imagine how disappointed Laframboise and Puyi-Jin are going to be."

Edmund paled. "They're not going to believe the treasure doesn't exist. They're still going to hunt us." He looked at Annja. "Aren't they?"

"Unless we can stop them or make them believe it doesn't exist."

Fiona returned with two cups. "That's going to be hard to do, I'm afraid. Now that we've had the lantern in our hands, even if we give it back they'll assume we've already figured out whatever secret was there. We're dealing with greedy men. I daresay they may not even trust themselves."

When Edmund tried to pick up his teacup, the porcelain tapped against the saucer because his hand was trembling. "We're in an impossible situation, aren't we?"

"Getting the lantern didn't help as much as I'd thought it would." Annja felt bad about that.

"In one respect, no, it didn't." Fiona opened a tin of short-bread cookies. "However, we have definitely set Laframboise and Puyi-Jin at each other's throats, so that should buy us some time. Otherwise, either of them could have pursued you, Professor."

"Perhaps we should go to the police at this point." Edmund looked hopeful. He squared his shoulders. "After all, it is me those two want. Me and the lantern, actually. If I were to turn myself over to the police, they could provide protection and the two of you would be left out of this whole sorry mess."

Fiona snorted. "I must apologize. I'm not very polite, am I? The police have their uses, Professor, but they're not so good when it comes to protecting individuals."

"But as long as I'm with you, I'm putting you in danger."

"Annja and I are adults, perfectly capable of making our own decisions. We involved ourselves. We could have let you go hang, after all, instead of showing up to rescue you."

Edmund smiled slightly. "I'm awfully glad you didn't."

"Of course you are. Now you need to have a little faith and let us work through this situation." Fiona leaned back in her chair. "Now, we can kill Laframboise and Puyi-Jin, or we can solve the riddle of the lantern."

Edmund's jaw dropped.

"The first will, of course, take some time, but it can be managed. I am not without my resources, and—given the base natures of our opponents—I am not without resolve." Her eyes glittered like glass. "And after all we've been through, I am certainly motivated."

"Doesn't sound like I'm going to be getting back to my life anytime soon."

"That wouldn't happen until we manage this problem, anyway, would it?"

"No, I suppose not."

Fiona glanced at Annja. "Not to put any pressure on you, dear, but a solution on your part would certainly be faster and involve less bloodshed and less potential police interest than anything I can offer at this point."

"I know." Annja stood. "Let me have some time."

"Of course. We're perfectly safe here for the moment. You tend to your investigations, and I'll see about making more arrangements."

Annja took the lantern and her backpack, then headed to her room.

THREE HOURS LATER, ANNJA sat cross-legged and short-tempered on the small bed in the room she'd been assigned. She wished she was back in her loft apartment in Brooklyn. There, surrounded by her books and her personal things, she thought her best.

She stared at the lantern, perfectly balanced on the bed. The dragon looked like it was perched and ready to leap out at her.

"Try it. Just give me any excuse." Annja shook her head. "Talking to the artifact isn't a good sign. Threatening it is even worse." Carefully, she got up, put the lantern back in its case and headed out into the living area.

The television was on, replaying a story about the shoot-out at the office building. She'd watched the footage in her borrowed bedroom. So far Laframboise and Puyi-Jin had been mentioned, but no one had dropped Annja's or Fiona's names. Magdelaine de Brosses had stated that thieves had broken into her office and stolen the object Laframboise had brought her.

No fingers had been pointed, but Annja knew the fortune-teller was more involved than she was letting on. Puyi-Jin's men hadn't found the second room by accident. Laframboise had been set up, and he was probably aware of that, as well.

Although Laframboise probably wasn't going to be held accountable for much more than defending himself and his property, the legal entanglements would at least slow the man in his pursuit.

Edmund sat on the couch with a deck of cards. He kept making them disappear and reappear mechanically. His eyes were unfocused, unseeing, and he didn't notice her until she stepped directly in front of him.

"Going somewhere?"

"Rooftop. I need to clear my head." Annja looked around. "Where's Fiona?"

"She went out with Georges. They're up to something, but she didn't say what." Edmund squinted at her. "What's on the rooftop?"

"Peace of mind, I hope."

"You still haven't gotten anywhere with—" Edmund

stopped himself and sighed. "Of course you haven't. Otherwise, you'd say."

"I would."

"Are you going to be all right on your own?"

"Yes. In the meantime, why don't you look back through the Dutilleaux material. See if there's some new angle. Anything."

"What should I look for?"

"If I knew, I'd tell you. Hopefully we missed something. We need a new trail."

Glumly, Edmund nodded and reached for his computer.

Annja went down the hallway to the fire escape. The window was unlocked and she went out it.

The traffic noise from the street below was muted as Annja looked out over the city. Cooing pigeons lined the roof's parapet. Occasionally one or a small group of them took flight in an explosion of gray and white.

Annja started slow, limbering up her body with stretches, then falling naturally into martial-arts katas. Her muscles loosened and warmed, taking less and less thought as she worked into the familiar routines. She'd started different martial arts while still in the orphanage, and she'd stayed with them all of her adult life.

After a few more minutes, she reached for the sword and pulled it onto the rooftop with her. The keen blade cleaved the air and reflected the late-afternoon sun. She whirled and danced, feinted and struck and blocked and counterstruck. The blade was a part of her, an extension of self. Continuing her workout, a fine sheen of sweat covered her and cooled her body.

Her mind freed up and went dormant. In her mind's eye, she studied the dragon lantern, turning it over and over and around.

The secret is incomplete.

The realization jarred Annja, but she continued to exercise, to become one with the sword. How was the lantern incomplete? The missing lens? That was one way.

But was there another?

There was something there. She sensed it. All she had to do was grasp it.

Her phone rang and she had the immediate impression she should answer it. She came to a stop with the ease of a leaf falling and was suddenly at rest. Holding the sword in her right hand, she fished her sat-phone from her cargo pants.

Doug Morrell.

Annja didn't want to deal with Doug at the moment, but she knew she had to answer. "Hello."

"Just checking in." Doug sounded relaxed, and Annja chose to view that as a good thing. "How's it going with the magic lantern?"

"I've got it."

"That's great, Annja." Doug suddenly started whispering conspiratorially. "You haven't used up all the wishes, have you? Because we had an agreement. You know, a wish each and then—"

"I remember." Annja stared at the Eiffel Tower in the distance. "I'm afraid I haven't figured out how to get it to work yet."

"That's cool. We can figure it out somehow. We just gotta find the instructions."

Instructions.

A chill ghosted through Annja and she felt certain she had part of the answer she was searching for. "Thanks, Doug. I've got to call you back."

"Wait—"

"As soon as I know something, I'll call you."

"But what—"

Annja closed the phone and tucked it back into her pocket. When she turned to face the fire escape, she spotted Fiona sitting there, watching.

"How long have you been there?"

Fiona smiled a little. "I honestly couldn't tell you. Long enough to tell that you and that sword were made for each other." She shook her head. "I've never seen anything like that. Was that dancing?"

"I don't know." Annja blushed. "It's just…natural when I'm with the sword."

"Don't be embarrassed. That was one of the most beautiful things I have ever seen, and I can tell you, I've seen some beautiful things."

"Thank you." Annja didn't know what else to say. "I just realized that we missed something. Is Edmund still downstairs?"

"Poring over his records of Anton Dutilleaux when I left him."

"I've got to talk to him." Annja started for the fire escape.

Fiona stood. "Maybe you shouldn't take the sword. He might get the wrong impression."

Smiling ruefully, but no less excited, Annja released the sword and the weapon disappeared before it hit the rooftop.

32

When they returned to the flat, Edmund was pacing the floor with nervous energy while he spoke on the phone. "Yes, yes, of course. No, this is *very* important. Those things should have been together. No, I'm not placing any blame on you. Do forgive me if I sounded that way. It was not intended." He continued apologizing for a moment longer. "Please let me know what you find out."

Fiona sat in the easy chair in the corner and steepled her fingers together. She smiled inquisitively at Edmund. "You sound like you've had an epiphany, Professor."

"Not an epiphany. That would be putting a happy face on it. No, I've made a dunderheaded mistake is what I've done." Edmund turned to Annja. "Do you know what I missed?"

"There were papers in the lot that had Anton Dutilleaux's magic lantern." Annja was so thrilled with her breakthrough that she forgot to let Edmund have his victory. "Papers that had belonged to Dutilleaux."

"That's right." Edmund looked troubled. "How did you know that?"

"If Dutilleaux took the lantern, if there was a treasure somehow attached to it, then he might have had something else, as well. Other belongings."

Edmund grinned. "Exactly. It came to me as I went back through the original auction I attended that the lantern might not have been the only thing Dutilleaux left behind. There was an assortment of magic books, and I had all those, but—as it turns out—there was a diary."

"But it wasn't his."

A frown knitted Edmund's brows. "You're more magician than I am. How are you coming up with this?"

"I didn't know there was a diary until you told me. I was hoping there might at least be papers or letters."

"I don't know if there were any papers or letters. I should probably ask."

"Tell me about the diary."

"What? Don't you already know?"

"It's written in Chinese."

Edmund shook his head in disbelief. "Perhaps I should venture up to the rooftop, as well."

"And so…?" Annja prodded him.

"The sellers were going to list the lantern and the diary together. Those items, after all, were discovered together. But they had no way of knowing that Anton Dutilleaux had ever owned the diary. In fact, I was only guessing that he might have. I was looking for anything written that had been in that lot. The sellers thought they might get more money offering the lantern and the diary separately. But I should have thought of that."

"You went there looking for the lantern."

"I did." Edmund scowled. "Once I'd heard of it, and of its possible history, I'm afraid that was all I could think of. Blindness on my part."

"Why would you have wanted a diary written in Chinese, and probably not even written by Dutilleaux?"

"True. There was nothing in his past that mentioned his knowledge of written Chinese." He shook his head. "Though, in retrospect, given my awareness of his history as a banking employee in Shanghai, I should have at least considered that."

Annja grinned. "Tell me about the diary."

"Not much to tell, I'm afraid. The diary popped up with the lantern when Robertson's assistant's things were found in an old boardinghouse three months ago, and is listed as having belonged to Dutilleaux, but that's all that's really known about it."

"No one's had it translated?"

"No one's cared to. It's over two hundred years old. The sellers figured that whatever was in the pages of that diary surely weren't of interest to anyone in this day and age. They thought it was a keepsake. Nothing more. Possibly a volume of Chinese literature or a family history."

"It may yet be that."

"I know. I can't imagine what it might be, but surely it must be something. Anton Dutilleaux wasn't the kind of man who would travel from the Orient carrying things that were useless to him."

Annja nodded. "Where is the diary now?"

Edmund frowned. "It was sold. I asked the sellers if they could let me know the name of the person who bought the diary. They're not in the habit of disclosing information, but I pointed out that Jean-Baptiste Laframboise certainly got hold of *my* information."

"Did they admit to that?"

"Not even, but it cut some difference with them. Their resolve weakened. They're certainly more receptive to the idea of putting me in touch with the purchaser."

Fiona spoke up from the other corner of the room. "Perhaps I can be of assistance."

Annja had almost forgotten about Fiona. She smiled. "Of course you can."

"I'll put Ollie on it right now." Fiona took out her sat-phone. "I'll just need the particulars of that sale, if you please, Professor."

WAITING FOR OLLIE'S IMMINENT success was hard. Annja occupied her time with her work. Chiefly, the Mr. Hyde investigation back in London. Detective Chief Inspector Westcox was the star of a half-dozen media interviews, four on television and two on radio, and he was collecting a lot of ink and rising in Google stats as more and more people wrote about the murders and speculated on the killer's identity and continued interest. And the helplessness of the London Metro Police Department.

Annja felt bad for the dead women. She looked at their faces and wished she hadn't. The photographs revealed on the various websites were garish.

You're not a detective. She had to remind herself of that. You're an archaeologist. There might be some overlap in skills, but you don't have the resources of a police department. Westcox will find the murderer. He's good at that sort of thing. If there was something in that investigation you could help with, you would.

There were several emails from Doug, letting her know he was collecting the media reports for her, covering for her while she was off trying to find the magic lantern.

Mr. Hyde continued to taunt the police. He'd written in twice more, claiming his victory, that they wouldn't catch him and that he would kill again.

Soon.

Annja felt torn. She knew she wasn't equipped to help out with the police investigation, but she still felt a need to be there. Despite her lack of police training, she'd gotten involved in the search for the killer and that chafed at her.

"Why so pensive?"

Startled, Annja looked up to see Fiona standing in the doorway. "I'm sorry. I didn't hear you come in." The woman was developing an irksome habit of popping up without Annja knowing.

"No wonder, what with the material you're looking at."

Guiltily, Annja closed her computer down. "I shouldn't be. Keeping up with all of that just makes me feel useless."

"Those murders aren't something you can do anything about."

"I've been reminding myself of that."

Fiona regarded her. "But you feel guilty, anyway."

Annja hesitated and wanted to deny that, but she couldn't. "Yes."

"Because of your involvement through the television show?"

After everything she'd seen Fiona do in the past two days, Annja wasn't surprised the woman knew about her Mr. Hyde investigation for *Chasing History's Monsters* even though it hadn't been mentioned. "Yes."

For a moment, Fiona was silent. "Have you always been so aware of this need to feel responsible for people?"

"What do you mean?"

"Most individuals wouldn't take on the responsibilities that you shoulder, Annja. If they'd met someone like Edmund Beswick, they would have felt badly for him and wished him well, maybe drop a donation into a bucket, but that sense of responsibility would have ended there."

Annja hadn't thought about that. "Maybe."

"There's no maybe to it." Fiona's voice was soft. "You stepped right into the young professor's battle without an instant's hesitation."

"Seems to me you did the same thing."

Fiona arched her brows. "The pot calling the kettle black?"

"Something like that."

"Not so. I took you on at the express request of an old friend. You didn't even know the professor, except for a few phone calls and a couple meetings." Fiona shook her head. "Not the same thing at all. Furthermore, I'm in the business of dealing with other people's troubles. You are an archaeologist."

"And a television personality." Annja smiled.

"I rather think you happened into that one and are using it to your own ends. I don't believe for an instant that being a television personality was ever an ambition of yours."

Annja couldn't disagree.

"What I have to wonder, though, and I am concerned, is how much that sword influences your sense of judgment."

"What do you mean?"

"I'm thinking perhaps it pushes you in the direction of helping others rather more than you would if left to your own devices."

"Couldn't I just be a good person?"

"I wouldn't think you could be anything else." Fiona was silent for a moment. "But I saw you with that sword up on the rooftop. It was like…like you and that sword know each other. As if you're in a relationship."

Annja would never have considered using those words.

"I know about the *troubled* things that Roux searches out. I know how bad they can be for people, and the horrible things that some of them can do."

"I've never seen anything like that."

"Then you're fortunate." Fiona shivered. "My point is that perhaps that sword might carry some trouble with it, as well."

"I don't believe that."

"I didn't think you would, but I wanted you to at least consider the possibility. The things you do, Annja, the bad situations you're drawn into, they may be brought on by that sword. It may well be that the sword doesn't push you toward these troubles, but perhaps it draws them to you."

Annja took a deep breath. "I've thought about that, Fiona. But I'm more of the opinion that—if anything—the sword lets me see the bad things that are happening. There's no forced involvement. The choice is mine."

"I hope that's true."

"Let me ask you a question."

"Of course."

"You searched for the sword with Roux, even found a few of the pieces."

"That's not a question, and you already know that I did."

"Here's my question—how do you know that the search you went on with Roux, that the contact you had with those sword fragments you helped him find, didn't somehow influence you and what you're choosing to do?"

Fiona held Annja's gaze, then smiled uneasily. "That sword was put here to change the life of one young woman."

"I've met several people whose lives have been changed because I was able to help them."

"Touché."

Annja smiled. "Did you just come up here to offer advice?"

"To pry, you mean?"

"If I thought you were prying, you wouldn't have gotten a word out of me. I was raised by nuns. I know how to keep my mouth shut, and when to shut it and disavow all knowledge of anything."

Fiona laughed. "You are a treat, Annja. I can see why Roux is drawn to you."

"I don't think *drawn* is the word he would use. The last conversation I had with him? I called him an asshat."

Fiona laughed. "I wish I had been there."

"I had to explain the term to him. That kind of took some of the sting out of it."

"No worries. I'm sure Roux was still considerably stung."

"I hope so." Annja sighed. "Roux can be a real jerk sometimes."

"Yes, he can. He is only a man, after all, and proof that even if a man lives five hundred years—or more—he is limited in what he can learn." Fiona shook her head. "I came up here to let you know Ollie has located the missing diary."

33

Night had fallen over Paris. The glow of the City of Lights pulsed against the windows of the flat as Annja took a seat on the couch beside Edmund. She hadn't realized how late it had become.

Fiona sat on the other side of Edmund. The professor's computer was open on the coffee table, displaying Ollie Wemyss, as immaculate and unflappable as ever, center stage in Fiona's office back in London. The view showed him from the waist up, and Annja was certain the man had staged it.

"Good evening, Ms. Creed."

"Hello, Ollie."

"As I was telling Ms. Pioche and Professor Beswick, I have had a bit of luck locating the contents of the diary you people are looking for."

"Wait." Annja held up a hand. "The *contents* of the diary?"

A small frown turned down the corners of Ollie's mouth. "Yes, you see, there was a problem with the diary. At about the time Professor Beswick went missing and Laframboise's people were breaking into his storage unit—with Puyi-Jin's people vectoring in at that moment as well, all very exciting—the purchaser of the diary had her house burgled. The diary appears to have been the target of the invasion."

"Was the woman harmed?"

"No. Fortunately she was out of the house when the theft occurred."

"Then how did you end up with the contents?"

"Ms. Creed, when you're about to deliver a lecture, do you allow the audience to pester you with questions—which you plan to answer in their proper due course—at the outset?"

Chagrined, Annja restrained her curiosity. "I apologize."

"We'll have time for the Q and A afterward." Ollie smiled. "As I said, the original document was lost. Whatever secrets might be in the architecture of the book itself, I'm afraid, are beyond us at this point. Though, I am told, the new owner had checked the volume quite thoroughly."

Annja curbed her impulse to point out that a hidden message could have been contained in the weave of the material comprising the cover, or that there could have been bumps or irregularities, or any of a dozen different things. If Ollie knew about such things, and she was almost certain he did, then he knew what they had lost. And if he didn't know for a fact, he was too clever not to realize that a facsimile wasn't as good as the original document.

It was gone. They had to concentrate on what crumbs they had left.

"Mrs. Rollison—quite an invigorating old bird, and I use that as a term of endearment—took it upon herself to photocopy all of the pages. She found me absolutely charming when I presented myself on her doorstep and asked after the diary."

Annja made herself be calm, but she was exploding with questions.

"I had to endure a lot of cheek pinching, but I persuaded her to part with a copy of her computer file. I'm sending it along now through the FTP site Professor Beswick has accessed. Since Mrs. Rollison is quite the expert in Chinese written language across the ages, and a suitable person will take some time to locate even with my connections, I also got her to share her partial translation with us. She's still working on the document."

Fiona interrupted at that. "Even though you're quite taken with Mrs. Rollison and her translation abilities, I'd like to have the translation double-checked."

Ollie put a hand over his heart as though wounded. "Seriously, Ms. Pioche?"

Fiona sighed. "Sometimes, Ollie, dear though you are to me, you are insufferable."

"How very magnanimous and eloquent of you. I've currently got the document with two other learned souls who shall get back to me forthwith because I bribed them heavily with your money. Since you're a woman of means, I saw no reason not to get the best available."

"I trust they're working independently, as well?"

"Definitely."

"How long will their translations take?"

"Days, I'm afraid. But since time is of the essence, I asked them to work the diary backward, believing that the last entries would be the most beneficial."

"Thank you, Ollie."

Ollie gestured broadly. "I live only to serve, Ms. Pioche." He smiled. "From the pages Mrs. Rollison has translated, the diary belonged to a man named Tsai Chien-Fu. At the time of the writing, he was a Chinese official working with the Shanghai banks in the late 1790s."

Excitement flared through Annja and she couldn't help grinning.

Edmund was smiling, too. "Looks like we're back in the race."

"I don't want to dim your spirits, but I would like to put things in perspective for you." Ollie looked serious. "Mrs. Rollison has been quite diligent in her translation, and I gave it a read-through as I was preparing it to send to you. There is no mention of a treasure. Tsai Chien-Fu appears to have been a very thorough Chinese bureaucrat working for the emperor. And quite boring."

Fiona waved that away. "But is there any mention of Anton Dutilleaux?"

"As it turns out, Ms. Pioche, there is. Tsai Chien-Fu worked with Anton Dutilleaux."

FOR OVER AN HOUR, EDMUND'S computer downloaded the graphic-intensive files through the server. As each page of the diary came through, he printed it out and sent it to Annja's computer so they could all look at the work being done.

Most of the reading was dry material. Tsai Chien-Fu wrote mostly about the day-to-day business of Shanghai banking as he learned it. He was fastidious about his recollections of the people he met and the transactions that were made.

"Typical bureaucratic documentation." Sitting at the table, Fiona leafed through the pages of translation she'd been passed.

"The Qianlong Emperor wasn't known as a generous person and was very conservative." Annja kept her focus on the images on her computer, blowing up the characters and searching for hidden meanings. It was mostly wasted effort on her part, though, because she couldn't read Chinese and only had the barest acquaintance with the characters. "He abdicated the throne in favor of his son, the Jiaqing Emperor, so he wouldn't rule longer than his grandfather, the Kangxi Emperor. That didn't really matter, though, because he ruled his son, anyway, until his death three years later."

Edmund stared at her. "No one plays Trivial Pursuit with you, do they?"

"I knew Dutilleaux was there during the Qianlong Emperor's reign. I read up on the history." Annja turned her attention back to the documents. "The point is that Tsai had every reason to make sure he had a separate record of what he was doing. In case the emperor's accountants took his books."

"This isn't going to help us much."

Fiona held up a printout. "Tsai seemed quite enamored of Dutilleaux, though."

Annja looked at the paper. "When's that from?"

"October 22, 1790. This details how the two of them met."

Edmund consulted a small notepad. "Dutilleaux was in Shanghai from 1786 to 1792. He went to work at the Shanghai bank in 1790."

Annja thought about that. "So the two of them met in 1790,

and two years later, Dutilleaux left. Did he have another job offer?"

"No. He returned to Paris and began his career in magic."

"He didn't have much time to work on it."

"On the contrary, Dutilleaux was a magician before he went over to Shanghai. He just didn't have his act together. Before then, he'd toured the small Parisian theaters but didn't have much success. He took the accounting job in Shanghai to avoid debtors' prison. Over the next few years, he was able to pay off his creditors and sharpen his craft."

Fiona sipped her tea. "Tsai was quite impressed with Dutilleaux's sleight of hand. In some of these references, Tsai calls Dutilleaux 'Xian.'"

That caught Annja's attention. "I don't know enough Chinese to do much more than survive in the country, but that's a word I know. The literal translation is *magician*. Or wizard or shaman. Among other things. But if Tsai was calling Dutilleaux that, I'd be willing to assume that's why he did."

Tilting the paper, Fiona started searching. "All right, if we now know that Xian was a pet name for Dutilleaux, then this later part makes more sense." She handed papers over to Annja. "In this section, Tsai refers to putting all his hope into the Xian."

"The translator could have inferred the article. Tsai might have been referring to Dutilleaux." Annja leaned over to more closely examine the paper. It didn't do any good. She still didn't have enough of a command of the language to make a difference.

Fiona looked at Edmund. "Do you know when Dutilleaux left Shanghai to return to Paris?"

Edmund consulted his notes. "July 15."

Nodding, Fiona smiled. "On this page, Tsai talks about how the Xian carried all the seeds of his family's future to more fertile pastures. This is dated July 15, and if memory serves me correctly, that corresponds with the Chinese Hungry Ghost Festival, the traditional day the deceased are believed to visit the living. By all accounts, a most singular day."

Edmund looked hopeful. "Then perhaps there's reason to believe that Dutilleaux stole nothing. Whatever treasure he was carrying was something he got from Tsai."

"There's still the question of what happened to Tsai." Fiona returned to the printouts. "Tsai's diary goes on for five more weeks, then stops abruptly. The last few entries are filled with his concern that the emperor's men have discovered what he has done, and that they are going to kill him. He goes on to say that they didn't know Xian was already gone." She looked up at Annja. "You said that some of the information you had dug up indicated the Qianlong Emperor's men were searching for Dutilleaux?"

"Yes." Annja pulled up the information and scanned it. "According to this, there was a theft from the royal treasury. Several bank employees were executed."

"Was Tsai one of them?"

Annja shook her head. "The information doesn't say. But the time frame appears right. Sometime in the early days of September." She took a deep breath. "We need to find out what happened to Tsai Chien-Fu."

Fiona's phone rang and she answered it. She talked briefly to Ollie, then took down a URL. When she was finished, she thanked her major-domo and passed the slip of paper to Annja.

"Ollie said we need to access that site. He says he got lucky and got video footage of the break-in at the Rollison home."

Annja quickly typed the address into her computer and waited as the site came up. A video dawned on her screen and black-and-white footage rolled.

On the screen, Asian men got out of a nondescript sedan in front of what Annja assumed was the apartment building where Mrs. Rollison lived. The scene cut, then opened up again on a hallway view of the three men as they broke into a flat. This time the camera revealed that they were Asian. They returned seventeen minutes later carrying a box. The time lapse sped up to get through the waiting.

Fiona looked grim. "We have to believe that the diary is in

Puyi-Jin's hands now. He could well be caught up with us at this point."

Annja pushed herself back from the table and took her computer. "Then he'll probably be looking for Tsai Chien-Fu, as well. We'll just have to find him faster."

34

Searching back two hundred years of history while looking for one man was an arduous task. It was easier to track an event or political climate, or even an environmental one. Finding people lost in history could be hard. Fortunately, it was *only* two hundred years. Though, the task would have been much easier if Tsai Chien-Fu had been more than a drone at a Chinese bank filled with drones. Killers and kings were much easier to locate.

Consumed by her mission, Annja worked through the night. The Tsai family name was one of the less common in China, and the country had a lot of genealogical documentation despite the wars and unrest that had torn it apart at different times. Annja had hoped the name would be enough to help her find Tsai Chien-Fu.

It wasn't. She failed and failed and failed again to the point she was ready to put her computer through the wall. In the end, it was the alt.history site that pointed the way.

At 5:53 a.m., a new posting came through from New Shanghai Girl. At Annja's request, the young woman had investigated her friend's family.

Ni hao again, Lantern Girl!
I'm glad my posting helped you find what you were looking

for. Wouldn't it be cool if your lantern was the same one my friend's family had lost? Or if the two lanterns were somehow related? I mean, I know there are probably a million dragon lanterns, but this one's gotta be special, right?

Anyway, my friend's family still lives in the same place. They own a flower shop in Nanqiao Town, the largest city in the Fengxian district. The shop's name translates to Beautiful Moon Petals, which has got to be one of the corniest names I've ever heard of. Her father's name is Li Shusen, or Shusen Li if you want to write it in English.

But my friend's mother's maiden name was Tsai. Which, I think, is the name of the man in the picture. The Chinese one, not the European one.

My friend's name is Guifang, but we call her Amy. Can I tell her that you may have found her family's long-lost lantern?

Gotta go. *iCarly* is coming on and I have a paper due in Anthropology tomorrow!
New Shanghai Girl

Ni hao, New Shanghai Girl,
Don't mention this to your friend yet. I'm planning on coming to Shanghai soon and can arrange a meeting. Maybe it will be a great surprise.

I appreciate all your help. Give me a post address and I'll send you a few seasons of *iCarly* as a thank-you.
Lantern Girl

Annja woke Fiona and Edmund, then went to the kitchen and started the coffeemaker and put on a kettle of water for tea. Evidently her two companions had been up late because they were slow to rise. Working on nervous energy, Annja pulled sausage links and orange juice from the refrigerator. She found pancake mix in the pantry and set a frying pan on the stove to heat.

Taking a few apples from the bowl on the countertop, she

washed them and chopped them into small pieces, then dropped them into a pan with a little water and set it to boil for applesauce. Turning her attention to the sausage links, she plopped the links into the frying pan to cook. She turned the sausages to brown them while she made pancakes.

By the time Edmund was sitting up and Fiona arrived fresh from the shower, Annja was placing the food on the dining table. She added fresh melon and grapes.

Fiona sat and arched an eyebrow. "You're still in your clothing from yesterday. Did you sleep at all?"

"No." Annja sat and dug into the meal. "But I think I found the Tsai family."

Edmund paused in the middle of forking pancakes onto his plate. "Truly?"

"Yes." As they ate, Annja told them the story of her discovery.

AFTER ANNJA HAD FINISHED relating her tale, they were well into the meal.

"Are you planning on contacting the Li family and finding out if they are indeed the family we're looking for?" Fiona carved a sausage link with a knife and fork, then popped a piece into her mouth and chewed.

"By phone?" Annja shook her head. "I don't think we could get the answers we need by doing this over the phone. I think we need to go there."

"Actually, I agree. This is something that will be best handled in person."

"Wait." Edmund held up his hands. "You're seriously talking about just jetting over to Shanghai?"

Fiona nodded.

"You do realize there are people looking for us?"

"Not a thing we're likely to forget, given the nature of our arrival and all the trouble we got into yesterday."

Edmund sighed in exasperation. "How do you plan on getting out of Paris? Laframboise, and possibly Puyi-Jin, will know about your private jet by now. You can't just hop on that and take off."

"I wasn't planning to. In fact, after the debacle that occurred at the airport, I had the pilot take my jet back to London. I didn't want to risk Laframboise or Puyi-Jin targeting the jet just for spite. People could have gotten hurt because it might become a target." Fiona sipped her tea. "I'm certain Georges can find us a way to Shanghai. He does business with that side of the world, as well."

Annja was ready to go. She didn't like the idea that Puyi-Jin might already be closing in on the family they hoped to see. "How soon can we leave?"

"Let me give Georges a ring, but I'm willing to bet we can leave fairly quickly." Fiona reached for her phone.

GEORGES REACTED A LOT MORE quickly than Annja could have imagined. Within an hour of getting Fiona's call, he had a flight available for them aboard a cargo jet that would be flying non-stop. They had to hurry to pack and get to the airport on time.

Georges drove them himself and talked with the flight crew to make sure everything was in order. He stood at the loading gate and talked with Fiona as the plane was prepped for departure.

"Everything will be in order for the customs people when you arrive in Shanghai." Georges handed Fiona a thick manila envelope. "I've provided paperwork that will show all of you as consultants for an investments business that I'm associated with in Shanghai."

Fiona regarded him with interest. "Doing a bit of piracy, are you?"

Georges smiled. "You've got a suspicious nature, Ms. Pioche."

"Only when I'm around suspicious people."

"Rest assured, the business I'm doing with these people will not reflect onto you. Your trip should be uneventful, and I'll keep hoping that you find whatever it is you're looking for."

"Thank you, Georges. You've been very kind."

He bowed slightly and kissed the back of Fiona's hand. "Your presence always reinvigorates whatever poor kindness resides within me." He straightened. "I do wish you'd have been able to stay longer. I would love to take you to dinner."

"I would have enjoyed that, as well, but that would be better at a time when someone isn't gunning for me."

"True."

"I'll see you again soon, Georges."

Standing in the shade of the small warehouse, Georges waved them off.

Mechanically, dreading the eleven-hour flight ahead of them, Annja carried her baggage to the waiting cargo jet. Once aboard it, she discovered the passenger section was larger than she'd expected. She chose a seat against one of the windows, stowed her gear and settled into the chair.

Within minutes before takeoff, Annja was asleep.

ELEVEN AND A HALF HOURS later, Annja woke to find Fiona shaking her gently by the shoulder. Annja looked up at the woman, realizing that the vibrations of the plane were caused by it taxiing. She got up from the seat in the back of the plane and started grabbing her gear. She slung her backpack over her shoulder.

"I can't believe I slept so long." Annja unplugged her sat-phone from the charger and tucked it into her pocket. Her computer was at capacity, as well.

"I think we all did." Fiona picked up her bag, but one of the flight crew came over and took it from her.

"No. Please. I was given very specific orders." The man smiled politely at her. Then he called over to another man.

Annja surrendered her carry-on, but she kept hold of her backpack. That never left her sight.

Edmund still looked tired. "I envy the two of you sleeping the way you do. I watched you do it, and I still can't believe it." He ran a hand through his hair. "I've never been one to sleep on a plane, and this thing jumped and bounced nearly the whole way."

Fiona patted him on the shoulder. "If all goes well, we'll be in a hotel tonight. Unless you wanted to stay there this morning."

"And leave you two to go off and figure out the secret that everyone is looking for?" Edmund shook his head. "That's not going to happen as long as I have a breath of air left in me." He fisted his bag and followed them out of the plane.

AS GEORGES HAD PROMISED, their passage through the China Inspection and Quarantine was relatively uneventful. There were a lot of passengers deplaning, though, and that took almost an hour. They had left Paris shortly before noon. With the eleven-hour flight and the time change between countries, they had landed at Shanghai Pudong International Airport at 5:40 a.m. It was now almost seven, but still too early to go calling on the Li family. There was still over an hour of travel time to reach Nanqiao Town.

Once they had cleared customs, Fiona led the way to the Avis car rental area and surprised Annja by speaking fluent Chinese.

"You can speak Mandarin?"

Fiona nodded. "I can speak it, but I can't read it. I came here a number of times with Roux. There were all kinds of interesting things we found while we were in this country."

Annja recalled the jade ogre Roux and Garin had destroyed when they had been at the Loulan City dig. China was thousands of years old, and the country jealously held on to its secrets because there had been so much turmoil, and because the emperors hadn't shared their knowledge. So much of it had been lost.

"I didn't think you could rent a car here. The last time I tried, I was told I had to have a Chinese driver's license and that it took about three weeks to get one."

"I have a Chinese driver's license." Fiona took the document from the small handbag she carried. "And it's up-to-date. As I said, I've been here a number of times, and I still have business that brings me here on occasion. Having a license is just smart."

Silently, Annja agreed. Otherwise, they would have been stuck with public transport or have to hire a driver. They would have been more or less stranded on foot or forced to give up part of their privacy.

"You're amazing."

"I've had an amazing life. As I'm sure you're going to have. The trick is to always manage to survive such a life."

AFTER THE CAR WAS PROMISED within the hour, which Fiona said would be more like two hours, she took them to the Canglang Ting restaurant, which was already open and business was booming. The scent of the spices and herbs made Annja's stomach growl. They sat and ate in relative silence, putting away an enormous amount of noodles and rice cakes.

When they finally pushed away from the table, Edmund sighed in discomfort. "I'll never be hungry again."

At the car rental agency, they picked up a gray Volkswagen Passat. Fiona drove them to the nearby Ramada Pudong Airport Hotel. Inside, Fiona walked directly to the Executive Lounge desk and the well-dressed man there greeted her by name.

"Not the best hotel we could stay at, but certainly the most convenient. And I don't expect our stay will be long." Fiona booked them into rooms.

A few moments later, they all had keys and agreed to meet back in the abbreviated lobby in twenty minutes.

Annja arrived first, five minutes early, freshly showered and in a change of clothes. She'd thrown her bag onto the bed but she'd kept her backpack. Seated on one of the chairs in the lobby, she pulled up a map site and plotted their route from the airport to the Li family flower shop.

"You know, the car does come equipped with GPS navigation."

Annja glanced up. Fiona stood just behind her. The woman

wore business casual, dressy enough to ensure respect, but not so much that it would intimidate a small business owner.

"I know, but I'd rather know my way around when I can."

Fiona nodded. "I'm the same. I had Ollie upload street maps to my phone so I'll be able to navigate with that if I need to. You'll also find them in your phone now, as well."

"I didn't think about that. Everybody needs an Ollie."

"Maybe one day you'll have one."

Edmund arrived only a few minutes later and apologized for his tardiness. Then they headed for the car.

35

Li Shusen's Beautiful Moon Petals flower shop wasn't far from Guhua Park. From the passenger seat of the rental car, Annja looked out over the trees and waterways. Though she could barely see them as they passed, several red and white temples with peaked roofs sat at the ends of paved walkways or stood on stilts. The whole area looked quiet and serene, and part of her wished they were headed there instead.

Fiona guided the car through the morning traffic into one of the business districts. Fiona swore on several occasions as bicyclists shot out in front of her and she had to swerve to avoid them.

Several of the bicyclists carried farm produce for the morning markets, and some of them even had crates of chickens on the backs of their bikes. Annja heard the strident din of traffic chaos even through the closed windows and limited soundproofing.

A few minutes later, Fiona pulled onto Renmin Road and took it to their destination. Trees and single-story shops lined the street. Shoppers and tourists were already out in full force. Unlike in the United States, where strip malls and shopping areas tended to be uniform, Nanqiao Town was a mix of old and new.

Miraculously, a block from the flower shop, a delivery van pulled out and left a vacant spot. Amid the shrill squeal of brakes and the blare of car horns, Fiona claimed the space at once.

In the backseat, Edmund sighed. "My God, I thought we were about to die."

"We had closer calls in Paris." Fiona checked her hair in the mirror. "I had everything under control." She opened the glove compartment and took out a sleek Walther PPK. "I could only arrange the one, I'm afraid." She tucked it into her small handbag. "I notice you don't carry a purse, Annja."

"Not if I can help it."

"Of course, having a sword you can pull out of thin air trumps a handbag."

Annja smiled. "It does." She got out of the car, backpack over her shoulder, and retrieved the case holding the dragon lantern from the trunk.

Edmund watched, clearly torn.

Annja held up the case. "Having second thoughts?"

He shook his head. "No second thoughts. Regrets, yes. That lantern belonged to Anton Dutilleaux, and it would have been a coup in my collection."

"I'm told the worst thing that can ever happen to a collector is to have everything he wants."

"I don't subscribe to that particular line of logic."

Annja laughed. "Totally understandable."

"All right. If I'm to give up that lantern, which I've owned for too short a time, I can only hope we'll get some answers about Anton Dutilleaux."

A SMALL ASIAN MAN SWEPT the walkway in front of Beautiful Moon Petals. He worked in swift, economical movements. He was thin and bald, perhaps in his forties, and neatly dressed in black pants and a white shirt with the sleeves rolled up. He noticed Annja and the others, but he only nodded until he saw that they were headed straight for him.

Then he rolled down his sleeves and reached for the black

jacket hanging on the handle of the open door. He pulled it on and smiled.

"Good morning." The man waved to the baskets of flowers lining the table behind him. "Would you like some flowers? Very pretty. Smell very nice."

Annja had to agree that they did smell good. "Mr. Li?" she asked.

A troubled look stole over the man's face. "I am Mr. Li."

"My name is Annja Creed."

Li looked uncertainly at the three of them.

"This is Fiona Pioche and Edmund Beswick. Friends of mine."

"I see. You are not here to buy flowers." Li sagged a little. "You need directions?"

"Is your wife here?"

Li hesitated for a moment. "In shop, yes. Working very hard. We have many orders to fill. Very busy time right now."

"We'd like to see her if we could."

Li shook his head. "My wife not know you. If she know you, I know you. I not know you."

"Mr. Li, we came here today hoping to return something to her. And to get some answers." Annja opened the case and revealed the lantern to the shopkeeper.

Li's face darkened and Annja knew she had his full attention. "Is this Tsai Chien-Fu's lantern?" he asked.

"We think so. We've traveled a long way to find out."

Nodding, Li motioned them into the shop. "Come. Come. We talk to my wife."

Li shut the door after they entered, hung up a Closed sign and drew the drapes. He cleared a space on the wooden counter beside the big, old-fashioned cash register.

"Please. Put lantern here. I will go get my wife." He turned and disappeared into the back of the shop, through a heavy curtain.

Annja shivered. She'd learned that having someone she had just met vanish wasn't always a good thing. On several occasions those people came back with weapons they were eager to use. She reached for the sword, brushing it with her fingertips.

"Easy." Fiona's voice was quiet and reassuring at her side. "He's only telling his wife about the lantern. She's excited, but she doesn't believe it."

Edmund fidgeted. "Frankly, neither would I. Family heirlooms usually don't reappear two hundred years after they went missing."

A moment later, Li returned with a tiny woman about his age. She wore a black dress and had her hair in a bun. The couple talked hurriedly, and the woman kept touching the dragon's face on the lantern as if to make sure it was truly there.

Finally, Li focused on Annja. "This is my wife, Xiaoming. She is very pleased to meet you, and she wants to know if you have eaten."

"Ni chi le ma" or "Have you eaten" was one of the standard greetings in many provinces in China.

"We have just come from breakfast. Thank you."

Li translated for his wife. "She has very little English."

That bothered Annja because it was the woman's family that had been entwined with Dutilleaux.

"She wants to know how you find lantern." Li licked his lips hesitantly. "And I want to know why you brought it here."

SEATED ON THE COUPLE'S RED couch behind the shop in the living room, with the Chinese husband and wife in small chairs across from them, Annja told the story. Li translated for his wife and had to stop only at a few points to clarify a word or a phrase. Fiona hadn't offered to translate, but the woman probably thought keeping her knowledge of the language to herself might prove beneficial.

Perhaps it was, because the Li's seemed to be involved in an argument.

Xiaoming's husband shook his head. She glared at him balefully, but he refused to budge.

And then Fiona said something in Mandarin.

Xiaoming looked shocked, then happy, and addressed Fiona

with renewed excitement. Li got up and walked away in apparent disgust.

After the exchange went on for a time, Xiaoming left the room.

"What was that about?" Annja asked Fiona.

"Mr. Li doesn't believe his wife should tell us anything. We are *gweilo*. White people. Outsiders. He's afraid we are here to do something bad, and that having anything to do with us will only bring bad luck to them."

Edmund snorted. "Explain to Mr. Li that we are the least of his worries, that he could have been found by someone a lot less friendly than we are."

"I don't want to bring that up if we don't need to. I'd rather communicate on a need-to-know basis."

Annja nodded. "We're the outsiders here, and these people didn't ask for any of this."

After a few minutes, Xiaoming returned carrying a small lacquered chest. As she spoke, Fiona translated for her.

"My family has carried the story of the dragon lantern and the Frenchman named Anton Dutilleaux for many generations. My ancestor, Tsai Chien-Fu, was a low-ranking administrator at one of the Qianlong Emperor's banks and worked with the Europeans and Americans. He became great friends with Mr. Dutilleaux because the Frenchman was a magician.

"One day, Tsai Chien-Fu told Mr. Dutilleaux that he would like to disappear from Shanghai. My ancestor's life here was very hard and he was a young man. After hearing stories of France, he believed he could make a better life for his family in Paris.

"My ancestor and Mr. Dutilleaux made a pact. They would raise money to move the family that wished to come. It was a very big thing they planned to do. Almost an impossible thing."

Annja thought of how dangerous it would have been to try to take a family so far to unknown lands—without aid of modern technology.

"Together, Tsai Chien-Fu and Mr. Dutilleaux invested in shipping. They made money. They were very good at what they did, and they were motivated. Mr. Dutilleaux had dreams of becoming a performing magician in Paris.

"They traded the money they made into pearls and gems, always saving and saving, always dreaming of the future. They put the savings into the dragon lantern that my ancestor got from his mother as a wedding gift. When the day came that they filled the lantern and it could hold no more, they decided Mr. Dutilleaux would return to Paris and prepare a home and send for Tsai Chien-Fu."

Edmund couldn't wait. "Did Anton Dutilleaux steal from your ancestor?"

Surprised when the question was translated, Xiaoming hurriedly shook her head. "No. Mr. Dutilleaux was a very honorable man. They were good friends. Mr. Dutilleaux was in love with my ancestor's sister." The woman grimaced. "It was that bad luck caught up with them. My ancestor was not a greedy man. You must understand this. He was just desperate. And he wasn't dreaming for himself. He was dreaming for his whole family. A large family. A very large dream."

For a moment, the room was silent. They waited patiently for the woman to resume the story, and Annja feared for the worst.

"In his desperation, my ancestor made a mistake. A terrible mistake." Xiaoming looked miserable and her eyes were wet with unshed tears. "This story I tell you now, it is not one my family likes to share. We have told no one."

"I understand, Mrs. Li. But this lantern has drawn the attention of several bad men." Annja kept her voice soft. "And if we do not solve this mystery, those men may one day show up here."

36

For a long moment, the woman made no reply. Annja knew no amount of pushing would make the woman decide any faster. Trusting someone was always a big decision, and she'd known them for only a few minutes.

Xiaoming glanced at the mantel to pictures of what might've been a daughter. In the photographs, the girl aged from a baby to a teenager. The woman shook her head. "We were not blessed with a boy. My husband works very hard, but he knows that he has no son to give this shop to. There is no one to care for us in our old age. The day will come when our daughter will marry and she will go live with her husband's family. But I do not want my daughter harmed."

"We're going to keep this away from you. If we can.... Please."

Xiaoming sipped her tea. "Tsai Chien-Fu took something of the Qianlong Emperor. He should not have done this, but he was desperate. He knew, that were he to be caught, his life would be forfeit. But he wanted to ensure his family's survival."

"Do you know what Tsai Chien-Fu took?"

"The Qianlong Emperor was a writer and an artist. Did you know this?"

Annja nodded. "Over forty thousand poems and more than a thousand texts."

"Yes. And the Qianlong Emperor also added calligraphy to paintings and other works of art. In the bank where Tsai Chien-Fu worked, there was a royal seal. The Qianlong Emperor's seal."

"Your ancestor took the seal?"

"That, and some jade figurines the Qianlong Emperor himself had carved to be hung in a museum. Tsai Chien-Fu didn't know the figurines or the seal belonged to the Qianlong Emperor at the time he took them. They were only things. There was no name associated with them. He took them from the bank manager's office and thought they belonged to that man, who he had cause to dishonor. The bank manager was a very evil man."

"Why did Tsai Chien-Fu take those things?"

"Because Dutilleaux told him the Europeans sought out Chinese art. He thought they could sell those, as well. Besides, they fit in the lantern." Xiaoming gazed at the lantern on the small coffee table. "That lantern."

Edmund studied it. "Even if that were filled with pearls, would the amount really be worth so much now?"

Annja laced her fingers together. "You don't know much about antiquities, do you?"

"If they don't relate to magic, no."

"A royal seal that belonged to the Qianlong Emperor recently sold for over twelve million dollars."

Edmund's eyes widened. "Oh. My."

"Couple that with the jade figurines, which can also be tied to the Qianlong Emperor, and you can plan on the contents of that lantern being worth several millions more."

"But what happened to those contents?"

Fiona translated the question to Xiaoming.

"While my ancestor awaited word from Mr. Dutilleaux, the theft was discovered. The bank manager was going to be executed. Tsai Chien-Fu stepped forward and informed the

Qianlong Emperor's guards that he was the thief." Xiaoming's expression hardened. "At first Tsai Chien-Fu would not tell of his partnership with Mr. Dutilleaux, but he was tortured. My ancestor was beheaded for his crimes, as was the bank manager for allowing the theft."

Edmund sat enraptured, his elbows resting on his thighs. "And Dutilleaux had already left for Paris."

Xiaoming nodded. "They never found the things Tsai Chien-Fu stole. The guards killed him too quickly. In turn, for their failure, they were killed. My ancestor's immediate family was fortunate to survive. After that, their lives were very hard." She sat a lacquered chest on the table. "Weeks after Tsai Chien-Fu's death, a package arrived from Mr. Dutilleaux. This package. And there was a letter describing the contents of this chest."

Edmund looked hopeful. "Do you still have the letter?"

"No. It was destroyed as dangerous. But in the letter, Mr. Dutilleaux wanted to show his good faith to Tsai Chien-Fu. He said that the items in this chest would show him the hiding place he had found for their futures."

After unlatching the chest, Xiaoming opened the top to reveal three glass lenses sitting on rice pillows. Inscriptions in different colors stood out against the glass.

There was a moment of silence as they all stared.

Annja gestured to the lenses. "May I?"

"Please. I would like answers as much as you would."

Annja studied the first lens. The glass was uneven, proof that it had been hand ground, shaped and polished. The lines painted on the lens made no sense, though. They weren't any kind of symbols that Annja recognized as language or a glyph.

"Do you have a candle I can borrow?"

Xiaoming got up and quickly fetched a candle and a lighter.

Annja lit the candle and placed it inside the lantern. When she closed the lantern, a spray of light erupted from the dragon's mouth and threw an oval of light onto the wall behind the couch. They all shifted so they could see it.

The lenses only fit into the dragon's mouth one way, as Annja had expected. She popped them in one at a time. The first lens projected a pile of skulls with red serpents running through them.

"This looks like one of the images Dutilleaux might have used in his phantasmagoria show."

"It has to be more than that," Fiona said. "Why would he send a phantasmagoria image to Tsai Chien-Fu?"

The second lens projected a moldering corpse with the bones showing through the skin. And more red snakes.

Xiaoming spoke up and Fiona translated. "When my ancestor's family first received the lenses, they almost threw them away, thinking they were the work of a demon."

Annja removed the second lens and inserted the remaining one. A black-cloaked figure pulled a skeleton from an open grave. More red snakes.

"Well, that's macabre." Fiona tapped her chin with a forefinger. "But I fail to see what point Dutilleaux was trying to make."

Annja cycled through the images again, then again. "They all focus on death."

"Morbid, but it hardly gives us a direction."

"I think it does. We know he hid the treasure in Paris. And there's one place Dutilleaux knew intimately that focuses on death, skeletons and bodies being removed from their graves."

"The catacombs," Edmund whispered.

"Where he was killed." Annja nodded. "I don't think Dutilleaux went far from the wealth he and Tsai Chien-Fu collected."

"People have been searching that chamber where Dutilleaux was killed for years." Edmund shook his head. "The story about the curse and the possible treasure brought out all the fortune hunters. If anything was there, it would have been found."

"Yet no one ever admitted to finding anything."

"Perhaps the treasure had been lost in one venture or another."

"And it may still be there waiting. You and Xiaoming both believe Anton Dutilleaux was a good man, Edmund. Do you think he was the kind of man to steal from his partner?"

"I want to believe in Dutilleaux, Annja. But this was over two hundred years ago. Whatever was there is surely lost."

Acting on impulse, Annja placed two of the lenses in the dragon's mouth.

The images created a confused jumble on the wall, and the red snakes ran rampant.

Carefully, Annja adjusted the lenses, gently turning them in the dragon's mouth until they overlapped each other. Then, slowly, the snakes lined up and made longer snakes.

Annja picked up the third lens and fitted it into place. Again, she twisted and adjusted. The glass ground and squeaked against the groove. Then, after a moment, the red snakes on the third lens lined up with the others and made a solid line.

"It's a map." Edmund's voice was a croak.

Annja nodded. "It *is* a map. Probably through the catacombs, and hopefully to where Dutilleaux left the treasure he and Tsai Chien-Fu collected."

"But there are nearly two hundred miles of tunnels and rooms beneath Paris." Edmund shook his head. "You're still looking for a needle in a haystack."

"Dutilleaux was killed in 1793, right?"

"Yes."

"The catacombs would have been smaller then. The work of moving the bodies didn't start until 1786 and continued until 1814. I think we can start at the beginning—Place Denfert-Rochereau, which was called the Barrière d'Enfer when Dutilleaux was alive. I can match this up to a map and see what we have."

Walking over to the wall, Annja examined an interlocking image on one side. Lines from at least two of the lenses came together there and formed the barest outline of a gate.

Fiona joined her. "That is your starting point, you think?"

"The Barrière d'Enfer remains the main entrance to the catacombs. It was located inside the old Wall of the Farmers-General. The wall was originally built to keep merchants from evading taxes, and they called it the Barrière d'Enfer."

"The barrier of hell." Fiona smiled. "I imagine merchants didn't think highly of the tax collectors."

"And once the catacombs opened up, the name took on a whole new connotation." Annja tapped the gate. "That could be the marker for the wall."

"If this is a true map, then there has to be a legend. In order to follow the route, you have to have a reference, a scale to estimate the distance."

Annja searched the combined image projected on the wall. Fiona was right. Dutilleaux wouldn't have made the map without a key.

Xiaoming came close and studied the image, as well. She spoke briefly with Fiona. Judging from the intonation, it was a question. Fiona replied and gestured with her hands, showing different sizes. The woman peered more closely, then pointed to something.

"This one." Her English was heavily accented, but she got her point across. "One equals eighty-eight." Her finger indicated three characters.

Annja didn't recognize either one of them. One of the characters was a single vertical line, which might have represented the number one, the next looked like the Roman numeral III only with the right crossbar missing and turned on its side. The second number was next to the same symbol, sitting upright to the III with the lower crossbar missing.

"What is that?"

Understanding the question, Xiaoming spoke to Fiona, making her grin.

"That is your key. We were looking for numbers written in English. These are written in Chinese. Very old Chinese, actually. Suzhou numerals."

Annja closed her eyes. "Missed that. The Suzhou numerals were also called the *huama* system. It was used in the Chinese markets before Arabic numbers replaced them."

Edmund shook his head. "Maybe you've heard of it, but I haven't."

"The Suzhou numerals were based on the rod numeral system involving horizontal and vertical strokes. There were two different styles, the traditional and the Southern Song. The Southern Song replaced symbols for the numerals four, five and nine to reduce the number of strokes necessary to make the symbol. Like changing the symbol for the number four from four vertical or horizontal strokes, depending on which way you were writing on the paper, to an X. That was quicker and more efficient."

"Eighty-eight seems like a strange number to use as a base."

Annja traced her finger over the combined lines, following the path along and counting marked divisions that showed in the changes of snake scales. "The number eight is considered a lucky number. It sounds like the Mandarin word for *prosper.* Same in Cantonese. The Summer Olympics in Beijing started on August 8 in 2008, at eight minutes after 8:00 p.m., just for that reason."

Annja followed the winding trail to its final destination. There was no marking, just the end. "And if we can follow this correctly, if Anton Dutilleaux's hiding place has been left undisturbed, we'll find the treasure."

Fiona already had her phone out. "I'll have Ollie get us back to Paris."

Annja stepped back from the map again and took in the bigger image. Excitedly, she realized they were in the final stages of the hunt.

"You're smiling pretty big there, Annja Creed."

Self-consciously, Annja turned to Edmund. He was smiling, too. "This is magic to me. Tracking something down through history, finding stories that were thought forgotten. This is what I live for."

"I see that." Edmund glanced back at the image projected through the dragon's mouth. "Do you think it's still there?"

"I don't know. I hope so. We'll see soon enough."

37

Sixteen hours later, jet-lagged this trip, Annja got out of the SUV in an alley not far from the public entrances to the catacombs. She wore black and wore a black watch cap to keep her hair out of sight.

Similarly dressed, Fiona walked at her side. Edmund brought up the rear but did so reluctantly.

They'd landed in Paris at 7:00 p.m. and decided to wait till after midnight to begin their search of the catacombs. Georges had equipped them with urban exploration gear—primarily flashlights, gloves and durable clothing—and small-arms weapons.

So far, there had been no news about Jean-Baptiste Laframboise.

Annja led the way down the narrow alley and flicked her flashlight beam around. Cats and rodents exploded out of the shadows and disappeared. The pervasive smell of rot formed a thick miasma in the alley, pouring off the garbage bins.

Edmund flicked his beam around, as well. "What are you looking for?"

"Markings on the wall. They'll show us the way into the catacombs."

"I thought we were going to enter through Place Denfert-Rochereau."

"It's locked up this time of night, and we're going to be wandering off the tourist routes. Exploring the catacombs on your own isn't legal. If we get caught, we'll be arrested by the catacombs police, the *cataflics*."

"Great. Probably not a good idea to explore at night, either."

Fiona patted Edmund on the shoulder. "During high noon, the catacombs will still be dark, Professor."

"Still...I'd feel better if we were underground during the day."

Annja spotted the markings she was looking for in a space behind a bakery. Urban explorers were obsessed with the vast underground and had developed symbols to help their fellow explorers. Annja had been down in the catacombs before and was acquainted with some of it, but she'd spent some time on Skype with a few people she'd explored with before to bring her up to date. They'd given her this location.

There wasn't much room behind the bakery, but a manhole cover gleamed under her flashlight beam. She checked around and found a brick with more markings. She removed the brick and took out a crowbar that fit into the manhole slot. Working carefully, she pulled the manhole up and placed the heavy cover aside.

"Those markings told you the crowbar would be there?" Edmund held the flashlight on the wall as Annja returned the tool and replaced the brick.

"Yes. They're left there by *cataphiles*." Annja aimed her flashlight beam down into the manhole. "Urban explorers whose focus is the catacombs."

"How do you know about them?"

Annja grinned up at Edmund as she climbed into the manhole. "This isn't my first trip down here."

Annja shifted her flashlight, gripped the iron rungs mounted on the wall and started down into the waiting darkness. Climbing into the catacombs was frightening, but she relished the adrenaline spike.

JEAN-BAPTISTE LAFRAMBOISE knelt in the shadows across from the alley where Annja Creed and her companions descended into the underground labyrinth. He watched them through the lenses of night-vision binoculars. Campra, in black Kevlar hung with weapons, knelt next to him.

"Have you ever been in the catacombs before, Gilbert?"

Campra shifted slightly. "No."

"I don't care for it very much. I may be a touch more claustrophobic than I care to admit."

"I've been underground before," Campra said in a monotone. "Out in Africa and the Middle East, a lot of people use catacombs for defense, storage, shelter from the heat…and to bury their dead."

Laframboise checked his watch after the professor was the last to disappear. Someone reached back up and replaced the cover. "We'll give them a five-minute head start."

"They can cover quite a distance in five minutes. They've already been to Shanghai and back in the past twenty-four hours."

That was true. In fact, they'd gotten lucky catching Annja Creed and her companions coming back into the country. Laframboise's people had been watching for the group to try to leave Paris, not return.

Campra shifted again. "Do you think Creed has solved the riddle of that lantern?"

"Why go down into the catacombs otherwise?" Laframboise glanced over his shoulder at the man. "Are you certain your device will work underground?"

"I've used the tracking chips under similar circumstances." Campra held up the small computer-tablet-size device. "As long as we stay within a quarter klick of our target, I can find them."

When they'd first captured Professor Edmund Beswick, Campra had insisted on injecting the man with a subcutaneous RFID tracking chip in the event that he escaped. The insertion wound hadn't been any more noticeable than any of the other damage the man had suffered in London.

Laframboise checked his watch again. "All right. Let's go." He led the way across the street. Campra and the other men followed after him. He was excited about the thought of learning what secrets the lantern hid, what the *hope* was that Magdelaine de Brosses had talked about, but he kept remembering how the fortune-teller had promised him that the lantern would be his death.

But his greed drew him on.

As ALWAYS, THE ORDERLY STACKS of corpses on either side of the catacombs inspired Annja with dread and awe. She played her flashlight beam over the wall of yellowed bones. Leg and arm bones lay neatly stacked. Skulls with missing teeth and missing lower jaws sat on top of the walls or were interspersed among the other bones. Given the neat order to the bones, it was almost possible to forget that the bones had at one time belonged to six million people. They seemed like something artificial, like a movie set.

"Oh, my," Edmund said softly into the emptiness.

Annja turned her beam onto the wall nearest Edmund, deliberately not shining the light on him. "Are you okay?"

"I will be. This is all…just a bit much."

"On several levels. On one hand, these are the remains of a lot of people. On the other, a lot of work went into bringing them here." Annja started forward, her voice echoing eerily around them. "Legend has it the priests worked at night so no one would see them disinterring and transferring the dead. The priests supposedly sang the burial service while transporting the bones." She smiled at Edmund's discomfiture. "Must have been a sight."

"Okay, that's enough." Fiona stepped between them. "After everything I've seen, I don't blanch easily, but I've only been down here once before, and I promised myself I'd never come again."

Annja grinned and continued down the tunnel. She had the map in her head. During the flight back from Shanghai, she'd studied what she knew of the catacombs and what she could pull up on the internet and through various urban-explorer sites. Some of the people she'd been in contact with had been very helpful.

Certain parts of the map Anton Dutilleaux had left on the lenses weren't on anyone's maps, though. That had been expected. There were a lot of areas in the catacombs that were still being discovered—rediscovered.

"Were these tunnels always under Paris?" Edmund flicked his light around the wall of bones nearest him. "Some kind of natural system?"

"No. This is where the stone was quarried that was used to build the city. The construction crews found natural veins of gypsum and plaster." Annja kept moving forward, halted at an intersection and chose the left fork. The dark pressed in at her, barely kept at bay by the flashlight.

"Why did they dig under the city?"

"The mines were dug in the fourteenth century. Most of them at the time were open-air pits that allowed the workers to haul rock up out of the earth. But the stratification was deep. It made more sense to dig into the side of a hill and empty out all the rock through an underground mine. For the next five hundred years, Paris kept growing, until it finally grew over the mines."

"It's a wonder the tunnels didn't collapse."

"They did." Annja turned left at the next turn. Her flashlight beam skated over a wall covered with graffiti, probably kids who came down into the catacombs on a dare, judging by the content. "Sometimes they still do. Erosion is a problem."

"Lovely thought." Edmund's voice was tight.

"Sometimes whole buildings have dropped into the mines."

"We climbed down, what? Forty, fifty feet?"

"At least. But there hasn't been a cave-in for a long time."

"So once they finished taking all the stone out, the city administrators decided that it would be easier to transfer skeletons here to reclaim the land as the city grew?"

"Reclaiming the land was only part of it. Paris, like London, had grown fast. Buildings sprang up almost overnight. The growing population also aged. Bodies had to go somewhere.

While it's true that the graveyards filled up quickly, and funerals were using the same casket over and over again, space wasn't the most important issue. Buried bodies were decomposing, and the various body matters were returning to the soil. Paris depended heavily on well water. The water table is quite close to the surface. The upside was that wells were easy to dig. However, the downside was that the water table often flowed through the cemeteries."

Out of the corner of her eye, Annja saw Edmund flinch.

"The resulting sickness from the bad water triggered the removal of the bodies." Annja couldn't help smiling. "I guess that kind of lends a whole new meaning to *urban decay.*"

Edmund sighed. "All right, I am grossed out quite enough, thank you." He paused. "I don't know why anyone would want to come down here."

"Same reason Anton Dutilleaux drew crowds down to watch his phantasmagoria. For the atmosphere. And the illegality of the adventure." Annja hesitated for just a moment at the next intersection and checked her sat-phone. She no longer had a signal, but she'd uploaded maps into the device's memory. "One of the caverns down here was even set up as a movie theater."

"You're not serious."

"I am. The police discovered it in 2004. The operation was set up by La Mexicaine De Perforation, the Mexican Consolidated Drilling Authority. It's just another name for a group of *cataphiles,* a splinter off the UX."

"What's that?"

"Urban Experiment. La Mexicaine De Perforation is dedicated to delivering clandestine artistic events. They had a movie screen, a bar and a kitchen down here."

Annja continued. "After the police came back for a more in-depth investigation, all the equipment had vanished."

"Vanished."

"Like magic. There were whispers that the whole thing was run by ghosts. Rumors get out of hand pretty quickly."

Fiona snorted. "Children. All for the momentary thrill of being afraid of the dark."

"A lot of criminals have used the place, too." Fiona flicked her beam across a section of graffiti. "Marijuana growers, mushroom growers, any number of drug dealers..."

Edmund cleared his throat. "I suppose there's a chance of bumping into them, too?"

Annja turned another corner and was surprised by the steep descent in front of them. The map hadn't indicated that. She headed down thirty yards, measuring the distance by counting her strides. If it became necessary, she had a Leica DISTO D2 laser distance meter to measure spans. So far the way had been easy to follow.

A moment later, her flashlight beam revealed the calm surface of a gray-green pool of water that blocked the tunnel mouth.

38

"What's wrong?" Edmund pressed into Annja, adding his flashlight beam to hers.

"The tunnel's flooded ahead." Annja moved her beam around, looking for intersecting tunnels that might offer another route.

Fiona stepped up and did the same. "The walls look solid. It doesn't appear to be a cave-in."

"No. Probably caused by the rising water table. Groundwater levels reroute themselves occasionally." Annja took out her sat-phone and opened the file she had that contained the catacombs maps.

"So the adventure ends here?" Edmund stuck a foot into the water.

"Not necessarily." Annja slipped off her backpack and set it on the stone floor. She opened it and withdrew a scuba mask and small oxygen tank. There was also a pair of swim fins. "I knew some of the tunnels in the catacombs were flooded. I thought maybe we'd encounter them. So I came prepared."

Fiona shook her head. "Surely you're not planning on going down there."

"I am now." Annja tied her hair back and pulled on the scuba mask. She took out the yellow-and-black canister of Spare Air.

The small tank was a little over a foot long and about two and a half inches in diameter. She slid into a harness and attached the tank over her shoulder.

Fiona looked worried. "That can't hold much air."

Annja smiled. "You've never used one of these?"

"No."

"They come with the equivalent of fifty-seven breaths. Three or four minutes if you space it out, and you can't deep dive because you'll use the air up faster. Enough for a little exploring."

"Enough to get you into serious trouble, you mean."

"That's why I brought spares." Annja reached into her backpack and took out another cylinder. She'd left her computer and cameras in the car to make room for the gear. The foray into the catacombs was about exploration, not documentation. "Georges was able to get me a half-dozen tanks. Should be more than enough to get through this." She attached a second tank. "They transfer quickly. If the dive is longer than that, we'll come back with proper scuba gear."

Edmund gaped at her. "You expect to descend into those stygian depths, search for a way through that tunnel *and* keep track of how many breaths you take?"

"Actually, I figure if I run out of air in the first cylinder, I'll switch over to the second and head back. Kind of keeps things simple, don't you think?"

"I think you're barking mad to even consider diving into that." Edmund flushed deeply enough to be seen even by the secondhand glow from the flashlights. "No offense."

"As I recall, I had to watch you do the whole water torture chamber thing."

"That was staged."

"I know what I'm doing, Edmund. If I didn't think I could do this, I wouldn't."

Fiona snorted. "I don't think you're in any way close to a litmus test for safe precautions."

"I can do this." Annja strapped a long knife to her right shin, tested the grip the holster had on it and stood.

Fiona grimaced. "Before you do that, we could look around. There could be another tunnel that intersects this one past this point."

"That would take time and we could get lost."

"Annja, that whole tunnel could be flooded."

"If it is, we'll come back prepared for that."

Fiona sighed in resignation. "Show me how to use one of those. In case I have to come after you."

"You've used a scuba?"

"Yes."

"These aren't much different." Annja went through the procedure, showing both of them. Then she strapped on the swim fins. "I'll be back in minutes." She turned and stepped into the pool.

The cold water quickly rose to her ankles, then to her knees and thighs and hips. The tunnel took a severe incline down, but she didn't feel any debris that would suggest there had been a collapse. The flashlight was waterproof and remained on, but the viscosity of the pool dampened the beam so that it only illuminated up to a few feet. She wouldn't be able to see much underwater.

A few steps farther on, the water came up to her chin and the tunnel roof angled down to meet the pool. She filled her lungs with air, then clenched the Spare Air mouthpiece between her teeth and dove.

WITH THE NIGHT-VISION GOGGLES in place, the catacombs stood revealed in multiple shades of green to Jean-Baptiste Laframboise. The flashlights held by the two people ahead of him churned his vision with too much brightness when he rounded the corner, though, and he had to raise his goggles.

Campra was at his side, their men behind. Laframboise looked at Campra in the darkness, and the man nodded and raised his machine pistol. Moving carefully, Campra went ahead.

Laframboise trailed after the man. They wore Kevlar vests from neck to knees, and Kevlar military helmets.

In the pool of water, the flashlight Annja Creed had carried with her dimmed and grew steadily smaller.

For a moment, Laframboise wondered if they should have closed in earlier.

Then he decided letting the woman forage on had been best. Although the three people weren't going to be able to put up much resistance, having them split up—and inattentive—was advantageous. Laframboise could capitalize on surprise, as well.

You will never see the treasure.

He forced Magdelaine's words away and concentrated. There were riches waiting.

The woman, Fiona Pioche, must have sensed something at the last moment. Laframboise was certain Campra had made no noise, but the woman reached into her pocket and came up with a small pistol as she spun around.

Ruthlessly, Campra moved in and smashed his rifle butt in the woman's face. She went back and down into the water, and the pistol flew from her hand.

The woman tried to get back up, but Campra pointed the rifle at her and growled, "Stay down or I'm going to kill you."

For a moment, she looked as if she was going to lunge at him, anyway. Then she remained still. "The water's cold. May I get out?"

Campra gestured with the rifle and directed her against the wall to the left. They took the professor into custody easily enough.

"Hello, Ms. Pioche," Laframboise said, pistol in hand.

She was bleeding from her mouth and nose, and her right eye was already starting to turn black. "Laframboise. Sorry. It took me a moment to pick you out from all the other sewer rats down here."

He grinned at her. "I'm still deciding whether I need to keep you alive."

She didn't reply. Instead, she drew her sleeve across her face. It came away bloody.

"Where is Annja Creed?"

She just smiled at him through her split lips.

He smiled back. "Be stubborn if you wish, I won't have you killed." He pointed his weapon at Edmund Beswick. "I'll start with the professor."

THE WATER WAS ALMOST ARCTIC and the cold leached into Annja's bones. She swam effortlessly, gliding through it with both hands ahead of her. In her left hand, the flashlight served only to create a lighted cone for her to swim through. Still, when she was close enough, she could see either the tunnel's floor or the roof. Either was fine. Both together would have meant the tunnel was narrowing and the way was coming to an end.

She counted her breaths as she went, and made sure she stayed oxygenated. The movement warmed her slightly, but she still felt cold. After twenty-two breaths, the cone of light flattened at the top. She angled upward and came out of the water at about the same time her flippers touched the tunnel floor.

Cautiously, she walked out of the water and sniffed the air. It was fetid and stank of mold, but there was no noxious odor of harmful gases. She took a deep breath and held it, checking for vertigo or any other indication that there wasn't enough oxygen. She felt fine, so she started breathing normally.

She estimated the time she'd been underwater and figured it was something over a minute based on the number of breaths she'd taken. The average adult breathed between twelve and twenty breaths a minute based on physical shape and circumstance. She guessed she'd been breathing about fifteen breaths a minute and revised her underwater trip estimate to just over a minute and a half.

If she'd known that, she could have simply held her breath.

Except that there had been no way to know.

She took the flippers off and left them at the water's edge. Then she widened the flashlight beam and moved forward. She had to guess at the distance she'd covered swimming. Olympic swimmers averaged a hundred meters in a minute. She wasn't an Olympic swimmer even with the fins. Her best estimate was that she'd covered forty or fifty yards underwater.

The tunnel rose only a few feet, just enough to keep it from the water. According to the map on the sat-phone, there was only one more intersection.

Annja found the four-way juncture another twenty-six yards ahead. She had to use the laser distance meter to accurately measure the distance, but the intersection was clearly marked on the map. She took the left turn and ended up in a short corridor that dead-ended.

That had been on the map, too.

Excitement tingled through Annja. The map had shown a door, a secret place that existed just beyond the door. She widened the beam again and played the light over the moldy surface of the wall.

Like the rest of the walls, the surface was uneven and irregular. The stones hadn't been shaped into any kind of standard dimensions. But there was a difference in the mortar. The grouting between the stones was smoother, and it wasn't pitted. The color was almost the same, and if she hadn't been looking for the differences, she knew she would never have found them.

Anton Dutilleaux was an illusionist. Why wouldn't he hide his treasure behind an illusion?

Edmund would love it. For a moment, she felt guilty that she was seeing everything before he did. This had been his mystery. He deserved to be here for the discovery.

She ran her hands over the wall, but felt only the rough surfaces of the stones, no irregularity. Turning the flashlight beam toward the stone floor, she studied the surface in front of the wall.

There were no scars, no scratches, to show that the door swung outward.

If the door didn't open outward, it had to open inward.

Annja fisted the flashlight and put both hands on the door. Gently, but with increasing pressure, she pushed. Just as she was about to give up, the door moved.

Grinding over loose debris, it slid backward about two feet and stopped. No matter how hard Annja pushed, the door wouldn't move any farther.

Using the flashlight, she spotted openings on either side of the door. She chose the one on the right and went through.

The air inside the room was thicker and stank more of rot. Evidently the door had been shut for a long time.

A square room forty feet across—measured by the distance meter—sat empty except for an obelisk in the center. Twelve feet tall, flush against the ceiling, the obelisk was carved of what looked like stone. It was only three feet wide.

Upon closer inspection, Annja realized the obelisk wasn't carved from a single stone the way a true monolith was. Instead, it was pieced together with large stones. The mortar looked like the same that had sealed the false door. Several of the stones had carvings on them. Faces and strange figures.

Slowly, Annja walked around it. There were no openings that she could find, and no marked areas that indicated hidden places. She had no doubt that Dutilleaux was responsible for the creation of the thing, though. Some of the engravings revealed rough figures from Chinese mythology—dragons and koi and ghostly apparitions.

Maybe it was there as a final warning to anyone who happened into the room, or maybe it was a puzzle Anton Dutilleaux intended for his friend Tsai Chien-Fu. Annja didn't want to touch it until Edmund had had a chance to study it and give her his thoughts on the matter.

Shining her flashlight around the room, she discovered that two of the walls were piled high with bones. At one point in the tunnel's history, it had been a storage area for the relocated Parisian dead. The skulls sat neatly among the long bones.

She walked back into the hallway and tested the door. It moved easily forward. Evidently Dutilleaux had used some kind of counterweight to keep the door shut. She directed her flashlight beam toward the ceiling, which she hadn't checked, and spotted the metal rod that extended through the ceiling.

Further examination of the ceiling over the entrance to the

room revealed that the ceiling had been lowered there and a false floor put in. Only the length of the shadows gave it away.

Annja was impressed. Dutilleaux had gone to a lot of trouble to disguise his treasure trove. But that only stood to reason. The Qianlong Emperor's warriors were searching to kill him and recover their ruler's lost belongings.

She'd just put her flippers back on when she heard the gunshot.

39

With the sharp report of the gunshot ringing in his ears, Laframboise spun around toward his men, ready to threaten whichever of them had fired. Instead, he stared in confusion as one of his men fell forward, his face a bloody mess.

Then Campra was at his side, bumping him roughly and shoving him toward the wall. Back the way they'd come, the corridor suddenly lit up with muzzle flashes.

Campra lifted his machine pistol and opened fire. Brass tumbled out of the gun. Instinctively, Laframboise brought up his pistol and added to the thunder and lightning, but he was only firing into the mass of muzzle flashes and didn't see any actual targets. The pistol bucked in his fist.

His men fell, torn to rags by withering fire. The ambush had caught them all off guard. The muzzle flashes lit up the tunnels and threw impossible shadows against the walls one moment, then ripped them away in explosions of light the next.

Laframboise fired his pistol dry, then tried to reload. He stood behind Campra, partly shielded by the man's bulk. Then Campra fell back on him, taking him down with his dead weight. Laframboise hit the ground hard. His elbow struck stone and he felt the pistol squirt from his fingers. He lay on his side and stretched for it, trying desperately to get his fingers around the butt.

When he realized he wasn't going to reach it, Laframboise twisted and sat up, pushing himself forward with one hand while he reached for Campra's machine pistol with the other. Campra's head turned with a sickening looseness. In the light from a nearby dropped flashlight, Laframboise saw the bullet wounds in Campra's eye and throat. Blood streaked the man's face.

He curled his fingers around the machine pistol and started to haul the weapon up. A black-garbed figure dashed forward and kicked Laframboise in the face.

Knocked backward, senses spinning, he struggled to hang on to consciousness. His head felt too big, wobbly, and his neck felt as if it was trying to support a pumpkin. A bright light in his eyes blinded him.

"Jean-Baptiste Laframboise." The voice was harsh and foreign. French was not the speaker's native tongue. "Can you hear me?"

He blinked until he could see Puyi-Jin. The Asian warlord was in his fifties, a grim-faced man with hazel eyes. His black hair was graying at the temples.

"I hear you." Laframboise licked his lips and tasted blood.

"Where is Annja Creed?"

"She dove into the water. The tunnel's submerged." Laframboise didn't want to answer, but he didn't want to die, either.

You will never see the treasure.

He tried to screw up the courage to grab for the machine pistol again, or maybe to spit in Puyi-Jin's face. But his mouth was so dry he couldn't manage it.

"You should not have betrayed me." Puyi-Jin pointed his pistol.

"The lantern's cursed. That's what made me to do it. The curse." Laframboise wanted to face death bravely, but he couldn't. His teeth chattered. "If you go after it, the curse will get you, too."

Puyi-Jin shook his head. "I do not believe in curses." He squeezed the trigger.

Bullets hit Laframboise in the face, then darkness closed in around him.

ANNJA SWAM THROUGH THE water, her flashlight barely lighting her way. Then she saw two figures in the water ahead of her, backlit by a flood of lights in the tunnel on the other side. She could barely make out Fiona. As she came up for a breath, the other woman grabbed her arm and pushed her back under. Muted gunshots echoed through the water.

Edmund was beside Fiona, also barely recognizable in the dark water. He wasn't a strong swimmer. Annja pulled him past her, then grabbed his belt and swam on top of him, dragging him along at a faster clip since she had the fins. A moment later, he started flailing in panic.

Realizing that Edmund thought he was about to drown, Annja took the Spare Air mouthpiece from between her teeth and passed it over to him. The short hose just reached to him. He shoved the mouthpiece between his teeth. Annja kicked strongly with her flippers and got him going again.

Twenty or thirty seconds later, she angled up and the three of them were safely on the other side.

Annja shone her flashlight over them. Fiona's face was bruised and swollen, but she was concentrating on the machine pistol she'd brought with her. Water drained from the barrel and the empty magazine space. She held the magazine in her other hand.

The gunfire continued sporadically.

"What's going on?" Annja kicked her flippers off and wished she had her boots.

"Laframboise's men were following us." Fiona held up the machine pistol's magazine and checked the load. The magazine was taped to another. She reversed the magazine and shoved the other one back into the weapon.

"How did they follow us?"

"Let's figure that out later." Fiona glanced around. "Does this tunnel continue?"

"No. It's a dead end."

Fiona cursed. "Not good."

The gunfire ceased.

"Laframboise and his people aren't shooting one another." Annja led them toward the room where she'd found the obelisk.

"I think Puyi-Jin and his people arrived." Edmund looked pallid in the dark. "I didn't see much because Fiona grabbed me by the shirt and hurled me into the water, but the men I saw looked Asian."

"One thing was for certain." Fiona flicked on a flashlight attached to the machine pistol. "We couldn't stay there." She glanced back over her shoulder. "I should think Puyi-Jin's men will be along shortly."

A single gunshot rang out.

Annja glanced back and spotted light dawning in the darkness of the flooded tunnel. Swimmers were on their way. "Come on. Dutilleaux managed to hide a room. If we can get there, we might be able to hide, too."

Annja guided them into the room, then turned and forced the door closed. She shut off her flashlight because she didn't want the glow leaking around the door. For a moment all she could hear was Fiona and Edmund's ragged breathing in the darkness.

Then they heard footsteps out in the hall. Voices filtered through a moment later.

Annja couldn't tell how many voices there were. The sounds were too confusing and her hearing was blunted from the gunshots. Certainly there were more than three opponents. She stood behind Fiona, who held her captured machine pistol at the ready. Quietly, Annja reached for the sword and pulled it into the chamber.

Someone spoke in Chinese, angry and commanding.

Fiona whispered just loud enough to be heard. "That must

be Puyi-Jin, or perhaps one of his lieutenants. He doesn't believe we've disappeared."

Light glared along the bottom of the hidden door. Annja focused on keeping calm. They could see the light on this side of the door, but the men on the other side couldn't see the crack.

Water dripped from Annja's wet clothes, curling around her ankles and running between her toes. Suddenly she knew that their hiding place wasn't going to remain secret for long. With all their wet clothing, they'd left a trail.

"Let's hope they muddied our tracks with theirs before anyone noticed," she whispered in Fiona's ear. "The door will only come into the room a couple feet. For just a moment, they're going to be trapped there."

"Good. It will give us a temporary kill box. I'll make the most of it." Fiona adjusted her grip on the machine pistol.

Annja waited tensely. The men out in the hallway stopped talking and things got quiet.

Then a deafening blast ripped through the chamber and the secret door flew into chunks of debris that ricocheted off the walls. Light flashed and ripped away the darkness for a moment. The concussive wave knocked Annja backward off her feet. She lost the sword and it vanished. She barely clung to her senses as vertigo slammed through her and sickness twisted her stomach. She swallowed to ease the pressure in her ears.

Dizzy, she tried to get to her feet to pull the sword back. Before she could, an Asian man dressed in black pressed a pistol against the back of her head.

"Move and you die."

Annja remained still, struggling just to stay on her feet even with the man holding her.

Only a few feet away, Fiona tried to get up, as well. Her hand flashed out for the machine pistol, but one of the men in black kicked the weapon away. Her opponent pointed his weapon at Fiona's face and Annja knew he was going to pull the trigger.

A man's voice barked out of the darkness.

The other man pulled back his weapon, then grabbed a handful of Fiona's hair and yanked her roughly to her feet.

Edmund quietly got to his feet and stared at their captors. Eight men all dressed in black stood in the room. All of them heavily armed.

The man Annja figured must be Puyi-Jin strode in and trailed a flashlight around the room. She recognized him from his pictures. He gave orders and, within seconds, the men had lanterns set up around the room.

Most were trained on the obelisk.

The Asian crime boss surveyed it in silence for a long moment. Then he turned back to Annja. "Miss Creed."

The man holding Annja jerked her forward to within arm's reach of Puyi-Jin.

"You are surprised to see me here?" Puyi-Jin smiled broadly, but there was nothing friendly in his expression. "You found your way into Shanghai very easily, but I have informants among airport customs. I knew when you arrived, and I knew when you left. Following you here was child's play. I had men on the flight with you."

Annja wasn't about to give the man the satisfaction of a reply.

He shrugged. "The only thing I want to know from you, Miss Creed, is where Tsai Chien-Fu's treasure is."

Annja glared at him.

Puyi-Jin motioned to the man holding Edmund captive. The warrior pulled out a sharp blade and pressed it against Edmund's throat, slicing just enough to draw blood.

"Now, Annja, I want to know the location of that treasure."

Reluctantly, Annja thrust her chin at the obelisk. "This is what I found when I got here. Evidently the treasure's gone. Maybe the Qianlong Emperor's assassins got it when they tracked and killed Dutilleaux in the catacombs."

"No." Puyi-Jin's hazel eyes glittered. "I would know that if it had happened. I know the story of the captain assigned to bring Anton Dutilleaux back to Shanghai—*with* the things

Tsai Chien-Fu took from the Qianlong Emperor. One of his assassins killed Anton Dutilleaux before locating the treasure. The captain himself was killed when he returned to Shanghai. The Qianlong Emperor had no mercy for those who failed."

Annja's ears still rang from the explosion. Out of the corner of her eye, she watched as Fiona and Edmund were brought closer. Fiona was measuring the opposition, memorizing the locations of the men and their weapons. Edmund was staring at the obelisk.

"The treasure has not left this room." Puyi-Jin gazed at the stacks of bones and at the obelisk. "It remains here, and you must find it."

The man holding Annja released her with a shove. She held out a hand. "I need a flashlight."

One of the warriors passed her a flashlight.

Annja switched on the beam and approached the obelisk. She studied the carvings, trying to make sense of them. The dragons, koi, ghosts and foxes didn't appear to have any real order.

"Hurry."

With deliberation, Annja trailed her fingers over the obelisk. Some of the stones seemed more deeply set than others. "*If* the treasure is still here, Dutilleaux might have set a trap. You might want to consider that."

"There is also the chance that someone heard the gunshots in this tunnel. If someone else arrives, I will have you and your friends killed at once."

Annja considered the problem and tried to put herself into Dutilleaux's mind.

"He was an illusionist, Annja," Edmund said quietly. "Whatever Dutilleaux hid, it wouldn't be in plain sight."

The warrior guarding Edmund chopped him in the throat with the edge of his hand. Gasping and coughing, Edmund dropped to his knees. Annja started toward him, but two warriors intercepted her.

Puyi-Jin glared at her. "Find the treasure. You are running out of time."

Annja turned back to the column. Edmund was right. Dutilleaux wouldn't have hidden the treasure in such an obvious spot.

She glanced around the room again, taking in everything. It would have to be something Tsai Chien-Fu would know to look for in case something happened to Dutilleaux.

Her gaze settled on one of the piles of bones across the room. For the first time, she saw the pattern in the lower left corner of the stack. Skulls had been placed there in front of the bones but tucked back so they matched the bones.

Eight of the skulls sat in a horizontal row. Under the second, fourth and sixth skulls stood three skulls, two skulls and three skulls. There were eight skulls across and an aggregate of eight skulls piled under those in vertical columns.

Annja knew then where the hiding place was, and that the obelisk was a trap. Glancing up, she again noticed how the obelisk touched the ceiling, and the way the ceiling curved over the front door.

She looked at Puyi-Jin. "I know where the treasure is."

"Then reveal it."

"It's a magic trick. Have you heard of the disappearing woman?"

Puyi-Jin shook his head irritably. "Show me the treasure."

Annja glanced at Edmund and Fiona. "The disappearing-woman trick works like this—a woman lays on a table and a cloth is dropped over her. The audience doesn't realize that the cloth has an internal wire structure that blends to the woman's body, then *collapses* when the magician yanks away the cloth." She turned to Puyi-Jin. "For all intents and purposes, the woman vanishes."

"Now, Miss Creed, or the man dies."

Hoping that Edmund and Fiona had understood her warning, Annja turned back to the obelisk. She grabbed one of the carved stones on the column and pulled.

40

For a moment, the carved stone Annja pulled on held. Then it grudgingly came away from the obelisk. It wasn't just a stone, though. The carved rock had been attached to a three-foot-long iron rod that was pitted with orange rust.

Something shifted inside the obelisk.

Behind Annja, Fiona said one word. "Jenga."

Annja nodded. "Exactly." She searched for another stone to remove. Evidently Dutilleaux had hoped his ostentatious structure would draw the attention of anyone who didn't know the room's secret. At least Fiona knew what was going on and what would probably happen.

"Shut up." Puyi-Jin stepped forward with a small automatic in his hand. He pointed the gun at Annja's head. "No more talking."

Annja grabbed another stone and pulled. The obelisk moved again, and this time a tremor ran up to the ceiling. Puyi-Jin and his warriors stared around the chamber, trying to fathom what was going on.

Ignoring them, Annja grabbed another stone and pulled another rod from the obelisk. This time when the grinding inside the obelisk started, it didn't abate. The sound continued to escalate in the space of a heartbeat and became a thunderous ripple of cracking that filled the chamber.

The mortised area over the door that concealed the counterweight shattered and a rock slide poured out of the opening. Fiona broke free and grabbed Edmund by the shoulder, yanking the professor back as the avalanche toppled from the ceiling. She forced him against the wall. With all the dust rising up from the rock slide, Annja quickly lost sight of them, but she believed they'd managed to avoid the brunt of the falling rock.

Throwing herself forward, Annja dived clear of the obelisk as it came apart in a cascade of tumbling rock. Puyi-Jin had time to shout, then he was knocked down by the falling stone. Dust plumed up and the lantern's light hit the cloud of particulates and filled the chamber with a milky-gray fog. The light-reflecting properties of the gypsum dust was almost as bad as the dark. Through the haze, Annja could only see vague images of the others.

She rolled to her feet in a squat, her left hand before her for support. With her right, she reached for the sword and pulled it into the chamber.

One of the black-clad warriors came at her from out of the dust. He had his pistol pointed in front of him and started firing immediately. Bullets struck the stone floor where Annja had been, but she was already running toward the man, angling for his right side. He wheeled and tried to come around, his pistol still jumping in his fist.

Annja swung the sword and the blade passed above the man's outstretched arms and through his neck. The man's head toppled down one shoulder and the body slid to the floor. Choking on the dust, her eyes watering, Annja got her bearings and headed back across the pile of rubble that had dropped where the obelisk had been. She searched desperately for Fiona and Edmund.

The column was now just debris covering the floor. The carved rocks were mixed in with the rough stones. A warrior tried to push himself up. Blood covered his face, but he freed his machine pistol.

Without breaking stride, Annja kicked the man in the head and he fell back, unconscious. Another warrior came out of the dust at her with his machine pistol chugging. Knowing she couldn't throw herself across the rock-covered floor without sustaining injury and that she had no hope of sliding away, Annja leaped up as hard as she could, trusting her enhanced speed and strength to get her clear.

She flipped over the man and came down on her feet behind him. Reversing the sword, she thrust the blade behind her and felt the point crunch through the man's chest. The resistance gave way at the last and she knew she'd pierced him through.

Spinning around, she put a foot into the man's back and kicked him off the blade. Her breath came in hoarse rasps as the dust coated her mouth and throat. She searched for more opponents, remembering where they'd been before the rock had knocked them all down. Five were left. And Puyi-Jin.

Frantic, Annja raced toward the wall near the door. She'd last seen Fiona and Edmund there. The rubble appeared to thin. The swirling shadows created by the multiple lanterns caused even more confusion. She caught sight of a gunner slightly behind her in her peripheral vision. Planting a bare foot, feeling the sharp stone bite into her flesh, she pushed herself sideways as bullets split the air where her head had been.

Annja went into a low crouch and spun to face her attacker. He was ten feet away and content to keep his distance advantage. She watched him, hoping that she would know which way to move before he started firing again.

Harsh gunshots thundered through the chamber.

Confused, certain that she'd seen no muzzle flashes, convinced that the man would not have missed her at that distance, Annja watched the man fall back limply as his face came apart.

At Annja's side, Fiona stepped out of the swirling dust holding a machine pistol in her hands. "How many?"

"I've put down three."

Fiona nodded grimly. "Then we're up to five. When I liberated this weapon, I killed the man holding on to it with his knife."

Annja stood. The dust was still too thick for her to see far in any direction. Her eyes ached and burned and required constant wiping to clear the dust.

"Where's Edmund?"

"He's fine. I left him by the wall." Fiona strode to the left, circling the biggest section of the fallen rock. Puyi-Jin and his warriors had been struck by most of it.

"Annja! Look out!"

Whirling at the sound of Edmund's voice, Annja tried to bring the sword around, but the man who had risen behind her was too far ahead. He shoved his pistol muzzle toward her face and pulled the trigger.

Annja dropped in a loose sprawl, falling on top of the rock and below the pistol. Three shots thundered, and the muzzle flashed over her head. Lying on her side, she swept her right leg forward and knocked the man's feet out from under him. The warrior went down as more gunshots rang out from Fiona's position.

The warrior landed on his back and struggled to get up. Annja rolled over on her side, rose to her knees and grabbed the man's gun wrist in her left hand. The sword couldn't be effectively used in such close quarters. She released it and it promptly vanished. Surging forward, she caught the warrior's face in her palm and banged his head off the stones until she felt him go limp beneath her.

Annja picked up her attacker's gun and threw it aside. She didn't want to risk ricochets inside the chamber. No one else involved in the firefight seemed to worry about that. She reached for the sword, found it and walked forward.

A shape stood about fifteen feet in front of her. Annja wasn't sure if it was just a trick of the gypsum fog or if it was Fiona. Almost too late, the fog thinned and she recognized Puyi-Jin. Evidently he'd been waiting for his vision to clear, as well.

He pointed his pistol at her.

Reversing her grip on the sword as it hung at her side, Annja rocked her body forward and threw the blade underhanded, then raced toward Puyi-Jin. Even if the sword didn't hit him, she hoped that it would be enough of a distraction to cause him to miss.

Instead, though, the sword sailed true and sank into the Asian warlord's chest just below his heart. He looked down at the sword that transfixed him. Stubbornly, he tried to aim the pistol again, but the weapon dropped from his nerveless fingers. He sank to his knees and started to fall forward.

Annja reached for the sword and it disappeared from Puyi-Jin's chest and was once more in her grasp.

"How did you do that?" Edmund said from a few feet away as he stared at the sword.

Annja grinned. "Magic." She searched for Fiona, who was trudging across the rubble.

Fiona glanced down at Puyi-Jin. "That will be the lot of them."

"What about Laframboise?"

"I'm pretty sure he's dead. Puyi-Jin and his people were thorough about wiping them out." Fiona gazed around the room.

Most of the dust had settled and less than half of the lanterns had been broken so there was still plenty of light.

Fiona wiped blood from her face. "So this is it, then? There is no treasure?"

"We'll have to see." Annja walked over to the wall of bones. "The obelisk wasn't Dutilleaux's hiding place. That was only window dressing."

"And a rather nasty trap."

"Yes." Annja looked at Fiona. "You don't see the clue, do you?"

Fiona wiped grit from her eyes and looked at the wall of bones. "All I see are a lot of poor souls who ended up as landscape."

Annja shifted her gaze to Edmund. "But you do, don't you?"

Excitedly, Edmund nodded. "Dutilleaux marked his hiding place with a symbol that Tsai Chien-Fu would understand."

He approached the wall of bones and knelt in front of it. "The secret's here. In these skulls." He traced a line with his hand. "See? The long line of skulls here."

"Eight of them." Annja released the sword and knelt beside him.

"And three columns. Again, only using eight skulls."

Fiona nodded in understanding. "The numeral eight in Suzhou. Very clever."

"Unless it's just an anomaly."

"Surely you don't believe that."

Annja reached for a skull. "No, I don't believe that." She pulled the first skull away.

Edmund joined in the efforts and they quickly cleared the space of skulls and bones. Behind the bones sat a brass box. Annja leaned back and gestured to Edmund.

"Your lantern is what brought us here. The honor's yours."

Edmund shook his head. "I'd never have gotten this far without you." He removed the brass box and set it before Annja. "You do it."

Carefully, Annja opened the box and tilted it so the lanterns' light better illuminated the contents. A jumble of gold coins, pearls and gems.

Reaching in, Annja plucked out the royal seal of the Qianlong Emperor. As she did, her fingers brushed against another hard surface in the pile of coins and gems. Digging through them, she found two books, one of them written in Chinese and the other a collection of sketches, but there was an English translation on the title pages.

Poems of the Qianlong Emperor and *Sketches of the Qianlong Emperor.*

Annja couldn't believe what she was holding. She turned the pages reverently.

"What is it?" Fiona leaned in more closely.

"These books are supposed to have belonged to the Qianlong Emperor." Annja studied the pictures of loons, petrels and pelicans. There were other birds she couldn't recognize, and animals, as well, including tamarin, alligators and pandas. "If they are, if that can be verified, they'll be worth a fortune."

Fiona stood and looked around the room. "I think we need to be going. We should probably notify the Parisian police before they end up catching us down here, don't you think?"

Annja nodded and closed the brass box. "I'll need to get my backpack first. We don't want to get those books wet." She handed the box to Edmund. "Well, Professor Beswick, how does it feel to find your first treasure?"

Edmund's eyes gleamed. "Like nothing I've ever felt before." He shook his head. "But this isn't the first time for you. I suppose after a while an experience like this loses its luster."

Annja grinned. "Never."

Epilogue

"So you're back in London?" Roux sounded only vaguely interested.

Annja walked through the winding alley in the East End. It was two in the morning and darkness draped the buildings. Sorting out the discovery of the treasure and accounting for all the bodies in the catacombs had taken three days and a host of Fiona Pioche's lawyers.

In the end, though, the law-enforcement agencies had cut them loose, but none of them had been happy about it, and Annja had gotten the distinct impression that her presence in Paris wouldn't be appreciated anytime soon.

"I am back in London. And I'm looking for Mr. Hyde. *Again.*" Annja turned her collar up against the chill and watched a group of college-age men walking down the streets. Judging from the way they were walking, they'd been on a pub crawl.

"I read about the catacombs find."

The story had made international news, and that was one of the things that had mollified Doug Morrell and the *Chasing History's Monsters* production management. Doug was working on cobbling some of the story together for a feature. It wouldn't be quite Mr. Hyde caliber, Doug had been quick to point out, but they were going to heavily work the Chinese curse angle. After all, a lot of people had ended up dead.

"Congratulations on your success."

Annja smiled. Roux was digging for something. He'd pried himself away from a Texas Hold'em table long enough to make the call. She'd ignored it, then returned his call when she was ready. "Thank you. So how's the table action?"

"I'm making my way. What is your professor going to do with his share of the treasure?"

"Need a backer for your gambling?"

Roux made a grunting noise.

In the end, Edmund hadn't been able to hang on to the find. Tsai Chien-Fu had given his life in the hope that he would provide a better future for his family. Two hundred years later, Edmund felt that the original effort needed to be honored. He had returned the treasure to the Tsai family, but Li Xiaoming had insisted that her good fortune be shared. She had given half of it to Edmund, Annja and Fiona.

"He doesn't know what he's going to do with the money yet. He gave the treasure to the Li family. He's a good man."

"If he invests it wisely, he wouldn't have to work again. Neither would you."

"I'm investing my share wisely."

"How?"

"By leaving it with Fiona. She's smart and capable, and I don't like the idea of managing money. I never have. Mostly, I have what I need. I'd rather pile up experiences and memories than try to hang on to material things. Physical things just provide a lot of clutter."

"You forget, I've seen your loft. You have boxes stacked everywhere."

That was true, but most of the antiquities were there for classification and validation. Some of it she'd asked for to pursue her own studies. "Most of those artifacts go back as soon as I finish with them. I enjoy seeing them in museums when I get the chance." It wasn't often, but it was enough.

"As much as you have found over these past years, you could retire."

"Not all of us can spend all of our days playing Texas Hold'em." Annja knew that would never happen. As long as she was able to take up the chase, she wanted to be doing exactly what she was doing. Success wouldn't change that. Financial gains weren't what made her life good. It was the hunt, the challenge of the unknown and the friendships she made along the way.

Roux harrumphed. "There will come a time when you grow jaded."

"I don't think so."

"Trust me."

"If things do change, money will be there waiting for me. Besides, the way I live? I don't think retirement is part of the package."

"You shouldn't talk like that." Roux's voice softened. "It's depressing."

"You know who else hasn't lost that zest for life and become curmudgeonly?"

Roux didn't reply.

"Fiona." Annja kept walking, but she heard the echo of someone's footsteps behind her. She turned at the next corner to put a streetlamp behind her. Long shadows of things behind her stretched across the cobblestones. "I've been with Fiona these past few days. She hasn't changed. She still enjoys the danger and excitement. Probably more than I do. Or, at least, she's more comfortable dealing with it."

"She is an exceptional woman. I told you that when I sent you to her."

"Why did you leave her?"

Roux was silent. Annja felt certain he was going to duck the issue. She hoped he wouldn't.

"When I first started working with her, I didn't really think about the danger I was involving her in. I never considered the consequences," Roux said thoughtfully. "Do you know how many times she was nearly killed working with me?"

"No."

Roux sighed. "I got up one morning and I realized I couldn't watch her get killed. After everything I've been through, and I've been through some horrific events, I could not bear losing her in such a fashion."

"So your abandonment had nothing to do with the fact that Fiona was getting older? Or that you hadn't ever loved her?"

"I love her with all my heart, Annja. I just couldn't protect her. My life was spent looking for the sword that you now carry, and that search took me into dangerous places." Roux paused. "And I couldn't give her children. I wasted twenty years of that woman's life before I knew it. That was how much in love with her I was." He drew in a breath. "I suppose, in your parlance, I had been something of an asshat."

Annja felt sorry for him. "Nothing in return? Roux, did you ever stop to think that maybe all she wanted was you?"

"Annja, you're young in so many ways. You're not ready for commitment. You live for the adventure each day brings. Tell me that you're looking forward to settling down with a husband and a house filled with children."

Guilt stung Annja when she realized she couldn't. "Maybe Fiona felt the same way."

"The life I lived then, it was too big. You have trouble keeping up with what that sword brings you, and that's the truth."

Annja had no argument.

"Now, if we've discussed this enough, I've a game to get back to."

"Sure."

"Maybe we should plan to get together again soon."

Annja heard the loneliness in his voice. He wasn't all hard bark and bluster. "I'd like that. But it can't be Paris. They don't want me back there for a while."

"Well, then, we have all the rest of the world, don't we?" Roux broke the connection before Annja could reply.

She stayed on the phone and sucked in a breath. The footfalls behind her grew louder. "Fiona?"

"I'm here."

Before she'd called Roux back, Annja had dialed Fiona and included her on the three-way call. She'd wanted to give the woman something.

"He didn't leave you, Fiona. Not in the way you thought."

"I heard." Fiona's voice was brittle and sounded far away. "At least I'll have better memories, and I thank you for that."

"You're welcome."

"Roux would be livid if he knew what you did."

"That's part of what made it worth doing."

Fiona laughed. "I suppose so. Do you know when you'll be leaving London?"

"Soon." The footsteps behind Annja were definitely closing in on her now.

"We should have lunch before you go."

"Definitely."

Annja hesitated. "You know, you could reach out to Roux. Maybe give him a call."

"Out of the blue?"

"Yes."

"For good or bad, he has his life and I have mine. Perhaps that's for the best."

"And perhaps it's not."

Fiona sighed. "I enjoy you, Annja Creed. Truly I do. Roux was right about one thing—you are still so very young."

"But—"

"Is there someone you care for very much, who could change your life if you let them?"

Immediately, Annja thought of Bart McGilley. They had been friends for years, and she knew they could be more if she would just stay still.

"I can tell by your silence that you know exactly who I'm talking about. Now ask yourself why you don't let that happen."

The question made Annja unhappy. Fiona was right. Right now her life was one thing and there wasn't room in it to be another.

"Now let me know when you plan to leave London. I do want to get together."

"I will."

Fiona said goodbye and hung up.

Annja took a deep breath and placed the phone back in her pocket. Instead of being thrilled at putting one over on Roux, now she felt depressed and irritable.

The footsteps behind her accelerated and she saw the long shadow of her pursuer closing on her. She sidestepped at the last minute and the big man ran past. His heavy boots clomped on the cobblestones, but he stopped himself and twisted around.

He stood a little over seven feet tall and would have shamed an NFL linebacker. His skin was pallid, almost fish-belly white, and his face looked like a cinder block stretched across his thick neck. Intelligence gleamed in his milk-white eyes, but there was no shred of compassion or humanity.

"Annja Creed." His voice was a low rumble.

"You know me."

"I've seen you on television." He started to circle her. Annja stepped to put her back against the wall.

"Mr. Hyde, I presume."

"And I'm going to kill you."

"Why?"

He grinned at her. "Because I'm a monster. Everyone has always said so. Killing you will make me even more famous. Besides, I have learned to enjoy killing. The bones in those women snapped so easily, and you could hear it. Snap, snap, snap." He sighed. "I look forward to hearing your bones snap."

"You're going to be disappointed."

"Why?"

"Because I fight monsters. And you picked a really bad night to make yourself available for me to vent my frustration." Annja reached for the sword, felt the hilt brush against her palm, then decided not to use the blade.

Hyde rushed in and she let him. His size and weight were advantages he was used to, ones he counted on.

Annja ducked beneath his outstretched arms, but only

barely. He was quicker than she'd believed possible. She rolled away as he threw one hand against the wall and halted himself, turning amazingly quickly. But his size worked against him in the end. She rolled to her feet behind him and slightly to one side. Coldly, with calculated precision, she kicked hard at his right knee.

The joint went violently sideways and shattered in a staccato of sharp cracks. *Snap, snap, snap.*

Crying out, Hyde threw himself at her, trying desperately to get those big arms around her. Annja stepped back slightly, batting his arms aside with her forearms, and brought her right knee up into his face. Blood spurted and his nose broke.

Hyde went to the ground, caught himself on his knees and reached for her again. He howled like a rabid animal.

Thinking only of the women the man had killed, Annja grabbed Hyde's outstretched right hand, slid her grip down to his ring and pinkie fingers, and twisted them viciously. The fingers dislocated and fractured. When Hyde drew his hand back, Annja twisted and delivered a side kick to the big man's face that broke his jaw and knocked him out.

Broken and bloody, Mr. Hyde lay stretched on the cobblestones as a crowd from a nearby pub started to gather. The last few moments of the fight had attracted an audience. Conversations gained momentum and volume.

Annja took out her phone. It was a toss-up whether to call Doug Morrell or DCI Westcox first. She decided on Doug. Judging from the glowing lights of the cell phones in the hands of the crowd thronging the street, the inspector would know soon enough.

* * * * *

The Executioner
Don Pendleton's
LINE OF HONOR

American medics fall prey to terrorists in the Sudan in this latest exciting episode of The Executioner!

When several American medics are held captive after a Janjaweed war band takes control of their camp in Darfur, Mack Bolan launches his own rescue mission. But the Janjaweed group has become an unyielding force in the region, and as the enemy troops close in, Bolan realizes he could be leading his men into a death mission.

Available in June wherever books are sold.